DARCI O

DARCI O

William Nona

Copyright © 2002, 2006 by William Nona.

Library of Congress Control Number: 2006905383

ISBN-13: 978-0615570655 Nona Publishing

ISBN-10: 0615570658

Registered with The Writers Guild of America, west, Inc.

This book was printed in the United States of America.

THE PYRAMID

Prologue

Celebrities and High Rollers came from all over the world to the grand opening of the most talked about gaming resort since Monte Carlo. The Hotel at Sundance Lake had been booked for more than six months by invitation only guests. Private jets of every size and shape filled the executive terminal and transient parking areas of McCarran International Airport. The overflow was directed to the Henderson Executive Airport a short eleven miles south. As an entourage of limousines made their way along the highway to Sundance Lake the outline of a pyramid rose from the water, and cast an eerie shadow across the Hotel and Casino at Sundance Lake.

The Pyramid is rumored to be the home of Darci O. It was first seen by the Resort's architect during the final stages of his design. Many local residents have seen the phenomenon for the last year and a half but regard it as an illusion or some kind of desert anomaly or mirage.

Resort clientele congregated in the hotel lobby, the casino lounges, and on the veranda that separated the main casino from the lake while they waited for the official opening. The Grand Opening Gala would start with the casino opening, which was scheduled for one hour before sunset.

Intrigued by the Pyramid shadow, and the stories that the Ghost would appear at the Grand Opening, many of the clientele moved to the veranda. Suspense heightened as the sun started to set over the mountains.

THE ENCOUNTERS

Chapter One

It was an August afternoon with clear blue skies, sprinkled only with lenticular clouds and magnificent jet airplanes, when the Blue Angels made their final pass for the VIP's as a parting salute to the El Toro MCAS. The delta formation executed a beautifully synchronized final approach and concluded their performance with a dazzling touchdown on two parallel runways.

Michael Orcini walked along the front of the airplane maintenance hangers with his long time friend, Col. John Rojam. "The end of another era," Colonel Rojam, a former Air Force Ace remarked, with a hint of regret. "This used to be one hell of a base." He continued, "Now they want to turn it into a shopping mall or replace John Wayne Airport. Damn-it, they don't even know what they want to do."

Many years ago, Captain John Rojam met young Lieutenant Michael Orcini in a mock battle over Nellis AFB, when the Ace was outwitted and 'shot-down' by the rookie. Lt. Orcini swore that it was just a lucky maneuver, but 'Jo-ro' knew he had a tiger by the tail. They became the best of friends from that moment.

"Yes, John, they're closing a lot of these bases," Michael commented. "Next thing you know, they'll do away with the Angels."

"I know that you're joking, Michael, but that might be coming sooner than any of us like to think about." He took a deep breath. "There have been discussions to abandon the group," the proud Colonel choked, with a distinct sadness in his voice.

"What?" Michael exclaimed, with clear-cut surprise. "They're an American Icon. Is anyone doing anything about this ridiculously stupid political. . . ." He was so upset that he couldn't find the words to show his anger. He continued, "Some idiot politician, who never served his country in uniform, probably came up with a dumb idea to save taxes and look like a hero, or just wag the dog."

Michael's outrage was interrupted when an Air Force Captain approached them on an oblique collision course, stopping just short of their path, and saluted. "Sir, the program is complete and all personnel are ready to be discharged."

"Thank you, Captain." The Colonel returned the salute. "Signal for closure."

The captain spoke into his walkie-talkie. "It is taken care of, sir."

"Michael, I would like you to meet Captain Nugari. The Captain is not on active duty, but participates in special events." He looked at the Captain. "Perni, this is my ol' flying buddy and personal friend, Michael Orcini."

"Haven't we met, Captain?" He questioned, putting out his hand and knowing they had somewhere.

The captain shook Michael's hand. "Yes sir we have, it was last year in Barcelona. You were with that gorgeous woman. Looks like a movie star. Bobbi." He stated with absolute assurance.

"And you couldn't keep your eyes off of her sister. Wait, didn't you. . . ."

"Ah . . ." his response lingered, "Yes. She wanted to see the Basilica of Saint Eulalia and the wood carving of the Cristo de Lepanto. Do you see her?"

"Sure. I see her from time to time. But how do you remember all that?"

"Captain Nugari never forgets a lady," the Colonel said with admiration, and quickly followed with a definite, "Gentlemen, I must be going. Michael can I drop you?"

"I have my car, John. Thanks."

The Colonel shook Michael's hand, "See you soon Michael," he paused, "give me a call, I'll take you up in one of our newest birds."

Michael's entire face beamed. "Absolutely, Jo-ro." This was a name he only called his friend when they were flying. "Give me a couple weeks. OK?"

"I'm heading to Nellis. Be there for the duration. You can find me there."

Michael offered a cordial civilian salute, while the officers mechanically saluted each other. The Colonel nodded and turned away.

Perni pushed back his hat and loosened his tie as he accompanied Michael to the parking lot. "Do you have time to go somewhere and get something to drink?" Pernicious Nugari had heard, from some of the other officers, that Michael was not only a pilot, but also a real estate developer. Perni would try to establish a business relationship with Michael and some offshore investment groups.

"I have an appointment," looking at his watch, "but it's not for another two and a half-hours. I have some time," he affirmed. "I have to meet someone at LAX."

'I'm going that way myself. How about the Proud Bird?"

"Sure, I know exactly where it is. See you in a little while."

The Proud Bird restaurant occupies a strategic location at the East End of the Los Angeles International Airport, for those who love to watch airplanes land. Michael arrived first and settled in at a table by a window, overlooking an old WW II war bird.

"The Lightning P-38 has always been one of my favorites," Perni announced as he motioned to the waitress. He had changed into 'civies', a sport coat and slacks.

A WWII airplane mechanic, posing as a cocktail waitress, approached. "What can I get for you fellas?" She said, in a voice matching her appearance.

Perni motioned to Michael giving him permission to order first. "I'll have a cup of your finest coffee, please. Black."

"Aren't you going to have anything stronger," Perni inquired?

"No thanks; I have a long night ahead of me."

"I'll have a rum and coke," sounding like someone out of the forties.

Michael looked at the waitress with a slight shrug acknowledging his disdain.

They talked for an hour or so, mostly about flying and girls. Michael was sympathetic to Perni's recent divorce situation, but the mention of his friendships with extremely wealthy Europeans and Asians fascinated Michael. He wanted to know more.

"What kind of people are they and what kind of money are you talking about."

"Well Mike it's. . . ."

"Michael. My name is Michael."

"Sorry, Michael," pronouncing it deliberately. "My people tell me that the Chinese have over two billion to invest, but they're looking for a way to get into Vegas. So unless you have a casino in Vegas?"

"First, Nugari, I don't go for this, 'my people' crap, and second, I do have a hotel casino project in Nevada." He paused. "We're looking for a financial partner who has eight hundred mill--i-on dol--lars." He stretched out the last words, studying Nugari's apathetic face and staid body language. Michael continued, "If you and 'your people'," he emphasized, "are for real, then I would like you to set up a meeting as soon as possible." Michael had heard this discourse before from would be money brokers. "Here's my card. Call me when you have something." Michael did not wait for a response. He looked at his watch and stood up. "I must go now."

Perni stood up. They shook hands. Perni motioned to the waitress and took care of the bill. "My treat this time, Michael."

"Thanks. Hope to hear from you soon."

Pernicious Nugari gestured with a small salute. They went their separate ways.

Michael went to the Bradley International Terminal at LAX for his scheduled appointment. The monitor indicated that the plane was going to be about thirty minutes late. He looked around, spotted a Starbucks, walked to the counter and ordered. "A cup of your finest coffee, please."

"That would be our House Blend, sir," replied a young girl dressed in a starched uniform that was too small for her. "What size do you want?"

"A small cup would be fine." He answered.

"You get twice as much for just a little more, if you order the medium size," a soft raspy feminine voice suggested from his side.

With a furtive glance, "Better make that a medium size--thanks."

He found an empty 'high top', adjusted the position of a stool so he could see the planes and began to sit when a raspy, "This seat taken?" Interrupted him.

"No . . . Please." He pulled the stool out for her. "Here." He took her coffee and large chocolate chip cookie, and placed it on the high top while she fumbled with her bags. She brushed her crumpled three-quarter-length skirt and squirmed onto the stool.

He was tall, tan, well structured and dressed with a sort of careless elegance, which seemed to encourage women to introduce themselves. He was not particularly handsome, but had a strong, sincere and magnetically playful face.

"My plane is late and I hate waiting alone in the airport. Do you mind?"

"I will force myself to enjoy your beautiful smile," he said deliberately.

"Thank you, kind sir." She anticipated a smile in return, but instead his eyes penetrated hers for a brief and uncomfortable moment. She looked away.

"Sorry for staring, but you are very lovely." He tilted his head apologetically.

She had an olive skin tone; almond shaped dark brown eyes set above high cheekbones surrounded by tussled brown shoulder length hair.

"Thank you again, kind sir." She did not look at him. "Where are you off to?"

"Nowhere. I'm meeting someone. The plane is late."

"Your girl friend?" She questioned, noticing the absence of a ring on his finger.

"No, a business associate," he offered, and then sipped his coffee. "Where are you off to?" Knowing it had to be out of the country. "Some exotic island?"

"I'm going to visit my uncle in Caracas. He's very sick and it may be my last chance to spend some time with him."

"Sorry," not knowing how to respond to someone that he just met, "I mean . . ."

"It's OK. He has lived long, ninety-seven. It's, well, I just need to see him."

They sat quietly for a while. "What do you do when you're not traveling?" He broke the silence.

"I'm an interior designer. I do mostly hospitality projects," she said proudly, "like restaurants and hotels." She nodded with a sales affirmation. "You?"

"I'm a real estate developer," he said trying not to encourage her sales pitch.

"You meeting some bazillionaire foreign investor for some outrageous project?"

He studied her face. Was he that obvious, or did this stranger just make a wild guess? "Yeah, as a matter of fact, he is coming in from the Cayman Islands."

He lifted his cup knowing he would probably never see her again. "We're going to build a casino resort," he told her as a matter of fact.

"Sounds great." She reached into her purse. "Here's my card.

Would you give me a call when you're ready for an interior designer?"

Shit! He knew this was going to happen. "Sure." He reluctantly manufactured an affirmation. Her card was beautifully and artistically done in a Southwestern style with her name, Gina Santiago Interior Designer, and an unusual quote, "Rules and models destroy genius and art."

"Interesting card, Gina." Looking at his watch, "I must find my associate."

"What's your name, kind sir?" She eased off the stool, brushing her skirt again, then putting out her hand. "Gina Santiago."

"Michael Orcini, Miss Santiago, and I'm very pleased to meet you."

"Will you call me, sometime?"

"Yes," he lied.

"Promise?"

"Promise." He compounded his falsehood.

She smiled and sat back down as he walked towards the gate where his associate would arrive from the Cayman Islands.

Hans Geller was transplanted to the Grand Cayman Island with his father, shortly after his mother's death in the mid sixties. Now he controls his family's financial interests, and is a strategic player in the International Marketplace. He came into view just as Michael reached the ramp. Recognizing each other by the photos they had faxed made it appear that they were long time friends.

The short blond German spoke. "Mr. Orcini, Ah con only spahnd a short time witd you today. Mah plans havf changed, ahn Ah must cun--ten--ue on to Vey-gaas varry soon." He paused to allow his statement to be understood. "Ah apol-o-gize, and pro-miss to spand ahs much time ahs you want, but nut today." He checked his watch. "I havf about on hour. Con we find ah place close by ahn talk?" The blue-eyed oxymoron spoke like a natural-born Jamaican.

Michael had prepared an elaborate presentation. Disappointed, he accepted the well-disposed expression of regret. "How long do you plan to be in Vegas?"

"Juss a few days, ahn thon on to Canada before returning humm. Perhaaps you would be mah guest ahn spand some time at mah villa in de eye--londs. What do you think, mon? You con bring your wooh-maan"

"Perhaps," he echoed. "Shall we get down to business?"

"Yes." Hans looked around, "Ah! Starbucks," he paused. "Coffee?"

"Yes, Starbucks is perfect."

Gina had been watching the encounter and purposefully followed their walk to the coffee bar catching Michael's eye. He nodded recognition as he passed by. "A medium size cup of your finest coffee, the house blend, please. What would you like, Hans?"

"Just a small cup, mon."

"The medium size is a better buy," he deliberately said bending around to see if she heard. "Want a dessert?"

"No tank you, mon."

As they went to a corner table, he saw Gina with a coy smile and thumbs up.

They reviewed the portfolio while a special chemistry transpired that formed an instant friendship. A bond that soon would be put to a test.

* * * * * *

The sailboats sat still in the harbor. The storms from El Nino had passed south of here three days ago, devastating Baja and moved through to Arizona. The presence of this eerie calm kept everyone busy. They were preparing for the unknown, lashing their little boats to docks that might not withstand a storm. Like the one that just hit Ixtapa.

The La Jolla Beach Yacht Club hosted many of the richest, and a lot of the 'plastic want to be rich', people on the West Coast. These plastic people attached themselves to the clubhouse like barnacles to the bottom of a ship.

Pernicious Nugari was one of the plastics that had just lost his meal ticket. The divorce left him floundering, trying desperately to maintain some sort of station with his fellows in this small Southern California beach town. He managed to keep the 'Dos Equis', a fifty-two foot trophy winning sloop, which he just renamed in honor of his two previous wives. Jana, the latest, wasn't too happy since he screwed her out of her rightful ownership. He looked out at the sloop from the Club bar thinking that he must move or sell her before she was lost to a storm or worse, to Jana.

Claude deVillefrance, the Commodore of the Yacht Club, entered, nodding recognition to the sailors, and would be sailors. His sanguine complexion was topped with yellow gray hair that emerged from under a dark blue, weathered, Greek Captain's cap. His squinty eyes mirrored his cautiously deceptive character. At forty-two Claude was just finding out who he was. Being an abused child and having his inheritance withheld until his thirty-fifth birthday, left him without a meaningful identity, and a condescending attitude that keeps most people at arms length. The advent of his fortune had reduced his previously unsavory ventures, but he still engages in endeavors of some indiscretion.

Perni went over and sat next to the Commodore. "Claude my friend. How goes it today?" He motioned to the bartender, "Another, and one for the Commodore, sweetie."

"Manhattan. Up, Commodore?" she sang.

"Yes, my dear," as if she were.

"Claude, I've been talking to this Chinese fellow about some investments. Says he knows you. Name's Jami Wu. You know him?" He didn't wait for an answer. "You think he's real? I mean, do his people really have that much money to invest in projects here in the US of A? I know they like our politicians and so forth, but, we-ll?" He had run out of intelligent things to say and decided to stop.

The Commodore cleared his throat aware that the bartender was listening. "It's like this, Perni." He puffed on his cheap cigar. "If you want something from him, you'll have to go through me. You know what I mean? I can make it happen." He eyed her;

being sure to say what he thought would impress her. "You got something special, Perni?"

"Got a fellow, Michael Orcini, with a hotel-casino project in Nevada. Says he needs $ 800 million to do everything, including adequate reserves for gambling. He has an option on the land and all the people to build and operate it."

"He got a proposal?"

"Says he does. Haven't seen it. He did send me some artist's conceptions and an overview. Do you have time to look at this stuff?"

"Let me see what you have." He patronized. They looked over a small portfolio. Claude smiled a little. "An unusual concept, but I like what I see. Tell him to get all the figures together and then I will set up a meeting, I'll talk to Wu. He may want to meet Orcini first, to find out if they can do business together." He swiveled on his stool and looked out over the harbor. The conversation was over.

How well the military taught Nugari to remove himself from any chance of a misinterpreted encounter. He wanted to talk about some other generally social things but, nevertheless succumbed. "Good day, Commodore," he said graciously, but tight-lipped.

The next day Perni called Michael and told him of his meeting with Commodore Claude deVillefrance and about Jami Wu. "You might get a call from them directly. We must meet and work out our arrangement before then."

"Fax me a proposal showing exactly what you want for yourself. If I like it, we can move forward."

"You'll have my proposal before the end of the day."

Later that day, while working in his home office, Michael received an overture faxed from Nugari, and scowled with an anger that he generally would exhibit after a bad play in racquetball. "This idiot thinks he can get a piece of my project," he shouted at the ceiling as he rose with a thunder knocking his chair over. He swung at some imaginary figure, "Ah--ha! Uff--huh--huh--yah!"--A heavy sigh--a moment. He picked up the chair and set it back facing the computer desk.

Disgusted with himself for getting so upset he walked to the kitchen, ground-up some coffee beans, and prepared his favorite brew. His mother would have cautioned him, "Slow down, Michael," reminding him of his tendency to leap before looking. "Don't go so fast that you get caught in something that makes you helpless." Then she would almost always segue into her prayer, "Slow me down Lord. Ease the pounding of my heart by the quieting of my mind," and finish with, "that I may grow toward the stars of my greater destiny."

There in the refrigerator was some Brie and a slab of Petrone Italian sausage.

"A few crackers and I'm set." Looking up, "Thanks mom." The coffee was done. He went back to his computer. "You are going to be a challenge Nugari," he spoke to the computer as he drafted an alternative. "I will give you one half of one percent when the funds are in escrow. Anything more will have to come from 'your people'. Respond." Pleased with his calm business-like reply, he worked the keyboard a little more and sent the fax on its way.

* * * * * *

It was the first of many trips that Michael Orcini would make to the desert in his newly acquired antique dream car.

As the shadows crept across the sand like a Dali masterpiece, the 1957 Mercedes 300 SL Gull Wing roared down the four-lane highway like a rocket to the moon. Tchaikovsky's Capriccio Italien was blasting on the after-market stereo. God was in His heaven, and it's vacation time. He planned to spend half of his time on business.

He knew it was going to be a long night as the effects of the black coffee made him squirm and wish that he had stopped at that service station a few miles back. As a matter of fact, he instructed himself, "Best be on the lookout for a rest sto . . . where the heck did you come from, you crazy son of a buck. . . ?"

Michael looked down at his speedometer. "85," he shouted, as if anyone could hear. "That idiot must be doing a hundred-ten . . .

wah--uh, hey." Slowly he eased the pedal to the floor, reached over
and reassured himself that the radar detector was fully operational
and watched the indicator move, 100-110-120-125. She purred
to his gentle touch, gracefully hugging the road as she closed the
gap. The Mustang convertible certainly was no match for the SL.
He honked the horn, but at this speed, he could barely hear it and
figured that she couldn't either. She? Better check it out. "Do it
slowly, Michael my boy, ya don't want to scare her," he ordered
himself.

He checked her out with a little smile as he came along side.
"Oh-Oh."

She was sobbing so hard; she didn't even know he was there.
He slowed and eased to her six where he stayed for what seemed
like an eternity. Finally she slowed and entered a roadside rest
stop. "Thank the Lord." He made his move to a place he always
liked to refer to as 'the used coffee department'.

A sliver of a moon cut into the steel gray overcast, a soft breeze
came down from the northwest. "I love the fall. Don't you? Smells
like rain, hey?" The old lady let a little more leash out on her
shepherd as if to warn him to shut up and go away, or else.

He moved on past a gray-haired man. "Good evening sir." The
old man put his head down and walked away.

As he approached the girl, he somehow knew that this would
not be a good time to try to strike up a conversation. Her face was
laced with pain, the kind she would feel if her very soul were on
fire. A few raindrops kissed her face and blended with her tears.
She looked at him as if he were not there.

Darci sat on the hood of the Mustang, cuddling her little dog,
fondling the end of a long, black braid, and staring back down the
highway. Slowly she slid off, chuckling a little, as though she had
just come to intimate terms with her surroundings. "Better put
the top up, Puca, or we might get wet on the outside, too." She
glanced at Michael, slid into the white leather and pulled the lever
that brought the top into position. She sensed his concern, and
looked back once more, this time there was an ever-so-small smile

that seemed to say, "thanks". With Puca in her lap, she drove away. Michael watched until the taillights were just tiny spots. Varoom, the SL seduced the road once again.

It was almost three in the morning when Michael pulled under the Porte-cochere at the hotel. The valet was excited. "You don't see a lot of these, ya know?"

"One scratch and I'll have your balls bronzed," Michael grumbled a tired order.

"Oh, no sir! No sir, you can just bet that I'll take good care of her. Just like she was my own." He wiped the hood with his sleeve, took off his hat, bowed a little, then handed a ticket to Michael, and waited until he was in the hotel before parking the SL next to the hotel Rolls-Royce at the front door.

The casino was buzzing for the Tuesday after Labor Day. Michael made his way down the center row of Black Jack tables towards the hotel registration desk. His eyes were drawn to the tall Asian girl standing by the shotgun seat of the last table. Her head tilted, causing her dark, silky hair to fall clear of her mostly bare waist. The blue dress looked like it grew on her, and enjoyed every minute. His eyes quickly peeled the dress away. It wasn't difficult to imagine the fruit lying under those peels. Cheers at the roulette table distracted him. During the short moment he had turned away, she was gone. "Oh, shit!" He almost knocked over the bellboy.

"I beg your pardon, sir."

"Um-uh, do you know who that girl is? The one who was standing right over there, over by the last table? You musta seen her, she's a knockout."

"Blue dress.. Asian . . . looks like she was poured into it?" The boy queried.

"Yeah, that's her."

"She comes here a lot, don't know who she is, sorry sir."

"Thanks kid."

The girl at the registration desk smiled, "May I help you sir?"

Michael put his gold card on the counter. "I don't have a reservation."

"Let me see what I can do for you," she glanced at the card, "Mr. Orcini." She worked the keyboard of the computer, glancing up now and then, catching his eye. "Here we are, Mr. Orcini. I can fit you in a deluxe suite with a Jacuzzi, unless you would prefer something else. The Jacuzzi is wonderful," she assured with complete knowledge.

"Ah, the Jacuzzi sounds great, I'll take that one."

She went aback to the keyboard. Without raising her head, she looked over her glasses. "How long will you be staying with us, Mr. Orcini?"

"A week, maybe two. I'm not really sure. It depends, you know." He planned to stay only a week, but something was tugging inside. It was like having a Courvoisier and wanting more, but knowing that it's not a good idea on an empty stomach.

She finished, returned his card, and called the bellman. "Twelve forty-two for Mr. Orcini. I hope you enjoy your stay with us. If there is anyth. . . ."

He interrupted, "I'll be sure to call. Thank you, Miss.. ?"

"Gordon. Jeri Gordon." She removed her glasses as she inspected him.

"I like your perfume. Is that Lilac, Miss Gordon?" He received her nod and smile, turned and followed the bellman to his room.

It was a large, southwestern style room with a king-sized, four-poster canopy bed with pillows, lots of pillows. A simple carved bench finished the foot of the bed. "It takes just a few minutes to get the tub going. Want me to start-'er up, sir?"

"Sure, I could use it after today, thanks."

"It has an automatic shut-off when it gets full. You're all set sir."

"Thanks, here."

The bellman put his hand out, and smiled. "Thank you, Mr. Orcini." He looked again, "Thank you very much, Mr. Orcini, sir. Shall I. . . ?"

"That will be quite enough," raising his hand to emphasize.

As the door closed behind the bellman, the phone rang. Michael stared at the white antique French style phone. He ignored the sound. It rang a few more times and stopped. He finished unpacking, tested the Jacuzzi, undressed, and sank into the hot, swirling water. "About ten minutes, then to bed," he instructed himself.

He slept like a newborn babe, way beyond his normal hour of six-thirty, when he was awakened abruptly. "Hoozekeepeen, are jew der?"

"What the . . . who's there?" He got a glimpse of a pink fuzz that he figured was hired to torment him. "Go away, I'm trying to sleep."

The maid retreated and quietly shut the door.

Michael rolled over. The digital clock showed 10:22 am. He slid off the edge of the bed, grumbled some unintelligible sounds, scratched his butt with one hand and his thick brown curls with the other, and let out an "O sole mio, la-dah-de-daaah," which soon was absorbed by the sounds of the shower.

The restaurant had a line extending around the corner, into the casino. He moved away though the already crowded casino, towards the valet service area. A nod here, a smile there. With a smirk on his face he acknowledged that *they* are all over the place.

"It's the silver SL," he ordered the valet as he pointed.

A nerd, dressed to imitate a valet, turned where he pointed. "Right on," he squealed, as he hopped up and ran to get the silver rocket. Varoom . . . screech . . .

"Want your balls bronzed on a shelf?" He repeated yesterday's crass overture.

"Sir?"

"Do that again and it will be my personal pleasure to. . . ."

"Sorry, sir. No sir, it'll never happen again, sir," whined the nerdy kid.

"Nice car," came a soft voice from over his left shoulder. She walked by him and placed Puca in the front seat of the convertible, which had just been brought around in front of the SL. "I'd like to apologize for last night." She turned her eyes down, away from his and walked to the driver's side.

"It's OK, I. . . . uh . . ."

Darci looked back at him with a small, sweet smile. "I'm sorry for being such a prude yesterday, and I want you to know . . . well, I just want to say thanks, thanks for taking the time to see that I was all right." She turned and opened the car door.

"Hey! What's your name? How about?"

"My name is Darci Tashmit, I'm in the book."

"Tasmet?"

"TASHMIT," she spelled, slid into her seat, placed Puca on her lap and drove off.

He turned the SL north, towards downtown, and wondered about this girl that he had encountered twice in less than twelve hours. What was she doing at his hotel? He reached for his cell phone, and punched a code in the speed dialer. "Hello. Is Charley there? Yes, tell him it's Michael Orcini and I'm buying lunch. What? The Golden? Oh yes, sure, where? OK! Twenty minutes is fine, thanks. Bye."

"M--m--Michael, you ole ff--fart, how the hh--heck are you?"

Michael's face lit at the sight of his old friend. "It's sure great to see you, pal." They embraced. Not the pat on back hug that most macho guys give, but a long, honest, sincere hug.

They talked about girls and airplanes mostly. Michael liked girls and airplanes. They had been flying together since the first time Charley gave him the controls on the way to Big Bear, a dozen or more years ago. Michael kidded him, "You still dating that child?"

You're just jealous 'cause she's c--cute and has big t--tits." He changed the subject. "You seeing anyone s--special?"

"Still seeing Bobbi, on and off, if you know what I mean?"

"Yeah, you g--guys never g--get ser--ii--ous, just p--playin' a--r--round."

"She's a lot of fun, great in bed, you know, but I don't think we'll ever get serious. She's flying in on Sunday to spend a couple of days."

Michael had been seeing Roberta Azure for almost two years. They do all the things that people should do who are in a long-term relationship, except talk about permanency. Bobbi had suggested alternative living arrangements, but Michael insisted on keeping his independence.

"Any b--body else?"

"No, I think that I'm gonna play it safe for now. But you know, there is this girl I'd like to know. Just met her." He went on to explain about Darci.

"S--she s--sounds like t . . . troub--b--ble," he snickered, pausing momentarily, "You g--got t--time to airp--port huh--hop Mikey?" He snickered because he knew that he was the only person who called him Mikey, and got away with it.

"You bet I do," with a sarcastic, "*Chucky*. How about first thing in the morning."

"You g--got it." They exchanged a warm handshake.

"See you at the airport. First light?"

"Yup."

He reminisced about his friend on the way back to the hotel. Charley only stuttered when he was excited, rushed, frustrated or had to make a major decision. With a smile he wondered if Charley stuttered while making love. He could ask the child. Eh, maybe. He turned up the radio and sang along with Sinatra, "Blue Moon, you saw me standing alone . . ."

He changed his mind and drove out past Sundance Lake then to Boulder City Municipal Airport. He checked in at the FBO to see what planes were available for rent. Nothing he liked, so he went back to his hotel.

The valet recognized him. "Good afternoon sir. We'll take good care of your car."

He played Black Jack for the rest of the afternoon, and into the early evening, winning a little. After a while he realized he was hungry, went to the buffet, stuffed himself, then retired to his room.

* * * * * * *

Darci settled into the corner of the loveseat with a book on The Secret Knowledge of Dreams, placed one leg under the other, and pulled it back until she was comfortable. "Ah that's good." She sipped herbal tea from her favorite cup and looked at Puca, knowing that he wanted to jump up. "OK." He snuggled in a corner just under her elbow. "He's kinda cute, don't you think, huh, Puca?" He looked up as if he approved. She named him Puca T after the supernatural being from Irish folklore that often appeared in animal form. The T for his last name, of course, and like his namesake, he was harmless but very mischievous. She snuggled, adjusting her position a little more into the small couch, looked down at Puca telling him, "Well Puca, we'll just have to see what this fellow is all about." She was sure he would call. She found the bookmark and began reading the chapter describing the dream world of children and pets.

She had been reading only a moment when the phone rang. She waited while the machine picked up. "Hello caller, I'm not here right now, but if you leave your number, I'll get back to you as soon as I return."

"I'm sorry to hear about your loss," he told the machine, "call me if you need to talk. You know the number."

She didn't want to talk. It wasn't fair. He was so young. Why didn't he listen? Those damn small planes, you just can't trust them. Sobbing, she threw the book at the wall. It caught a small picture. Crash! The picture caught the top of a marble statue of an Indian. The glass broke, exposing a picture of her mom and dad. She held it to her breast. "It's not fair, it's not fair, it's not . . ." Her words faded into her sobs.

She awoke to the sound of the phone. "Hello."

"Hello, Darci?"

"Yes. Who's this?"

"We met last night and again this morning. You said to call. Is this a bad time?"

"What time is it?"

"It's about eight o'clock."

"Look, can you call back in the morning? I'm a little stressed right now."

"Sure, I can do that. Any time. What's good for you?"

"Oh, I guess about nine. Let me look in my calendar. Hold on. . . . What did I do with that dumb calendar?"

"What?"

"No not you. I was just trying to find my, oh here it is. Let's see . . . yes, nine will be fine. I'll talk to you then." She started to hang the receiver. "Wait, wait. I don't even know your name. Are you still there?"

"Yes, um, Michael. That's my name."

"Ummichael, what kind of a name is that?" she teased.

"No it's just Michael, Michael Orcini. That's my name, Michael Orcini."

"Mike Orcini, I like that."

"It's Michael."

"Hello Michael Orcini, I'm pleased to meet you, Michael Orcini."

"Were you asleep? Did I wake you?"

"No, it's all right, I had to get up and answer the phone anyway." They laughed. "So you won't forget? You'll call me tomorrow?"

"Yes, I mean no. I mean--I'll call at nine in the morning."

"Goodnight, Michael Orcini."

"Night."

Darci took a long, hot shower and put on her favorite sweats. She fed Puca, then rummaged through the pantry to see what to fix for herself. She wasn't very hungry, but some crackers and cheese, a little wine, sure. "I hope he calls, Puca."

* * * * * * *

The morning was bright with a slight chill and a calm breeze that whisked across the desert towards Lone Mountain in the west. Not a cloud in the sky, a perfect day to fly.

Charlie had already inspected the plane thoroughly by the time Michael got to the airport. "Climb in s--slow p--poke," the pilot commanded. He set the radio. "North Vegas ground, Cherokee, Nevada niner tha-ree foh-war niner sierra papa ready to taxi to the active with information." Charlie announced into his headset.

"Cherokee, niner sierra papa, taxi to the active and hold." was the response from ground control.

"Niner sierra papa. Ready Mikey?"

Michael showed his thumbs up as he mapped out their first leg. Charley almost never stuttered when he was the 'pilot in command'. Michael would navigate and Charley would fly the first leg to Bullhead City, then they would go across the river in Laughlin for breakfast. They would change seats, Michael would pilot, and Charley would decide where next, and so on.

"North Vegas tower, Cherokee, Nevada ninner tha--ree foh-war niner sierra papa, holding for a right turn departure."

"Cherokee, niner sierra papa, clear for departure. Have a good flight, Charley."

"Let's go." Thumbs up. "Full power, twenty, thirty, forty, fifty---sixty-five, an--d rotate," shouted Charley over the sound of the Lycoming engine.

Charlie maneuvered the Piper Cherokee over Lake Mead and Hoover Dam, then down along the Colorado River. He notified the Aeronautical Advisory Station at Bullhead City when they approached Cottonwood Cove. "Bullhead City Unicom, this is Cherokee Nevada niner tha-ree foh-war niner sierra papa over Cottonwood, airport advisory." He tried again. There was no response.

"Why don't they answer, Charlie?" Michael looked bewildered.

"You got the right frequency?

"Bullhead City, Right? I dialed in 122.7 Oops, there's two Bullhead Cities." He reached for the radio and redialed 122.8. "Try it now, Charlie."

Charlie repeated his call to the new frequency. "Bullhead City, this is Cherokee Nevada niner tha-ree for-war niner sierra papa, ten North on the Colorado for landing, advisory."

"Cherokee niner sierra papa, sixteen active, calm wind, five knots. Cessna 172 reports inbound fifteen southeast."

Charlie announced his position at two more intervals prior to landing.

They 'tied down' the Cherokee and caught the shuttle across the river. "Let's try the Belle. I hear they've got good hotcakes there."

"S--sounds ok--kay to me."

The waitress took them to a deuce near the buffet setup. "This okay?" They nodded.

"A couple cups of your finest coffee." Michael ordered. They studied the menu.

"What timezit, Charlie?"

"N--nine f--fif--t--teen."

"Shit. Where's a phone? I left my cell in the plane." He stopped a bus boy that pointed towards the far corner. "Good thing I've got this calling card," he thought, as he placed the call.

"Hello caller, I'm not here. . . ."

"Darn machine where is she? Hi, this is Michael Orcini, sorry that I'm late calling. Got hung up. I'm in Laughlin. Umm, I--uh. I'd like to see you. Would you like to, ah, well, maybe have dinner with me tomorrow night. I'm staying at Caesar's, room twelve forty-two. Call me there, and I'll get back to you. Okay?" He squirmed a little as he hung up the phone. He stopped to reflect on what he had just done. The uneasy feeling he had with this girl was not a normal reaction for him. He tilted his head, bewildered at his desire to be with this mysterious girl.

When he got back to their table Charlie had ordered the hotcakes. "I asked her to b--bring you s--some eggs."

"That's great, thanks."

"W--what's wrong? S--she turn you d--down?" Charlie noticed his friend's perplexed expression.

"She wasn't there, got her machine."

Darci laughed, as she monitored the call. "He's gonna be fun, Puca. Sounds a little shy. I like that." She frowned, not wanting to start up with another guy who would jump right in and try to control her, like her last encounter. No more dominating macho guy, except, maybe. . . . She hugged herself, picked up her little dog, and went into the kitchen.

Before they took off again, Michael made another call.

Everything had slowed down at the travel agency. With Labor Day out of the way and all the kids back to school, Keleigh would be able to take some time for herself, and she'd better do it now, before the Thanksgiving rush. She planned quietly to go to Tahoe.

Her daydream was interrupted by the sound of the phone. "Good morning, Cody Travel. How may I help you?" her assistant announced. "Yes, Miss Ives is here. Who's calling, please? Oh! Mr. Orcini, yes I'll tell her, just a moment." She turned around with her hand over the mouthpiece, "It's that gorgeous Michael Orcini for you."

Keleigh smiled. "Hi! Michael, where are you this beautiful day?"

"I'm over in Laughlin with Charlie, doing some airport hopping. I'd like to see you. What are you up to tonight? Want to get some soup, and catch up on stuff? It would have to be later, like nine or so?"

"It just happens that I'm free tonight, and nine would be just fine."

"Can you meet me at Grandma's House at nine?" He referred to a coffee shop where they often went after playing racquetball. He couldn't remember exactly why they called it that. It certainly wasn't because of the food.

"I can do that, see ya, bye."

He never had a chance to say goodbye, she always said that and hung up when she's through. He put the cell phone in his pack, looked at Charlie and said, "Where to?"

The Sedona airport sat on a five hundred foot Mesa. The winds were calm and CTAF indicated runway 3 for landing. Charlie wanted to meet a friend at Red Rock Aviation and check out a Comanche that was for sale. Michael parked the Cherokee in front of Red Rock. "You never told me why you want such an old bird."

"She a fast b--baby, lots of r--room too, and I aw--all--ways w--wanted one. Izat Oh--k--kay with you? Besides, she's a part of my heritage."

Michael smiled, and climbed down after Charlie. She was parked right in front, a beauty all right, had a tiger shark cowl, and a Hartzell prop. Charlie had bragged all the way over that she was one of the last made before the Piper plant was inundated when the Susquehanna River swelled from the rains left by Hurricane Agnes in '72.

"That's a great 260-C," hollered a weathered old guy, in a World War II leather flight jacket, as he walked toward them.

"Hey Jack."

The old guy smiled at Charlie.

"How much time do you need, Charlie?"

"About an hour," he said without a stutter.

"Okay, but be sure to be back by then, I have to get to Las Vegas by eight-thirty."

Charlie looked at his watch, gave him a 'thumbs up' and got one in return.

Michael was looking out the Airport Restaurant window when Charlie eased the old bird onto 'two-one'. The wind had changed and was gusting at 15 knots. Michael finished his coffee and joined Charlie. "I got the standard briefing and checked for NOTAMS. Everything is AOK. Ready to go?"

"Soon as I finish checking this b--baby." He double-checked the fuel level. He was satisfied. "Let's go."

They went over their route, checked the weather briefings for winds aloft and set their course. "You gonna buy that bird?"

"Think so, if I can get that old b--b--buzzard down on his price." Charlie was excited about the prospect of buying the

Comanche. "She's in real g--good shape, only thirty-s--seven hours s--since her last major, and t--the p--prop's b--brand new."

Charlie took off from the plateau without climbing more than fifty feet, made a steep turn, and flew right passed Bell Rock through the heart of a beautiful red rock canyon before easing her up and back to Las Vegas.

They silently drank-in the sight of the last rays of an auburn colored sunset as it highlighted the canyon rim, and created deep purple shadows against God's awesome red rock creation as Charlie pointed the nose of the Cherokee at the black sky just above, and a few degrees north of the setting sun before he established the final heading that Michael would plot as they reached altitude. Michael established a heading that took them back over Bullhead City and Laughlin. From there Charlie would fly his normal route back. He kept a powerboat at a friend's house on the Colorado, and had made the trip to the 'River' many times.

Michael stared out the window. "The sky was as black as God could make it, with a lot of little holes to let His light through," he could hear his mother say, as if she were right there with him. He looked up to the heavens and just knew that she was. God and his mother, they were both right here with him. He would call her when they landed. He loved to fly. It was so peaceful.

The flight from the river was smooth and uneventful. Charlie landed precisely 'on the numbers' as he had done a hundred times or more, and taxied to the tie-down area.

Michael started to help with the 'tie-down', and realized that it was almost eight thirty. "I've got to run, Charlie. Do you mind?"

"No, go ahead. S--say h--hi to K--Keleigh for m--me?"

"Absolutely! It's been a great day."

Charlie stuck his head out from under the wing where he was tying her down, and smiled with his usual 'thumbs-up'.

Michael jumped in the SL and headed for Grandma's house.

* * * * * *

Jami Wu sat nervously in a lawn chair, and listened as 'Connie' Contedetto laid out a strategic plan for the financing of a hotel casino project with his group.

Jami's people, from the central province of Hupei, China, sent him to the 'States' to invest a great deal of money in a gaming operation. They originally wanted to find experienced developers to build and manage casinos on Mainland China, near Wuhan along the Yangtze River.

The developers would come and build, but the Chinese could not find a soul who could stay long enough to get the casinos 'up and running'. Their alternative plan was to gain experience in Las Vegas, return to China, and complete the primary plan. Jami was in the States to joint venture with 'Donna' Una Ceres. They planned to put up an equal amount of money, but the Donna would get a larger return because she had the political contacts to make it happen. The quandary, for Jami, was to combine funds with the Donna, and then act out the role of a sole financial partner for purposes of the State Gaming Commission.

Now Jami T'ing-fang Wu, named after a turn of the century diplomat, was reduced to taking orders from undesirable business associates, a situation he would tolerate long enough to get what he wanted. What he did not foresee was that the Donna had ideas of her own, which did not include him. In addition, there was Nugari, and the other greedy factions within his own team. Jami moved on like a horse with blinders, seeing only what had been, and ignoring what was just around the corner. Just yesterday he had called his associates on Mainland China, and requested a retinue of his own to offset Una Ceres' henchmen. Jami readied himself for a conflict, but being prepared for a power encounter with Connie and his men was not the same as a physical face-to-face encounter with them. He would soon confront these obstacles.

Ermano 'Connie' Contedetto was the final person to see before having an audience with Una Ceres. "Donna Ceres wants to be sure for you should completely understand that what must be finalized with your people before she should to allow our group a participation in this venture of considerable financial undertaking." Connie always spoke with a surly voice, emphasizing the important words with his hands as though it made a difference.

Wu looked over his shoulder. First his eyes moved along a flagstone pathway, then in the direction of the white two-story mansion. There was a massive terrace with patterned brick paving, and large pastel clay pots in groups of varying colors. The pots were freshly planted with pink, red and white flowers. Tables with colorful umbrellas were organized along the outer edge. There was a shapely woman in a white tennis outfit leaning against one of the tables and talking on a cellular phone. A man came out of the house, walked around in front of her and spoke softly. She looked at Jami then followed the man into the house. Looking up Jami could make out the image of an old woman standing on a balcony protected by an ornate pink balustrade and flanked by two very large men in black. He instinctively knew who she was.

The 'Donna' raised her hand above her head with a sovereign wave. Connie got up. "Excuse me Mr. Wu", he bowed slightly, "make yourself comfortable. If you want something, ask Mario. He will get it for you." Connie motioned to a man on the terrace, "I must see to the needs of my employer. I will return in a few minutes."

Jami watched as Connie walked at a fast pace and disappeared into the house.

"May I get you something, Sir? A drink perhaps?"

"The woman on the terrace!"

Mario's eyes pierced into the uncomfortable Asian, "Sir?"

"A glass of white wine, dry, not sweet," he requested, hoping it would erase the uneasy feeling in the pit of his stomach.

"We have Liefraumilch, an excellent Rhine wine. It's delightfully dry. Would you like to try a glass of that, Sir?" the moose of a man asked.

"Yes, thank you, Mario, thank you," Jami said with some trepidation thinking that Mario was probably better used as a hit man than a butler.

Jami sat and studied his copy of the proposal he had already memorized days before. "What are they doing?" he wondered, looking at his watch. "It's supposed to be the Chinese who take a long time, agree and then change their minds, not the Italians," he assured himself talking out loud to the lawn chair across the table. He threw the document on the table and stood up. He was prepared to accept alternatives without having to go back to his superiors, but the waiting made him nervous. He began to amble about, being careful not to move toward the house fearing that one of those somber men in black would return to admonish him.

Connie returned forty-five minutes later. "I am very sorry. Please accept my very sincere expression of regret, I did not mean to have you to wait for such a long time," he articulated every word. "Donna Ceres has reviewed your proposal, and has consented that I am to accompany you to meet with Mr. Orcini tomorrow for dinner." He took a Turkish cigarette from an engraved silver case. After tapping it on the case, he lit it with a wooden match that he struck on the bottom of the table. "I will call you at your hotel to let you be aware of the location of the restaurant." Connie gestured away with a palms up hand indicating it was time for Jami to leave. "Mario will show you the way."

Connie headed for a bungalow near the pool as Mario ushered Jami out.

The shapely woman reappeared on the terrace just as Jami reached the top of the stairs. She was the most intriguing Asian woman he had ever seen. The change of attire went from a simple tennis outfit to a seemingly painted on, full-length gown of pink with pearls all the way down her right side emphasizing her fully exposed leg. She tossed her head sending her silky black hair over her shoulder, and smiled at Jami as he passed.

Jami paused only to receive a gentle nudge from the bull of a butler behind him.

The man waiting in the bungalow was savoring the Manhattan that Mario had prepared for him a little while ago. He sat in the overstuffed leather chair in front of the fireplace still watching the closed circuit TV, even though the primary subject had just left. "Why the fellow behind the bush with a gun?" he asked as Connie entered.

"Nona insists on the added protection of these measures when she is in the company of someone that is not of her acquaintance or trust."

"Why do some of you call her 'Nona'?"

"Nona means grandmother in Italian," he said reverently, "and only if you are accepted as Family can you address the Donna in such a manner of esteem."

The large man, wearing a Greek sea captain's cap, rose and went to the bar. "You are family?" he spoke in a tone of disbelief. "Do you think that you could have Mario fix me another drink?" He eyed Connie with disdain, as he turned his empty glass over.

"No!" Connie said with authority, then took the glass from him and placed it on the bar. "It is time for you to go. I will call you to make you aware of the time and the place for which we will have our meeting tomorrow with Mr. Orcini." He motioned for the Commodore to follow him. "You have heard on the television what I have spoken to Mr. Wu in regards to the wishes of the Donna?"

Claude deVillefrance followed behind Connie without hesitation as the two men in black, who seemed to appear out of nowhere, silently enforced the command. "I heard that we meet tomorrow for dinner."

Connie nodded to the men in black, and they ushered their guest along the path, past the woman in pink and out to a waiting car. "Good night, Sir," one of them said.

* * * * * *

Keleigh stepped out of the shower, modeling the lavender towel in front of the full-length mirror. She dropped it to her hip; a slight twist pushed her ample breasts forward. A little more turn and she exposed the profile of her back as it flowed into a soft curve. "Those racket ball games sure do pay off," she said admiring her small, well-shaped, firm butt. "I could drive him crazy," she told the mirror. She went to the closet and began trying on her sexiest things. A short, tight, black, show-all, no room for underwear dress. "This was made for Michael," a little above a whisper, as she bent and touched her toes, still looking back at her reflection in the mirror.

"Crazy, heck why not drive him all the way to insane," she informed the looking glass once again as she auditioned a short skirt and teaser top. She danced in front of the mirror. "Shit, this won't work. He'll just make some silly remark." She put on an old S.C. sweatshirt, some baggy Dockers, her Nikes and left to meet him.

Michael was reworking some notes in a corner booth.

"Hi."

"Hey, kiddo, you look great," he got up hugged her, took her face in his hands and kissed her, as you would a child, on the lips. Still holding her with one hand, he picked up a single yellow rose he brought, and placed it gently in her hand.

She squirmed away and plopped into the booth like a shy little girl. She smelled the rose. "I'm glad to see you, Michael. How long will you be in town this time?"

"It could be permanent if this deal works out."

"What deal? What are you saying? Tell me. I want to know everything!" Her face lit up like the sunshine of a spring day, right after a warm rain shower.

He always loved her enthusiasm. "You're the greatest. If I were ten years older, I'd make an honest woman of you."

She frowned, as if to scold him, "I'm a girl and I'll always be a girl, you know that, Michael, and I don't want you any older, either." She liked being a girl. There was something about being called a woman that didn't feel right, made her squirm.

"Yes. I'm sorry Keleigh. Forgive me?"

Her green eyes blazed under her auburn bangs. "Tell me! Tell me!" she demanded.

"Let's order something. They have your favorite. Corn chowder."

"Why do you always tease me? I want to know. Michael?"

"Let's order first, Okay?"

"You know me, Michael darling." She submitted to his wish.

"Check your menu, here comes the waitress. I'll have the BLT on wheat toast; hold the mayo, and a cup of your finest coffee. Keleigh?"

"Oh, I'm so excited, you order for me, Michael."

"Not a chance, I've tried that before."

"Can I get just a cup of that corn chowder? And some saltine crackers with butter, real butter, please?"

"It only comes by the bowl. Want anything to drink, Dearie?" scowled the Nazi drill sergeant, dressed like a waitress.

"Some herbal tea, please. With honey."

"Dearie," they said together, after she was out of range.

"Keleigh, how have you been? It's been so long since I've seen you. Tell me everything that you have been up to since, well, since the last time we met." He put his hand on hers, like she was his dearest friend.

She pouted, and slowly withdrew her hand. "Later, Michael, but now I must know what you are up to. What is so special that you would even think to move here?"

"Keleigh, Keleigh." he took both of her hands. This time he held tight. "I want you to be the first to know. I haven't even told Charlie."

He took a deep breath and looked deep into her eyes. "I have an option on some acreage out at the lake and I am going to build an exclusive resort. Five Star hotel, the finest casino anywhere and a spa to die for and I want you to run the casino."

"Michael!"

"What do you think, Kiddo?"

"I don't know. Let me catch my breath."

They sat and stared at each other for a long time. They didn't have to talk, they communicated with their eyes. He was unaware that he was still holding her hands.

She looked down. He released his grip. When Keleigh spoke, it was like a child opening the Christmas present that she always wanted, with tears of joy breaking into an emotional, "You want me to run the casino? Oh, Michael, I love you." She didn't realize what she had just said. She kissed his hand moving it to caress her cheek with his palm.

It was his turn to withdraw. "Not only do I want you to run the Casino, but you've got a piece of the action if you want. What do you say? Miss Keleigh Cody-Ives?"

He had only called her that once before. It was after her divorce when they got drunk together. Keleigh moved over to his side of the booth, put her arm through his and laid her head on his shoulder. "I must be dreaming. This just can't be true."

He touched her cheek. She looked up. "Well?" He said softly.

She felt like he was asking her to have sex with him. The excitement was so powerful; she thought she was going to have an orgasm right there in the restaurant. She released his arm and moved back across the table. After a moment, "I would just adore being your casino operator, sir," she expressed in a nasal, snooty fashion.

He laughed, "I love you too, Keleigh."

The Nazi returned with their order. "Want anything else?"

They looked at each other. "No thanks," Michael responded.

Michael shared his entire plan with his best friend. They talked and planned for hours. Exhausted, they walked with their arms around each other to the parking lot. They stopped at her car and embraced.

Keleigh couldn't let go, she had to hold on to the dream, and it didn't seem real. This was something she had always wanted.

It was like he could read her mind, "It's real baby."

She pulled back slightly. She was tired.

"Say good night Gracie." He patted her on the butt as he always did. "Night."

"See ya, bye," she whispered as she turned. "Michael," she turned back and raised her voice a little, "why'd you give me the rose?"

"Because I love you, Keleigh." He turned on his heel and slowly walked to his car. He reached the SL and glanced back to make sure that she was safe in her car.

She took a while, and then slowly drove away. "You're the best, Keleigh," he reassured himself as he watched. "This is good." He said to himself, pleased with her commitment. Michael went back to his hotel tired and excited.

The desk phone indicated messages. He turned on the small desk lamp. "This message is for Mr. Orcini," the voice sounded more like a machine than the recorder. "This is Pernicious Nugari calling. I would like Mr. Orcini to call me when he gets in. My number is . . ." Michael didn't bother, he had it in his book and would touch base with him in the morning. He took off his shoes, and waited for the next message.

"Hello, Mr. Orcini, my name is Jami Wu. Mr. deVillefrance asked me to call you. Would you please call me. . . ?" This was the call he wanted, the fellow who could provide the finances for his project, if Hans didn't. He'd call him first thing in the morning.

"Hello Michael Orcini. I'd love to have dinner with you tomorrow. I can be ready by 7:30 if that's all right with you. Let me tell you how to get to my house."

He sat and wrote down her address and very specific directions. "See you then SWEETHEART," sounding a little like Bogart. "Oh . . . you're not there yet . . . of course not . . . I . . . um . . . oh. . . . h . . . ," a disappointed voice drug out the message, "thanks for the rose and everything Michael, see ya bye." "Hmm," he sniffed, "housekeeping must have sent up some flowers." He enjoyed the pungent smell of lilac. He took off his shirt, unbuckled his belt, and paused with the realization that lilacs were not in season. Puzzled, he started for the bathroom.

"Come on in, the water's fine." A recessed light above the Jacuzzi came on to reveal an invitation from within the bubbles.

"What are you doing. . . . ? How did you get in? Miss Gordon?"

"It's part of the perks for working here. Well--ll?" she stretched out the invitation. "Do I have to come out and get you?"

"Ah, the lilac. What the hell," he undressed and she turned on the jets.

The mirrors surrounding the Jacuzzi steamed as they enjoyed each other. She was very intense. Michael became unsure if he should continue.

"I need to cool down," he pulled up and sat on the edge leaving his legs in.

She moved to wipe the soap from him, then stood up, took his hand and invited him out holding the bath towel to blot the excess water from him as she led him to the four-poster.

After a while, she looked up to see the mirror above his bed. She paused, "Nice ass," grabbed it with both hands, and they continued.

"Thanks." he graciously acknowledged her compliment.

Michael's internal watch told him to open his eyes, but he was a little afraid at what he might encounter. He mustered the strength, opened his eyes, "Good morning," he said to his reflection in the mirror above the bed. He expected the reflection or, 'what's-her-name,' to answer. He waited a moment. Perhaps it was just a dream. He slid out of bed, as he always did, and inspected the suite. "Just a dream. Oops, guess not."

She left a beautiful floral arrangement, with a note, on the vanity where he would be sure to see it first.

"You definitely come and go as you please," he admonished her as if she was still there, and not entirely sure why he participated in her little party.

He read the note and recognized that it was from a poem by Susan Polis Schultz, one of his favorites:

'Once in a while everyone needs to know that they are wanted
. . . . I just wanted to tell you that if you ever feel this need.
I would like to be the one to reassure you . . . ' Jeri

He smiled and said out loud, "What a quaint mixture of raw sex and morality." Then he quietly dismissed his part in the night before as he passed by the bed, smiled and continued to the desk phone.

Michael loved coffee in the morning. He 'dialed' the phone. "Room service? Ah good, I'd like a carafe of your finest coffee, a Danish, no nuts. Yes that's right, and a very large glass of orange juice. Yes, twelve forty-two. Ten minutes? Thanks."

He got out of the shower as the doorbell rang. "Room Service."

"Just a minute."

He threw on a hotel robe and opened the door. "Just put it on the desk," he motioned to the bellgirl, as he picked up his pants, rummaged through the pockets and handed her a satisfactory tip.

"Thank you, Mr. Orcini, sir." The bellgirl made an abrupt about face and left.

"Best get on with business," he mumbled to himself, listened to his messages again, lifted the receiver, and punched in Wu's number.

The voice on the phone said that Mr. Wu was out, but she would be talking to him soon, and she would ask him to call back.

"Tell Mr. Wu that Michael Orcini called him from Las Vegas. . . . say again please . . . he's here? Here in Las Vegas? OK . . . yes that's right . . . Caesars . . . yes, thank you."

"Well, let's see what Perni is up to . . . hello, may I speak with Mr. Nugari?"

The female voice responded, "This is Kimberly, I am Mr. Nugari's assistant." She paused, "One moment please. Mr. Nugari is on a long distance conference call, but would like to get back to you as soon as he is finished. Where can you be reached?"

"Pretty darn formal," he thought. "I'm at my hotel in Las Vegas. He has the number, room twelve forty-two."

"Thank you, Mr. Orcini, good bye."

"Good bye."

He 'dialed' another number. "Hello caller, I'm not here. . . ."

Perplexed, he talked to the machine. "Hi, This is Michae. . . ."

"Hello Michael Orcini," she cut in on his response. "Did you get my message?"

"Yes, and 7:30 is perfect."

"What should I wear? Dress-up? Casual? I must tell you that I don't own any old blue jeans or anything like that. So where are we going? I hope it's a really nice, quite place for our first date and all. Am I talking too much? Maybe I should shut up."

"Casual will be just fine. Any special requests?"

"Just be on time, that's all. Oh, and I don't really want to go anywhere near a casino, if you don't mind. Do you know how to get here? Can you find it?"

"Absolutely, see you promptly at 7:30. Bye."

"Good bye, Michael Orcini."

He wondered if she was being cute with his name or what. "Maybe Charlie was right," he pondered. "She could be trouble."

Shaving wasn't one of his favorite things to do, but he didn't like the alternative of clipping and trimming a beard either. He made gestures at the face looking at him from the mirror.

"Wonder what was bothering her the other day?" he questioned the lathered face, while seeing her pain and the tears, as her face appeared instead of his, in the steamy mirror. He blinked and shook his head. Her face was still there. "Where did you come from?" As if there should be an answer.

The phone rang. "Thank God." He splashed warm water on his face, wiped the water and cream off his face and neck, threw the towel over his shoulder, walked across the room and picked up the phone.

"Hi, Michael. Did I wake you? Did you sleep well?"

"Hi, Keleigh. Uh. Yeah. I guess so. How about you? You Okay?"

"I couldn't sleep. I was so excited about the project Michael. When I got home I poured a large glass of Chardonnay and settled in with my scrap book."

Michael smiled, sat back, put his foot up on the desk, poured some coffee, bit into the Danish, and switched the phone to the other ear. He knew it was going to be a while, but did not mind it at all. He actually enjoyed her meandering conversations, and always felt totally at ease with her. Sometimes it felt sort of strange to have a girl as a best friend, especially when they shared their innermost feelings about other relationships.

She frowned, tilted her head and continued without missing a beat. "I was remembering the days when my dad and uncle ran the casino in Monaco. Dad used to set me on his lap and tell me stories about all those rich and famous people who came to the casino. Just like he knew them personally. Michael, Did I ever tell you about the time when he introduced me to Princess Grace?" She didn't wait for an answer, she just kept rambling. "Now I'm going to be just like my dad. Isn't it just the greatest, Michael?" She took a short breath, "What are you doing tonight? I thought that maybe I could make some dinner and we could have some wine and talk some more, or I'll get some of your favorite brandy. You know I never did get the chance to tell you what I have been doing the last few months. So . . ."

"Hold on sweet cheeks, you're going too fast. Besides, I have something planned. Let's get our bearings on this, and I'll call you in a couple of days, okay?" He didn't wait for an answer, either. "I have to meet with those guys, Nugari and Wu, about the money, remember? I told you about them last night."

Keleigh sighed with disappointment, "A couple of days? I want to get started right away. What can I be doing? I can't just sit around while you have all the fun. Sweet cheeks? Why'd you call me that?"

"Because you have a nice butt. Now you can start by calling all those people that you want to work for you and get them to commit to the project. Work up an incentive plan, you know. That kind of stuff. Oh, and check with your friends in the business and get some stats on the ultra-rich. Where they've been spending their money, how much they bet, you know."

"Since when did you started noticing my butt?" she continued without missing a beat. "I can do all that with no problem, and I have some standard forms at home for the other stuff. What about non-disclosure documents and so forth?"

"Yes. Sounds great, kiddo. Round-up whatever you think, and we'll take a look."

"I'm really excited about this, Michael. So, when did you notice?

"What?" He pretended quizzically.

"My butt. When did you. . . ?"

"You should really wear something other than those baggy pants."

"I'm excited. Okay. I know that you're busy, see ya, bye."

"I know," he said to the dial tone. Keleigh hung up just like she always did. He loved listening to Keleigh, and would have let her go on and on, but he had business to take care of, and a date with a woman that was a definite distraction to his somewhat scheduled life. He looked at the receiver. He had always known that she had cute buns. Always.

The phone rang as he put it down. "Yes?" It was the hotel operator. Wu had called, and she offered to place the call for him. "That would be fine, thanks."

Wu came on the phone, "Mr. Orcini?"

"Yes, this is Michael Orcini."

"Hello! My name is Jami T'ing-fang Wu. Mr. deVillefrance asked that I call with regards to your casino project. Is it possible for you meet me for dinner tonight? I have someone that I want you to meet." He spoke very good English.

"Not tonight, Mr. Wu, however, I am free this afternoon, how about lunch?" Something pulled at his gut. He couldn't put a handle on it, but his entire substance resisted the thought of not being with Darci tonight. He had never had such an ardent desire to be with someone before.

"Let me make a phone call, Mr. Orcini. I will call you soon."

"Thank you Mr. Wu."

"Hello, room service? Can you send up some of your finest

coffee? . . . Yes, that's right . . . thanks. What? Yes they did, it was fine, but I want some more."

The operator called again. "Mr. Orcini. Kimberly from Mr. Nugari's office called. Do you want me to connect you with that number?"

"Yes, but if Mr. Wu calls, would you please interrupt? I must talk to him."

"Yes Mr. Orcini. Please hold while I get that number for you." It only took a moment and she was back. "Here's Mr. Nugari's office, sir."

"Thanks."

"Michael, I'm glad I caught you in. Wu wants to meet with you and his group tonight. They are very interested in your project. I am going to take the next flight out. So clear your calendar. We should plan an early dinner so there's enough time to go over all facets of the project and answer all their questions. Wu should be calling you soon."

Michael took the receiver away from his ear, and with the instinct of a private eye recognized the proverbial balls on this son of a bitch. Nonetheless, he waited as his blood pressure started to rise.

"Michael, did you hear what I just said?"

"You're not in the Army anymore Nugari." He paused to allow the knot forming in his stomach to loosen. "I'm not one of your little privates, or whoever it is that you're used to pushing around, and I don't take orders. Got it?"

"Air Force, I was in the Air Force."

"I don't give a damn what force you were in, Nugari," he said loudly. "Look, can you call me back in about fifteen minutes? I need to calm down."

"I don't know what you're all hot about, buddy, but I guess I can call back."

"Fifteen minutes, give me fifteen minutes. Talk to you then." He slowly replaced the receiver, holding back the urge to slam it down. "Buddy? This guy really knows how to get on my nerves," he mumbled.

The phone rang again. Michael took a deep breath, and answered with a very soft, "Hello, this is Michael Orcini speaking."

"My, but you are so formal my darling," an equally soft, but decidedly more sexy voice responded. "I hope that you haven't gone and changed on me."

"Uh, right." His brain was on overload. He wanted to ask who it was, but instinctively knew he should not. He spoke, "I'm sorry, darling, my mind is somewhere else at the moment. Forgive me?"

"What's wrong, Michael?" Still talking in a forced sexy voice.

"Nothing, I'm just stressed a little. What's up?" Still not recognizing the guise.

"Well, I know something is wrong, 'cause you never call me darling," she announced with the voice of a woman who wanted an honest 'darling' from him, but knew deep in her heart that it would never happen.

It finally clicked in. "Bobbi!" He realized who she was. "Where are you, and why are you talking like that?"

"Don't give me that, 'where are you' stuff. I'm still at the ocean where you left me." She sensed that he just recognized her disguised voice. "Doesn't sound like you miss me."

"Bobbi, Bobbi," he grasped, now that he was into it. "You know me, I'm just playing with you. So--oo, what's up?"

"Sometimes I feel like I could understand where you're at, if only I could understand who you are. Oh well, I just wanted to let you know that something has come up and I won't be able to come and play with you in Vegas on Sunday. Sorry, darling."

"It's just as well, Bobbi, it looks like I'm going to be busy with this project. Some people are in town and want to see me," he said, relieved that she wasn't coming. The relief was more than just being able to make time to spend time with her. He felt a sense of ease now that he wouldn't be obligated to entertain her. She did like to be entertained.

"Don't make it sound so . . . Damn it Michael, you could at least be a little sad or something. You could tell me that you had big plans and I screwed them all up."

Roberta Azure was doing it to him again. She purposefully moved in and out of her childlike actions, first blaming him, and then making him apologize for *her* actions.

"Actually, I did have plans for us, Bobbi," he said smoothly. "Perhaps another time, soon?"

She waited. "You're forgiven, Michael," she sang softly to a little tune.

"What do you mean, I'm forgiven? You're the one who canceled." He raised his voice slightly, trying not to play her game, and not to sound too relieved.

Bobbi made a soft sweet laughing sound as if she had just attained some small victory over him. "Call me when you get back. Michael darling. Ciao", she completed.

"So long, Bobbi, I'll see you when I get back."

Wu called with news that a lunch meeting would work out, but Nugari would not be able to be there. "Is that okay with you, Mr. Orcini?" He asked apologetically.

"Yes that is just fine with me. We can get all the preliminary dialog out of the way and get to know each other," he decided, but qualified, "I always like to know who I'm getting into bed with." They laughed, while Michael remembered that wasn't exactly true with Jeri last night. "Will you call Nugari and let him know, Mr. Wu?"

"Yes, I will call him. I can send a car around for you at one o'clock, Mr. Orcini, if that is acceptable."

"Thanks Mr. Wu that would be more than acceptable." He marked his calendar, and assessed how easy it was getting accustomed to these guys catering to him. Yeah, ve--ry easy.

Michael grabbed his brief case, moved to the couch by the window placing the case on the coffee table. He stopped for a moment, went back and retrieved the carafe of coffee and his cup. "Now I am ready," he professed to the world outside his window. Before getting down to the work at hand, he opened the sliding door and went out on the balcony, took a deep breath of fresh air, closed his eyes and let the sun and soft breeze warm his body.

Images of Darci filled his mind. It was like he had his own private movie screen right there. It seemed strange. There was no sound. He listened as he 'watched'. Finally she said in a whisper, "A quiet place for our first date. I don't want to go anywhere near a casino."

He shook his head, to clear the daydream, so he could get on with matters at hand. A navy jet soared at a relatively low altitude. "I've got to call John," he told himself, went into the room picked up his daytimer calendar and wrote himself a note; 'Call John R'. He paused for a moment, and jotted, 'Call Mom. He studied his watch then gathered the papers into his briefcase and went down by the pool.

He soon realized that sitting by the pool, in Las Vegas, and trying to work was not going to be fruitful. There were too many distractions. He put the papers back into the case and started back by way of the casino. "A little blackjack will relax me," a small persuasive voice suggested from somewhere inside his replete brain.

"Will you send this to my room, please?" he asked at the front desk without looking to see who would respond while he searched his jacket pocket for his room key.

"Of course, Mr. Orcini, would there be anything else I could do for you today?" Miss Gordon said in a demure voice.

"Shit!" he winced in a muffled voice only he could hear. "Oh, hello, Miss Gordon. Thank you, but not right now, I mean . . . I just want my case put in my room so I can play a little, a little cards. Without carrying it around. Can you take care of that for me?" She smiled. "I'll have the bellman take care of your case, Mr. Orcini."

"Thank you Miss Gordon."

He started to look for an acceptable table, even though they all looked the same. Then as if a lightning bolt had struck, he changed his mind and went to the Porte-cochere where the valet kept his car.

"Good morning sir. Would you like me to bring your car?"

"Yes. It's the Gull Wing."

"Of course, Mr. Orcini. It will be a pleasure."

The SL was still parked under the Porte-cochere next to the hotel Rolls. The valet started the car and slowly brought her to rest in front of Michael. "Your car, sir." He tipped his hat, clicked his heels, and bowed slightly as he handed the keys to Michael.

"Thank you." As he tipped the valet he looked up to see a group of admirers. This seemed to be commonplace anymore, and he was getting used to people wanting to get a closer look at the classic Mercedes.

"Nice caaa," a fellow obviously from Massachusetts sang out, "a '58?"

"It's a 1957," Michael responded.

"Fast, huh?" A teenage boy in blue jeans questioned.

"Very fast. Want a ride?" Not knowing why he offered.

The boy turned, "Mom, is it Okay? Can I?" He turned to Michael with a helpless look on his face, then back to his mother questioning her with his eyes.

The valet intervened. "This is Mr. Orcini, ma'am. He is a gentleman."

"Are you a safe driver, sir?" she asked, half hoping that he would say no.

"Yes ma'am. I'll be gone for about an hour, or so. The boy is welcome to come along, providing of course, that you approve."

"Clay, my son, has been bored ever since we got here," an apologetic voice from a woman who appeared much too old to have a teenage son. "He can be a pest and I don't know what to do for him. Maybe a little ride won't hurt. I guess it's Okay."

"It's done then. Let's go, Clay." He motioned to the boy.

Clay hugged his mom and went to the car, not quite sure how it opened. The valet came to his rescue, "Permit me, sir," as he raised the gull-wing door.

"Buckle-up," Michael commanded.

"Yes sir!" He struggled with the custom made restraints, but finally succeeded.

He carefully wheeled the SL out the hotel's main drive, around to the Interstate highway and headed north.

"How long are you and your folks going to be in town?" he asked keeping his eyes on the road.

"I don't rightly know, sir. My dad wants to find a job and move us here."

"First of all, Clay. If we are going to be friends, you'll have to start calling me Michael."

"Yes sir, I mean, Yeah. Right on. Okay. Michael. This car is awesome."

"What does your father do for a living?"

"He has a catering business back home, but he wants to hook up with a hotel here and manage their catering department. I work for him at home," Clay pronounced with pride and raised his head to accentuate the self-importance.

Michael retrieved the cell phone from its cradle and punched in some numbers, "Colonel John Rojam please, Michael Orcini calling. Yes thanks, I'll wait."

The voice on the phone rang out, "Michael, where are you?"

"On I-15 heading your way. Got any birds that need warming up?"

"I'll have one by the time you get here. What's your ETA?"

"Fifteen minutes."

"The guard at the gate will direct you. It will be good to see you again."

"I have a young friend with me. Is it okay?"

"Sure, what's her name?

"I'll see you in a few . . ." He replaced the phone and turned to his new friend, "Ever been on an Air Force base?"

"No. Is that where we're going?"

"Yes. What do you think?"

"Coo--ill," he dragged out the slang affirmation, "coo--ill."

They drove beyond the city limits taking the Craig Road turn-off and headed east to Nellis Air Force Base. The guard at the gate expected them. "Good morning, sir," he executed an informal salute. "Colonel Rojam is waiting for you." He handed him a map with a route high-lighted. "Just follow the green line and you shouldn't have any problem locating the Colonel." He stepped back with a courtesy salute.

"Thank you, sergeant." Michael nodded and drove to meet his friend.

"Wow! That guy saluted you. Are you somebody important like a General or an Admiral or somethin'? Who are we going to see?"

"Patience, my young friend, patience. You'll find out soon enough."

As the SL approached the designated hanger, a woman wearing Air Force dungarees directed them to park inside the hanger beside a restored F4-U Corsair.

Michael loved WWII war birds and this baby was a beauty. "Is this the one?" he shouted as John Rojam came near.

"Sorry, Michael. That one is not mine to give out. And who is this?" Pointing to Clay, then whispering to Michael, "I thought you were bringing a girl."

"Must it always be a girl? Besides, you just assumed that it was," he snickered as he spoke. "This is my friend, Clay." Turning to the boy he said, "Clay, this is Colonel John Rojam."

The teenager didn't know if he should shake hands or salute. The colonel made it easy for him by extending his hand, "I am pleased to meet you, Clay."

"Me too, sir. I'm pleased to meet you, sir."

Michael took the officer by the arm and lead him away, "Could you have one of your pilots take the boy for a short ride in a trainer, as a personal favor to me?"

"I thought that you wanted to go up, but I can arrange it," the Korean War Ace stated with absolute certainty. "How old are you, young man?" he demanded.

"Seventeen, sir." He stood at attention.

"If anyone asks, you're eighteen. Understand?" Not waiting for a reply, "Mr. Orcini says that you want to fly in one of our airplanes. That right?" Again he did not wait for the boy. "Sergeant Drake," he called to a non-com inspecting one of the hangered planes.

Sgt Drake 'hopped-to' the officers command, saluting and shouting. "Yes, sir?"

"Have this young man prepared for flight, on the double, and have Lieutenant Morris report to me."

"Yes sir," he snapped a smart salute. "Come with me." He motioned to Clay.

Clay looked at Michael with a question on his bewildered face. Michael motioned for him to follow the sergeant. "Go. Go. I'll be right here when you get back."

The excited boy ran after the sergeant.

An officer in flight gear marched up and saluted the Colonel, "Sir." John Rojam put his arm over Lieutenant Morris' shoulder and walked giving him private instructions. They stopped, turned to face each other and saluted. The pilot walked towards a row of parked jet trainers. He waived for his crew chief to join him as he continued on his way pointing to a specific airplane. Others joined them and prepared the plane for flight.

"John, can we get some coffee?" a very concerned voice asked.

"We can go to my office." He sensed that privacy was going to be important.

"Sergeant Mills," he alerted his attractive assistant, "this is Mr. Michael Orcini. Please bring us some coffee, and we do *not* want to be disturbed."

"Yes sir," she acknowledged his instructions and moved away quickly.

He beckoned Michael to follow him to his office. "Sit there, on the couch, you'll be more comfortable," as he sat in a large, overstuffed, herringbone wing chair. "What's so serious that you have to come to me with the pretense of giving a boy a plane ride?"

The Colonel's office was masculine in nature, but not entirely military. The walls were finished with a fine plaid wallpaper treatment, extending from the heavy wood light cove a foot or so below the ceiling down to the carved wood wainscot. There were elegantly framed paintings of hunting scenes on two walls. The wall behind his desk had glass shelves displaying hand carved toy soldiers. The credenza below was neatly arranged with personal photographs of family and special friends. The wall to the right of his desk revealed a soft, human side of the officer. There was a bay window, overlooking a unique flower garden, complete with a traditional window seat, and plaid cushions.

The informal sitting area was in front of his desk and near the bay window.

Michael completed his observation, and responded to his friend's question. "John, I was wondering just how much you know about this fellow, Nugari."

Sergeant Mills knocked and slowly opened the door. "Your coffee, sir."

"Come in, sergeant."

"Here you are, sir." She placed the tray with a carafe, two cups, cream and sugar on the coffee table in front of them, bending only at the waist, and not looking at either of them, "shall I. . . ?"

"This will be just fine. Thank you."

She was used to being interrupted by her boss. "Will there be anything else, sir?"

"No. Thank you, sergeant." He looked back to his friend, "Nugari?" He waited.

Sergeant Mills closed the door slowly and quietly.

"Nugari," he repeated. "Can he be trusted? Just how well do you know him?"

"He flew my wing in Korea. A good dependable pilot, but I have not been involved with him at a personal level. Are you getting into something with him? A business deal?"

"You remember the hotel casino project that I told you about?" John nodded that he remembered their telephone conversation. "Well, Nugari says that he has some Chinese businessmen that want to invest in Las Vegas, in my project. There's something about him that I can't quite figure out, and I thought that maybe you might shed some light on my suspicions."

"He just went through a very messy divorce and came out

smelling like a rose. But, I actually think that the whole thing smelled rotten. Jana, his ex, came up on the short end of the stick. He took her for a bundle. She had all the money to start. He got her yacht and a condo in La Jolla and a bunch of money." John reached over and picked up a box of Havana cigars, offering a prize to his friend.

"I thought these were illegal in the States," he said, clipped the edge and leaned down as John snapped an ancient Zippo lighter. He took a long puff, leaned back and blew several smoke rings. "What else do you know about him? " He released the rest of the smoke and stared at John.

"Sounds like you don't trust him, Michael."

"There's something that I can't quite put my finger on . . . I'm not sure."

Colonel John Rojam was a highly decorated flying ace that always went by the book and never let his own feelings dictate his position on any circumstance. Personal opinions were not a part of his daily vocabulary. It would be difficult for him to tell his friend that he might be getting in bed with the enemy. He had no facts. He contemplated the situation. "Would you like some brandy in your coffee?"

Michael shook his head no, puffed on the Havana and waited for an answer.

"I think that you have to constantly watch your six with Nugari. Even when you think you're covered, he'll sneak up on you, have you locked in his sights before you know it, and, WHAM," he slammed his thigh, "you're dead. Here I tell him what to do, but out there he does whatever suits him. No. I do not trust him as a civilian." He gulped his coffee and fell back in his chair, as if he had just unloaded an albatross from around his neck.

"Well, John," Michael announced, "if you have anything that you want to say, please don't hold it back on my account." They laughed. Michael always tried to lighten up a serious situation even when it was extremely important to keep focused on the issues.

"More coffee?" John felt the serious part of their visit was over.

"Only to see Mills," he smiled mischievously. "Does she always wear that stupid uniform? Ever let her hair down? Bet she looks good wh. . . ."

"Don't go there Michael." The officer stiffened a little, offering a friendly decree.

He waved his arm between the door and the embarrassed officer. "You and the sergeant? Isn't that against the rules?"

"That's what I like about you, Michael, you don't miss a thing."

"How could I? You're like an open book." A smile. "Is it serious?"

"She submitted her resignation. It's just a matter of time. We plan to get married."

The intercom buzzed. "Colonel Rojam, the young civilian pilot is back."

"Give us a minute sergeant," he spoke in the direction of his desk, pausing for a moment. "Her name is Traci, and she is the best thing that ever happened to me."

"It's been a long time since Beverly passed over." Michael never referred to dying or passing away. 'Passing over' to the other side make more sense than something so permanent. Michael bowed his head; "You deserve a good woman in your life." He looked at his friend; "It must be very difficult calling her sergeant all the time."

They stood up and hugged like the good friends that they were. "It won't be much longer, but we still have to be careful not to rush things, and be open to Air Force scrutiny. You know the military has their rules." They reached the door, shook hands and went out to greet the young pilot.

Michael went over to the sergeant, "Thank you very much," then whispered her name, "Traci," he took her hand in both of his hands, squeezed softly, smiled and quietly he said, "He's the best."

Traci turned her face down, and whispered back a soft, shy, "I know."

He did an about face, looked at the teenager and said, "Well, kid. Let's go."

Several officers and non-coms were admiring the SL. A Lieutenant stepped forward saluting Michael. "Permit me, sir," as he opened the Gull Wing door.

Recognizing him, Michael acknowledged with a handshake. "Thank you, Lt. Morris. You are a gentleman. I appreciate what you did for my young friend, if ever.. "

"Perhaps we could fly together sometime, Sir. I hear that you're the best."

"Sounds like Colonel Rojam has been exaggerating again," he said looking him square in the eyes, "but, I would be honored to fly your wing, Good day Lt. Morris."

* * * * * *

A dark green Lincoln stretch limousine, bearing a coat of arms detailed on the side panel between the doors, was waiting for Michael at the hotel entrance. A huge man in a black suit with the same coat of arms embroidered on the breast pocket, and sporting a little black cap, approached him asking, "Mr. Orcini?"

"Yes, I am Michael Orcini."

"I will drive you to your meeting. Please come with me." He abruptly turned and moved toward the limousine, stopped and opened the door. Michael got in to find that he would not be alone. Mario shut the door behind him.

"Good afternoon, Mr. Orcini. I am Ermano Contedetto. I am to be escorting you to your destination, and in anticipation that you should be most comfortable in your journey. Mr. Wu will be joining you and the other persons of whom you are to meet at the restaurant," he dictated in his forced unschooled grammar.

"Good afternoon, Mr. Contidino," trying to remember the name that was mixed up somewhere in all that gibberish. "But I thought Mr. Wu was sending his car."

"It is Contedetto," he emphasized, "but you should call me Connie, if it is your desire to do so. Mr. Wu is on his way to the restaurant with the other participants."

"I am very uncomfortable with your arrangement. I don't like being told about a change in plans after the fact. Do you understand?"

"We will be there at the restaurant in just a few minutes, Mr. Orcini."

"Get this straight Contadano, or whatever your name is, you don't tell me what to do. Capicci?" He raised his voice and sensed that the bull of a driver was watching in the rear view mirror, and became even more unsettled. "Whose idea is this?"

"It is the wish of Donna Ceres for me to escort you to the restaurant."

"And, just who is this Person? I don't have any business with anyone by that name." Not knowing if Ceres was a man or woman.

"The Donna, she is the head of a very powerful group, of whom is interested to be involved in your casino project. What ever it is that the Donna wants, it is to be sure that she will have such a desire fulfilled to meet with her absolute wishes."

The limousine pulled up in front of a small Ristorante with a half-dome dark green awning over a single carved wood entrance door. Mario jumped out and circled around to the rear passenger door and opens it saying, "This way Mr. Orcini," with a palms up motion of his massive hand towards the restaurant entry door.

Michael got out, and made his way to the entrance, not looking at the bull. Mario rushed past and opened the door. "Permit me, sir."

He snarled an unintelligible, "Thanks," and entered the quaint Mediterranean style café, stopping short as the host came directly in front of him.

"This way sir, please follow me." He chose some menus from a rack, and ushered the unwilling customer to a table in a corner under a trellis, where two men waited.

The men stood up. "Please let me introduce myself." Michael recognized the voice from his phone conversation. "My name is Jami Wu, and this is Claude deVillefrance. I must apologize for the shift in our arrangements, and I sincerely hope that you were not inconvenienced. Please, sit down," pointing to a stuffed, high-back, winged chair.

Michael shook hands, "Mr. Wu." Then looked suspiciously at the ruddy man in quasi sea captain attire as he slipped into the worn antique chair. "Mr. deVillefrance," he nodded, "I'm not sure just who you are or . . ."

"I am here as liaison between, Mr. Wu and his Chinese investors, Mr. Nugari, Donna Ceres and you, of course," he stated as-a-matter-of-fact.

The waiter asked, "Sir, may I get you something to drink?"

"A cup of your finest coffee, black, thanks." He looked at deVillefrance, "Who is this Donna Ceres, and what is her involvement with you and Mr. Wu?"

The waiter brought his coffee. "Would you gentlemen like to order now?"

Michael sipped his cup as the others picked up their menus like puppets. "This tastes like it was cooked last week. Is this the best you have?" He pushed the cup away, not bothering to acknowledge the waiter's presence.

Connie was hovering just within earshot. "You should be more careful of what you are serving to a special guest to the Donna. Go and bring to Mr. Orcini the special coffee that you have only to serve to your best of customers." He took the cup from Michael. "I will be sure to have the finest cup of coffee for you in just a moment or two. Please, I apologize for this most disagreeable . . ."

"Forget the coffee, and bring me a Courvoisier." He had a feeling this was going to be an arduous meeting.

The waiter quietly took lunch orders from the others at the table. Michael waved a palm down-and-away gesture to indicate that he wasn't going to order.

Wu spoke, "Mr. Orcini, perhaps if I explain why we are all here, and who the players are, then you will be more comfortable." He looked for a response, and getting none continued. "First, we thought that it would facilitate matters, and bring all parties together with a better understanding of what needs to be done.

Second, as you know, Mr. Nugari arranged for you to meet deVillefrance and me. We will handle the negotiations with you and my people with regards to financing your casino. My people do not know how things are done here in Las Vegas, and Donna Ceres can help us with the politics, licenses and so forth. Mr. Contedetto represents her group."

The waiter brought his drink. Michael waited. deVillefrance looked around the table stopping at Michael. "Nugari showed me drawings of your project. I like your basic concept. It's not a proven niche, but you just might get away with it, if you were to make some adjustments."

Michael smiled, but still waited. He would take control of the meeting, and any future negotiations with these people and their superiors.

He continued, "We must see your package and review the projected income stream and your estimates on costs to build and run the casino and hotel."

Michael moved his eyes from Claude deVillefrance to Jami Wu and waited.

Jami squirmed under Michael's stare and finally said, "We understand that you need eight hundred million dollars. If you have the right project, we have the money."

Michael sipped his brandy, and continued to stare at Wu . . . waiting . . . waiting. deVillefrance spoke. "How many rooms do you plan to build?"

Still staring at Jami, "Tell me what you want for your eight hundred million." He glanced around the table. "How you intend to get it, and when. Also, when you will prove to me that you actually have this much money, and, and your ability to transfer it to my account for this project. You must also explain, to my satisfaction, how all these other people will participate, how much they each think they will get, and from whom."

Michael gained control of the meeting. "deVillefrance. I heard that you're a Commodore at a yacht club in La Jolla. Is that true?" He quickly maneuvered the conversation to his advantage.

"Yes." deVillefrance straightened up in his chair, massaged his unshaven face, and adjusted his cap with a curt salute of acknowledgement. "Yes, sir. I am."

"Why do you sit in judgment of my project, sir?" He repositioned his control by putting deVillefrance on the defense. "Are you an expert on casino development?" Michael looked away from the commodore to observe the other men's reactions.

Wu interceded. "Mr. deVillefrance brought the project to me, and is just protecting his position with my people." He reached for the sugar bowl. "I sure that he meant nothing disrespectful, Mr. Orcini."

Michael sat quietly, sipping on his brandy, as Wu and deVillefrance exchanged surreptitious glances.

It was Connie's turn to save face for the group. "Mr. Orcini. We want that you should take our absolute presence here as a sign that we should want to talk in a very serious nature about the financial constitution of your project. Mr. Wu, and his associated persons, can bring to you all the money that you need for your casino. The Donna, of whom I am in the employ, will take care of all the business and political people. You will only have to construct and operate the casino, with the Donna's general outlook, of course." He looked at Wu for approval.

Michael once again sat silent, and waited while they ineptly dug themselves a hole that would be difficult to climb out, at least today.

Wu spoke without looking at Michael. "We understand that you might want to look at other offers." He found Michael's eyes. "However, Mr. Orcini, we are ready with the funds right now. Perhaps we could open a discussion with regard to the basic details." Jami Wu was not accustomed to Michael's method of doing business, and became obviously unsettled waiting for a response.

Michael reached into his jacket pocket, withdrew a pad and pen, and jotted a note. He tore a page from the pad, and handed it to Connie without acknowledging Wu or deVillefrance.

Connie read the message that asked the Donna to prepare a proposal and to schedule a meeting for everyone.

"I will inform the Donna of your request, Mr. Orcini." He motioned to Mario with an unmistakable gesture indicating that the meeting was over.

Michael rose, picked up his glass, finished his drink, and said. "Gentlemen."

Surprised at the abrupt ending, Wu began to stutter. "But, but. Mr. Orcini?"

Connie interrupted. "We will tell you as to when the Donna wishes to discuss the continuation of our conversations with Mr. Orcini." He paused, looking down at Wu and deVillefrance. He turned to Michael, and said, "Mario will drive you to your hotel, Mr. Orcini." He deliberately stared into Michael's eyes with a subordinate look of displeasure that translated into contempt. Connie knew his position, and executed the directive with the precision of a well-trained soldier. "Good afternoon, sir."

* * * * * * *

Happy that the day's work was over, Michael maneuvered the SL up the winding roads and into the hills where Darci lived. The clock in the dashboard indicated that he still had more than enough time to arrive before 7:30. On the seat next to him was a single Sterling Silver rose. He had instructed the florist that he wanted something simple, but special, for this lady with 'just a few of the baby's breath twigs', and a lavender ribbon.

The worsted slacks and patterned Armani silk shirt, topped with his leather flying jacket, was about as casual as he would be on their first date.

He drove into the cul-de-sac at the end of the road. The address between a single carved wood door and the garage was difficult to see. "This should be it," he told the SL as he backed up, then eased forward onto the short drive. A motion sensor turned the light on over the door and verified the address.

He pushed the illuminated button, and stepped back.

When the door opened, he was greeted by a smile and scintillating eyes that invited him in before a word was spoken. Michael felt a quiver inside his chest and an instant connection with this intriguing woman.

Darci stood motionless in the dimly lit entry hall presenting a different image than their two previous encounters. Her hair was piled on top of her head, fashioned loosely with narrow tresses on each side of her face. She wore a simple patterned full-length skirt, topped with an elegant teal colored silk blouse. "Hi, Michael Orcini," a delightful voice broke the spell. "Welcome to my home." She stepped aside allowing him to enter.

Michael moved through the doorway, paused, and with a shy, almost boyish transferring of weight from one foot to the other, presented the single rose.

"My favorite," she said with a softness that matched the rose itself, "my absolute favorite in the whole world. How did you know?"

"It was the most beautiful at the florist. It seemed appropriate."

"Help me get a vase down from the cupboard." He followed her down the stairs to the main level where full height windows of the two-story living room exposed the entire length of the breathtaking Las Vegas light extravaganza. They paused for a moment, then without a word continued on through the dining room and into the kitchen. "There on the top shelf, the tall tear drop crystal in the center." She pointed, as he opened the glass door of the cupboard. He reached in and looked back at her with a questioned look. "Yes, thanks," she said, being quite able to reach the vase herself.

Darci put some water in the vase and arranged the 'baby's breath' around the rose. Satisfied, she picked up the vase and walked into the living room. "Here by the window." She glanced at Michael, "I'll move it to my bedroom later."

Michael became aware of a small dog, sitting on a loveseat in an alcove, staring at him, but not making a sound. "Who are you?" he asked, not really expecting an answer.

"That's Puca T. Say hello to Michael, Puca."

"Arf. Arf." The little critter responded in a sound matching his size.

"Hello Puca T." Michael went over and sat next to him, and petted him on the head.

"Arf. Arf." Puca laid his chin on Michael's lap.

"I think he likes you. He doesn't usually like strangers. I'm famished."

"Me too! Ready?"

"Yes."

"Then, let's get going."

Darci picked up an exquisite Indian shawl, and handed it to Michael. He unfolded the woven artifact and placed it over her shoulders, allowing his arms to fold around her for a brief moment.

"Thank you, sir," she said, catching his eye as she glanced over her shoulder.

When they reached the top of the stairway she stopped and set the alarm.

They drove down the winding road. "This must be a scary drive in the winter with ice and snow on the ground," Michael commented, shortly before he reached the bottom of the hill, and headed away from the bright lights of the 'Strip'.

"Everyone on the hill is up in arms about this road. We're constantly trying to do something about it. It's been going on for a long time. This time I'm heading up a committee to get some barricades installed along the edge. They probably won't do anything about it until someone gets killed."

The conversation was sounding strained, so Michael changed the subject.

"Puca T. How did you arrive at such an unusual name for your little dog?"

Darci smiled, sensing he would rather talk about something less complicated.

"When my very, *very* Irish girl friend gave him to me," putting a definite accent on the second 'very', "she made me promise to give him an Irish name befitting him. Even though he's not any kind of Irish dog."

"I've never heard of Puca as an Irish name."

"Well," she said quite proudly, "in Irish folklore, 'Puca' is a harmless, but very mischievous supernatural being. It is also said that they sometimes appear in the form of an animal. He got into all kinds of mischief as a pup. I think that he is an old soul, so that sort of takes care of the supernatural part."

"An--d the 'T'. What does that represent?"

"Tashmit, the 'T' stands for Tashmit. His last name."

"Of course it does."

They pulled into a circular drive that was bounded by several small, but exquisite old world style buildings. A nearby fountain echoed a tranquil sound.

The valet helped her out as Michael came around to receive his claim check.

"I love this place, Michael. I didn't know it existed." She sounded like a little girl who just saw her first dollhouse. "This is great."

He put his hand on her back, and with a light effort indicated the direction they were to go. "This way, Darci."

She came along side of him and slid her hand into his hand. Michael instinctively caressed her hand, as if it belonged there. The trembling inside his chest increased as the pounding of his heart filled with an excitement he had never experienced.

Darci squeezed back and looked up into his eyes. "Me, too!" she whispered.

Then, still walking, with her other hand she clutched his upper arm, and pulled herself to him, like a child in a small embrace, and sensed complete security. He released her for a moment to open the restaurant door, and accepted the natural return of her hand to his, like they had been doing it all their lives.

The maître d' approached. "Mr. Orcini. It is good to see you again. It has been a very long time." He nodded attentively to Darci. "Your table is ready. Please, come."

The restaurant had an ambiance of old world charm. The lengthy mural depicting a Mediterranean port with rows of tiled rooftops always seemed to be a bit ostentatious to Michael, so he had asked for the other room. Their table was in the center of the dimly lit dining room, and adjacent to a small statue of a gilded nymph pouring water into a pool.

"Is this satisfactory, Mr. Orcini?" in a definite British accent.

Michael looked at Darci who smiled approvingly, "Yes Winston, this is fine."

"Would you like something to drink?" Winston motioned to a nearby waiter.

Michael looked at Darci. "Do you like champagne?"

"Yes."

"Bring us a Louis Roederer champagne, 'Cristal' please."

"Yes, sir. Would you like something to start, an appetizer?"

"Absolutely! We are ravenous," Darci announced.

"Do you still serve that wonderful appetizer combination?"

"Yes, sir."

"We'll have that to start."

Darci accessed the eclectic room styling, the ceiling with it's Rococo style molded metal panels and contemporary pendant light fixtures, the walls of strong masculine earth tones and whimsical primary colored accents, and the flowered carpet with a highly polished black marble border. She stopped at the symbolic nature goddess next to their table, and studied her form.

With her head still facing the statue she turned her eyes to Michael. "Hi," she smiled at him, "I was on a little trip around your eatery."

"I know," he apologized, "but the food is a thousand times better than the interior design. It's the reason that we're here."

"This place smells wonderful." She sniffed. "The aroma of the garlic and all the different spices are out of this world. I feel like I'm in that painting." She pointed.

Michael smiled.

"The English maître d' in a Mediterranean restaurant?" she questioned.

"A definite oxymoron, but a necessary part of the eclectic charm of this place."

They were lost in each other's eyes.

The waiter placed special stemmed glasses on the table, and displayed the bottle with its label for Michael's approval. "Achhem.," not wanting to be disrespectful, "Sir?"

"I think he wants you to confirm his selection."

He studied the bottle, then Winston, the maître d', cocked his head in a manner, such as the assurance of a father to his son, signaling that it was the right decision. "Thank you Winston, this is exactly what I want."

"Very well, sir. I am confident that it will meet with your approval." He instructed the waiter to serve the wine. "Your appetizer will be here in a moment, sir." A small tilt of his head and he turned to attend to the adjacent table.

"No Dom Periniogn?" Darci kidded.

"This is better."

"What should we toast, Michael? We must make it very special, because of the way that we met, and all. Is that okay?" She didn't wait, raised her glass, "To Michael and Darci, may they always be the best of friends."

"The absolute best of friends," he responded, "always."

As they sipped from the long stemmed glasses, she moved her hand across the table to meet his with a gentle but electric connection. "Always."

Their eyes journeyed into each other's souls experiencing the warmth of what seemed to be a past, and continuing friendship.

"We've been together before, Michael."

"Is that what it is? I know I feel a strong chemistry with you, as if . . ."

"We have plenty of time to sort this out," she knew instinctively. "Lets enjoy this time, now." She caressed the rim of her glass, with her finger in a counter-clockwise motion, as she waited for his acknowledgment.

The waiter brought a garnished platter of assorted antipasto, arranged like an original Picasso. "We can't eat this," she pouted, "can we?"

"What's wrong?"

Her grimace turned into a small shy smile.

"You're cute," he laughed. "You're lucky that we're such ol' friends or . . ."

"Or what? Would you spank me?" She helped herself to the platter taking one of each different hors d'oeuvre, then handed her selection to him. "Here." The smile he saw when she first opened her door, returned with sparkling hazel eyes, inviting him to receive her offering. "Would you?"

He accepted her presentation exchanging his empty china. "Would I what?"

"Spank me." She read his smile and knew he wouldn't answer.

Michael watched with delight and waited until she completed her meticulous selection and placed it on the table. They ate the antipasto in silence, exchanging glances, and communicating without words.

The waiter returned asking, "May I take your dinner order, sir?"

"Would you order for me, please, Michael?"

"Sure." He thought for a moment. "A Caesar salad," he raised his brow and watched for her approval, but she could have been playing poker. "The Chateaubriand, but with potatoes au gratin, and snow peas in a light cream sauce." A small smile was all she presented to her glass as she took a sip. "The Chateau must be medium-rare." He checked her unexpressive face again. "And a bottle of Cambria Pinot Noir."

"Yes, sir." The waiter questioned Darci with a glance.

"That is perfect, just perfect, Michael."

They shared their first meal while discovering a new friendship, which according to Darci was actually a continuation of past incarnations. Darci learned that Michael was an only child, born in Chatham, Massachusetts of Italian/French ancestry. His father was a mechanical engineer and his mother was a homemaker who played the church organ in the oldest church on Cape Cod. She admitted to being a military brat whose father was predominantly Cherokee Indian. He was stationed in Tutuila, Samoa when he met her mother. Her olive-skinned complexion and distinct high cheekbones delineated her lineage. They savored their meal and each other as they talked about family, religion, reincarnation, places they have been, and things they would like to do. Darci and Michael were totally unaware of the universe outside their newly formed private world.

"Mr. Orcini." It was Winston. "I am sorry to interrupt you and your beautiful lady, but we have closed the restaurant for more than a half an hour.

He looked at his watch.

"What time is it?" Darci asked, looking around the empty room.

"Both hands are pointing to Mickey's nose," he said jokingly, partly in disbelief. "We should go, huh?"

"Your check, sir."

Michael gave him a credit card.

Winston returned with the check. "Here are the keys to your automobile. The valet has parked it in front."

Michael reached in his pocket and pealed-off some bills. "Would you please take care of the waiter and valet? The rest is for you."

"Thank you, Mr. Orcini."

"Can we walk for a while?" She pressed his arm.

He didn't have to answer.

They walked along the tree lined path, discovered an outcropping of rocks, climbed ten or more feet to the top, and sat holding each other while Darci pointed to shooting stars.

"Look! See that?" She would say each time, turn, and kiss his cheek.

"Where?" he questioned with an, "Ah-huh." after she pointed again.

She repositioned herself in front of him, and leaned back against his chest. "Do you always bring your first dates here?"

Michael put his arms around her, feeling the thrust of her breasts against his forearms, as she nestled into his embrace. "No. I have never even walked out here, or sat on these rocks before."

She laid her head back, and with a sigh, settled in. After a long while, he gave her a squeeze. She knew that the signal meant it was time to go. They discovered there was a path down the backside of the rock formation, and easily retreated to the SL.

They didn't speak until he pulled into the drive. "Michael?"

"Hmmm?"

"Oh, nothing." She reached in her pocket. "Here's my key."

As he helped her out of the car she inclined against him, and he had to reach around her to shut the gull wing. He touched her cheek and she pressed her head softly against his chest as they walked the short distance to her front door.

They were greeted by an "Arf-arf."

"Poor baby. You must have to go outside." When they reached the bottom of the stairs she opened the side door on the main level, let him out, and waited until the little dog returned.

Michael admired the selection of books along the wall near the alcove. She put her arms around his waist and pressed her forehead against his back.

"Edgar Casey? You have several . . ."

She released the hug, slid down to sit on the floor, extracted a few books from a lower shelf, and handed them to him. As he sat down next to her, she released the hair piled atop her head, shaking carelessly, to reveal a length that reached to the floor where she sat. They sat on the large pillows in front of the bookcase talking about Joel Goldsmith, Richard Bach, and Paul Twitchell. He was amazed at how much more they had in common.

Then, suddenly, came spot lights from the sky, high up into the windows, all around, helicopters, muffled sounds coming from a bull horn, then understandable words, "The house is surrounded. This is the sheriff come out with your hands up."

"Michael, what's happening?" The phone rang. "My God, it's almost two a.m."

"I'll get it. . . . Hello . . . Sheriff? . . . What? . . . Michael Orcini . . . that's right . . . yes . . . no, I'm here with Darci Tashmit, the owner . . . the what? . . . The alarm? . . . Just a moment. Darci, it looks like the alarm is still on. It's the sheriff, and he wants to talk with you."

She took the portable phone and held it against her breast, not knowing just what to do. After a moment she said in a frightened voice, "Hello, this is Darci Tashmit. Yes sheriff . . . no sir . . . yes . . . front door . . . um.. well . . . okay.. okay." She looked sheepishly at Michael, "He wants you to stand in the light with your hands on your head, and I'm supposed to open the front door."

"Check the peep hole first, be sure it's the sheriff before you open the door."

"It's the sheriff, all right." She pulled the door open and stepped back. "Sorry."

Several deputies rushed in with guns in their hands, ready for the worst kind of encounter. Two deputies stayed with Darci while she reset the alarm code.

One of them took the phone. "You wont be needing this Miss. May I see some identification?" he scowled, as he admonished her negligence.

His partner asked who owned the car parked in the drive. Michael affirmed that he owned it. "We'll have to check it out," he informed Michael, "since it has California plates and looks very expensive." After twenty-five or thirty minutes the deputies were satisfied, and left only after a lengthy lecture on responsibility.

Darci plopped herself on the loveseat in the alcove. "Sorry, I've never done. . . ."

Michael knelt in front of her, took her face in his hands, and kissed her sweetly on the lips. "Are you okay?"

"Yes, just very tired all of a sudden," she yawned.

"It's been a long night, I'd better go." He got to his feet.

"I'll walk you to the door." She stretched her arm for him to pull her up.

As they got to the stairway she tugged at his arm, and put her arms up around his shoulders, lifted herself up off her feet, and hugged him like she had never hugged anyone before. Michael responded with his arms embracing her back as their lips met in a savage concert. Her arms stretched, and her hands caressed the back of his neck while he moved his hands down, beneath her hair, to her butt, and raise her up to him. After a moment he eased her down slowly. She stood on her toes and pulled her head back and looked at him, studying his lips before kissing them.

She caressed his mouth with a single finger, "Yummy," kissing the air between them. "Yummy."

They were glued together.

"This was our *first* date, huh?" she asked, emphasizing 'first'.

"Yes," He kissed her nose, both her cheeks, her forehead, and then his lips caressed her eyes before releasing his hug. He moved his hands up the length of her back, along her neck and finally he held her face for what seemed an eternity before he adopted her lips with his mouth. The kiss was short but delicious, and completed their first date.

Darci walked with him up to the door, "Call me," she commanded, half pleading.

"Absolutely. Night."

"Good night Michael Orcini, drive safely."

She watched as he pulled out of the drive and slowly disappeared into the dark morning. She shut the door, reset the alarm and chuckled as she picked up Puca. "What a night," she explained to her little companion. "I can't wait for our next date."

Like an angel on a mission she descended the staircase and went to her bedroom, put Puca in his little basket, and twirled around and around and around, finally throwing her backside down on the bed. With her arms stretched out as if to receive blessings from above she shouted, "I can't wait! I can't wait!" Studying the room, she wondered what he would think of the massive painting of an Indian maiden hanging over the headboard. She remembered her mother telling her, every time she visited, to get rid of it or she would scare the right man away, and she would always respond that with the right man, it wouldn't matter. But now, as she lay there, she wondered what Michael would think of the painting. She hugged herself as the words 'the right man' echoed in her mind. An angelic smile filled her entire face. She *knew* he was the right man.

After brushing her teeth, she washed her face, removing the small amount of natural make-up she wore, and applied a moisturizer.

At the foot of the bed she undressed, allowing her clothes to fall to the floor, something she would never do, and glanced at her image in the mirror. "Skinny kid with the big tits, they used to call me," chuckling. "Still true, I guess." She slid under the sheet and pulled the comforter up to her chin. "Darn, I forgot," she told herself, "darn."

She jumped up, ran into the living room, picked up the vase with Michael's rose, and sauntered back to the bedroom. The cold night air felt extraordinarily erotic on her naked body. She paused by the side of her bed, plucked a single petal from the rose and stroked her already aroused nipples. "Thanks, Michael Orcini. If you only knew." She placed the vase on the nightstand, the petal on her pillow, and nestled back into bed with a shiver. "Yummy, yummy." She hugged herself, and almost instantly slipped into a peaceful sleep, the kind she had not known for a long time.

* * * * * *

Michael drove slowly back to the hotel. He found himself driving down the 'Strip' instead of the interstate. Everything was going fine until Darci. He silently cursed that night on the highway when he followed her, and again when he found out her name and called her. He didn't have time for romance. This wasn't going to be an affair or a one-night stand, he was sure, and he'd have to make a commitment. He considered the absolute inequity of it all.

How impossible to be involved with someone, especially like Darci, and deal with the complexities of building a hotel and casino! But with other women. . . . Bobbi, to be sure, he could come and go without commitment. This was different. Darci was different! Somewhere in his mind, the sound of responsibility rang out, but Darci was occupying so much of his thoughts that he couldn't get anything into a logical order. Michael felt confused.

Michael had stopped in the middle of the Las Vegas Strip to sort things out. There were crowds of people everywhere you looked. Some peered inside his window with drunken faces while others rushed by on their way to another show or casino, or wherever you go in Las Vegas at three in the morning. Cars sounded their horns.

He shrugged off the momentary annoyance and eased forward to notice that his hotel driveway was just ahead. He had to put on his turn indicator and move over two lanes. Out of nowhere came a traffic cop, dressed in a tuxedo, waving a nightstick that looked like a martini glass, and directed the other cars to let him by. Having accomplished his task, the formal cop danced off to join his friends as Michael gave a light beep on the horn in recognition of the good deed.

The casino was bursting with people, a huge crowd for the weekend after Labor Day. There was laughter and shouting and an air of excitement. Old men with young women in tight dresses, each trying to out-do the other, while these mistresses of the night made passes at every other man that walked by. Michael surveyed the room, somehow expecting to see the 'bod' in her painted-on dress, but not really caring if he did.

Michael had no intention of hanging around the casino. He stopped and looked about the room once more. There at a Gui-pow-pan table was deVillefrance with Wu. He started toward them just as a bell went off, indicating someone had just won a jackpot. He hesitated as a cold sweat came over him, and decided it was a foolish idea.

Even the elevator was full, stopping at almost every floor. The air was oppressive with the lingering stench of stale cigar smoke, and fat, smelly women whose faces looked pinched with exhaustion, wearing their cheap perfume, and rubbing against him. They forced their overworked voices to brag on how much they won. The twelfth floor couldn't come soon enough. Walking might be better. Oh well, not tonight.

The stillness of his room greeted him with an ominous calm. He switched on the light at the desk and stood still for a moment, sensing the presence of another. He moved irresolutely toward the center of the room. Cautiously past the bed, stopping, a minute went by and then another. A few more steps to the bathroom. No girls in the tub, none in the bathroom . . . a breeze from the sliding door . . . he looked to the window and back to the couch. Nobody here. He turned on all the lights in the room. An empty cocktail glass was on the coffee table with the stub of a half-smoked cheap cigar. It was the same smell he encountered at the lunch meeting in the Italian restaurant. He immediately knew who had been there. The question was, how did he get in, and what was he doing there?

Michael went to the phone and called the front desk. "This is Michael Orcini in room twelve-forty-two. Somebody's been in my room and I want the locking code changed right now. . . . Ten minutes?. . . . Fine, but not any longer, I'm very tired.

The technician was there in less than five minutes, and had the code changed in two or three minutes.

With that taken care of, he could settle in. One more thing. He called the front desk and asked that all calls be held until at least noon. He went to the bathroom, brushed his teeth, washed his face, and looked into the mirror. He expected to see her face like before. Her image was not there, but he knew that she would be right there with him in his dreams. "You are like nobody I've ever met before, Miss Darci Tashmit," he sang as he retired to the four-poster. "Nobody." He looked at himself in the mirror above the bed, "I wonder, I wonder." He closed his eyes and saw her face. Sleep came quickly.

* * * * * *

The sun was setting with a sizzle into the ocean off the coast of Big Sur, California as Roberta Azure arranged the fresh cut autumn flowers in an oversized antique ceramic vase. For a moment she seemed petrified as she stared at the sunset. Her mind raced with thoughts of the day. It was just this afternoon when she gave in to an impulse so childish that she capriciously invited an old friend to dinner.

Bobbi had gone to town to pick up a gift for Michael, and have lunch with her sister Norah. She wanted to buy something that had to do with golf, so she went to the pro shop at Pebble Beach. She was on her way to the clubhouse for lunch where she ran into Guy and his friend who had just finished a round of golf.

Guy Nestor was in Carmel for only two reasons; to search for a boutique hotel site, and to play a few rounds of golf with a movie star friend. He had made a fortune in real estate, and his vast real estate holdings included a number of small hotels, Bed and Breakfast Inns, quality restaurants, and a string of retail shops. It was time for a new venture. He wanted to add some high quality, four-star inns to his portfolio

Fall was almost here, and the brisk wind tossed Norah's shoulder length raven colored hair across her face as she took her final step to the clubhouse door. A young man, who resembled Tiger Woods, scurried to open the door for her. "Good afternoon Miss Laude," taking off his cap, "you're lookin' fine." She sauntered by, and he watched her soft derriere as it moved under her skirt. She glanced over her shoulder, catching the acknowledgment of his hand simulating her rhythm, smiled at her admirer, and continued on to meet Bobbi in the lounge.

"Over here," Bobbi announced, her voice rising and falling. "Look who I found."

The sisters embraced, kissed each other's cheeks, and whispered their hellos.

Both Bobbi and Norah looked so young and vibrant that it

was hardly possible to believe that they both had been married for almost ten years, divorced, and now single mothers with eight-year-old daughters. They both met and married Frenchmen after their trip to Paris. Bobbi's marriage lasted two years, while Norah could only make it for one year. She just couldn't stay in the relationship any longer. Norah couldn't be still about anything, she was always doing something, even as a child she was fidgeting, fussing, and playing with her hair. So much so, that she was nicknamed 'Busy'. A name that remained with her throughout the years. Busy always liked to go to places where she could be noticed, she didn't have to wear or do anything special to stand out in a crowd, just enter a room. The unique combination of her tall slender beau ideal form, and wholesome features complete with the grace of a princess, demanded attention from men and women alike. Country Clubs were among her favorite places to 'show-off' what she knew she had to offer.

"Well, isn't this just a coincidence," half questioning the man sitting on the couch. "Haven't seen you in quite some time."

Bobbi knew Norah was struggling for his name. "You remember Guy Nestor."

"Oh," she lowered her voice sending him a sweet quick look, "I remember Guy." She remembered she didn't like him. "You and Bobbi are old friends. Hello."

Guy stood and politely shook her hand. "So nice to see you again. My, how lovely you both are." He turned on a forced smile, "You know Jon Astor."

She put out her hand, "No I don't." Again she lowered her voice, "Hi!"

"Please sit down." Jon motioned to a place next to him on the couch.

"Thank you." She preferred the high-back chair next to Bobbi.

Guy was as handsome as Bobbi remembered, but something about him was very different. It wasn't the slight stoop when he stood that bothered her. It was something else. This tall, handsome, well-dressed, unattached man in his late fifties whose hair had turned to silver, except for a small streak within a curl that fell on his forehead, just came back into her life. Why? Something was gnawing at her, it had been only three or four years since they knew each other in San Francisco, but somehow he seemed more intense, not the animated, open book she remembered. She had never seen him so austere and consumed. Bobbi was intrigued. She had to know what was going on, besides, he made it clear to her that he wanted to get together and renew the friendship. It would be easy to convince him to open up and share his deepest desires. She had done this before, and would use everything at her disposal. Nothing would be left untried. Guy Nestor was the same *challenge* that her sister had counseled her on a few years ago. He could be easily conquered, and business just might have taken a back seat to her *primary* goal. But why had she been such a fool to cancel her time with Michael . . . oh . . . damn . . . damn . . . damn. She could have bitten her tongue for having jumped at this chance to set him up again. Bobbi only wanted to use another one of her new smart tricks to prove that she was superior, and could gain control of one more business situation with him. She knew that her access to many influential and wealthy people on the Monterey Peninsula could help her old friend, notwithstanding the fact that it could result in a considerable fee. But, something else is going on. She didn't like being perplexed.

Her preoccupation with recollections of the afternoon's encounter was interrupted by her own voice on the telephone answering machine. So deep in thought that she didn't hear the phone ring. She waited, the caller seemed rushed. "Bobbi, this is Guy, and I've been delayed with some people at Pebble Beach. I'm sorry. . . ." She turned down the volume not listening to the rest of the message, instead she went back to her daydream. Both her business and personal accomplishments were always prearranged in her mind, as in a movie where she was director, producer and actor. All the other players, except for Michael, did exactly as she directed. She would have to set the stage. Guy Nestor would play the part she wanted, and she would direct. She was confident.

Suddenly she began to laugh, oblivious to the sudden gusting of winds progressing down the coast, rattling the windows. With a quick swipe, she grabbed a pillow from the overstuffed couch facing the ocean, and began to dance to the music in her mind. Stopping almost as quickly as she started, for a moment she hesitated by the table, her self-justification lifted her spirit, and she rewound the phone message. "Bobbi, this is Guy, and I've been delayed with some people at Pebble Beach. I'm sorry to call at the last moment. I really want to see you. I wonder if it would be possible, well, for you to meet me for a late dinner, about nine-thirty. It's a major boost for me, I have some potential investors, and all. I can explain latter. It's probably unfair for me to ask you to drive here, but if you can, I promise to make it up to you. I'm staying at the Lodge, please call me."

Still holding the pillow, the well-shaped, size three coquette laughed quietly, "I'll be there Mr. Nestor," squeezing the cushion to her breast. "I'll be there." She would wait a while before placing a call to the Lodge, leaving him a message to meet her in the bar, but now she must call her sister.

Busy lived in Pacific Grove, a short distance north of Pebble Beach, but was not home when Bobbi called. "There's a change of plans," she told the machine, "and I'm going to meet Guy for a late dinner at Pebble Beach, but I'm not really sure why. Can you drop over there about nine-thirty or so? I think that I'm gonna need some reinforcement. I really, really, would like you to be there." She replaced the portable phone in its cradle, grabbed an old quilt, and settled into her favorite chair on the balcony.

The silence of her sleep was broken by the startling smash of a palm branch against the side of the house, near where she sat all snuggled and warm. Bobbi rubbed her eyes, like a child who wasn't quite sure where she was or what time it was. The crescent moon had disappeared behind the storm clouds, and the waves were orchestrating a crescendo upon the rocks below. She sat mesmerized by the faint moonlight dancing on the crest of the waves. There was a lone seagull flying high and circling. She wondered what a gull was doing out at night. SNAP! Swish, Another palm branch fell to the beach below. As if it were a sign, she got up, went inside to the phone and left a message for Guy to meet her at the Stillwater Bar & Grill.

"Oh, my God," she said out loud as she looked at the clock on the wall, "it's past eight. Now I'll have to rush. Nah, he'll wait." She resolved.

Bobbi was a master at getting ready for an evening out with a man. She languidly started up the stairs, then paused as she reached the second level and her bedroom suite. She could set her beauty in motion without a second thought. She went to the closet and chose a long charcoal wool skirt, grabbed her three-quarter-length leather coat, and carefully placed them on her bed. Across the master bedroom was the armoire where she kept her sweaters and hats. She took a moment and walked over, opening the sliding door facing the ocean. Hugging herself, she recalled her grandfather building this level on top of the old shack of a beach house when she was just a little girl. "Thanks Gramps," a soft prayer was dispatched over the ocean. "Thanks for all of this." The night wind sent a chill to her bones as she stepped onto the balcony. For a moment she watched the waves, and that dumb gull. He's still flying out there at night.

"Brrrr . . ." she shivered as she shut the door behind her and went to the armoire. The ocher turtleneck that Michael purchased for her in Spain will be perfect, a part of him would be with her tonight, she contemplated. A quick shower, make-up and hair. She would be ready in half-an-hour. Bobbi was not tall or stately like Norah, but at five foot four, with a well-proportioned, sultry body, and dramatically resplendent natural blonde hair, she commanded the attention of the more sophisticated set. She was ready. Her gray eyes wandered to the chiffonier where the framed picture of her daughter, Alexandra, seemed to stare at her. As she studied the picture, her eyes danced and her cheeks bore deep dimples while her smile lit the rest of her face. She lifted the receiver on the French style phone next to her bed, started to dial then placed it to her breast, remembering the nine hour difference between California and France. The smile diminished. "I'll call you tomorrow, baby," she told the photo.

The top was still down on the Jaguar. Bobbi contemplated the situation, and decided it was too cold and it just might rain. She snapped it into position in a flash. The clock on the dash indicated eight forty-five, plenty of time.

There was a light mist in the air and the wind was coming down from the north, bringing a chill, the likes of which she couldn't remember. Gramps told of the 'williwaw' that blew out to sea as it came down the coast off the cliffs when he was a boy. But those haven't been around for a long, long time. This was probably just some residual from El Nino. She left the contemplation behind her as she turned up the stereo and sang along to 'Friends in Low Places', from her favorite Garth Brooks album, 'No Fences'.

Suddenly, the rain came down like God had opened the skies and emptied a humongus bucket right down on the two-lane coast highway. And the dark road, the dreadfully dark winding road seemed to become narrower by the minute. The wipers could not keep up with the downpour. It seemed like she was driving into the storm, and she became frightened and slowed to thirty. There was thunder and lightning, a lot of lightning. She drove for another five miles or so, squinting through the movement of the wipers, scanning the darkness ahead, What? What's that? She instinctively recalled the day she was learning to drive the old Ford pick-up, and Gramps instructed her that she must never hit the brakes in the rain. Bobbi eased the brake pedal and slowed the car to a stop.

A huge tree lay across the entire road. "Damn . . . damn . . . damn. Shut up Garth," she unharnessed her anger at the sound from the stereo. Punching, punching the buttons, furiously until the stereo responded with no sound at all. She sat back and took a strained and penetrating breath.

Into her irritated mind came a rush of thoughts. "I can find a way around, or go back home. Somebody will come along. Damn . . . damn . . . damn" she was scared. Her heart quickened and she began shaking. Frantically she put the gears in reverse and knew that she must hurry home. Back and forth a couple of times and she was on her way. "Twenty minutes at the most, and I'll be safe at home." She assured herself. But it was only a few moments before she heard a thunderous crackling sound. Lightning struck a short distance down the dark road illuminating everything in sight. "Oh, God. I'm scared," she cried, "help me get home." She drove only a short distance when her worst fear loomed before her. The lightning sent a fiery hazard across the road. There was no way around the fallen burning tree. She fumbled with her purse. Her search was futile. She tried the glove compartment, and realized that she left the cell phone at home. "Damn. . . . damn." Oh, if only she hadn't been so quick to leave. With all of her training and accomplishments, she wasn't prepared for the fear that bore deep into the very center of her being. She began to weep uncontrollably as the fear took hold. She tried to pray but wasn't sure if God could hear with all the thunder going on around her. "I can't stay here," she pounded on the steering wheel, "I gotta get home." She couldn't be more than five or six miles from home, but in this storm it could take forever. There was a flashlight and a poncho, and oh, she hoped that her tennies were still in the trunk. She got out and went around to the rear of the Jag. Pausing, afraid that she might have left *them* at home too. She finally popped the trunk lid. "Thank you God, they're here," she exclaimed.

Bobbi wrote a short message with her name and phone number, put it inside the windshield on the dashboard, and set out for home. She made a path down to the beach, figuring it was the safest way back. The wind was howling around her, pushing at her back, and sending a chill up her spine. She was grateful that she put on the wool skirt and warm sweater, but the leather coat was absorbing the rain and getting heavy.

The moon had completely disappeared, and the beach ahead was a dark dreaded path that would surely eat her up. Lightning cracked across the sky, delineating the endless stretch of sand before her, and she realized that she would soon reach the cliffs.

Angry waves attacked just a few feet away, telling her to go to higher ground. She must find a way back up to the road before it was too late. "God, I'm not dressed to climb," she talked to the blackness in front of her, making sounds like children running past a cemetery, "I'd better find a path soon." CRACK! Her prayer was answered. The sky lit up again. There was a worn trail through the ice plant leading up to the road.

The wet asphalt of the Coast Highway was a relief from the awesome waves below, and still, the sanctuary of the road struck terror in Bobbi as she looked around. There weren't any lights. Anywhere. The terror soon turned to panic as she began to run, stumbling on small rocks and branches strewn along the road. She fell, tore her skirt and skinned her knee.

"Gramps. Gramps, help me," she cried out, "help me." She huddled with her face to the pavement for what seemed an eternity.

"Get up child," her grandfather's voice echoed from within her heart. "Get up, and keep going. Come on child."

A gasp of joy rose from her chest, but stopped as it got to her lips. "Gramps?"

She felt something tugging her arm.

Bobbi screamed, and trembled in absolute horror.

"Let me help you," the deputy said. "Are you Miss Azure?"

"Huh? What? Who are. . . ? Oh, yes," she started to cry. "Thank God." She whimpered.

"Take it easy, we'll have you home in a few minutes. Here, the car is right here."

She crawled into the cruiser, drenched and fatigued. The weariness from exertion and fear had caught up with her, and she laid her head back. In a scant attempt to speak, she asked, "How did you find me?"

"Your sister called when you didn't show up in Carmel. We drove this section twice before we saw your light. Couldn't get past the tree on the road," the second deputy said, as he gently covered her with a heavy wool blanket.

"My light?"

"Yeah, the flashlight," he said. "By the way, where's your car?"

She told them of her experience, and where she had to leave the car. He asked for her keys, and assured her that they would have her car delivered tomorrow, as soon as the road was cleared.

The few miles seemed like an eternity. "Here we are." The deputies helped her into the house. "Will you be okay? We can send someone over to stay with you."

"Thanks, I'll be all right."

"Call your sister," the senior deputy commanded, and waited for her response.

Dripping and cold, all she could think of was a hot tub.

"Miss Azure?"

"Oh, yes, yes, I'll call her, thanks. Thank you very much." She shut the door and painstakingly drug herself up the stairs to her bedroom. She took off the long leather coat and carefully hung it over the high-back chair in the corner. Slowly, she crossed the length of the room to the bathroom and cranked the faucet at the oversized tub, dropped her clothes where she stood, put on a terry cloth robe, and poured a large glass of the brandy she kept for Michael. She was still shivering when the phone rang. She whispered a delicate, "Hello."

"Bobbi. Bobbi, are you okay? What happened? The sheriff just called and said he took you home." Busy was shouting her concern, but continued without waiting for a reply. "Why didn't you call me and let me know where you were."

Bobbi painstakingly explained her ordeal as she drank the brandy. Not the way Michael had taught her to savor the bouquet, but with a long, discernible swallow. She poured another, set the glass on the edge of the tub and sank into the steaming bubbles while talking to Busy. "Would you call Guy and give him my apologies, and tell him I'll call him tomorrow? He's at the Lodge, the Stillwater Bar," she pleaded with her sister as the brandy and swirling water started to warm her.

"Sure, honey. You rest now. I'll call you in the morning. Night."

"Thanks, Biz, I love you."

"Love you too, bye."

"Bye."

She laid back and soaked for a while void of any thoughts, then sadly she wondered what Michael was doing, and, and why had she ever let him and that damn decorator talk her into black marble in her bath, especially with a gray tub, and little accents of red tile. "How depressing when you're depressed," she thought. She realized that she must get out of the tub before she fell asleep. She grabbed the large bath towel, wrapping it around her warmed body, poured some more brandy and drank it down like a sailor, and slowly moved toward the bed stopping at the chiffonier. She dropped her eyes to the picture of her little Alex. "Night, baby." The towel fell to the floor as she pulled the pouf back, and slid between the satin sheets.

* * * * * *

The phone rang as the noon-day sun streamed through the skylight above Bobbi's bed. "Hello," a tired voice uttered, clearing her throat, "achem, hello."

"Bobbi, this is Guy, Guy Nestor. Did I wake you?"

"What time is it?"

"It's just about noon, and Busy and I are driving down to see you. We're on the coast highway heading your way. We should be there in about twenty minutes or so.. "

"Look, I'm . . ."

"We won't take no for an answer, besides we're half way there already."

Reluctantly, "Okay, I'll leave the door open for you. Biz knows the way."

Bobbi picked up the towel she had left on the floor, and went to the bathroom. She inspected her torn skirt and crumpled sweater.

The skirt was history, but the sweater from Michael was just a little soiled. She stuffed the skirt in a small trash basket, put the sweater into the antique pannier, threw on her robe, and went down to unlock the front door. On the floor she noticed her keys. She peered through the sidelight and saw that the Jag was in the drive. It was all coming back. The deputies must have . . ."I must call and thank them," she told herself, as she started back up the stairs. At the top she paused for a brief moment, "Damn brandy." She put her hand to her head wishing she hadn't drunk quite so much. "This'll do it," she affirmed, as she swallowed four double-strength aspirins and a large glass of water. She turned on both faucets of the oversized shower, hung her robe on the hook and stepped in for a quick, cold shower.

"I've got to call Alex," she told herself as she slipped into her blue jeans and cuddled herself in one of Michael's old S.C. sweatshirts. She sat on the bed and dialed the long distance number. It would be after nine and Alex should be getting ready for bed.

"Bonjour," a small voice answered.

"Alexandra," she shouted, "Comment allez-vous?"

"Momma," came an excited response. "Tres bien. Ou est . . . Oh--h," she pleaded, "Where are you? Are you here in Paris?"

"No darling, I'm at home. I just wanted to hear your voice."

"Oh, momma," an excited cry came, "daddy took Danny and me to Montmartre today. We walked through the artists' square. It's called Place du Tertre," she proudly spoke like a Parisian. "I just love all those artists. One of them painted a picture of me. Daddy drank some coffee and watched. I was cold, but I didn't tell daddy, 'cause I knew he wanted the picture. It's not a very good picture, but it was sort of fun . . ."

Bobbi listened with absolute delight, while her daughter rambled on, telling of her adventures of the day. She wanted to hear everything she had done the entire week, but Alex only lived for today. In the distance she heard someone calling her name.

Busy was downstairs. "I'm up here," she called back. "No, Alex, I was talking to your aunt Norah."

"Oh, let me say hi to Auntie Biz, momma."

"Just a moment darling. How is your father?"

"He's just fine. But well-ll he has a new girl friend, and, and . . ."

"And what, don't you like her?"

"I guess she's okay, but she's not pretty like you. She just has big boobs, and.. "

"Well your father must like her. Enough of that, here's your aunt Biz." She handed the phone to Busy as she entered the bedroom. "It's Alexandra."

"Bonjour, Alexandra. How's my favorite niece?"

Bobbi went into the bathroom and finished getting ready. She spun her wet hair back in a bun, and came out in time to hear Busy finish her talk with Alex and her daughter, Danielle. She took the phone. "Hi, baby, did your father get you email yet?"

"Yes, it should be ready to use in a day or two. I can't wait. You'll be the first one that I am going to write to. I'll tell you everything. How's Michael?"

"He's fine, I just talked to him yesterday. He's in Las Vegas."

"What's he doing there without you? You know that you shouldn't let him go alone, especially to a place like Las Vegas. You better. . . ."

"Well, well, look who knows so much about everything. Look, sweetheart, I must go now. Biz is here with someone that I must talk to, business and all, so I must sign off for now. Give my love to Danielle. Au revoir, baby."

"Au revoir, momma."

Bobbi replaced the phone, and hugged Norah for a long time.

"I don't understand it, Bobbi."

"Understand what?"

"How can you go through all this stuff, take ten minutes, come out looking like you just stepped out of a fashion magazine, and be ready to meet the world?"

"It was twenty." She winked. "Let's go down and join Guy."

Guy sprang to his feet as they entered the living room. "I'm so sorry about your horrible experience last night. It's my fault. If only I hadn't asked you to drive up and all, you wouldn't have had such a frightful time of it. I . . ."

"Well, she's okay now, and that's that," invoked Busy. "Let's sit down and talk."

"I'm going to put on a pot of coffee. Anybody want something to drink?" Bobbi went to the kitchen and started the process of grinding the beans and carefully measuring the spoonfuls of coffee grounds into the basket above the special thermos. "How about a sandwich or something? I've got just about anything you might want."

Guy, who had been looking about and nostalgically remembering the house from a few years ago, chimed in with an affirmative, "I'll bet you do."

"You know I do," she replied with out missing a beat. "Sandwich, Guy?"

"Sure, let me help."

The kitchen was designed like an open-exhibition cookery, the kind that you would find in an elegant trattoria. The cooking surface with a large copper hood above was on the back wall, and the sink was strategically located within a large island that provided places for guests to sit and eat.

Guy went into the open kitchen. Approaching her from behind, he put his hands around her tiny waist and kissed her on the neck, just below the ear. As she snuggled back against him, his hands moved up under her sweatshirt, finding her unprotected, firm breasts. "Hmmm," she whispered, as she pushed her posterior against him. "Later."

He caressed her nipples for a brief moment, and reluctantly moved away, remembering how temperamental she could be. "How about if I slice some of this ham." His manner was like a school boy who just got caught with his hands in the cookie jar. "Biz, d'ya like some ham?"

"No comment," she played with her voice, "but a sandwich would be great."

He managed a coy, "What kind of bread? Cheese?"

"Rye, Swiss cheese, and mayonnaise, lots of mayonnaise."

"I don't remember you looking quite so beautiful," he said softly, so Busy wouldn't hear. "You look radiant. I--uh. . . ."

"It must be the sweatshirt."

Guy recalled how Bobbi always tried to manipulate their time together. This time he would take charge. He has what she wants but, was determined that it's going to be pleasure before business. He must not appear overly anxious to get her to help him, even though she knows all the right people. "If I play my cards close to the vest, then. . . ." his thoughts were interrupted.

"How come you're so quiet all of a sudden?" Bobbi nudged him with her hip.

"I . . . uh. I was just off in a fantasy?"

"Having fun?"

"Not yet."

Busy shouted from the deck. "How're the sandwiches coming?"

"Come and get your drink. We're almost ready." Bobby yelled.

They sat at the huge, hand carved, Philippine mahogany dining table where Bobbi and Busy enjoyed many meals with their grandparents. Gramps always sat in the middle, with the ocean at his back, so he would be close to everybody, and Gramms sat across from him. "So I can look at him and the sunset at the same time," she would say.

The sisters talked about their daughters and all the things that sisters and mothers and best friends talk about. Guy listened in amazement, thinking how wonderfully different these two women are . . . not just social beauties with scattered interests as he perceived, but warm, loving and intelligent women.

His silence was rewarded. "Guy, you are so marvelous to sit there and listen to us talk about everything," Bobbi said, as she kissed him on the cheek, and picked up the empty plates. "Tell us all about your project, and what we can do to help." She started towards the kitchen. "Be still, we can manage. D'you want more coffee?"

He raised his cup to affirm that he did.

Busy got up and finished clearing the table. They finished in the kitchen, and rejoined Guy at the table.

Guy had not intended to share any more than just the peripheral elements of his project. His voice was soft at first, but there was a discernible amount of excitement that somehow energized him to reveal most of the concept. He stopped himself short of divulging how much he had to invest, and who his partners were.

For a moment Bobbi considered asking him how much he had to invest, but quickly rejected the idea. She knew from past experience that he would be cautious about sharing any aspects of his business.

"How can we help you, Guy?" Bobby inquired.

"I'm not quite sure," he lied, "but I thought if you could introduce me to the right people, then, maybe, just maybe--ee, it would speed up the process."

"You know that *we know* everybody around here, Mr. Nestor." She emphasized.

"I guess I do," He admitted.

"What do you want?"

Guy looked at Busy with one of those, 'I wish you weren't here', looks. He wanted to rekindle the personal relationship with Bobbi before establishing a business association with either of them.

Busy took the hint. "Excuse me. I'll be right back." She went upstairs to Bobbi's bedroom.

Bobbi quizzed Guy with her eyes.

"I thought that we could get to know each other again before we got into . . ."

"Bed?" She questioned.

"No. Well--ll."

"Oh! So you want to *do it* without getting reacquainted." She started to play with his mind.

"How about that dinner I promised you yesterday. We could talk about it, alone."

"If you want to be alone, why don't I fix something for dinner?" She decided to set the stage for her own production.

"I like that idea, Bobbi."

"Then it's all settled. Come around about eight." She got up, and kissed him on top of his head. "Biz?" She called out to her sister.

"I'll be right down."

Bobbi ushered Biz into the kitchen, and informed her of the change in plans. "I'll let you know all about it in the morning," she paused with a smile, "after he leaves."

"Don't forget a little something for your sister."

"I won't."

"Let's go," Busy shouted.

"Right after I go to the little boys' room."

* * * * * * *

It was nine o'clock in the morning, and Darci wasn't ready to get out of bed when Puca jumped up, frantically to let her know that he must go outside. The bright mid-morning sun streamed into the south window through the Paisley curtains her mother had made for her thirtieth birthday. She rushed to put him out the side door of the main level, gently encouraging him to hurry. Puca seemed to take an extra long time. "Puca T. You just hurry up now," she called into the cool morning air. "Where are you, you little rascal?" She looked down to see him walking slowly with his tail between his legs. He wasn't used to being shouted at, and thought she was scolding him. "Oh, I'm sorry." she said apologetically as she picked him up and cuddled him between her bare breasts.

Still naked she went into the kitchen, set Puca on the floor, and prepared her ritual drink. She kneaded a lemon slowly and precisely on the beige ceramic counter top until it was soft enough to cut and squeeze. She added instant hot water from the special tap, to the juice and pulp, and mixed it with just enough purified water to make it tepid and easy to drink. This was just an old Indian remedy her father taught her as a little girl. It was to purify the body, an absolute necessity, before attempting to bring the chakras into proper alignment. She drank her potion with satisfaction, believing that the natural process would begin, and in twenty minutes or so she would be ready to meditate.

Puca watched her, as he always did, waiting patiently for his little biscuits. But today she was humming a tune and seemed totally oblivious to his routine. A little, "Arf, arf." brought her back to the reality of their traditional morning procedure. She took four of the treats from a box under the counter, and said, "Let's go to my room, Pukie." It seemed that four was a special amount for him, something she never could figure out. If she gave him less, he would fuss at her until she gave him all four, and he always stopped at four, even if she tried to give him more.

That tune. She was trying to remember. It was playing in Michael's car on their way home last night. She had never heard it before. It was haunting, sort of opera, but with a sad classic love song feeling. She would have to ask him what it was called.

Back in her room she stopped and looked in her hand . . . the biscuits . . . she placed them on the floor next to where Puca slept. She had a gauche look on her face. She never allowed him to eat in here. Then with an equally dumbfounded expression, looking in the mirror of the sliding closet doors, she realized that she had not put anything on, not even her robe, or an old shirt. Nothing. She stood there for a moment, inspecting the unfamiliar image looking back at her, waiting for some sort of discourse from this naked stranger. She realized that she never walked around the house unclothed, sometimes quickly between the bath and her bedroom, or from the Jacuzzi with just a towel, if it was dark enough, but never, never to walk about the house totally exposed.

The aria from last night filled her mind, and she began a slow, methodical dance. Stopping in front of the large sliding doors to the balcony, she drew the curtains back, positioning the transparent fabric to shield her from some unwanted observer. She slid the door open, allowing a cool, fragrant breeze to enter. Oblivious to the world around her, she stepped out on the balcony, placed her hands on the railing, and drank in the sweet smell of the alyssum and gardenia blooming in the clay pots surrounding the large deck. A blackbird hovered for a brief time, then sailed over to settle in an adjacent pine, while cumulonimbus clouds gathered in the northwest. The smell of a distant rain storm mixed well with the fragrance of the flowers.

Darci drew a picture in her mind, of Michael lying beside her on a tropical beach with his head propped on one hand, while the other hand applied lotion to her thigh. There wasn't another person anywhere. They were alone except for a half-dozen or more seagulls floating in a jet stream to an island in the distance, and then back again. She imagined the warm ocean breeze across her entire body, the sand against her skin, and the steady waves crashing softly on the beach. Michael had dug two holes in the sand for her breasts, so she turned over and settled in as he brushed the sand from her feet and then purposefully along her legs and thighs. Her fantasy, coupled with the cool breeze over her bare breasts created a sensuous feeling that sent a shiver, causing her to move her hands up from the railing and across her eager breasts. The magic of the moment was shattered by the sound of the phone.

By the time Darci got to the beside phone, the machine had answered the call. She couldn't hear the machine in the other room, and really wanted to succumb to her reverie. It was a sweet contemplation that needed more time to enjoy. She tried to get back into the daydream, but the moment was gone.

Sitting on the edge of her bed without a stitch of clothes on, she became aware that it was thundering and she'd better close the door. Reality somehow persuaded her to get up and grab an old oversized shirt from the closet, pull it over her head, cross the room, and close the door. A chill came to her, not from the outside air, but from the tacit voice within that penetrated directly into her heart. "What if he doesn't feel the same way that I do?" She dismissed the idea.

She stood upright. Her mother never told her what to do if his feelings didn't match hers. Past experiences were no gauge for these feelings. She pouted, which she did very well, turned on her heel and went to the bathroom. Stopping quickly, she looked at the wall beyond her bed. "I hope you're not right, mom," she told the thoughts of her mother, as she remembered what she said about the ominous painting over her bed. Darci looked around the room . . . the pale beige walls . . . the dark stained wood . . . the dark brown carpet . . . she wondered if he'd think that she was too boring. She would have to entertain him, hopeful that he would enjoy her method. Her instincts told her that she must, or lose him. She turned and continued to the bathroom, filled the combination tub-shower, sprinkling bath salts, and tested the water from time to time.

The bathroom was small compared to the rest of her custom-built home. She told the architect that she needed more room for closets, and the bath could be of a size that fit the plan. She realized, much too late, that he was an idiot who should have been fired after drawing the first line. The tan tile, with images of leaves imprinted, as well as the tan lavatory, water closet and tub, were to represent her character and to be as natural and *earthy* as possible, but the spaces in between were his responsibility. She shouldn't have to pull-in her knees every time she sat on the john, and, and, oh well, too late.

Darci piled her long hair on top of her head, and eased into the hot tub. As she settled in, letting the water warm her, she realized what she had just done. Letting the dog out, walking around the house without any clothes on, and . . . and . . . standing totally naked on the balcony. "There must be . . . What's going on? I never . . ." she cursed at herself. "You dumb broad, what if somebody saw you, what if. . . ?" After a long pause, and with absolution, "I hope they got a good look, hah." She smiled and wondered what Michael would say if he knew that she ran around without any clothes on. She kicked her foot out of the water and let the bubbles drain down her leg. "Bet he'd be furious at first, but then he would love it. He'd laugh at me, and call me a child, or something. Yes, that's what he'd do," she said, and splashed her hand into the soapy water. "He won't find *me* boring," she affirmed.

She patted herself dry and applied oils to her skin, then put on a very loose-fitting jogging suit. In the corner of her room, by the fireplace, was a small three legged table. She had restored the old milking stool and used it to hold the incense and candle she used when she meditated. She reached over and switched off the phone so she wouldn't be disturbed. It was important to shut out the unnatural sounds of the world while she became centered and got in touch with her higher power. She read many books by Edgar Cayce and learned a lot about meditation from studying Joel Goldsmith. She lit a special bayberry candle and incense given to her by her father. Darci meditated for about a half-hour.

Refreshed and peaceful, she went to the kitchen, and prepared an apple spice herbal tea. While it was steeping, she checked the answer phone, hoping the call was from Michael. "You haven't called since the accident. Let me know if you're okay." It was her old boy friend calling again. Darci didn't want to talk to him, especially about something she was trying to forget. Instead, she decided to call Michael. He wasn't in, so she left word for him to call.

Darci worked at home a lot of the time. She took over her father's real estate business when he retired. He taught her about property values and estate management. Most of the estate management was for property he put in trust for her. As a broker, she was very active in exclusive residential properties and high end retail stores. Recently she got involved with leasing exclusive shops in the major hotels. She found that these opposites actually complemented each other, promoting her business among the affluent .

Today she had to prepare herself for an 'appointment only' open house on Sunday. It was for a large ranch owned by a popular Las Vegas entertainer. She scheduled a number of interested celebrities to view the property through out the day. She pondered how these privileged few became aware of prestigious property for sale. She wondered if Michael would like to help her with the open house. "Nah." She told herself.

* * * * * * *

Banging sounds in the hotel corridor woke Michael from a dream that seemed to real too be true. He was on a tropical beach with a naked girl with long dark hair and, he was scooping out two holes in the sand for her. . . ? He shook his head to clear the lingering dream. It was her again, invading his mind.

For a short moment he thought about the possibility of asking Darci to go to the Cayman Islands with him. After all, he promised Hans that he would come and discuss the project. He didn't think that Hans would mind if she came along. "Perhaps I'd better ask her first," he surmised aloud. "No," he cautioned his pillow, with a punch to its center, "Bobbi would be much less demanding. She wouldn't expect it to mean anything special. Sometimes," he continued to talk to the pillow, "sometimes I wish I could shut these thoughts off, and, we-ll, who do you think I should ask? Okay Whom?" Suddenly he realized that he was asking a pillow to tell him what to do. He socked it again. After knocking it out cold he got up, slid out of bed, and went to the bathroom. Looking in the mirror, he said, "Tomorrow, I'll call her tomorrow," assuring himself that it was only proper dating etiquette to wait. Besides, he shouldn't even call her until Tuesday. Monday is too soon, and if he waited until Wednesday, she might think he didn't have a good time, or wasn't interested." Certainly Sunday was much too soon and today was absolutely out of the question. "I'll call her later." He knew that she wouldn't expect him to call too early after their first date.

Michael showered, shaved, dressed, and went across to the Flamingo Hotel. He liked the New York Deli. There was a short line by the entrance, so he got in line with the tourists, and watched the crowds gathering outside in the gardens. There was a show going on. Penguins? Here in the desert? Why not? After all, this *was* Las Vegas. It was said, that right there by the swimming pool was the place where Bugsey Segal first built the 'Original Flamingo'.

He sat by the railing along the promenade where he watched the people come and go on their way to and from the casino. Many counted their chips, while others argued about how much they really should have wagered. It was amazing to Michael that so many came 'to win' and most of them lost. Many lost more than they could afford. His casino was to be for the super rich who used money as a plaything, something purely for their own enjoyment, and would not be angry or even care about 'how much' they won or lost. Some would get caught up in the power of the game with the high stakes, and might even get upset if they lost, but it would never be about the money. It would always be about winning or losing. This he was sure was the purpose of the people destined to be his clientele and regular guests.

He ordered a bowl of chicken soup and a sesame seed bagel with cream cheese, and of course, a 'cup of their finest coffee'.

A tall, gray-haired man, dressed in an elegantly tailored silk suit, but sporting a distasteful neck ornament, stopped at the rail. "Good day to you Mr. Orcini," he said in a strong European accent. "How are you?"

Michael recognized the senior executive of a prominent hotel, and returned his salutation. "I am very well sir, and how are you this fine day?"

"I am feeling a little tired."

"Do you have time to join me for a cup of coffee?"

"Ah, if only I could take the time, but thank you, I have an appointment. Perhaps another time? How is your project down by the lake coming?"

"We're ahead of schedule," Michael lied, wondering how he knew. "Putting all the right people together, and all, you know."

"Still planning on stealing my M.I.S.?" he questioned with

absolute confidence that Michael would not admit to a head hunting expedition.

"People move around a lot in this town, but I didn't think that she was ready to make a move out to the lake." He evaded the obvious question. "But now that you mention it, I just might have a talk with her. If you don't mind?" They exchanged artificial, but guilefully correct laughs.

Michael extended his hand over the railing. "I am going to spend a lot of time here, perhaps we can get together for dinner."

The lanky man took a small gold case from his inside coat pocket and handed Michael a business card. "Call me, and we can arrange a time," he responded as a man in charge of a business situation. "I have a favorite restaurant that I'm sure you'll enjoy."

"I welcome the opportunity," Michael assured him.

"Then it's settled. I will expect to hear from you. Good day Mr. Orcini."

"Good bye."

Nodding, the hotel executive continued the journey to his next appointment as if he had only stopped to tie a shoe lace.

Michael wondered just how veritable the offer for a casual meeting could be coming from this man, and why was he so interested in this project. Or could he be suggesting something more than just a casual dinner? Michael opened his daytimer and jotted himself a note to review this encounter in about a week, but now it was time to go over the dossier he had compiled which included all the candidates for executive positions in his project. He was amazed at the accomplishments of the people he was introduced to, and their willingness to leave their secure positions to join him. It must be that they were drawn to the idea of a super elegant hotel and casino, like Monte Carlo was in the past. Of course that's what it must be. No need to dwell on it anymore. He moved on.

A problem was growing in Michael's mind. How to know which of these people should fulfill the positions, and how suitable would any or them be, not only to complete the roster, but also to fit into and carry out his mission statement. Keleigh and his architect were the only definite selections at this time. He contemplated the meetings scheduled for next week. It was most important to establish a selection of his chief financial officer, then the remaining choices would be made by a joint effort. He wished that he had an honorable partner, but a coadjutor like his last one was the last thing he wanted in his life.

Michael spent more than an hour analyzing the notes he had made to the document, thinking, thinking that something was missing. It was like the time when he bought a sailboat, and didn't know the difference between a jib and a mainsail. He had been researching the organization of gaming hotels and casinos for over a year now, but something was tugging at his insides. Something was not right. Michael's instincts cautioned him to go slow with the selections, and he realized that he'd better let his best friend, Charlie, in on the situation. He had a sixth sense about things like this. He sat back in his chair and let out a copious sigh with sound effects that resembled the gasp of a runner just completing a marathon. He immediately became aware of two senior ladies staring at him, and smiled with a little nod. "Ladies," he chanted, then gathered his papers and got up. He placed the appropriate amount of cash on the table, nodded to his matronly audience, and left.

Half-way across the casino, he decided to try his luck at the wheel of fortune. The wheel did not have very good odds, but the petite Asian girl spinning the disk to an empty table looked very lonely. His impulses never seemed to work in situations like this, but he would only play a few turns and be on his way. "What's your best number?" he asked, as if she really could name a winning number. "What do you suggest?" He sat down and waited for an answer as he laid a twenty down, covering it with his hand. "What?" He touted her, "tell me."

"There are more 'ones' than any other number, but the highest odds are the forty to one. My favorite is fibe," she said with a bashful curl to her lip.

"Then five it is," he said, with the authority of a judge who just slammed his gavel. He slid the bill to her, indicating he wanted chips.

The girl, whose nametag indicated she was from Oshkosh, gave him four five-dollar chips and reached back ready to spin the wheel.

Michael placed all the chips on the five dollar marker in front of him and said, "You're a long way from home," pointing to her badge. "Oshkosh."

"Oh, yes it is a long way," she reacted to the obvious misnomer designated on her name tag. "I'm really from Namdinh, North Viet Nam. I just thought Oshkosh sounded very American. It is okay?" she qualified, in an unmistakably foreign vernacular.

"It's perfectly okay with me. Now let's see that fiver."

"Feeber?" she questioned.

"Yes, it's an American slang for five."

The wheel click . . . click . . . clicked slowly until it stopped. Landing on the five. "What number do you like now?" he asked, watching for her expression.

Without any change in her unexpressive face, she placed four twenty-five dollar chips next to his original bet, and said looking down, "I still like the feeber." She looked up for his approval of the latest addition to her vocabulary.

"Well then, we'll just let it ride, and see if little feeber can come up again," he mocked her inability to pronounce the 'V'. "So, how long have you been in the States?"

She glanced down to look at the reflection of the wheel in the mirror on the table. The disc was still spinning very fast. She looked past him and answered, "Only seeks months and one week by today."

The wheel's small clicking noise came to an end as the indicator came to rest on the five once again. "The gentleman wins again." She waved her arm as a proclamation for the sake of any passersby within the sound of her voice.

"Hmm." Michael sang. He had never won two in a row on the wheel. Without looking up he mumbled, "Still like five?"

She stacked his winnings next to his previous wager, and said in a very low voice, "The house forty wins the most."

A small crowd gathered on both sides of Michael as he reached over and removed his original twenty, and slid the remaining chips to the forty-to-one long shot.

"It's your money. Let'er go!"

Two young girls followed suit, except they each placed a dollar on the other forty-to-one marker. No one else placed a bet.

"That's the wrong one," Michael informed them. "The other is going to win." The girls smiled curtly, and turned away as Oshkosh spun the wheel.

This time it seemed that the wheel was never going to stop. Clickity click . . . clickity click . . . slowly . . . slowly . . . very slowly it came to rest on the house forty-to-one space. The crowd that gathered shouted and screamed as Oshkosh collected the losing wagers, and prepared to pay the winner. "I'll have to call someone," she notified Michael. "They will have to pay you."

"Thanks."

"How much did he win?" A voice cried.

"Over twenty thousand," someone replied.

One of the casino officials checked Michael's wager and wrote a voucher for twenty thousand and instructed Oshkosh to count out the remainder in chips. "Here you are sir," she said as she placed the chips over the voucher on the table.

"Thanks." Michael was enthralled with the circumstances of the last few minutes. He slid some of the winning chips over to Oshkosh who put her hands together as to pray and bowed slightly. He picked up the voucher and the remaining chips, and turned to leave. He paused, looked at the unbelieving dollar girls and said, "Got to go with the flow, ya know." He went to the cashier's cage and exchanged the chips for cash, and the voucher for a cashier's check, gave information for the IRS, and left for his hotel.

"She'll never work for me," he promised himself.

The indicator on the phone showed that he had two messages. He punched the code. "M--Mikey, c--can we d--do din--n--ner?

C--call m--me at home." Charlie seemed to have a second sense, knowing when Michael needed a confidante. The message center continued. "Hello Michael Orcini. I don't know if it's proper or not for me to call you so soon after our first date, but I just had to talk to you, please call back "

The message from Darci was totally unexpected. Michael felt humbly triumphant in tandem with a strange calmness that permeated his entire body. He felt his whole world changing, and knew he was nothing more than a brittle body and soul, open and vulnerable. Michael sensed where this was heading. Darci kept referring to their 'first date' with the solid conviction of an umpire that there would be many more. Everything inside him kept insisting to hold on to who and what he knew best, to protect his right to be . . . To be what? To be safe with Bobbi, or just have friends like Keleigh? Suddenly he hated her with an antipathy that challenged her right to enter his world, and it exasperated his entire being. The calmness was replaced with anxiety, and he felt drained of his triumph. He sat down and after an exhausting moment felt something impractical tugging at his heart. A small endearing voice from within said, "Don't be afraid Michael, it's okay."

Michael went over and sat on the edge of the bed, picked up the bedside phone, and punched in Darci's number.

"Hello," came a somniferous response.

"Hello, sleepy-head. Did I wake you?"

"Michael. No, I uh, no . . . um."

"Something wrong?"

"Well, um. I had second thoughts about having called you," she confessed. "After I hung up I started getting scared that maybe I did the wrong thing. I was sort of hoping that you would call. You said you would. Is it okay? I mean do you. . . ?

"It's fine." He almost sounded condescending, but followed with, "I actually . . ."

"Don't patronize me, Michael Orcini," she scolded him, "I actually think that you take pleasure from the fact that I didn't wait for you to call. Don't you?"

"Why *did* you call?" He avoided her question.

"Well," she said sweetly, and paused to be sure that she didn't appear too anxious, "I'm leaving for Santa Monica tomorrow to house sit Steve's place while he's out of town for a week, and I didn't want you to think that I skipped out without telling you that I had a good time on our first date."

"Who's Steve, and why are you staying at his house?"

"Didn't you hear me say that I had a terrific time last night?"

Michael took a deep breath, wondering why she affected him this way. "Yes," he sighed, "I enjoyed being with you, too." He instinctively knew that the *too* in his response was not what she wanted to hear. On all his previous dates with other women, he simply lied to them, telling them what he knew they wanted to hear. Telling the truth, how he was feeling, was not going to be easy with Darci.

Darci graciously ignored his little tinge of jealousy. "He's my brother. Remember, I told you about him," she said definitely.

"Who?"

"Steve."

He swung his feet up on the bed, leaned back, and pushed his head back against the pillow, his eyes searching the reflection of himself in the mirror above the bed, for an easy way out. "Yes, of course I do." He paused to take control. "I slept-in this morning, how about you?" He was a master at directing conversations away from something he didn't want to talk about.

"Yes. I did too," she said proudly, "I even . . ." She started to tell him about going about the house without anything on, but decided not to continue.

"Even what?"

"Remind me when we're together. It's not . . . It'll be more fun if I can see your face when I explain. Are you going to be in Malibu next week? Santa Monica is just a short drive, you know?"

"I'm going to be here all week, but I do have to go to San Diego to meet with my architect. Maybe we could spend Friday afternoon doing something."

"Do you like the County Fair? I love all the animals, especially the horses." She sounded excited, like a little girl who was just given the honor of selecting her very own horse on the carrousel. "What do you think, Michael?"

"I haven't been to the Fair in a million years."

"Then it's all settled. Do you know how to find Cloverfield Airport?"

"Sure do. Why?"

"Steve's place is nearby, off Bundy. Got a pencil handy?"

"Just a minute." He got up and went to the desk near the door, and returned with a hotel note pad and pen. "Okay, I'm ready. Start with the phone number."

Darci gave very specific directions, including what to do if he got lost. She continued on about all the things they would do, especially the horse races, and that it was important for him to wear the right shoes, because they will be doing a lot of walking.

Michael looked at his watch. They had been talking for almost an hour and a half. Well, she had been doing must of the talking. Except for Keleigh, he couldn't remember the joy of talking to a woman, just for the sake of conversation. With Keleigh it was always more of an inconsequential nature, just words, never significant. This was different. Darci was special, and he knew that the next few weeks would impact his life forever.

"Darling, I must call Charlie. We're going out to dinner."

"Ask me what I'm doing right now."

"No, but you can tell me on Friday. Okay?"

"Umm . . . okay. What time Friday?"

"Late morning, ten or eleven. I'll call you."

"It's going to be fun."

"Bye."

"Bye, Michael."

He hung-up, and immediately called Charlie. They agreed to meet at the hotel registration desk at eight o'clock. Michael rang up the front desk and asked for a seven o'clock wake up call. A short nap, that's exactly what he needed.

Darci, all cuddled in her favorite love seat, stirred with pleasure as she felt a warm sensation fill her body. Her hands followed the eagerness from her breasts down her abdomen to a point where anticipation turned to ecstasy, and she began to squirm. "I can't wait," she told herself, knowing that she must wait until the right time. "I can't wait, yummy . . . yummy. . . . yummy." She hugged herself, and day-dreamed for what seemed like hours.

* * * * * * *

Michael was awake before the desk clerk called. He sat on the couch near the sliding doors facing the small balcony, and rummaged through the final draft proposals that he would present to Hans. He studied the scope of the project, and the justification of the cash flow figures. The outline that he got from J.T., his primary candidate for CFO, was remarkably on track with his own analysis. He sat back and relaxed for a moment, trying to picture the project on opening day. "Not too bad for a kid without a trade," he spoke to the idea in his mind. This was the last project he would develop. It was the end of the road. This would be his legacy. The only 'Seven Star' hotel in the world with a casino and health spa that would be revered by all the rich and famous. The unique salons and designer studios would be an assemblage of the most prominent fashion designers from Europe and New York. It will be like a rare gem, an accomplishment to be remembered.

A smile parted his lips as he watched the mental picture grow with many faces he had only seen in the movies, news papers and magazines. They were laughing, gambling, and having a wonderful time. They all stood up, and became quiet as he slowly walked down the Grand Staircase of the main casino with Darci on his arm. They stopped before reaching the final step, surveyed the majestic room, and were greeted by the thunderous round of applause. Darci tugged at his arm and whispered in his ear, "I hope they don't fall out." He looked down at her cleavage and smiled. They continued in his fantasy meandering through the casino, stopping to nod graciously to a politician or to acknowledge a celebrity, and of course the photographers, Darci would love them, he was sure. Many did not know who he was, but followed the lead of those who were 'in the know'. The Prince of somewhere shook his hand saying what an extraordinary place this was, while everything DeBeers had ever mined was draped around someone's neck or arm. There were women who had never worked a day in their life, with hands and skin softer than a baby's butt, and the men, ahh yes, the rich plastic men with more money than sense. They moved out to the veranda where they embraced until the phone rang, and Michael brought himself back to reality.

"Darn." He wanted to remain in the daydream.

It was the front desk with his wake-up call.

He placed a call to Hans in the Cayman Islands. "Hello, Hans? This is Michael Orcini calling."

"Gud eve-n-ning mon," he responded in a deep-toned refrain, "it is gud to hahr frum you. How hahv you ban? When are you comb-ing to de eye--lahnds, mon? I hahv ban waiting to hear frum you, I did . . ."

Michael took a deep breath and cut in before he could ask any more questions. "I've been fine, and very busy organizing my project. I thought that I might be ready to fly out to the islands in about a week or two. I should have everything in order by then, but I'd like to go over the highlights with you now if you are still interested."

"I ahm, I ahm. Do you hahv sumtin you con fox to me mon?" He sounded earnestly interested.

"Yes, I have some artist's conceptions, an outline showing projected costs, and an income stream. I'll have dossiers on all my key people by the end of next week.

"Dat is a gud start. I hahv ban tooking widt sum a-so-see-ates in Germah-ny a-boot your project, ahn dey want to know mohre."

"Thanks Hans," he said quietly, "but we must come to an agreement with regards to your fee and a timeline for the availability of funds."

"Ah, my mon. You are ahb-solu-tily right. Fox me your informa-see-on, and I will fox you my proposal. What is your fox number?"

They exchanged numbers and completed their conversation. Michael called the concierge to make arrangements to send and receive the transmittals. He went to the closet and checked his jacket looking through the pockets for a business card. Not there. He wondered what he might have done with it. Maybe the leather flight jacket. Gina Santiago, ah yes. Maybe he should have Henri give her a call, but where was Hans' card. Oh well, with the fax number, he really doesn't need the address.

He returned to the desk and rummaged through the scraps of paper he put in the drawer, extracting a napkin with a note '1994 Commander 114B and a phone number'. He dialed the number, "I would like to talk to someone about the '94 Commander you have for sale."

"Yer talkin' to him," came a quick answer.

"I'd like to check her out tomorrow, if you're available."

"Yeah sure. What time d'ja wanna come over?"

"I'm in Las Vegas. I can drive up tomorrow afternoon, say about one or two."

"That'll do jest fine. We're on the east side jest south of the tower. D'ya know how to git here?"

"Yes. As I remember, the airport is about a mile west of town."

"Thet's right. What's yer name ?"

"Michael Orcini."

"Mike . . . what, kin yeh spell thet?"

"O-r-c-i-n-i, Orcini."

"Okay, gotcha Mr. Oceny. See yeh tamarrah."

"Whom should I ask for?"

"Huh?"

"What is *your* name." He put emphasis on the 'your'.

"Jest ask for Seth, everybody knows me."

"Okay, thanks, see you tomorrow."

With that done he took a quick shower and went down to meet Charlie.

Charlie was on time, as always. He stood quietly by the registration desk, while every available female clerk vied for his attention. This shy, sensitive man, who looks like a candidate for the Mr. Universe pageant, always attracted women, even when he tried to be inconspicuous. Charlie was an imposing figure to say the least. The pearl white silk shirt under his worsted Zenga pin stripe suit accented the combination Cherokee and Black African lineage embossed in his deep bronze face. His anxious soft brown eyes searched above the crowded casino for the familiar face of his friend. The Tony Lama custom boots enhanced his six feet-four inch frame, and he could easily canvas the room without being obscured. His face lit up as he spotted his dear friend. The shyness lifted and he was no longer uncomfortable. "Hey Mikey," he invoked with a thunder characteristic of his stature

"Hey, ole pal. Good to see you," he responded from a distance.

"Mikey?" came a voice from behind the counter just as Michael approached.

"Good evening, Miss Gordon." He ignored her comment noticing the surreptitious glances exchanged between several inquisitive clerks. "Where to?" he questioned Charlie.

"How a b--bout a st--steak? I could go for the b--biggest, juiciest s--steak with all the tri--m---mmings, and some c--country musi--sic. What d'ya s--say?"

"Perfect." He glanced back at Jeri and smiled.

"You d--driving th--that sar--dine can M--Mikey?"

Michael nodded.

"We can t--take my tr--truck. Okay?"

"Sure."

The valet sprinted over. "Your car, Mr. Orcini?"

"No. We're taking his."

Charlie passed the claim check to the valet. "It's the b--black Expl--plor--rer." as if it were the only one there.

They drove to a place just off the strip where the country music could be heard with the doors closed, and the air was filled with the smell of stale cigarettes and beer. There were would be cowboys in their blue jeans and straw hats, and cowgirls wearing sequined boots with matching hats, and skirts that barely covered their pride and joy.

This would not have been Michael's first choice, but Charlie was a special friend and this is what he liked. Besides, they did have the finest Kansas bred beef this side of the Mississippi. They were led to a booth on a second tier where they could see the dance floor. The waitress was as sweet as she could be, and came back as often as she could to flirt with Charlie, hinting of her availability after hours.

As always, the two friends talked of girls and airplanes. Today, however, the particular topics of conversation were Darci and the Commander Michael wanted to buy. It was time to tell him about the project. The Commander seemed to be a good choice, and they agreed that they would fly up to St. George tomorrow to check her out. Charlie was brutally up-front and expressed his concerns about the fascination that Michael had for this girl. "S--she's t--troub--ble M--Mikey. S--she's got y--you m--mov--vin' to f--fast. J--just play f--for a lit--tle wh--while. G--get to know h--her." He stopped and starred questioningly

"What?"

"W--what's w--with the girl at the h--ho--t--tel?"

"What girl?" He pretended not to know.

Charlie queried him with his eyes.

"Oh. You must mean Miss Gordon."

"Miss G--Gordon? G--give me a b--break?"

"Okay. Jeri," he mumbled, "she's just trying to be nice."

"R--right and I'm P--Peter Pan."

"I'll tell you about her later. Can we get back to Darci?"

"I d--don't know." Then as a command, and without a stammer. "Besides I haven't met her yet."

"I don't need your approval," he retorted, "besides, she's grown up, not like . . ."

"S--so when can I m--meet her?"

"Maybe next week. But now I have another surprise for you."

He mapped out the project that he was going to develop and delineated all the particulars, from the design to the players.

Charlie listened to the entire dissertation without interrupting the obvious satisfaction that Michael had with planning his venture. He even dismissed the waitress with kind gestures denoting the seriousness of their conversation. After Michael finished, Charlie motioned for the waitress to come over, "Two d--double S--Scotch r--rocks." he pointed his finger towards the table and waved it back and forth like a pendulum between them. He changed the subject. "You told K--Keleigh ab--bout D--Darci? You know she's ca--ca--crazy about you. Wha--at ab--bout Bob--b--bi? How d--does she f--fit in?"

"What do you mean, Keleigh, crazy about me?.. Nah. We're just great friends. You think? Really? Nah. You're crazy. Let's get back to my project. Okay?"

The investors became a consequential argument for Charlie. He objected to the Chinese and their involvement with Ceres and her group, and he became livid with the contemplation of Nugari taking on any role other than a finder of funds. He did like Hans and suggested that Michael wait while he had his friend Dominic Poncerelli, the police commissioner, check them out. He said that even though the Gaming Commission checks these guys out, his friend could go underground for other information. Michael said that he didn't have the time, and thought with the state checking them it should be okay. Charlie admonished his anxious friend of the possible consequence of dealing with these uninvestigated people. The only ease he got from their conversation was that Michael had previously agreed to meet with Hans, and try to work out a deal with him.

Michael agreed to *sleep on it* and talk more tomorrow when they went to St. George, and promised he would enjoy the remainder of the evening.

Charlie got up and went to the restroom, only to return with two eager cowgirls. It was when Michael reminded him that they had a full day ahead of them that Charlie's little boy came out.

"Just a few dances with these lovelies," he begged playfully and without the slightest hesitation. "Just a little while, Mikey?"

Michael laughed knowing that a few more dances meant closing the place down. Tomorrow would prove to be an interesting day. He was glad that he made the appointment for the afternoon. He was also glad that he had a friend like Charlie.

* * * * * *

It was nine o'clock Sunday morning when the two men met for breakfast at 'Grandma's' house before going to St. George. Michael laid out some papers that a fellow pilot at the A.O.P.A. had faxed to him a few days ago on the '94 Commander. They ordered their breakfast. The way that Charlie ate always amazed Michael. He seemed to eat all the wrong foods, but still had the body of an Olympic athlete. They went over the particulars of the airplane.

'You said t--this is a s--special model M--Mikey?' he said with a question.

"Yeah, it's a 114B with a range of 725 nautical miles at a max cruise of 164 knots. She is fully loaded with the latest GPS, and she is 'sposed to have a gorgeous paint job. Dark blue-green, almost black, with silver and red stripes down her fuselage, on her tail and wingtips."

They spent their entire breakfast time discussing the 114B. They scrutinized the statistics, and compared the useful load, operating and maintenance costs, comfort, style, luxury, utility, and safety features.

They completed their breakfast, and went out to the parking lot. "I'm gonna leave my car at Nellis. Give them your name at the gate, and they'll let you know where I am."

"O--k--kay."

Michael had Colonel Rojam make arrangements for him to leave the SL in one of the service hangers. It was the same hanger where he parked on his last visit. A man was working on the F4-U

Corsair as he drove in. He turned as Michael got out of his car. "Good morning Mr. Orcini, Sir." He rendered a courtesy salute.

"Good morning Lieutenant Morris," remembering him. "This your bird?"

"Yes Sir, she certainly is."

"She's a beauty."

"The Colonel said that you were going to leave your car here today. She will be perfectly safe in the hanger. Sergeant Drake is on duty today," he said as a matter of fact.

Michael parked the SL in a corner near the overhead door, and waited for Charlie.

The men drove to St. George continuing their discussion from the night before. Charlie started as soon as Michael got into the truck. "The t--troub--ble with today's wah--world," Charlie stated, "is th--that the honest tra--trust the dis--on--honest without know--knowing that they're being ro--robbed bl--blind." Charlie was obviously, and profoundly concerned about Michael's involvement with Nugari and the Chinese investors. He went on to reprove Nugari, and the circumstances surrounding the involvement of Ceres and her Mafia group. He said that the whole cauldron of Wu, Nugari, deVillefrance, and Ceres with her henchmen boiled inside him like a concoction that reeked of Gresham's theorem. Charlie had become obsessed with investigating the 'scum', and suggested that Michael meet his friend the Police Commissioner. Charlie's dissertation was so lengthy that it took almost the entire trip to St. George to complete.

Michael listened intently to the discourse. "I would like you to meet these people before you render a final decision," he pleaded with his confidante. "You realize that they may actually have the funds ready to invest?" His statement ended in a question, which brought about a sudden anxiety in the center of his gut. He looked out the window, and contemplated just how much of Charlie's concern might be cause for investigation. Nugari was extremely aggressive in his approach to get started. Wu and deVillefrance were unknown factors in the equation, and Ceres, well, he hadn't even met her.

"O--k--kay M--Mikey. S--set it up, and I'll g--go there with you."

"I hate to say this, but you might just have a point here," he looked over at Charlie, noticing puzzlement on his face, and took a deep breath. "You know. About checking up on these guys"

Charlie nodded, and smiled the smile of a true friend. "Now, ole p--pal, I want to t--talk to you about your n--new l--lady."

"There," he pointed to the highway sign, "turn off here Charlie. The airport should be about a mile."

They spotted the FBO across from the main terminal, and figured it to be the most likely place to find Seth. As they approached the field, Michael spotted the 'Commander'. "There she sits, Charlie." The excitement rose in his voice. "Look! Isn't she a beauty? Turn here," he pointed, "park as close as you can."

Charlie glanced over at his eager friend, and said calmly, "O--k--kay, boss."

Michael jumped out, and walked briskly over to the airplane, and began an immediate inspection.

Charlie was impressed with its size. It was a big airplane. She stood tall and proud on a trailing-beam main landing gear. Michael walked with ease under the tailplane, which was mounted midway up the fin. The dark, almost black, color was most unusual with its streamlined stripes down the entire length of the fuselage, and on the wing tips and tail.

"I understand that some of these babies have actually landed on carriers," Michael sang out to his buddy.

"T--that's o--k--kay if your p--planning to l--land on wah--wah--one of t--them," Charlie shouted with a hint of sarcasm. He walked over to Michael, and told him that he would go and find Seth.

Ten or more minutes passed, and Charlie appeared across the tarmac with a tall thin man in coveralls. The man had rumpled sandy hair, and looked as if he should be guiding an old fashioned plow behind a mule.

"This is S--Seth," Charlie announced.

"Yew must be Mehster Oceney." He wiped the palm of his hand on the bib of the coveralls, down the side of his thigh, and extended it to welcome Michael. "Pleased to meetcha," He sniveled. "Didn't rightly know if'n yew were commin."

"Is this your airplane, or are you just keeping her for someone?"

"She's maihn alraight." He shuffled his feet. "Yew intristed in buying her?"

"It all depends on her condition, and the price."

"She's only got a hundrud an tirdy hours since her last major," Seth said, and handed Michael a file folder with all the maintenance records. "Da asking price is unda wat's goin fer out der," he pointed. "It's in the folder."

"Thanks." He thumbed through the folder. "We'd like to take her up."

"Gotcher license and log?"

"Right here," Michael extracted some documents from a small flight bag, "and my current medical." Michael referred to the required, up-to-date, medical certificate that all pilots must have. "Charlie has his too."

Satisfied, Seth unlocked the doors, and handed Michael the key. "Let's go." He said, motioned for Charlie to get in the back, and climbed into the right seat.

Seth directed Michael towards Mesquite for a 'touch and go', and an immediate ascent up and over Virgin Peak to prove how easily the 114B climbed to altitude. Michael circled around, and landed at Mesquite. "Your turn, Charlie."

Charlie 'put her' through many exhausting maneuvers, and returned to St. George.

"We'd like to get some coffee, and talk."

Seth escorted them to the pilot lounge where they spent the next hour going over the records, and discussed the airplane's performance. Satisfied that she was a good airplane, Michael and Charlie went for a walk outside and exchanged ideas on her value. They returned, and Michael wrote a number on a piece of paper. He handed it to Seth, who, without hesitation pulled some cards from his pocket, shuffled through them, and handed one to Michael. Michael raised his eyebrows, showed the card to Charlie, scratched through the numbers, got Charlie's approval, and returned it to Seth. Seth chose another card. They went through this silent, and unusual process a number of times until Seth simply said, "Okay. Yew gotta deal."

"I'll give you a deposit now, and the rest in two weeks. You must keep her in a hanger until then. Agreed?"

"Yew got it, Mehster Oceney," Seth said, pleased with the transaction.

Michael wrote a check for the deposit. "I'll have the title checked through my bank, and if everything is in order, the money will be transferred to you. Thanks."

They walked to the car. "I wonder where he got the money to buy her," Michael exclaimed. He doesn't look like someone of any substantial means."

"He w--won her in a c--contest."

"That explains a lot, especially the price." He settled back in the seat. "How about the cards with all those different prices? Have you ever seen anything like that before?"

"Uhh, uhh." Then without a stammer, "You got a good deal, Mikey."

"Thanks. And thanks for coming along with me. I really appreciate it."

They sat quietly for a long time before Charlie asked, "What about D--Darci?"

"What about her?"

"You n--never avoid t--talking about g--girls be--f--fore. What's so sp--special about her, any--w--way? You in l--love?"

"Don't know," he hesitated, "she affects me like nobody else."

"You're n--not gonna have enough t--time for hot--tels and casinos, and a n--new g--girl." He took a deep breath. "Bobbi's gonna k--kill ya."

"Naw."

Charlie spent the rest of the trip back trying to discourage

Michael's relationship with Darci. The sun was setting as they drove through the main gate at Nellis.

Sergeant Drake was still working in the hanger when they arrived. "She's safe and sound Mr. Orcini. I had one of my men wash her down. There's a lot of bugs out here in the desert, and she needed some attention."

"Thanks, but you di. . . ."

"It was *my* pleasure," came a feminine voice from the Air Force dungarees that appeared out of the shadows. "It was my idea." She shook her hair loose, and smiled.

"One of your *men* Sergeant? You'd better get your eyes examined."

* * * * * *

The next two days were grueling for Michael. He spent the entire first morning with Keleigh and Jan Thaddeus (JT) Popinski, his preferred candidate for the position of CFO. His propensity toward J.T. was more than his credentials. His willingness to move to Nevada or the fact that being a family man gave him a degree of stability. It was his reversal of attitude to fit a situation. The ostensible ease in which he changed hats from a logical, precise financial advisor to a *damn the torpedoes, full speed ahead* captain. Michael liked that quality, since it mirrored his own character.

Hector Ruby sat, talked and did almost everything as if he were acting out an operations manual for lawyers. The term, human being, could hardly be included in any definition of him. Michael used him for his expertise in gaming and corporate law. If the truth of the matter were to be known, and he could get the contracts completed by fax or mail, Michael would never talk to him .

They spent more than half the morning creating, and recreating agreements for just the one position. Although Michael and J.T. were not completed, they had resolved the major issues of primary salary and longevity. Michael knew the way to keep key people was to offer long term incentives, and he wasn't interested in anybody who wanted to make a quick buck. J.T. was sympathetic to Michael's desire to use a portion of the gross revenue for the homeless and otherwise unfortunate people before his own profit sharing. Michael looked to Keleigh, and she discreetly nodded her approval.

Michael was pleased when Keleigh agreed with the choice for this senior position. After all, she helped him pick out her own boss. When they got up to take a short break he walked around behind her and patted her lightly on her tight butt. She gave no indication of his little ritual, but wished there was some other meaning to his gesture. Then she threw him a curve on the selection of General Manager for the hotel. He was ready to go with J.T.'s recommendation when Keleigh introduced a dossier on Sumner T. Williams III.

The resume was impressive, later, when they were alone, he would tell her how incredible it was that she should find such talent that was available. "Can you get him to come here for an interview, Keleigh? We don't have much time. Got to keep moving."

Keleigh tossed her auburn hair as she stood up, and looked at him with an emerald sparkle that told him she was up to something.

"What? No. You couldn't. You didn't. Did you?"

She walked to the door of the conference room, stopping for a brief moment to look over her shoulder at the bewildered men. She eased open the large carved wood door and softly commanded, "Mr. Williams, we are ready for you now. Thank you for being so patient."

A tall regal, broad-shouldered figure stepped through the doorway. He looked like the ruler of a small forgotten empire somewhere in the midst of Europe. He was perfectly attired in a great two buttoned, nailhead worsted suit, custom tailored in England. He was balanced, yet formal with an elegant simplicity. In place of the customary tie he sported a deep plumb colored silk cravat. His eyes were guileless and intelligent, but mysteriously cautious. His smile was mirthful, but with a tinge of arrogance. He stopped at the end of the table. "I am pleased that you should consider me for such a prestigious position in your magnificent resort. Miss Cody-Ives has told me a great deal of your plans, and I am most anxious to know more." He spoke with a strong precise phonation that placed him in command of the interview.

"Gentlemen, may I introduce Sumner T Williams the Third. Sumner, this is Michael Orcini, Hector Ruby, our attorney, and J.T. Popinski, our Chief Financial Officer."

The seated men arose as if being introduced to royalty, not knowing whether to shake hands or bow. When the inevitable hand shaking was finished, Michael invited the prospect to sit for an interview.

"Well, Miss Cody-Ives, why don't you begin." He offered a sarcastic grin, but followed it with a wink that only she could see.

Keleigh asked Sumner to present his credentials to her colleagues. Once again he took-over the interview, questioning more than offering his list of achievements. From the first moment there seemed to be an almost magical bonding between Michael, J.T. and their *new* Hotel General Manager.

Hector excused himself soon after the interview started, acknowledging that his presence was not really required at this time.

Keleigh sat back and enjoyed her accomplishment while she watched Sumner control two strong leaders. She could never remember Michael giving up control of a meeting. She studied his face, assessing that he must have something up his sleeve. She squirmed when he realized what she was doing and winked at her. She couldn't wait to get him alone. He winked at her twice. He never did that.

After an hour and a half, J.T. suggested that they break and discuss the aspects of Mr. Williams' interview, and asked if he would be so kind as to wait for their decision, which he promised would be forthwith.

Everyone made their acknowledgments, while Sumner T. Williams III bowed graciously, and left the room.

"Well, Miss Keleigh Cody-Ives, what do you think of this fellow that you have unleashed upon us?" Michael inquired with a playful banter.

"I think you like him and, . . . No! I know you like him, otherwise you wouldn't have let him take control. That's it. Right?" She knew what was going on. It was as if a light was turned on, and the darkness of her doubt disappeared. "Am I right, Michael?"

He pretended to review the dossier, and waited a moment before looking up. "What do you think J.T.?"

"I think Keleigh is one-hundred percent right on this one."

Keleigh waited as Michael controlled the meeting once again. Now she knew for sure. Sumner was the right person. She was optimistic when she asked him to come to the States to meet Michael, and now, now she was sure.

He looked at her with the admiration of a lover. "Will you ask our new General Manager to come back in? I think that it would be appropriate if *you* gave him the news, Miss Cody-Ives. Don't you agree, J.T.?"

"Ab--so--lute--ly," came an approving response.

Keleigh beamed with the joy of her success, but quickly regained her composure as she got up to once again invite Sumner back to the meeting. She glanced over her shoulder before opening the door, but this time with authority and confidence.

"We're ready for you, Mr. Williams."

Michael closed the meeting with an invitation for Sumner to join them later for dinner. He graciously declined, explaining jet lag, and all the other symptoms that go with international travel. He left, and they continued to peruse the remaining dossiers.

"Tell me, Miss Cody-Ives, do you have any more surprises?"

"Oh, Michael," she pouted.

They all laughed.

"Let's call it a day," Michael intoned. "Back at eight a.m. sharp."

"Goodbye."

"Goodbye."

"Goodbye," came the last salutation as Keleigh stopped at the door, "I think you owe me dinner, Mr. Big Shot Michael Orcini."

"I think you're right, sweet cheeks," he said with a song. "I'll pick you up at eight."

"Right, but no Grandma's House. A nice place." She paused, not quite sure what she just heard. "Did I hear right? You're going to pick me up at my place?"

'That's right. Eight o'clock."

"Gotta run. See ya, bye,"

Michael chuckled at her predictable response.

It was precisely five minutes before eight when he pushed the button next to her condo door. He heard some shuffling, and a, "Just a minute."

Keleigh opened the door while striking a pose with her left hand slid to the uppermost point of the door edge, and her right hand, palm up was resting on her slightly elevated right knee. She was wearing a man's gray flannel pin-stripped suit coat over a lavender form-fitting sweater, and white pedal pushers complete with white four inch spike heels. "Hi." The sound of her voice was forced to complement her attire.

"Hi." His response echoed her, but in a somewhat shy unbelieving tone. He took a deep breath as she continued her pose. "You ready for dinner?"

"Oh, Michael." She fell out of her pose and right into her delightful pout, curling her lip and dropping her head. She lowered her knee swinging her foot as if to kick an imaginary can. "Don't you like how I dressed for you? Even a little?"

"You look fabulous, Miss Keleigh Cody-Ives."

"You called me by my full name several times today. How come?"

"How come what?" He stood by the door while she went over to a porter's table in the hall for her hand bag.

"Never mind," she scowled.

"Come on, sweet cheeks."

"Don't call me that unless you mean it."

"But I mean it, *sweet cheeks*. Let's go."

He took her to the Hard Rock Cafe. They talked about old

memories, college days, and many inconsequential topics. "It's almost midnight," he said with a yawn.

"You going to turn into a pumpkin?"

"We have an eight o'clock scheduled." He took her hand, holding it close to him, and led her out of the restaurant.

"Do you want to come in for awhile, Michael?" Knowing his answer.

He took her face in his hands, and sweetly kissed her on the lips, like a friend, and turned away. "Good night sweet cheeks."

"You don't know *how* sweet," she whispered.

Michael slept in past his normal six-thirty, skipped his workout and hurried down to the hotel conference room. Keleigh was pouring some coffee and handed him a cup. He patted her on the butt. "Good morning," he said. "You're looking mighty fine."

She ignored his transparent attempt at being alert. She knew all to well that he would be faking it until the coffee did it's job, and the excitement of the day's challenges would kick in the adrenaline.

J.T. followed by a moment looking fully rested, and ready for the task at hand.

"Everyone read the profiles?"

"Yes."

"Michael, have we narrowed the MIS Director down to just two candidates?"

"You have a surprise for me, Keleigh?"

"No, but I thought that you wanted to talk to the one over. . . . You know."

"The Flamingo?" He watched her affirmative nod. "No not at this time."

They interviewed the candidates for the MIS and Entertainment Director positions, and asked each of them to return at two that afternoon.

"Would you like me to order lunch for us, Michael?"

"Not for me Keleigh. I need to get out of here for a little while." He picked up his files, and headed for the door. He stopped briefly. "Let's be back by one-thirty. That should give us time enough to cast our votes. Don't you think?" He resumed his exit, not waiting for an answer.

"Okay."

Michael went to his room, and immediately called room service for a soup and sandwich combination with a large carafe of fresh-brewed coffee. He had become perplexed with his buddy, Keleigh. It seemed to him that the last couple of times he patted her butt, she would push back against his hand and allow it to linger against her. He liked making the gesture, but now his playful acknowledgement was beginning to become expected. He attempted to dismiss the thought as being only his imagination, but he realized that she did not resist or avoid his hand movement like she used to. Could Charlie be right or was she just playing with him because he'd given her a key position in the resort. He resolved that it was nothing, she was just a good sport, and an old friend. With that settled in his mind, he laid back and rested before going down to the meeting.

They unanimously selected Rebecca Greydove as their MIS Director, but labored over the Entertainment Director until they finally decided on Spike Hawley. Michael was relieved that this task was completed. He informed his new team that he will be about the business of completing the funding, and that he would meet with his architect over the weekend. He instructed them to organize around the CFO, and to prepare their outlines for a meeting next Thursday.

"Will you be meeting the money guys here, in town, this week?" Keleigh asked.

"No. I'm heading to Malibu first thing in the morning. You can reach me there. Oh, I'll be working with my architect all weekend," he paused. "Keleigh?" he asked, "Would you be an angel, and be sure that everyone knows how to reach me?"

"Sure, Michael."

"Good day everyone. I'll see you next week."

A mixture of various 'goodbyes' resounded as he left the room.

* * * * * *

After an extensive workout in the hotel exercise facilities, Michael showered and called for a bell hop to get his bags. He wasn't surprised to see an attractive 'bell girl' show up at his door. "I'm here for your luggage sir," she said abruptly as she brushed her endowment against his arm on the way to pick up the bags.

"Your name tag. Ennis Quintus. Bet you get a lot of kidding about that."

"He was an. . . ."

"An epic poet. I know."

"Too bad you're leaving. Do you come often?"

"As often as I can." He didn't look for her expression. "Please tell the valet that I'm going to stop for breakfast before leaving." He handed her his claim check and a generous tip.

"Thank you. Please come again." She turned, bent down at the waist to emphasize her round derriere, peeked under her arm to see if he was watching, picked up his bags with a quick wink, and left.

The hotel coffee shop was relatively quiet. Michael sauntered in beyond the hostess station, and looked around. He saw an empty booth in a corner, and motioned to a waiter that he was going to sit there. The waiter approved with a nod, and a short wave of his hand.

He ate and read the local paper in less than a half-hour and started back to Malibu.

"Hey, Mr. Orcini." Clay was running across the parking lot.

"Hi, Clay. How's it going? Have your folks settled in yet?"

"No, not yet. Dad hasn't found the right job yet. He's particular, ya know."

"Sure." Michael knew. "Have him call this number, and ask for Mr. Popinski. Tell him that I want him to talk to your Dad." Michael took out one of his cards as he talked, and scribbled J.T.'s name and number. "Don't forget. Okay?"

"Thanks, Mr. Orcini. Thanks a lot."

Michael called J.T. from his cell phone in the car. "If he's any good, put him on the payroll, and we'll talk when I get back."

"You on your way to Malibu?"

"Yes. I'll be there about mid-afternoon. You can get me at my home office."

The drive back was uneventful, and Michael arrived in Malibu just as he planned. He dialed his message center, and listened to the phone messages while he brewed some coffee and unpacked his bags. Most of the recordings were predictable. Except for the one from Biz telling about Bobbi's ordeal. He immediately dialed her number.

"Hello."

"Bobbi. It's Michael. Are you okay? I just got back, and heard Biz's message."

"It was days ago, and besides it's no big deal."

"What do you mean no big deal? Biz said the Sheriff had to rescue you in the middle of the night."

"I'm okay, Michael, and you know how those deputies exaggerate, especially when there is an available girl in a predicament."

"Oh, so now you're available."

"I've been available for a long time. Or have you forgotten?" She didn't really want to hear his reply, and quickly changed the course of the conversation. "Michael, do you remember my friend Guy Nestor?"

"Isn't he the one with those cheap little motels?" He remembered. "Oh, yes, it's all coming back. You were dating him for a while. Weren't you? And then there was his worthless son, Ivan or something like that. The one who just wants to chase skirts, and play tennis or polo. He tried to get into your pan . . ."

"Ian, and he didn't."

"Didn't what?" Try, or get in?"

"Michael!" she shouted, scolding him. "I've some serious things to talk to you about. So, can we get on with *my* conversation?" She emphasized the 'my' as she always did when she had something very important to say. Finishing with a sweet, "Please?"

"What's so important about Guy Nestor?"

"All those *cheap motels*, as you so eloquently put it, have made him very rich. By the way Mr. smart stuff, they're hotels."

"Well ex--cue--ue--ue--zzz me," he mimicked a Steve Martin comedy routine.

"Can we be serious for a moment?" She had a habit of not waiting for his answer. "I told him about your project. Well, the little that you told me on the phone. Anyhow, he's interested and wanted me to ask you if you'd like a financial partner. He really has the bucks. He told me, in confidence of course, that he has a half-b--bil--oh, it's so, like five-hundred mil . . . Michael, I can't even say it, it's so much."

"Are you trying to tell me that Guy Nestor has five-hundred million dollars that he wants to invest in a hotel?"

"Yes." She composed herself. "Isn't it wonderful?" She sounded like a real estate sales person again. "And he wants to talk to you about your project." The excitement rose in her voice. "Oh darling, isn't it marvelous? It's just what you've been waiting for. I'm so happy. Aren't you?"

"Whoa. Slow down. You're starting to sound like me." He needed to find out more of the circumstances surrounding his offer. "Tell me how all this came about."

Bobbi delineated the whole story. The chance meeting at Pebble Beach, the fact that he already knew something about the project, and that he trusted her to help him find a great hotel project.

Michael became skeptical when he heard that Guy knew about the project before he talked to Bobbi. "Are you sure that he had information on *my* project before you ran into him?"

"Yes. He mentioned Sundance Lake when he came to the house." She sounded perplexed. "Why, is it important?"

"Just overly cautious, I guess. Did he mention any names?"

"He said that he ran into an old friend of Biz's. Somebody she met in Spain when we were there. Remember Spain, Michael? Didn't we have the best time? The absolute best time?"

"Nugari? Was it Nugari?" he said, with a scowl in his voice.

"What's wrong? No! That's not it. It was a French name. Claude de.. something or other. What's he have to do with you?"

"He sure does get around. Look, does Guy want me to call him, or.. ?"

"Did I do okay, Michael? You sound a little upset."

"You did just fine, Bobbi. Does he want me to call?"

"Yes. I'll get you the number. I have it upstairs." She pressed the hold button on her phone, and he listened to country music in her absence. She was gone for only a moment. "Here it is. Ready?" Again she didn't wait. She enunciated the number to be sure he understood. "Got it?"

"Yes." He read it back so that she would know he captured her words on paper.

"When can we get together? I have something for you."

"O.. oh ?" he stretched out his inquiry.

"Not that, silly. I bought you something, a present. That's why I was on the peninsula last week when I ran into Guy. See it's all your fault. So when can I see you?"

"I don't know. My calendar in full for the rest of this week, and I'm going down to San Diego to spend some time with Henri this weekend."

"I could drive down on Friday. We could play around a little, and maybe have dinner."

"I'm leaving early Friday morning." He wasn't ready to tell about Darci.

"How long are you going to be there? Maybe I could come along and help out. I wouldn't be in the way. I promise."

"This is business. I'm going to be solid into the layouts, designs and so forth. You would be terribly bored. Remember the last time?" He had to make his explanation convincing, or tell her about Darci. The evasive commentary was the way to go. He was sure.

"When will you be back?"

"Sometime Monday afternoon."

"Can we get together then?" she implored.

He was starting to get impatient with her. "Look darling," he said surreptitiously, "I don't know what my schedule is going to be like. Could you call me on Monday?"

She sensed his avoidance. He called her darling, again. Twice in less than a week. He was up to something, and she was determined to find out.

"You can bet I will, *dahling*," her repartee came in a snip.

"I'll try to get Guy now. What time is it in Kansas?"

"Don't be smart. Let me know how it goes. Okay? I'll talk to you later."

"Goodbye, Bobbi."

He was glad that conversation was over.

He dialed Guy's office. He had left for the day, but would call-in for messages. Michael asked that he call back tomorrow. He settled in at his desk, and reviewed his new associates' contracts, marking them where he wanted Hector to make changes. He worked over the *scope of work* that he and Henri would use as criteria for the design. He was so involved that he worked into the morning hours. Exhausted, he went to sleep.

* * * * * *

Pernicious Nugari took the toll road through Laguna and Newport Beach, and finally turned onto the freeway that would eventually lead him to his rendezvous with Jami Wu in Marina del Rey. He selected the Marriot for its central location between himself and Wu. Additionally, he scheduled to meet later with deVillefrance who had other meetings in the area. He waited in a nook of the main lobby.

Wu was late. He rushed around looking, and looked right past where Nugari sat. Nugari saw his dilemma but relished in his inability to focus on specific people or groups as he scanned the room. Desperate, Jami asked a waiter who pointed to Nugari.

"Sorry I'm Late. I've looking all over for you."

"Yes, I know," he said, with a self-satisfied expression.

Jami peered down at him. A muscle twitched in his gaunt face. "You were watching me, and let me . . . I.. I don't understand your ways. You are very arrogant. If I weren't already involved, I wouldn't do business with you."

Nugari sat with a banal, almost expressionless face, starring right through Jami. In his mind was the remembrance of a Viet Nam officer during his last military encounter. He too, was admonishing him for his arrogance, telling him it didn't serve a purpose in the arena of military negotiations. This meeting was not unlike a diplomatic military confrontation. The rules of order were not as precise, but the outcome depended on strategy and flexibility. Oh, how he hated to give in.

"Nugari," came an anxious voice.

"Please excuse me. My mind was somewhere else." He adjusted his position, and motioned for Jami to sit across the coffee table from him. He called to the waiter. "Could we get some coffee?" Turning to Jami, "Would you like anything?"

Jami predictably ordered hot tea with lemon.

Nugari indulged in a Danish with his coffee.

"Let's get down to business," Nugari said as he drew some papers and a small calculator from his briefcase. "Orcini is hesitant about our group, and we must gain his confidence. I have outlined some possibilities." He handed an agenda to Jami. "Those Italians make me very nervous. Especially Contedetto. I think he'd cut his own mother's throat without any compunction. Is there any way we can do this deal without them?"

Jami Wu stated his concern and suggested that he could bring in the *Chinese Camorra*. He said that they could bring a balance to Ceres and her group. "Our family has been associated with the Camorra since World War II. We will regain control of the situation when they get here. I have talked to my father about this, and he is willing to talk to the family on our behalf."

"That could start a small war, and I don't want to be caught in the middle. Can't we just tell them that your people changed their mind, and don't want to invest in this project at this time?"

"But we do. We haven't changed our minds."

"You and I know that, but Ceres doesn't have to know."

"How do you intend to pull this off? You know that we don't understand anything about casinos or the gaming laws here."

"We set the theme for the proposal to Orcini in such a way that he won't accept it. We tell Ceres that we're out, and he has other people interested. Then, we bring your people in through another contact that I have." Jami frowned. "It's not totally untrue. I know that he is talking to some Germans."

They went on to discuss alternative proposals that would garner a larger profit for each of them without jeopardizing the deal. Nugari had ulterior motives. He wanted control, the same kind of dominion he enjoyed, for a short time over his former wives, except this time he would succeed. Everything in the setup must change, except for the appearance. The configuration must appear to be the same. No one must suspect his maneuver.

Jami's only interest was that of showing face with his family. To *show face* was the single most important part of his involvement. Failure to complete his assignment would mean disgrace in the eyes of his traditional Chinese family. They placed the responsibility of this investment squarely on his shoulders. He was destined to be true to the culture in which he was reared. The devious proposals Nugari was setting out had to be restructured to give an appearance of honest intentions. To continue in the historic family way, and with this unorthodox approach would be difficult. Jami felt a new definition creeping into his id. 'Oxymoron'

They finished their meeting, agreeing to explore the alternatives. Jami Wu left Nugari exactly where he was two hours before.

Satisfied with the outcome, Nugari gathered his things and went to the dining room for lunch. He set aside his work in favor of the Wall Street Journal. His next meeting was with deVillefrance at two o'clock.

Claude deVillefrance arrived early, wearing the same pseudo Sea Captain's outfit, complete with a repulsive smelling stogie. He saw Nugari in the lobby with Wu. He positioned himself in an obscure place across the massive lobby, while he carefully observed the exchange of emotions between them, and decided to keep his surveillance of their covert meeting a secret. He had just come from a meeting with Michael, and was remiss to share the outcome with Nugari until he found out what transpired with Wu.

Nugari eeked out a phony, "Good to see you Claude," as the unkempt figure prepared to join him in the restaurant. "How are you today?"

"Perni." He pulled a chair from the table. "I'm very tired," he said drawing a laborious breath while slamming his large frame down to sit. "Got to lose some weight."

The waitress came over. "I'm very sorry sir, but you must get rid of the cigar. It's not allowed in here."

He handed it to her. She took it with two fingers, deliberately holding it out and away with a disgusting grimace. "I'll be right back for your order."

"I know what I want."

"I'll be right back." She turned and left.

The waitress returned with a menu and her order pad. She gave Claude the menu, and looked disapprovingly at his hat.

He removed the hat, brushed his yellow-gray hair back, and said. "I know what I want." He handed the menu back noticing her nametag, "Kathy. I'll have your largest cheeseburger," he deliberately eyed her breasts. "With everything on it, and a large order of . . ." he intentionally looked at her hips, then back to her breasts, "some of your, umm . . . wonderful fries." He paused briefly. "And a diet coke."

"Rare?" she assumed.

"Yes, of course," he snickered, still eyeing her bounty.

"How do you want your meat cooked?" She motioned for the bus boy the refill Nugari's cup.

"Rare."

"I thought you wanted to lose some weight." Nugari chided him like a boy.

Claude ignored the comment, and began the order of business. "I am not happy with the agreement between Wu's people and the Donna. You've got to know him. You must tell Wu, without any reservation, that without an experienced group here in Nevada they won't get to first base with the Gaming Commission." A bus boy brought his diet drink. "You must let them know that they must be flexible. This is America, not China. Remember, my friend, without me you have nothing."

Nugari did not like deVillefrance's authoritarian attitude, but was willing to let it appear appropriate. "Of course," he responded.

They discussed the Orcini and Ceres proposals, while they both pretended that everything between them was the same as previously discussed, and without a hint of their individual agendas. They carefully maneuvered each other while drafting their proposal. Nugari wanted more than the money, he wanted power. deVillefrance was greedy, and prepared to play on the side that gave him a larger piece of the pie. They settled on their approach, and agreed that Nugari would draft the proposal for presentation to Michael on Monday. A double cross on each side was in the making. Time would tell if either would come out on top.

* * * * * * *

Michael sat on his deck, overlooking the Pacific Ocean, for what seemed an eternity, mesmerized, calmed by the ocean waves. God knows, he needed to be calm. It wasn't more than a half-hour ago that he stifled the impulse to tell Claude deVillefrance to *shove it*, even while his reasoning mind told him not to cancel the negotiations. Claude proposed that Ceres should get a much larger share of the project than originally suggested, because her group was more essential to the deal than the Chinese. The fact that her group was politically connected became the driving force in the new proposal. Michael still hadn't a clue that she would put up half the money, but want total control.

His mind was whirling. Guy Nestor's early morning call stuck in his memory. He had five hundred million to invest. They discussed the total budget, and Guy felt that his bank would cooperate. Michael wasn't quite sure exactly what that meant, but he was open to meet in a week, or so, to discuss the opportunities.

He wondered what J.T. thought about the aspect of these proposals. He would call him in a few moments, but right now he must collect his thoughts. This project was becoming more complicated every day. Michael was accustomed to dealing on a hand shake. All his previous associates knew that his word was as good as gold, and they could *take it to the bank.*

The sun warmed him as he dozed off.

The evening breeze was cool, and the sun had completely gone into the sea as Michael returned from his nap. Instead of calling J.T., as he planned, he called Keleigh.

"Hello."

"Hi, sweet cheeks."

"Michael!" she shouted, "What's up?"

"I just want to run some things by you, and get your opinion."

"Sure. Do I need to write it down?"

"No. I just want to talk to you about some things."

"Should I get a glass of wine and a box of tissues?"

"That won't be necessary, this is business."

"Okay, fire away."

Michael explained, point by point, the latest proposals from both Guy Nestor and deVillefrance, and that he wanted her opinion before he talked to J.T. or anyone else.

"I appreciate your confidence, Michael, but tell me something."
'What?"

"Who is Guy Nestor? You never mentioned him before."

"Oh, sorry. I thought I told you about him." Michael explained the connection with Bobbi, and how Guy became interested.

"Tell me that you're not interested in his proposal just because of Bobbi? That it's really a business judgment." She added a personal note, "You know that she's just interested in you for what she can get. She's probable sleeping with this guy too."

"Keleigh, Keleigh."

"Well, it's true, Michael. She's just using you, and the sooner you realize that the better it will . . ." she didn't finish.

"Suppose she is? What if he turned out to be a good deal?"

"Just as long as Ian isn't a part of the deal."

"His son? That's right. You and Ian had a thing a while ago. Didn't you?"

"That's history, besides it was all wrong from the start."

"Would it bother you if we made a deal with Nestor?"

"Like I said, as long as Ian's not involved."

"What do you think about the two proposals?"

Keleigh liked the simplicity of Guy Nestor's proposal, but was concerned about getting the balance of the funds. She was afraid of the people in deVillefrance's group, even though she never met any of them. "Do these people always keep changing their minds, or are they trying to leverage their position?"

"I think that leverage is a good word."

"I think that you should keep the door open for all opportunities, Michael. Besides, aren't you still talking with that German fellow from the Cayman Islands?"

"Hans Gruber. Yes, as a matter of fact, I'm going to call him in a little while."

"Then all the more reason to extend your options."

"I'm sure glad you're part of my life, Keleigh."

"Me too," she said, wishing for more.

"Okay, I going to call J.T., and discuss this with him. I'll talk to you later."

"Okay, bye," the familiar intonement came.

"Bye, Keleigh." He spoke once more to the dial tone, and smiled.

* * * * * *

It was a particularly cold September morning on the beach at
Malibu. The normal assortment of joggers was unmistakably ab-
sent as the threat of another storm hovered in a forbidding darkness over the coastline. Michael donned a heavy sweat suit with a
hood over his head, and set out to run off the stress that dwelt
within him. About a half-mile down the beach he hesitated by an
out-cropping of rocks, then climbed to the highest point and sat
for a long time, allowing the sounds of the ocean to replace the
thoughts of his hurried mind. Suddenly, he felt her presence, just
like their first date when they were sitting on the rocks near the
restaurant. He symbolically put his arm around the image of her
and sighed, "What am I going to do about you?" The waves crashed
a metaphorical answer, "Just let it flow, don't fight it. Easy, easy."
He knew this was the right way to handle her, to handle this new
relationship, but the timing, the timing isn't right. He sat for a
few minutes longer, then descended the rocks, and continued his
jog to the farthest point on the beach, turned and headed back.

He reached his beach house and ran up the lengthy stairs
continuing his cadence until he reached the top. Michael moved
to the exercise room where he spent the next half-hour with his
equipment. Exhausted, he looked at the clock on the wall. It
was nine o'clock, almost two hours since he started. He continued his normal agenda by grinding the coffee beans and prepared his favorite brew. After showering he poured a cup,
popped some whole grain bread into the toaster, went over to
his desk in the study bower and checked his computer for any
email. "Nothing that can't wait," he told the computer, and
went to the kitchen, grabbed the toast, went out on the deck
and ate. He was hoping for an answer to the email he sent
Darci a couple days ago but, knew in his heart that she was a
snail mail person not an email person.

He called Henri, and confirmed their appointment. Everything was in order. If Michael was late, the cottage at the rear of

their estate would be left open, and the dogs would be in their run. Satisfied, he showered, prepared his luggage for the weekend, and set out for his day with Darci.

Following her instructions, he turned his every day car, a Ford Explorer, down a middle class neighborhood near the Santa Monica Municipal Airport, referred to by many old-timers as Cloverfield, and alongside a neatly kempt golf course. He spotted her Mustang convertible in a cul-de-sac at the end of the street. He parked in the drive right under the basketball hoop. He had stopped at the florist. This time he bought a dozen roses, eleven pinks and one red one right in the center surrounded by baby's breath, and tied with a lavender ribbon.

A totally different image appeared at the door. She was wearing a knit sweater, blue jeans, and tennis shoes. Her hair was tied in two braids with rust colored ribbons at the ends. One braid lay over her shoulder and down between her large breasts, the other fell naturally down her back. Even with this unexpected transformation, her delicious smile and twinkling eyes were the same.

"I thought that you didn't own any blue jeans."

"I bought them especially for you. What do you have behind your back, Michael Orcini?" she teased him.

He presented the flowers with a bold, "For you, my Indian Princess."

"For me?" she sang. "Whatever shall I do?" she broke into a playful laughter, grabbed the hand holding the roses, and pulled him to her. She teased, pretending to kiss him, but kissing the roses instead. "One of them is different."

"So are you. One in a million."

"You're so sweet. Come in, I'm almost ready." She still had hold of his hand, and lead him into the living room. She finally released his hand, and took the flowers.

He immediately grasped the hand holding the roses, and turned it behind her pulling her to him, and kissed her. Long, soft and meaningful.

"Good morning, sweet prince," she said, and looked away.

He released her. "Let's get going. I'm excited about going to the fair."

"I'll only be a few moments." She laid the flowers on a marble top table, turned and went into another room. "We can take my car if you like," she hollered.

"It's okay, I'm driving my Explorer."

She came out with a little dance step and a twirl. "I'm ready. Lets go." She went over and picked up the flowers. "Can I take these with me?"

"They might wither."

"I want to enjoy them while I'm with you."

"You're a romantic."

"Absolutely"

It took more than an hour to drive through Los Angeles, and out to the fairgrounds. "Look Michael, we're just about there." She pointed to the freeway sign. "This is going to be fun."

They spent the entire day like a couple of teenagers on their first date. It seemed to Michael that every childlike action she possessed came out of Darci that day. She danced and skipped and tugged on him with a; "Can we go here, can we do this?" Then out of nowhere she would throw her arms around him and kiss him, and just as quickly she would grab his hand and pull him after her.

They ate at what seemed to be every concession stand in the park. The fresh, hot cinnamon rolls were their favorite. "I'm going to be on a sugar high for a week," Michael exclaimed," as she prodded him to have another.

When they reached the very top of the Ferris wheel ride, the rotation stopped. The chair swayed a little, and she tightened her hold on his arm. "Wow. I can see forever."

The animals were an absolute must before the day was over. "We should have seen the animals in the morning. They smell a lot at the end of the day."

He was certain that her comment didn't make any sense. They surely must smell in the morning, but it did not matter.

Not an inch of the fairgrounds was left undiscovered. Or so it seemed.

They walked towards the exit knowing it was time to go. The ride home consisted of a complete recap of their adventure at the County Fair.

"Let's stop and have some Mexican food." She pointed, "There's one at the next turn-off."

"You're going to burst.," he said.

"Don't know when we're going to go to the fair again. Gotta have Mexican food to finish the day."

He wasn't going to question her logic. "Ole," he laughed.

When they got inside her brother's house, he questioned. "Did you turn off the alarm?"

She puckered her lower lip, and lowered her head in a shy gesture.

Michael hugged this child masquerading as a beautiful woman, and whispered, "I have to go to San Diego now."

"I know." She snuggled tight against him, caressing every part of him. "Good night my sweet prince."

"Good night."

* * * * * * *

Michael's friend, Richard, left his Cessna 182 fueled and ready to use next to Garrett Aviation, at the southeast end of the Los Angeles International Airport. He went in and checked the computerized weather service. It was perfect flying weather. Next, he performed a *walk-around*, where he checked everything necessary for a safe flight. Satisfied, he checked ATIS, and contacted Control. He had to wait for a break in traffic. Finally he was cleared for immediate departure.

He was gratified that the flight was smooth and predictable. Earlier, while sitting under a tree at the Fair, Darci shared the loss of her nephew in a small plane crash out of the mountain airport at Big Bear. It happened the same day they first met along the highway to Las Vegas. She told him how she hated small planes. Michael elected not to tell her he was a pilot, and that he was flying to San Diego. He especially was not ready to tell her that he just bought a plane. He would tell her another time.

He wanted to fly into Montgomery Field, but they had restricted hours. The only alternative was Lindbergh Field. He touched down a little after two in the morning, picked-up his rental car, and drove to Henri Piaget's estate. The driveway sensors activated lights, and he entered the code for the security gate.

The guest cottage was at the end of the extended brick driveway, a contemporary structure with each room an extension of another. The influence of Corbusier, his mentor, was evident. An oval coppice, adjacent to the main room, had a portable drafting table set under a large skylight. The sleeping area was sheltered from the other areas by a massive, freestanding closet. The entire interior was completely white with a gray slate floor. Simple pieces of Berber rugs were placed strategically. The small kitchen was completed with glass cupboards, and a bright royal blue synthetic counter top. The steaming spa outside the French style bedroom doors was tempting, but Michael just wanted to sleep.

A little dog, no bigger than his foot, was yapping outside the French doors. The Dali clock on the wall indicated ten-fifteen while the morning sunlight filled the entire space as it filtered through the skylights and generous fenestration. He rubbed his eyes with one hand, and slid out of bed scratching his butt with the other.

The exterior wall of the bathroom was solid with immense hand made glass blocks with a slight blue-green hue. Directly in front, a white marble shower-tub combination sat unprotected, topped with a frosted glass skylight. A black toilet and bidet shared a marbled nook, and a pedestal sink stood guard in front of the full-mirrored wall opposite the shower.

The pulsating shower brought an immediate satisfaction. He breathed the steam clearing his lungs, and energized his muscles by stretching and flexing. A super large black towel, with a coat of arms embroidered at one end, hung on a chrome rack nearby. As he looked in the mirror he realized it wasn't steamed from the shower. He had to ask Henri about this phenomenon.

Camuela's voice came over the intercom by the drafting table. "Are you ready for some breakfast, Michael?"

"You bet I am. Give me ten minutes?"

"Come on in when you're ready."

Michael walked along the brick pathway to the main house. It was covered by a cantilevered arbor thick with wisteria, which allowed full view of the distant ocean along its open side. He thought of the lattice lined walkway at his parent's home in Cape Cod. The colors would start to turn soon. Indian Summer, his favorite time on the Cape was just around the corner. "I'll have to take Darci there, and have her meet. . . ." He said out loud, catching himself in mid-sentence.

As he reached the ostentatious pool arrangement, he heard Henri call out. "How do you like my pools?"

He stopped and surveyed the orchestration of three pools set within a polished slate decking, and guarded by granite fountains replete with Picasso style statues and a myriad of brass intaglio set in granite frames. By this time Henri was at his side.

"Why three pools?"

"It's my lucky number. Do you like the statues? They were done by a fellow up in Laguna Beach."

"I love the sculptures. We have to use him on my project. You'll explain all this other stuff for me. Won't you?"

"The first thing I have to explain to you, my architecturally ignorant friend, is that they're not *stuff*. Come along, Cam has prepared something special for you."

Camuela Piaget stood in her massive contemporary styled country kitchen, holding her arms out to greet him, like Moses before he parted the red sea. "Mon ami," she sang out in her exquisite French accent. "Come and give your favorite princess a hug." Camuela claimed to be born a princess in the Marquesas Islands of French Polynesia.

They exchanged the traditional kiss on each cheek followed by a sincere hug. "You're not my favorite princess anymore," he whispered in her ear.

"What?" she whispered back. "Just because I didn't have Snicker Bars waiting for you in the cottage?" She referred to the miniature candy bars that he had come to expect each time they met. She pulled back slightly, scrutinizing his face. "This sounds serious. Come sit down, and tell me all about her."

"You've got it all wrong. What's this?" He drank from a large earthen cup.

"You like? It's a special blend, all the way from my island. Just for you."

"You never buy me coffee like that. How come he is so special?" Henri kidded.

"Because he is, and besides, you're not a connoisseur like him. Now," she looked back to Michael, "I have made a special Belgian Waffle for you with real New England maple syrup, and powdered sugar. Some scrambled eggs and authentic Italian sausage." She sat down, put her elbows on the table, and rested her chin in her hands while she stared at him. "Good, no?"

"Good, yes." He looked up at Henri. "What about you? Aren't you going to eat?"

"We ate hours ago. I'll have a cup of *your* coffee, though." He winked at Cam.

"How was your flight?"

"It was smooth."

"Really? No thermals over the desert?"

"I flew in from LAX."

"LAX? I thought you were coming from Vegas." Henri questioned.

"No. I've been in Malibu since Wednesday."

"Wouldn't it have been easier to fly out of Santa Monica or Oxnard?"

"He's got a new girl that he's going to tell us about. Somebody special, not like the others. Right Michael?"

"What do you mean?" He looked quizzically at Michael. "You

don't have time for a new girl, especially if it's serious," he cautioned him.

"I just met her, it's too soon to tell," he lied, and winked at Cam. "Did you get my email with the sketches?"

"Yes. I downloaded them yesterday. Truthfully, Michael, you *should not* draw."

"I was just trying to illustrate an idea."

"How are the negotiations going with your investors?"

"I think that Nugari and the Chinese are having problems, and Ceres wants too much control for what she is putting into the project."

"What about Geller?"

"I talked to him the other day. He says that they're interested, but it won't happen overnight. I'm keeping him as a back-up. There is another player. An old friend of Bobbi's who says he has the money. We're going to get together next week."

"How is Bobbi?" Camuela chimed in. "You still seeing her?"

"I talked to her just a few days ago. She's fine."

"Henri, I want your opinion on this Chinese-Italian set-up."

"What do you want to know? I don't know much more than what I see on the surface, but I got a bad feeling about this guy Nugari. I think you should be careful with him. Make sure that your lawyer checks him out real good. What does Charlie think?"

"Charlie hasn't met him yet. Do you think I should have Charlie meet him?"

"Yeah. Charlie has a sixth-sense about people and that sort of stuff. Must be his Indian blood or something."

"Cam, this was an absolutely wonderful meal." He got up, went around behind her chair, and kissed her on top of her head.

The men went up to Henri's office on a loft overlooking the two story Grand Room. There they spent the next two days, planning the basic layouts for the resort, stopping only to eat and sleep. Michael established the criteria and nature of the operation, and Henri sketched. He always sketched with a charcoal pencil, using overlays upon overlays, adjusting, changing, and reworking the layouts before he would have a technician put his planning and design concepts into the computer. Henri was very old fashioned that way. He knew the computer was essential to his work, but still liked to *get his hands dirty*. Something about the artist in him, he would say to excuse his old methods.

Exhausted, they finished late Sunday night.

"When can you get some plans to me?" he asked.

"I'll put a couple people on this first thing in the morning. Should have these layouts in the computer in a few days. Just conceptual layouts, you understand?"

"Good. Can you whip-up some sketches of what this baby is going to look like for my meeting with Hans?"

"We already gave you some delineations."

"Yes, but this is quite a change from our original concept. What do you think about my new ideas. You haven't commented on the quelle and the gardens."

"My mind is still trying to assimilate everything. The basic idea is great, but we have a lot of work to do. When are you going to see Hans?"

"Don't know yet. A week maybe."

Henri looked over the top of his granny glasses. "A week? You think I'm some kind of a magician?"

"That's why I came to you. You're the best." He flattered him.

Michael retired early. He had to fly out first thing in the morning.

* * * * * *

A cold wind was blowing from the ocean and the cumulonimbus clouds were black with the threat of another El Nino onslaught when he headed the Cessna out on runway 28 right. It would be a short flight, but he didn't want to be diverted to another airport. He set the throttle at eighty percent, and kept his altitude as low as possible skirting the coast until he was thirty miles from LAX. He took her up to altitude, and was ushered in between a couple of commercial jets. He returned the Cessna back to Garrett, and drove to Malibu.

The rain had begun just as he passed through Marina del Rey. He looked towards the northwest, and hoped that the coast highway through the Palisades would remain open until he got home. "Just a little while longer," he pleaded with the weather Gods.

The sky burst just as he came to the outskirts of Malibu. The rain pounded the Explorer, and he was grateful he had his *minitank* instead of the SL.

He looked about the house checking the doors and windows as the waves began their crusade against the rocks below. He had razed an old weathered shack three years ago, and built his home on the highest grouping of rocks in the area. He remembered how the storms were on Cape Cod, and sank concrete pilings deep into the rock formations with reinforced concrete beams and floor slab. Henri assured him, "It will be standing long after you are gone."

"I hope you're right, Henri. I hope you're right," he exclaimed in retrospect.

His message service was full. He turned the volume up, and went to the kitchen where he ground the special beans Camuela gave him. Darci just wanted to say Hi, Keleigh had to go over *mounds of stuff*, and needed to see him ASAP. Charlie's call was a surprise. He met with his friend the police commissioner, and had some important information about Ceres and Nugari. Nugari, Wu and deVillefrance had to see him. Hans was ready to start negotiations, could he come to the islands. Bobbi *had* to see him, and *now* was her final word. Guy Nestor wanted to talk.

Rain was beating furiously against the windows facing the ocean, and the wind began to howl a mysterious song. He donned some sweats, put a few small logs in the fireplace, and lit the gas starter. The pot of coffee, a cup and his briefcase completed his toolbox for today's work.

He sank into the soft deerskin couch facing the beach, filled his cup, and placed the first call to Keleigh at the agency.

"Hi, Michael. Are you back?"

"Yes, just got in a few moments ago. But, I'm here in Malibu, not Las Vegas. How are you doing? Sounds like you've been busy."

"I've been a busy little beaver."

"Really, all moist and.. ?"

"Michael!" she shouted as she censured him, "can't you ever be serious? Why do you tease me all of the time?"

"What have you accomplished?" He transgressed.

She told him that all the key people she wanted for the casino had faxed her a commitment, and that she needed to have him approve her selections. She wanted to get together as soon as possible so she could respond to her staff. Her voice was soft and purposeful, but the excitement was evident. Keleigh had accomplished more in a few days than most experienced executives would do in months. She had acquired an up-to-date list of high rollers, including all of their recent gambling activities. Computer read-outs for this and that, charts and graphs, forms she created, and even a mission statement. Michael wormed himself deeper into the couch as he enjoyed her dissertation.

"So, boss, when can we get together?"

"Boss? Keleigh, Keleigh," Almost like a 'Tsk, tsk'.

"So, when?"

"I'll be in Las Vegas on Thursday, remember?"

"But, I need you to approve the candidate selections."

"You don't need my approval to run your casino, Keleigh."

"My casino?"

"Sure. Your casino." He paused a little to let it sink in. "But, you *will* share some of the profits with me, won't you?"

"You can have anything I've got." Her tone was intentional, but somewhat demure. "Anything."

"Then it's settled. Give them your approval, and I'll see you Thursday."

Her voice changed, "This is so exciting."

"I know, and I'd love to talk to you all day, but I've got a million calls to make."

The expected. "Okay, bye," echoed from the phone ending in a dial tone.

Charlie wasn't in, but expected in an hour or so. Michael asked for him to call.

He 'dialed' the next name on his list. The phone rang only once. "I want to cook dinner for you. When will you be back in town?" It was Darci's voice talking to an unknown caller.

He kept silent.

"Michael Orcini!" she scolded.

"What made you think it was me?"

"I just knew."

"What do you want to cook for me?"

"Never mind. When will you be back in Las Vegas? I want to see you."

"You're a pushy broad."

"When?"

"Thursday, but.. "

"I can't Thursday. Friday?"

"It'll have to be late."

"How late?"

"Nine."

"Nine will be perfect."

"Can I bring something?"

"A white wine, and that C.D. you were playing on our first date. Do you remember the one I mean?"

"Sure. It's still in the SL. How do you know what kind of food I like?"

"You're going to love it. Trust me."

"I had a great time with you at the fair."

"Me too. Are you rushed today?"

"Yes. Why?"

"Oh, nothing. I can sense it in your voice."

"I'm sorry. I didn't mean to.. "

"Don't apologize, it's okay. I know you're busy. I'm going back to Las Vegas tomorrow. So, I'll see you on Friday."

"Yes, Friday. It's a date."

"Au revoir, sweet prince."

"So long, darling. See you Friday." He was amazed with himself, he really meant it when he called her darling. It frightened and excited him at the same time.

He barely set the phone down, and it was ringing. "M--Mikey, I h--have s--some interes--t--ting news f--for you. Some of it you may n--not like.

"What's up Charlie?"

Charlie told him of his meeting with Dominic Poncerelli, the police commissioner, whom he referred to as *Ponci*. The Information they had on Nugari was mostly with regard to his military records, marriages, and children. He had a daughter from his first marriage that is in a shelter for battered children. Ponci was not able to find out if it was due to him or his former wife, since the court records were sealed. He had a number of failed businesses. He married twice for money, but hadn't been able to hold on to the wife or her money. Except for Jana's condo and boat he had little to show.

Ceres was another story. She was married to a Sicilian who was proscribed by his own people, and disappeared shortly after they came to the United States. It had been rumored that she was responsible for expunging him and his black mark against the family name, ironically, the exact reason that he was banished. She had numerous legitimate business enterprises with no corroborated ties to organized crime. Contedetto, on the other hand, had been arrested many times, but no convictions. They're still checking on the rest of her group. They have a long rap sheet on deVillefrance, all petty stuff, but Ponci thought there was more to him, and would keep checking.

Michael was concerned with the Chinese and Ceres, but thanked Charlie for checking on the others. Pressured by his friend, he agreed to meet with Ponci.

Both Nugari and Wu called back, insisting that it was important that they move ahead with the agreements with the Chinese before they change their minds and find another project. They all agree to meet in Las Vegas on Friday.

Hans was not in when he called back. Michael left word with his service.

There was a rap, rap at the front door followed immediately by a desperate pounding simultaneous with the ringing of the door chime.

Standing there drenched and crying was Bobbi.

"Bobbi? What are? Come in here." He grabbed her arm, and pulled her inside. "You're drenched. What are you doing here? I was getting ready to call you." He led her to the bath. "Get out of those wet things. There's a robe behind the door. I'll get you some brandy."

She called out from behind the half-open door. "They wouldn't let me drive any further. I left my car up the road."

"Who wouldn't? What are you doing here anyway?"

"Cal-Trans. There's a rock slide. I could have gotten past if the Highway Patrol wasn't right there."

"You didn't answer me. What are you doing here?"

"Don't be mad at me, Michael, but I had to see you."

"And, just what couldn't wait 'til tomorrow?"

She came out wearing a terry cloth robe, and a large towel wrapped around her head. She was ravishing, even in the worst of conditions.

"I swear, Bobbi, I don't know how you do it."

"Do what?"

"Look so gorgeous."

She sauntered over towards him stopping short, dropping the hand that held the robe closed. "Thank you sir."

He allowed himself a momentary view of her, handed her the brandy, and closed the robe tying the sash. "Here. This will warm you."

"*You* could warm me."

"You still haven't told me why you're here." He spun and went to the kitchen.

Bobbi knew he was upset, and remained silent. Sipping the

brandy she watched him over the top of the snifter. She knew that he would not speak first. She also knew that she must sound convincing. He rattled some dishes, and then dropped a large pan onto the slate floor. He picked up the pan, and slammed it down on the counter. Bobbi jumped. Her instincts told her that no matter how sexy, how much of her body she revealed, he wanted to know why.

He filled his cup from the coffee thermos, and sat on the couch. Shuffling the papers on the table, he waited for her answer. The phone rang several times.

"Aren't you going to see who it is?" She said demurely.

"Hello." He listened. "Of course." He waited. "Hans, it's good to hear from you." He waved his hand and motioned for her to leave the room. "Would you excuse me for just a moment, Hans?" he paused. "No, it's okay, I'll be right with you." He looked at Bobbi with authority. "Go dry your hair or something. This is private, it's business."

Bobbi left, but not without her famous coup d'oeil. She quietly closed the bedroom door behind her, and sat down on the bed. Cautiously she lifted the receiver of the bedside phone. Hans was telling Michael that his associates from Germany wanted to begin negotiations with him as soon as possible, but needed more information. Michael told him that the financial projections and up to date architectural plans would be ready in another week. Hans would try to set a meeting for the following week in the Caymans. As the conversation became less business and directed to his family and the weather in the islands, Bobbi carefully replaced the receiver. She left her hair slightly wet, teasing it to form ringlets. When she was satisfied, she went to the closet and retrieved a long sleeve silk shirt and put it on, leaving just enough buttons undone. Pleased with herself, she opened the door. "Is it okay for me to come out yet?" striking a coquettish pose with her finger to her cheek.

Michael knew that she had been listening, but decided not to comment. "There are a lot warmer things for you to wear in the closet."

"I like this. Don't you like how it suits my," she paused bringing her hand down from her cheek slowly across her breast continuing to her thigh, "personality."

"You have a great . . . personality, but," he tried to ignore her obvious intent to seduce him, "I've got a lot of work to do."

She moved slowly from the bedroom stopping a few feet from him. "I have a lot of interesting things to tell you, but can't we play first?" She moved to him, putting her hands under his sweatshirt. She knew he never wore anything under the sweat pants, and slowly, slowly, her hands found his tight buns.

He never could resist her, but it was different now. "You mustn't do this." He pulled away. "I don't have time to be distracted."

It was obvious that she had excited him. "What's this?" Her hand moved to his obvious excitement. "You are more than just distracted. Come on, let's play."

"Later. Maybe later." he said. "Now, please, go put some clothes on."

Angry, she pounded his back as he turned away. "You're incorrigible, damn it."

After a few minutes she came out wearing a sweater and beach pants with a cord tied around her waist. "Is this better, master?"

"It doesn't matter," he said as a quibble.

"What doesn't matter?" She knew what he meant.

"Never mind. You came here for more than just sex. Tell me what it is, or I swear, I'll put you back out in the storm." He looked at her sad expression. "Don't give me any of your tortured looks. Come over here and tell me what's going on in that pretty head." He pulled the screen back, and put another log on the diminishing fire, stoking until the flames took hold of their new fuel.

"Well, since you don't care about me," she continued to play her game, "I guess I'll just have to tell you the wonderful news first. Guy Nestor called me yesterday. He said that you talked to him."

"We had a brief conversation," not wanting to tell her too much.

"He knows *all* about that project of yours, the one that you won't talk about. Anyway, it seems that he was talking to people in the business, and they think that you're dealing with the wrong people."

"Really?"

"Don't interrupt! I'm getting to the good part. He wants to put up the money, and you can develop the project *your* way," she emphasized.

"What does he want in return?" He didn't let on about his talk with Guy.

"Sixty percent."

"What do you get?"

"Just your everlasting appreciation, *dahling*." She toyed with her words.

"It can't be that simple. He's not going to put up eight hundred million, and sit back while someone else.. Wait a minute. I seem to remember," he pondered for a while. "Doesn't he have a son, and didn't he and Keleigh have an affair?" It was his turn to play with her mind, knowing she knew more than she was letting on. "Is he trying to get Keleigh back with that worthless kid of his?"

"Michael, you're making too much of this whole thing. Besides, would it be so bad if Ian and Keleigh got together? You're not sleeping with her, are you?"

"Ian. That's that good-for-nothing human impostor's name."

"You didn't answer me."

"What?"

"Are you sleeping with her?"

"Keleigh? Heavens, no. She's just a pal."

"Then, can't you just let things happen?"

"You can be so callous at times, Bobbi. Keleigh is not a part of any negotiation."

"Anyway, I told him that I could set up a meeting with you and him. Will you see him? For me?"

"Sure."

"I'll call him now. Okay?"

"Use the phone in the bedroom. You know where it is." He watched for her reaction. She was nonchalant. "Do I need a quarter?" When Bobbi played a game she was in for the duration. She was there to win.

"He can meet you on Friday," she shouted from the bedroom.

"I'll be in Las Vegas. Make it in the afternoon."

"Perfect. Can you pick him up at the airport, at two?"

"Yeah."

It was another ten minutes before she came out. "See! What would you do without me?"

"The rain has subsided. I'm going to call the Sheriff, and get them to find your car. Where did you leave it?"

Sheepishly, "You're gonna kill me," she hesitated, "it's just outside."

Fire in his eyes, he got to his feet.

"I'm going. I'm going. She ran to the bedroom, gathered her clothes, and ran to the front door. "Ciao, Michael."

He stood for a moment after she was gone. The rain had started again, lightly, not like before. Michael wondered just how far Bobbi would take her venture. He was positive that he was in for a prolonged ride with her and Guy. Guy obviously didn't tell her about their conversations. He hoped she had set Guy up as her new quest, and was using the project as bait. Once Bobbi set her sights on something or someone she never let go until she got what she wanted. It certainly would ease telling her about his situation with Darci. But, why did she care if he might be sleeping with Keleigh? What prompted that question? She left him with a lot of questions that needed answers.

His next two phone calls resulted in what seemed like the same script, only with two different players. Both Nugari and Wu were worried about the other wanting more. Wu said that Nugari wanted to take control because the Chinese trusted his ability to organize and run complex projects. Nugari, on the other hand, said that Wu was getting tight with Ceres, and that they wanted more control.

Stressed and weary, he called Hector. "See what you can do to straighten out the agreements with these people," he implored. "Set a meeting with them for Friday morning if you can, and I'd like you and J.T. to be there."

Hector Ruby promised to make the necessary arrangements, and would call back to confirm the time. He felt that his office would be the most appropriate place. Michael agreed, but would meet at most any location, if it made things easier for everyone.

* * * * * *

Arrogantly in defiance of her visitor, Una Ceres shook her fist, letting him know that she would be in control of Orcini's resort. "We are *Family*," she commanded. "You and I are family." She set her chin while bringing her fist to her abdomen, "Just like you came from here. Family, Mr. Rubioso." She paused. "Your mother would turn in her grave," she proclaimed softly. "*Family*." She enunciated loudly and took a deep sigh causing her to waver a little. Immediately, one of the boys in black was at her side supporting her elbow. She shooed him away, brushing away imaginary wrinkles from her dress. Without looking up, she said, "Ermano will be at this meeting. He knows what must be done."

Hector Ruby whined. "He specifically asked for you, Donna Ceres, and he wants his CFO to be there"

"You will do as I say. Now go!" She glanced over her shoulder.

Mario appeared from the corner and escorted the mumbling lawyer out.

The Donna sat by the fire, as the other man in black brought her other visitors to the large room. Her cicerone led deVillefrance and Wu to her side, where they stood quietly until she gave them permission to sit. She waved her hand, with short papal like gestures, indicating that they should sit across from her. "Ermano, come sit by me," she pointed to the chair next to her.

"We are honored to be in the same room with you," deVillefrance spewed out like a babbling simpleton.

"Y--yes," chimed in a hesitant, Jami Wu, "very honored."

"You must wait until the Donna wishes for you to speak in her presence," Connie instructed the two men, while Mario appeared from nowhere to enforce the decree.

Una Ceres read from a portfolio on her lap, and spoke softly, "Tell the Chinese that they will get thirty five percent of the hotel and thirty two percent of the casino revenues for their participation. Mr. Orcini can have ten percent of the hotel and casino revenues, a ten percent developer's fee, and twenty five percent equity in the project. You can have an amount equal to five percent of the investment funding when the project is completed."

"But.. " Claude deVillefrance attempted to interject.

Mario edged closer as Connie Contedetto stood, and commanded. "You are not to speak to the Donna until such time as she is to give to you the permission to verbalize what it is that you might have to say in response to her wishes."

Ceres handed a paper to Connie, "Ermano, please give this to the gentlemen."

It was a detailed outline of her proposal set in a contractual form. The men looked at her, in disbelief, after they read the document.

"Do you wish to say something?" she asked.

They looked cautiously at Mario, and then to Connie who gave an approving nod.

Jami spoke first, "My people will never agree to your proposal. It gives you complete control of the entire project. They are investing a great deal of money, and want an equitable position. We are not even sure if you have your share of the money to invest." He paused when he saw Mario and Connie stiffen after his last remark. "I mean no disrespect, but you haven't shown any evidence of your share of the money." He sat back in his chair hoping that deVillefrance would come to his rescue.

The room remained quiet for what seemed like an eternity to Wu. He was not an accomplished negotiator, and broke the silence with a losing query, "Don't you suppose that you should rethink your proposal?"

His faux pas was instantaneously evident as the Donna executed her ultramontane signal once more, and Mario moved into his definitive escort position.

Claude spoke. "I believe that this proposal has considerable merit. I am confident that we can come to a reasonable and equitable agreement."

"Thank you, Mr. deVillefrance." The Donna accepted his plea.

"Mario will show you out," Connie said with the authority of second in command.

When they left, Una Ceres looked up at Connie, and said, "Ermano, they are puppets. I want you to contact the Chinese directly. Let them know what it will cost them to get the experience they desire, and the consequences of my wrath if they want to have more than I am willing to give."

Connie smiled, and said nothing.

"Ask our other guest to come in."

Connie bowed, and left, returning with yet another player who was instructed on their protocol.

Pernicious Nugari sat across from Una Ceres making only the slightest nod of acknowledgement to the Donna, and waited for her commentary, as he was advised.

She did not speak, but handed a paper from her portfolio to Connie. With her silent beckoning he gave it to Nugari.

This paper deliberately differed from the one previously given to the others. Here she offered the Chinese forty percent of the hotel, and thirty five percent of the casino revenues. The next offering was for Orcini, who was to get straight seventy percent equity position, and control of the design and management. Nugari was to receive a ten percent finders fee plus a five percent equity position. She recognized his greed, and knew how to dangle the preverbal carrot. She wanted him to sell her proposal to Michael, and cut out Wu and deVillefrance in the process. Her other motive was to eliminate competition from other potential investors.

Nugari took the bait. He nodded again, but this time with pleasure.

"You are pleased with my proposal?" she asked.

Nugari looked at Connie, who allowed him to speak by signaling with a slight motion of his head.

"Yes, I am pleased. May I ask the Donna a question?"

She nodded.

"Do you have any objections if I were to negotiate additional compensation, for myself, from Mr. Orcini?"

"I would be disappointed if you didn't," she said with a hint of ominous delight.

"I will get back to you very soon," Nugari said with the confidence of someone in charge of his own destiny.

Ceres signaled. "Mario will show you out Mr. Nugari, Goodbye."

"Goodbye, Donna Ceres." He stood with a proud posture and departed.

Connie sat with Donna Ceres by the fire and discussed the potential outcome of their different proposals, while Mario stood by. She told them that she knew these men would give their own interpretations to the other participants, and their individual agendas would create enough conflict among them to allow her to orchestrate the final agreements.

"You are being very generous with your proposal to Mr. Nugari, Donna Ceres. Is it your wish that he should succeed with Orcini and the Chinese?"

She explained, to her trusted associate, that she had no intention of giving away any of the equity percentages. These proposals were merely a tool to bring the players in line, an essential that would become nonessential once she had the project under way. She reasoned that they would fight among themselves, and ultimately look to her for a solution because of her experience in these matters.

"But, what if they do not fight?"

"You will see that they do."

Ermano Contedetto knew exactly what his employer meant. This was what he had been trained to do. To remove the opposition when they would not remove themselves.

* * * * * *

Yesterday's rain left a sweet smell in the cool Malibu afternoon. Michael needed to clear his mind, so he entered a code in his phone transferring calls to his cell phone, and walked along the coast highway to a small restaurant he favored.

"Hi, Michael," came an energetic voice from the approaching waitress. "Haven't seen you in a while. Where've you been?"

"Las Vegas and San Diego," he replied as if it was important for her to know.

She pointed to an empty booth. "I'll be right with you."

A squawking sound came from the next booth. "I hope my baby doesn't bother you. She's just a little tired."

He smiled at her, but didn't respond.

The waitress had a cup of coffee in her hand. "Fresh brewed, Michael. Anything else today?"

"Jose' bake any pies today?"

"Fresh blueberry, lemon, mmm.. "

"Stop! The blueberry with some ice cream, please."

"Comin' right up."

He felt like a nomad searching the desert for water, and stumbling into one mirage after another, each with sweet-smelling poisoned water. He had promised God that when he built this resort, he would set aside ten percent for the less fortunate people, the homeless and hungry, especially the children. Why was all this poison being placed in front of him? Maybe he should have his attorney and J.T handle the negotiations. This would allow him to work with Henri on the design. He was perplexed with this whole Bobbi situation. What was she up to?

The cell phone signaled a call. "Orcini." He listened. Hans asked him to come to the islands soon. "How about it if I come down on the weekend?" A pause. "No, Bobbi won't be coming with me. I'll be alone." A long silence as Hans briefed him on what will be expected for him to bring. "I'll have everything you need. See you then, Goodbye."

The ice cream had melted and was running off the plate onto the table. He reassured himself that it must be poisoned, and pushed the plate away.

During the remainder of the day, and into the next, he talked with his bankers and their associates in Nevada. Setting up accounts and transferring funds was burdensome, time consuming, but nonetheless necessary. Thank God he set up a corporation, at least that was behind him.

It was peaceful at the beach house. He wandered from the Grand room, with its eclectic furnishings and appointments, up the open staircase to the ultra-contemporary kitchen that overlooked the Grand room. He meandered around the curved cooking island stopping at the under-counter refrigerator drawer. A Haagen-Dazs vanilla ice cream bar with chocolate coating would satisfy his need for a snack. He went back down the staircase, stopping to survey the paintings and photographs, and wondering what Darci would do to his home. Would she want to redecorate? He went into the Master bedroom with the same thought. Suddenly he shouted out. "Redecorate?"

* * * * * * *

The contrast between the ocean serenity of Malibu Beach, and the opulence of this glittering city in the middle of a Nevada desert, was like a small sailboat surrounded by warships in the middle of a raging sea. Michael Orcini felt like Chinese and Italian warships had descended upon him, and he had to call for reinforcements.

Soon after he checked into his Las Vegas hotel, he placed a call to J.T. "I must see you before the others. Let's have lunch, and bring your cash flow projections."

"Sure, Michael. What's up?"

"I'll fill you in at lunch. Let's meet a little before noon at the New York Deli in the Flamingo. Do you know where it is?"

"Yes. See you then."

He grabbed his briefcase and left for a meeting at the bank. His banker from Los Angeles would be there to assist in the complicated paperwork. Nathan Gregory, his personal attorney, arrived last night, and would be there to protect his interest. He discovered that Nevada laws dealing with gambling revenues were complex, and he needed someone he could trust. Michael was exercising his option to purchase the land, and would transfer personal funds to the corporation. He had the bank's legal department prepare quitclaim deeds in his parent's names. A note of indebtedness was to be secured, along with the quitclaims, and placed in his safe deposit box in Los Angeles. The property owners were ready to close escrow at a moment's notice. "I want to close in a week," he instructed the bankers. It was imperative that he acquired title to the property before his final agreement with any financial partner. Michael gave further instructions to Nathan Gregory to prepare a duplicate quitclaim and forward it to his parents. His trusted attorney, Nate, assured him that it would be done.

"We're meeting J.T. for lunch at the Flamingo. Do you know where the Deli is?"

"Yes, I have a quick stop, but it'll only take about twenty minutes, See you there." Content with the preliminary arrangements, he left to meet with J.T. As he walked through the casino on his way to the deli, he heard, "Herrow, Mr. Feeber."

"Oshkosh. It's nice to see you," he lied politely, and continued on his way. Suddenly it hit him, as if someone had opened the book of eternal enlightenment. "That's it," he exclaimed to a couple passing by, who just shrugged and continued on. He realized what had been disturbing him since meeting Nugari and Wu, and all the rest. "They're planning to steal my Project" he said out loud. He knew the only people he could trust were Keleigh, Nate, and Charlie, and Charlie wasn't really involved.

It was a half-hour before he was to meet J.T. There was just enough time for a short detour to see about that dinner engagement with the hotel executive. Perhaps the old pro could help with some ideas on management. Administration wasn't the issue here. It was structure. Anyway, getting together for dinner was *his* idea.

His secretary said that he wouldn't be in today, but she knew about Michael.

"I can make an appointment for you. He's anxious to see you. I know he's free Monday night. Is that convenient for you?"

"Monday will be fine."

"He has a favorite restaurant. I'll write the directions."

She handed Michael a piece of paper with the address, phone number, and a little map with directions.

"Thanks."

"You're welcome, Mr. Orcini."

J.T. Popinski had taken over a corner booth with papers and charts spread from one end to the other. He slid across the seat and stood as Michael approached.

"Hello, Michael." He didn't add any superfluous greeting. His face told the story. He was happy and excited.

J.T. was born of Polish lineage on the north side of Chicago. His father was the chief comptroller for a major airline, and Jan followed in his father's footsteps. He earned his PhD. in mathematics, and his masters in business management at an Ivy League College. He married his high school sweetheart, Armella, and had two kids in college. Not an imposing man at five feet eight inches, but an absolute delight to be around. His eyes danced, and the dimples in both cheeks deepened when he smiled. His voice, deep like a Shakespearian actor, commanded attention when he spoke.

"Hello, J.T."

"You sounded very concerned on the phone. What's wrong?"

"This is extremely critical. What I'm going to share with you is confidential. You can only discuss it with Keleigh or me. Not Sumner or Rebecca. Not even Ruby. My personal attorney will be here in a few minutes. I'm going to bring Keleigh up to speed in a little while."

"You can count on me, Michael." He waited.

Across the table J.T. listened intently as Michael mapped out his options and alternative plans for financing the project. He told of his heightening concern with Nugari, Wu, and the Chinese and Italians. Popinski recognized the anxiety in Michael's voice, and posed all the same questions Michael had asked himself.

"Michael," a voice came from behind him.

"J.T., I want you to know Nathan Gregory. Nate is *my* attorney," he emphasized the exclusivity. "Nate, this is J.T. Popinski, my CFO."

They shook hands, and uttered the acceptable, 'nice to meet you' simultaneously.

They spent their entire lunchtime discussing a plan to secretly obtain alternative financing, and to work on options with Nugari and friends. Michael told them about Hans and Guy Nestor. They agreed on the sensitivity of the situation, and affirmed that Nate would review all proposals and contracts without anyone else's knowledge.

"It would be prudent not to share any of this with Armella." His suggestion came in the form of a subtle command.

The dimples shown deep, but his eyes were set and sincere. "Absolutely."

Finally. "Do your projections include input from Keleigh, Sumner, and Rebecca?"

"Yes, and I've adjusted them to work with the total picture.

"Let's go meet the others, J.T."

"Do you want me any more today, Michael?"

"No. Not today. Thanks, Nate."

They executed the conventional handshakes, and departed.

* * * * * * *

J.T. and Keleigh rented a small office off the 'Strip'. In a short time they completely furnished it, desks, chairs, computers, a secretary, and a few clerks.

Astounded, Michael did not hear the welcome from his new employees. He moved from office to office marveling at the arrangement of offices and equipment.

Keleigh came out and whispered, "Close your mouth, you'll catch flies. Come with me, and I'll introduce you to your employees."

"They're just temps, right?"

She introduced Candace, the receptionist, Maria, the staff secretary, and his personal secretary, Martha.

"She's very . . ."

"Matronly," Keleigh remarked with satisfaction. "She'll take *real* good care of you." She said with a slight snicker. "Keep you out of trouble."

J.T., Sumner, Rebecca, Keleigh, and his new secretary assembled in the conference room. Martha came with a fresh cup of coffee for her new employer. "Here you are boss," came a warm inflection.

"Thank you, Martha." Michael looked at Keleigh and mouthed without any sound, raising his eyebrows, "Boss?"

Keleigh smiled. She knew he was pleased.

"I was expecting," with a stern voice, then softly, "a double wide on a vacant lot. How did you do this?" They all looked at Keleigh.

"You did this?"

"Yeah," she said. Like it was nothing.

They spent the rest of the afternoon going over projections, wish lists, results of inquires for key personnel, and proposed budgets before opening day.

They completed everything on the agenda by five, except for the casino operations. "We'll finish this on another day. Thank you, ladies, and gentlemen." As they left, he looked up at Keleigh. "D'you have a moment?" scarcely ahead of her exact request.

"Yes." She moved to his side of the conference table.

"I, uhh, well I'd like to tell you what a great job you've done here, and.. "

"I listen to compliments much better over dinner," she nudged him with her hip. "And *I* get to pick the place this time." She prolonged the *I.*

"Eight?" he questioned.

"Seven-thirty."

"Shall I dress up?"

She scanned him from head to toe, and back up to his waiting eyes. "Seven-thirty. Coat and tie."

* * * * * *

He barely touched the button by the door when she appeared in an elegant two-piece business suit with no evidence of a blouse or bra. "I'm ready. Let's go."

"Which way?"

Confused at her abruptness, he drove silently, only responding to her directions.

"Turn left at the next light." She directed him out of town. "Let's wait to talk about business until after we have dinner. Okay?"

"Okay."

"You have to promise."

"Okay, I promise."

"Where's your other car?" She played with the radio, changing stations.

"It's at home. I had a lot of stuff to bring this time."

"There." She pointed. "Turn into that drive, and stop at the canopy on the right."

"Italian?"

The valet took the Explorer.

"You're gonna love it." She slipped her arm in his, and they went in.

"Reservation for Mr. Orcini," she evoked.

The host nodded without a word, and indicated that they should follow.

"He forgot the menus," Michael noted.

They followed him through the length of the dining room, and through large double stained glass doors where they were welcomed with a warm round of applause.

Keleigh stepped aside, and joined in the ovation. She returned to his side, squeezing his arm. "This is your new family." She ushered him around introducing the wives and husbands of his employees, and finally to his chair.

"Your idea?"

She smiled. "D'you like?"

"Yes, but what would you have done if I had other plans," he whispered.

She pushed herself against him, and whispered back. "I would have shamed myself, and seduced you into coming."

He glanced down at her half-exposed breasts.

Without moving away, Keleigh raised her glass. "A toast to Michael Orcini, and the Resort at Sundance Lake."

A resounding. "Hear, hear!" followed by clinking glasses.

"It really was no big deal," she finally answered his constant inquiry. A legal firm moved to larger offices, and this one was almost perfect. I got Charlie to do the rest. J.T. and Rebecca got the computers and Abigail helped with the decorating."

"Abigail?"

"Sum T's wife."

"You lost me. Abigail? Sumtea?"

"Sumner T. Williams, *the third*," she pronounced in a snobbish nasal sound. "Sum T. That's what I call him."

"Oh." Still not sure. "And what do you call me?"

"Depends . . . Boss. I think that I'm going to call you boss." She brushed a curl back from his face allowing her hand to linger for a brief moment.

He took her hand. "Thanks for everything, sweet cheeks."

He couldn't keep his eyes from glancing at her partially exposed breasts.

"You shouldn't call me that in front of others. They'll think we . . ."

"No one heard, and," he paused, "besides . . ."

Sumner announced that it was getting late.

"Boss," Keleigh looked apologetically at him. "I forgot to tell you something."

"What."

"You're paying for this."

"Give it to J.T. He's the CFO." He laughed boisterously, and waited a moment before handing her his gold card. "Here."

Keleigh hung on to his arm as they made their way to the car.

On their way home they talked about the spouses of the employees, as people do.

"Did you notice? Everyone except you and me are married."

"It's you and I, Michael," she corrected. "Yes, I noticed. Here we are already. You have been full of surprises the last few weeks. Anything else I should know about before I go into full cardiac arrest?" He pulled to the curb in front of her place.

She leaned over, completely and intently exposed her breast, and kissed him sweetly. She lingered a while, allowing him to see a little of what she had to offer. Then as if nothing happened, she answered. "Yes, there is more, but not tonight. I'll see myself to the door." She straightened her coat, and got out of the car.

He pounded the steering wheel. "Damn." A word he reserved for a bad play in racquetball. He couldn't figure her out. She teased him all night. And now? Charlie's words came back, telling him that she was crazy about him, and, and Bobbi thought she was sleeping with him. He tried to dismiss the emotion, but this time he knew there was more to learn about these recent actions of his dear friend and pal. He suspected that her playfulness would become evident in the not too distant future, and he wasn't sure if he would be ready for the real meaning. He surmised that all these speculations were without reason, and nothing short of her explanation would complete the puzzle.

* * * * * *

As he opened the door to his room he sensed a presence inside. He started in cautiously, but found himself being pushed in, hard, so hard that he fell to the floor. He felt a foot heavy on his back, pressing him tight to the floor. He didn't resist.

"Help Mr. Orcini up," came a voice from a shadow in the corner.

"We have been very patient with you, Mr. Orcini. You should not hold out on us."

"What the devil do you mean? Who are you?"

"It is of no consequence. Be mindful that our patience is wearing thin."

Michael was aware that he referred to patience twice, so he decided to do just that, and be quiet. He would let this shadow and the two goons behind him make the next move. He figured if they came there to hurt him, they would have done it by now.

It seemed like an eternity before the interloper spoke. "There are many people depending on this venture of yours. You must sign the contracts." He hesitated, "That is not the right word. Is it? But *you* know what I mean. Don't you Mr. Orcini?" He waited for an answer, and became impatient, as Michael remained silent. He raised his voice slightly to emphasize. "We are a peaceful people, Mr. Orcini. Peaceful." He instructed the goons with his hand, and they pushed Michael again, and again until he was face down on the bed. "Please stay there until we are gone."

Michael went to the bathroom, and washed his face in cold water to wake him from the reality of the last few minutes.

He called Charlie, and told him about the visit. Charlie suggested they get together with Poncerelli. He'd call to see if Ponci could get away for lunch. Michael agreed.

He dialed again. A sleepy voice said, "Hello."

"Keleigh, I need to see you first thing in the morning. Can you meet me for breakfast at Grandma's house?"

"What's wrong?"

"Nothing," he lied, "can you make it at seven?"

"Sure, bye."

Sleep did not come easy for him. He tossed and turned. His mind raced with thoughts of the thugs in his room, Wu, Nugari, Ceres, and deVillefrance out to steal from him. Bobbi. Then there was Bobbi. What was she up to? Fantasies of Keleigh, and Darci. Darci was there in every crazy thought, watching the whole thing. Then he succumbed to a fantasy with Darci, and fell off to sleep.

* * * * * * *

Keleigh was waiting in a booth at the far end of the restaurant. Her face lit up like a Christmas tree when she saw him. "Hi, Michael."

"Hi, sweet cheeks." He bent over and kissed her as he always did, only this time she kissed him back placing her hand on his cheek, sliding it under his chin, and pulling his lips tight against hers. He didn't resist at first, then pulled away slowly, and sat down.

"I need to talk to you," he regained his composure, "but first I need some coffee."

"I know."

"Keleigh, darling. I must talk to you about some very important business."

"Yes, Michael. I know."

"I don't think you do."

"Can I get you something?" the waitress asked.

"A cup of your finest coffee, and a Danish without any nuts for the gentleman, and a short stack for me. Oh, and a cup of hot lemon herb tea for me." Keleigh ordered.

"When you take over, you really . . ."

"You ain't seen nuttin yet pahd--ner," she seemed to kid, "wait 'til Ah git goin."

Michael roared a boisterous laugh until tears rolled down his face.

"If you were . . ."

"But, I'm not," she whimpered, "I'm not." She began to pout.

"Keleigh." He stopped, realizing that she wasn't playing.

"What important business do you have that can't wait until we get to the office?"

He sensed that she needed a moment to herself. "I have to run to the rest room for a minute," he said, and left without excusing himself.

When he returned she was composed and smiling. "Tell me what it is, Michael."

He told her about his meeting with Nate and J.T. He explained every detail, especially the other possible financing opportunities with Hans and Guy Nestor. When he came to the part about his concern with Nugari, Wu and Ceres, she turned white with fear. Michael wondered if he had shared too much. He tried to comfort her by telling her not to worry, that Charlie and his friend the commissioner were investigating everybody.

They embraced, as they always did. He patted her butt, and she put her hand over his, holding it there for a moment before she turned and said, "Bye, see yah at the office."

* * * * * *

The security gate was open when Michael arrived at the Ceres mansion. He proceeded along the palm tree lined double drive to an open circular auto court. The drive separated into a 'Y' and continued under a breezeway to a massive garage. He stopped short of the breezeway parking near the entrance just behind a silver Rolls, and walked to the front door passing a myriad of cars. The front door was wide open and unprotected. He proceeded with care, calling, "Hello, hello, is anyone here?" It was as quiet as an empty church. He was considering leaving when an exquisite Asian girl appeared out of no-

where; wearing a teaser top and the tightest hip hugging pedal pushers he had ever seen. It was the same girl from the casino.

"This way, Mr. Orcini. You are expected. They are waiting in
the library."

He caught up with her, touching her arm. She stopped
abruptly. "Not here."

"What is your name?"

"I will tell you sometime, but not now." she continued to a
massive pair of carved mahogany doors with ornate brass hard-
ware. She pushed the lever, and allowed him to pass, but not without a whisper. "Twelve twenty four."

Connie Contedetto stood up and walked to meet him extending his hand. "Welcome to Casa Trinacria." Michael graciously
shook his hand, but said nothing.

Surrounding an enormous wood table that extended at least
twenty feet, and looked like an antique from Old Italy, were the
gruesome threesome. Nugari spoke first, but did not come around
to meet him. "Good to see you Michael."

Wu also stayed on the far side of the table. "Good morning,
Mr. Orcini." deVillefrance arduously lifted his large frame, and
came around the table to greet him. "Mr. Orcini." was all he said
as he shook his hand.

"Hello." He looked at the others, and stretched out. "Gentlemen." Using the salutation because it was customary, and not for
any other reason. He looked for Hector. Anticipating his question,
Connie said. "Mr. Ruby called before you arrived, and said he was
detained, but would see you later."

"Might I have a word with you in private, Mr. Contedetto?"

"If it is your wish to do so. We can go into the office." He
looked down at the others. "You gentlemen should excuse us, as
Mr. Orcini and I have secluded things to converse about."

They sat facing each other over a small oval wrought iron table
with a glass surface, and a silver tea set magnificently displayed on
top. "What is of such concern that you should wish to speak with
me on such a personal basis?"

"Mr. Contedetto.. "

"Please. You should for to call me Connie."

"Connie." He told him, in detail, about the visit he had, and that he suspected that Ceres sent them. He concluded his discourse with a demand that Ceres be involved in their meeting, and he would be pleased to reschedule to a time that was more convenient if she was not available.

Connie listened without interruption, as he was trained, and when he was sure Michael was done, he asked to be excused. "You may remain here until I return. I will send someone to bring you a drink."

When the door opened, Michael expected 'The Bod', as he secretly called her, to enter. Instead it was that bull, Mario. "Would you like some of our finest coffee, sir?" He mocked him from his remembrance at the restaurant. "I brewed it fresh when I heard you arrive. Black. No cream or sugar. Is that right? Sir."

"Yes. Coffee would be good."

He went across the room, savoring the sight of fine objects at every turn. Finally he reached his destination. He scanned the titles of the books behind glass doors.

Mario came in and set the silver coffee service on a hutch nearby. "It's permissible to look at the collection, sir. You may open the lid." He gently grasped the diminutive brass knob, and lifted the lid, sliding it back and over the books. "Here, sir. Like that. It's quite simple."

"Thank you, Mario."

He inspected the collection. Goethe, Thoreau, Steinbeck, Dickens. Rudyard Kipling. He took a copy of 'Captains Courageous', and opened it. This was a treasure. He ran his fingers over a signature with the date Dec. 1897, and a small inscription. As he replaced the prize, he wasn't at all surprised to find Corti's Elizabeth, Empress of Austria, in the original German publication. What did surprise him was the original letter from Elizabeth to the Countess Festetics dated Oct 1872 that fell from the between the pages.

He was enjoying his trip through history when the door

opened, and Mario announced, "The Donna Ceres." Connie was close behind, as were two men in black.

"Good morning, Mr. Orcini." She came forward, and extended her hand. "It is a pleasure to finally meet you." She stopped short of his position making it necessary for him to advance, and complete the connection.

He was glad she put her hand out, otherwise he wouldn't know whether to bow or genuflect and kiss her ring. "It is an honor," he lied convincingly.

"You are Italiano, No? Come sit with me."

Connie administered to her chair, while Mario guided Michael to the proper chair moving it to a suitable distance from her.

She took a handkerchief from her sleeve, using it to signal the boys to leave. "Ermano tells me that you are upset. He says you think that I send some of my family to intimidate you."

"Ermano? Connie?"

"Yes. Is that what you think?" Her eyes became soft, but unsympathetic. "You think that I, Donna Una Maria Antonia Ceres, would do such a thing?"

He didn't like being on the defensive. He stayed quiet and waited.

Her eyes became cold and calculating. "They were instructed not to hurt you."

His poker face changed with a small curl at the corner of his lip. He had won this round, but would not anticipate her next move. He remained quiet.

Donna Ceres was becoming infuriated with Michael, but did not want to jeopardize the entire undertaking, so she decided to make a proposal. "We can do business Mr. Orcini, and I will promise that this," she thought, "*event*, will not occur again."

Finally, it was Michael's turn. "This event will *never*," he emphasized, and stood up, "*never* happen again. Our business is over. Good day Mrs. Ceres." He looked down at her pathetic expression, and went to the door. Connie was guarding the door. He turned back to her, and calmly said. "Tell him to move."

"As you wish, Mr. Orcini. As you wish." She used the handkerchief once more. Connie made a slight bow, and opened the door. Michael departed.

Michael paused, looked at the large doors, and went in. "Gentlemen! The negotiations are over. Find yourself another project." Without waiting for their reaction, he quickly made an about face and exited.

His heart was pounding as he wheeled the Explorer down the drive and through the gateway. A partly obscured car, on a parallel road, passed going the other way. It looked familiar, but he couldn't place it. He instinctively knew that this was not the end of her involvement. He also knew that the Chinese had deposited two hundred fifty million into an escrow account, and they were not going to be very happy. His mind told him to deal with Wu separately, while another part of him wanted to wait for Hans. He thought of Bobbi's friend Guy. He would see him this afternoon. Maybe, just maybe there's a deal to be made there. This was not like any of his previous developments. Get the land, find a banker who would lend the money, hire an architect and a contractor, and that was it. These people are greedy. He was stumped, at least for now. It was time to meet Charlie and Poncerelli for lunch.

Skyrider's Coffee shop at the North Las Vegas Air Terminal was Charlie's selection for lunch. Michael got there early, and watched the airplanes take-off and land. There was a structured peacefulness to the ritual 'touch and go' that small airplane pilots exercised.

"Michael."

He recognized the call.

The three men shared a simple coffee shop lunch, and Michael became an instant friend with Ponci. Charlie was right. This man had integrity and soul. They talked of common interests, their love of flying, but not girls this time. Ultimately they came around to the reason they got together. They discussed Michael's concerns about Ceres and her friends. Michael explained, in detail, the hotel visit and his confrontation with Ceres. Ponci and Charlie listened with concern. Ponci asked Michael not to meet with them until he checked on a few things. He wanted to talk to a judge he knew, who was one of the few honest ones left in Las Vegas. Michael agreed, but emphasized that he had to go ahead or lose the project.

They parted company, and Michael headed to McCarran International Airport to pick-up Guy Nestor. He arrived early and stopped by Sundance Helicopters, to say hello to an old friend, on his way to Eagle Flight where Guy was scheduled to tie down. The Cessna V Ultra touched down like a mother caressing her baby's butt. The corporate jet sported the Nestor Insignia on the side, setting it apart from any other. Michael crossed the transient parking area and met Guy.

Guy had made reservations at the same hotel as Michael. His suite was one of the gambler specials, extremely large and flamboyant. After a short social discovery time, Guy got right into his reason for being there. He never asked how much, or what Bobbi might have told Michael. He took out a short two-page proposal, handed it to him, and walked to the bar. "Would you like a drink?"

"Could we call for some coffee?"

Guy didn't answer, but picked-up the phone and ordered it to be sent up immediately.

It was amazing how much he put into such a short proposal. His bankers would deposit the money in increments during construction, and they would supply all the necessary start-up capital. Nestor would own the project until the initial investment was recovered. It would then revert to a sixty-forty partnership in Nestor's favor, but Michael would have equal voting power from the beginning. It sounded too simple, too good. There had to be a catch.

They discussed the offer at length, with Michael adding his concept of ten percent off the top for his other non-profit venture. Guy had to run this by his attorneys, and promised that he would get back to him soon. Design and furnishings would be left to Michael. Guy wanted to approve the key personal, even though Michael had made commitments. After an hour and a half, they agreed to continue the discussion in a few days.

The day felt long and it was only four thirty when Michael returned to his room on the twelfth floor. Suddenly it clicked.

Twelve twenty-four. The impulse to knock on the door was overwhelming as he passed by. Is that what she meant or was it? He wasn't in the mood to find out. What if she was planted by Ceres to get to him? He proceeded to his room.

"Hi Michael, darling."

"Bobbi!" he exclaimed with surprise. "What are you doing here? How did you get in my room?"

"I bribed the bellboy with a few dollars and a promise. I had to see you."

"A promise?" he shook his head. "Why?"

"Because," she started toward him, "I've missed you."

"And?"

"Isn't that enough?"

"That's never enough with you, Bobbi. Why are you here? You know that I don't like unannounced guests."

"I'm not a guest, Michael," she put her arms around his neck. "I'm your lover."

"Bobbi!"

"You look tense, darling." She started to unbutton his shirt. "Come over here, and I'll give you a massage."

A massage sounded good. He started to lie down, and she stopped him, unbuckling his trousers. He tried to stop her. She looked into his eyes. "Feet and legs too." He was too stressed out to argue, after all it was only a massage. Bobbi never meant the rubdown to be limited to his back and legs. He was thinking of Darci as she moved her skillful touch between his thighs. Aroused, he turned over to see that she was almost completely undressed.

He sat up with a new awareness. "I can't do this."

"What's wrong?"

"I can't. You'll have to go."

"What do you mean, can't? We've done *it* hundreds of times. What's wrong?" She sat on the edge of the bed, throbbing. She put her face in her hands, and started to cry. "What's wrong with me?"

"Nothing's wrong with you." He picked up her blouse, and handed it to her . "It's me." He stood up and looked at her.

"I don't understand. I know I excite you. It's another girl. Isn't it? It's Keleigh. I knew it all the time. You're spending a lot of time with her a lately. It's her. Isn't it?"

"No it's not Keleigh. It's someone new. I'm going to see her tonight. I'm sorry."

She got up, and began pounding his chest. He didn't stop her this time. He put his arms around her, and let her cry. After a minute she broke away from him, picking up her clothes as she hurried to the bathroom.

In a few minutes she came out looking refreshed and radiant. "You'll come back to me when she's gone."

She went straight to Guy's suite. "Surprise." She sashayed passed him.

He looked bewildered, but pleased. "What are you doing here?"

"I had to see you."

He smiled, and closed the door behind her.

* * * * * *

THE ROMANCE

Chapter Two

Michael remembered the last time he drove up the winding road to Darci's home. The excitement burning inside him was more intense than the first time he embarked on his first solo flight. A large scruffy dog ran across the road causing him to hit the breaks, intruding on his moment. The CD slid off the seat onto the floor. "I must remember to take that in," he reminded himself. It was almost dark. "Only a couple more weeks of daylight savings." He caught himself talking out loud, but continued. "Gotta stop talking to myself."

"Whatcha got behind your back?" she played like a little girl, twisting back and forth. "Somethin' for me?" Her hazel eyes twinkled.

"Aren't you even going to say hello? Must I always come bearing gifts?"

She threw her arms around his neck, pulling herself tight against him. "Yes." She pulled her hips tighter against him. "What do you have for me?"

"You're a shameless woman. What will the neighbors think?"

"I don't care. What do you think?" She wiggled her hips.

He leaned down, and kissed her nose. "May I come in?"

"I 'spose, since you're here." She released her grip. "I'm glad I excite you." She stepped back a little, making him brush against her as he came in.

He handed her eleven pink roses with one peach-colored rose in the middle, surrounded by the baby's breath.

"What's in the other hand? Did you bring it?" She reached around him.

"You must pay for this present."

"Anything. Anything you want, but I must have it."

"A kiss."

"You're easy." She rose up on her toes, and gave him a small peck on the lips.

"You'll have to do better than that Scarlett." He put his arm around her waist, drawing her to him, and kissed her. Hard at first, easing into a sweet caress of her lips with his tongue.

"I'm not sure if you just got here or if this is good night."

She took his hand, and led him to the kitchen. He put two packages on the table as he passed. He leaned against the counter as she fussed with the flowers. Darci pushed him gently out of her way as she reached up for the crystal vase. He put his hands on her waist to help lift her slightly. As her arms were stretched up he slowly moved his hands to her breasts. She settled back on her heals, and enjoyed his touch.

"Your dinner will burn up." She snuggled back against him.

"It's already hot." He kissed her hair, which was hanging full to her waist. Slowly he moved his hands down along her hips to her thighs, and moved away patting her butt.

"Whew," she breathed out loud.

He watched lovingly as her hands trembled while arranging the roses in the vase.

Darci tried to regain her composure. "Shush. Get out of my kitchen so I can fix your dinner, and please put these flowers on the dining room table. I want to look at them while I feed you." She gently pushed the arrangement into his hands.

The dining room was small, with an old burl wood buffet filled with pewter cups and plates, and a pair of matching urns. The table was set with white china trimmed in blue flowers, and set upon pewter plates. Two candles were ready and waiting to create the ambiance she wanted. Michael placed the roses to one side.

"Whatever you're cooking, it smells wonderful. What is it?"

"You'll know soon enough. Did you bring the wine?"

"Yes. It's here on the table. D'you want me to open it?"

"There's an opener on the hutch."

Michael put the CD in the player and made his surprise ready for her.

She spoke very softly as he lit the candles. "Sit down, dinner's ready."

She placed the food out in an old fashion family style. A platter of meat, a tureen with some unknown delight hidden under its cover, and small plates of various vegetables. Her face was radiant with excitement. "Please sit while I serve you."

She motioned for him to give her his plate, then carefully and precisely displayed her creation, and returned the plate to him. He waited for her. She bowed her head. "Lord, we thank you."

"How did you know? This is my favorite." He talked with a half-full mouth.

"You told on our first date."

"But, I didn't tell you how to prepare it. It's just like mom . . . Tell me you didn't."

She lowered her head. "We had a nice talk. Are you mad at me?"

"No, of course not. How did you get the number?"

"They're in the book, silly."

They ate in silence, speaking only with their eyes.

He helped her with the dishes, and they sat by the fire and talked. Excusing himself, he went to the CD player, pushed the start button, and rejoined her by the fire. "You remembered. I love you." They continued their playing, kissing, talking, kissing, and fondling. They became hotter than the fire.

She stood up gave him her hand, and led him to her bedroom,

stopping to take the flowers he gave her. They made love most of the night, until they could no more.

He awoke to the most delicious of morning smells--fresh coffee and bacon frying. She came in wearing the shirt he wore the night before, and pulled the curtains back, letting the late morning light in. "Come here, you delicious wench."

She jumped, landing next to him. "We can make love after breakfast." She kissed him and left. "You can wear a big old sweatshirt. There's some in the drawer. Hurry."

"Do I have time for a shower?"

"No. I conserve water around here. You'll have to shower with me later."

She prepared eggs and bacon exactly as he liked. They made love, and showered, and made love. They talked into the afternoon, slept a while, and made love again.

"I have to make a long distance call." He said somewhere in the middle of the afternoon.

"Do you want to use this phone, or the one in the alcove?"

"This one is fine."

"Want me to leave?"

"No. But, I do want you to tell me about that," he hesitated not wanting to hurt her feelings. "that painting that has been looming over me all night, and half the day."

"You don't like my princess?"

"I love it." He lied.

"Mother told me.. "

"You should listen to her."

"You'll love her."

"I already do."

He dialed Hans. "I am planning to come to the islands today, and I'm bringing someone special." He waited. "Yes. I have the plans and the projections. I'll call you later. Goodbye."

She looked astonished. "What? Who?"

"Wanna go wid me to *de I . . . lands*?" He tried to sound Jamaican.

"Do you do this often?"

"Invite a girl to the Cayman Islands?"

"No. Decide on the spur of the moment?"

"Wanna go?"

"Yes."

* * * * * *

Darci looked out the window of the 747, as they departed McCarran International, hardly believing that she was on a plane to the Cayman Islands. She hadn't a clue why they were going, except that Michael had some business. Suddenly all sort of thoughts came into her head. Orcini is an Italian name. The Mafia are Italians. The Cayman Islands are where rich people launder money, or put them in special accounts. "Oh God." She thought. "What if she had fallen in love with a Mafia hit man?" She wondered how he got the tickets so quick, he never even made a phone call.

"Penny for your thoughts."

"How did you get the tickets at the last minute? I never saw you make a call."

"That's simple. I ordered them on the Internet."

"The Internet? I didn't know you could do that."

"Well, Miss snail mail. You don't answer my email for a week or more. How do you expect to know anything about the Internet?"

As if he had been reading her mind. "Don't you want to know why we are going to the Caymans on such short notice?"

"I'm not going to be killed if I know too much, am I?"

"You're beautiful. What a wonderful imagination you have."

"Tell me. You're not a hit man, or anything like that. Are you?"

"Sure I am. Didn't you feel that lump in my pants yesterday?" He kissed her, and began to tell her about the project. During their previous conversations, he only skimmed the surface telling her the wonderful ideas he had, and how it would look. Today it was different. He told tell her everything.

"Why are you telling me this now?" She interrupted.

"Let me explain. On our first date, when you opened the door, and smiled at me, I knew something was happening." She wanted to speak, but he put his finger lightly on her lips. "Let me finish." She nodded. "Then when you took my hand, I got feelings that I have never had before." He looked into her eyes. "The day at the fair was the most incredible day I have ever known, until yesterday." He took a deep breath. "And then yesterday, after you cooked my favorite meal, you made love to me like I have never experienced before." She wanted to speak, and once more he touched her lips, only this time it was with his lips. "You're going to think that I'm crazy, and I am." Another deep sigh. "I'm crazy about you, and I have to tell you everything." He sat back, knowing she was going to hit him or, maybe tell him that he has no right to say things like that to her.

She didn't say a word. Her silence was making him squirm in his seat. At last he looked at her. Tears were streaming down her cheeks, but her face was aglow, and her eyes were sparkling through the teardrops. He wiped a tear from her cheek with his finger, and put it to his lips.

She put her hand to his cheek, and told him that she loved him with her eyes. Then she rested her head on his shoulder and fell asleep.

Hans was waiting at the airport with a limousine. "Gud day mon." Shaking Michael's hand but, keeping his eyes on Darci. "And who is dis maag--nif--ee--sant woo-maan?" He took her hand and kissed the back just below the wrist.

"This is Darci," he paused, "the future Mrs. Orcini."

Darci looked away in what appeared to be a moment of shyness.

"You did noot tell me mon. Come."

Hans pointed here and there, showing points of interest, as the sun set into the calm sea. He told them, that one week before, the seas and the winds were raging from the thrust of El Nino. "We did not hav no pow--waar for two days."

The limo turned onto a gravel road that wound its way to an enormous three story Mediterranean style villa. "It looks like it

just came out of a travel brochure for Spain or Monaco." Darci
exclaimed.

"You are very ob--sir--vaant, Miss Dahr-cee. I ack--tu--ally haad
my archi--tek copy one dat I liked on the western shore of Corsica."

A short, plump woman with dark hair set back in a bun welcomed them into the imposing entrance hall. Standing at the foot
of the grand staircase were two young dark skin girls dressed in
starched uniforms. "I am Marianna. This is Felicia and Simone."

The girls giggled.

She summoned the girls to take their bags. "Allez mes
paresseuses! Vite! Vite!" She emphasized with a quick clap of her
hands. Then Marianna turned to Michael and Darci, "Your rooms
are upstairs, at the end of the hall with a view of the sea."

"Rooms?" Darci questioned, in a whisper, as they ascended
the staircase. "I don't want to sleep alone. I want to be with you.
Would you tell them?"

Only a pair of very ornate doors separated the rooms. "Look
here, I can come visit you." Michael joked, and the girls giggled.

"It better not be just a visit. Remember, I am the *future* Mrs.
Orcini." She threw her arms around him, and whispered in his
ear. "I want to talk to you about that." She bit his ear.

"Ow," he cried, pretending it hurt.

"Besides," she inspected the rooms, "my room has a better
view."

"It sure does," he said, undressing her with his eyes.

"And don't you forget it."

"Dinner is in thirty minutes." Marianna said, and left.

"I can do that," Darci told Simone as she unpacked her case.
"But.. "

"It's okay." She took her arm, and led her to the door.

Darci went into Michael's room looking around. "Did you get
rid of your girl?"

"Heck no. I'm keeping her around, just in case." He joked.

"There ain't never going to be," she tackled him throwing him
on the bed, "any just in case." She smiled looking down at him.

"Now that I've got you where you can't get away. What's this *future* Mrs. Orcini stuff I've been hearing about?"

He wrestled over on top of her. "Got me where I can't get away? Huh?"

"You can just bet that I do. Now tell me before I hurt you." Her eyes danced.

"I just said that so he wouldn't try hitting on you." He held her arms alongside her head, and allowed the weight of his body to press against her as he kissed her.

"I don't think you ever *just* say anything."

"You're right." Now he took control of her. Raising his shoulders, and pressing a little more with his lower body.

"What are you saying?"

"You should be Mrs. Orcini." His face became very serious.

Without a moment's thought, she smiled and said, "Well, since I've got you where you can't get away. Okay. But, just so he won't hit on me."

They kissed and embraced for what seemed like only a brief moment, when a knock on the door reminded them. "Dinner in ten minutes, Sir" There was no similar knock on her door.

"Do you think she knows that I'm in here?"

"Of course not," he smiled, "hungry?"

"Yeah. But dinner can wait." She tried to wrestle on top of him, but failed. "In bed is the only time you get to be in control. Okay?"

"I love it when you're on. . . ." He kissed her. "Okay. Now lets go eat."

"Give me five minutes."

Marianna said that they would have supper in the small dining room.

"I wonder what the big one is like," Darci commented as she inspected the high vaulted carved wood ceilings and the paneled walls of the room. She went to the arched windows and looked out onto a magnificent garden.

"Cohm sit hahr, by me, Miss Dahr-cee."

They dined in elegance, and talked about the politics of the islands, the weather, and numerous other socially significant topics. Hans said he would arrange for them to use his yacht or go snorkeling, or any of a host of other activities.

"Is there a nice beach where we can go swimming?" Darci asked.

"We haav our own pri--vat beach. I will show it to you in the moor--nahn."

After dinner, Hans invited Michael to his study for the traditional cigar and brandy. "We caan discuss som bus-ness."

"Can I come too? I want to know everything." She put her arm through Michael's, and gave him her 'let's go' look.

"I know you don't haav these in the U.S." Hans presented a humidor.

"As a mater of fact, I had one of these just a week ago." He chose a hefty Romeo y Julieta robusto

"Can I try one?" Darci asked, as serious as she could be.

The men looked at each other, and simultaneously shrugged.

Hans offered her a different humidor. "The El Ray del Mundo is mil-door wid ah sweet-tah fla-vour. It woo-hd suit your pahr-son-ahl-uty."

"Thank you, sir."

He nodded and offered the bottle of Hennessy XO for Michael's approval, and suggested the Hine VSOP for Darci. "It's moahr fru-tay. You wheel luvh it. Trust meh."

The men discussed the project at length while Darci listened with amazement. The drawings from Henri, and the projections from J.T. were most impressive. Hans said that he would send the information to Europe on Monday.

"Hans?" he questioned, "may I use your phone? I must call Las Vegas."

"Of course, mon. Use de won in de staah--dee. Cohm wid me."

Michael followed him to the study. "I will use my calling card," he invoked.

"Nohn--cents. You are my guest. Call ahn--nee--whar, he enunciated the gentle command, "ahn--nee--whar in de wourl--dh." With a hardy laugh he departed.

The executive secretary took Michael's call. "He was looking forward to your dinner Mr. Orcini. I know he'll be very disappointed. Would you like to reschedule now?

"I'm out of the country, but I'll call as soon as I return, and we can set a time then. Would that be okay?"

"I'm sure that will be just fine, Mr. Orcini."

Michael and Darci played for the next two days. The yacht, scuba dining and swimming on the private beach. As he dug two holes in the sand they looked at each other, knowing they had been here before. "It's de-ja vu. I know exactly what's going to happen next." She said, turning over and placing her breasts in the double excavation.

"Me too." He brushed the sand from her feet, then along her legs and thighs. He had propped his head on one hand. "I'll bet there are seagulls sailing in a jet stream."

"No bet."

They returned to *their* beach the last night, and made love.

* * * * * * *

As they neared the end or their journey, Darci leaned over him to look out the window at the Las Vegas lights. "Nice cleavage," he said.

"I glad you like them. Did you know it's raining cats and dogs out there?"

"Cats and dogs?"

"I wonder if it's safe to land in the rain. Do you think its safe?"

"Yes. It's safe."

"How can you be so sure."

"I told you that I was a pilot."

"I forgot." She thought a moment, "But, you don't fly anymore?"

"Of course I do. As a matter of fact, I just bought a plane."

She became quiet. Then turning to him. "I guess it's out of the question to ask you not to fly anymore?" Soulfully, her eyes pleaded with him.

"Anything's possible. Can we talk about it later?"

"I love you, Michael Orcini." She put her head on his shoulder.

He kissed the top of her head.

Darci got the luggage while he brought the car around. "It really is raining cats and dogs," she said with a smirk on her face.

"How come you keep saying that. I don't see any animals." He teased as he put the luggage in the car.

"Be . . . cause," she said, lingering, "I just saw a man step in a poodle." She started to giggle, and then broke into unstoppable laughter.

He drove away. "You set me up. I don't believe you really said that." He joined her laughter. When they stopped, he said seriously, "I'll bet it's not raining in Paris."

Suspicious, she said. "Why?"

"I have an idea."

"I'm afraid to ask." She waited. "What?"

"Let's go to Paris and find out."

"You want to go to Paris, and find out if it's raining? What kind of a nut are you anyway?"

"Your kind."

He turned up the road leading to Darci's Home. "I don't see any reason for you to stay at that noisy hotel anymore. Do you?"

"Where should I stay?"

"Right here with me, unless you don't want to." They pulled into her drive. "Well, What do you think?"

"I'll get the bags," he said with a big grin.

Inside, at the bottom of the stairs he dropped the bags with a thud.

"What's wrong, Michael?"

He took the things she was carrying, and gently put them on

the dining room table. "I wasn't kidding about Paris." He took both her hands, looked lovingly into her surprised eyes, kissed her eyes and her lips, and fell to one knee. "Miss Darci Tashmit, will you marry me, and run away with me to Paris?"

The tears that poured down her cheeks could not put out the fire burning in her heart. She took his face in her soft hands. "Yes." She fell to her knees, and they embraced.

After a moment she pulled back and said, "You are definitely my kind of nut, but you had better get me now before I stop to think."

"Okay! Lets go find a minister. I'll call Charlie to be best man. You live here. Do you have a favorite minister?

"Yes. Pastor Jim at my church. I'll call Maggie. She's gonna kill me, but she'll stand up for us. You can use the phone in the alcove. I'll use the other one in my, our bedroom." She checked his reaction.

"Let's both use the phone in the bedroom," he grabbed her around the waist, lifting her and swinging her around in circles.

"You want to get married or have sex?"

"Dumb question. I'll call from the alcove."

"You're g--gonna wha--what, M--Mikey?" Charlie shouted. "You're ca--crazy!"

"You heard me. I want you to be my best man. So put on a tie and meet us at the Presbyterian Church at seven o'clock."

"She m--must reh--really be someth--thing. Where's the ch--church?"

Michael gave him directions.

Darci's friend Maggie stopped and picked up some flowers on the way. Pastor Jim wanted her to wait and bring her intended to pre-nuptial classes, but after a lot of Darci's groveling he agreed to perform the ceremony.

"I've made reservations out of McCarran at nine-forty-two non-stop to Paris."

"Michael?" Sounding more like a little girl saying *Daddy*. "Should I always keep my passport in my purse?"

"It'll probably be cold, so take a warm coat. Oh, don't take any white tennies."

"No tennies?"

"No white ones. Sure way to stand out as a tourist."

"What about rings?" She asked.

"Charlie has a friend that owns a jewelry store. He is going to stay open for us. Now, we've got to get going."

"What about your car?"

"Got it covered. Charlie will take us to the airport. He'll take care of it."

"You scare me Michael. You take control. I'm not used to anybody planning anything for me. Tell me that you're not going to try to take control of me."

"Only when I'm on top."

"Promise?"

"Promise!"

Charlie and Maggie took them to the airport

It was the middle of the day, and raining when they touched down at Orly Airport. "Well now that we know we'll just have to turn around and go home." She was leaning over him looking out the port.

"Know what?"

"That it's raining in Paris," she tarried. "Isn't that what started all this, anyway?" She hadn't moved.

"Yes, of course." He pushed her hair aside and kissed her ear lobe.

"I hope the driver is cautious. Would you ask him to go slowly?" Darci looked concerned as they got in the taxi.

"Plaza Athenee. Driver, would you go slow, S'il vous plait ?"

"Oui, monsieur."

Their driver extended their experience through the heart of Paris. First he pointed out the Cite Unternationale Universitaire de Paris, then Montparnasse, and on through the Left Bank with the Tour Eiffle on their left, across the Seine into the fashionable part of the Right Bank. An attendant was standing under the glass shelter waiting for them to arrive, or so it seemed to Darci. They were escorted to the lobby and seated at a Louis XVI Marquetry desk facing an antique Flemish painting.

The clerk asked how long they planned their visit.

Michael answered in fractured French. "Je voudrais une chambre pour une nuit."

"Monsieur?" he said abruptly.

He quietly tried to explain that they were just married, and would stay two weeks.

Darci wanted to act snooty, or run about like a child to break the spell, but she decided that Michael might not appreciate these antics. She decided to wait until they got to their room.

She pushed aside the taffeta drapes exposing a courtyard filled with climbing vines bordered by flowers. There were small tables sheltered by colorful parasols. The courtyard was unoccupied, except for a small girl running to an open door.

"I want to have morning coffee there," she pointed as he joined her, "when it's not raining. It will stop, won't it?"

He brushed her hair back, and kissed her neck. "Absolutely."

"Couldn't you find a better hotel?" She sounded serious.

"They were all full." He kept it serious, as he put his arms around her. "We should have planned ahead."

"What did you say to that man at check-in? He got a little short with you."

"I told him that I wanted a room for one night, because I had to get you home before your mother missed you."

"You did not! Did you?"

"Hungry?"

A late lunch in Grille Relais Plaza proved exciting with the entree of a number of recognizable personalities. Darci described the bright colors and decorations as *fun*. The long trip finally took its toll, and they decided to go back to the room and rest. They made love and fell asleep.

Darci woke first, and took a shower, soon to be joined by Michael. Their enjoyment of each other was more than physical, but now, here in Paris on their honeymoon, they experienced their sexuality to its fullest.

"I'm hungry," she said. "Lets eat."

They dressed and went down to the La Regence-Plaza. "You are very lucky, we just had a cancellation," the maître d'hôtel exclaimed half French and half English.

"We are *very* lucky." She squeezed Michael's arm.

The table was next to a large curved top window fronting the avenue Montaigne.

"How do you do this?" she looked at Michael quizzically.

"Do what, darling?"

"Get airplanes tickets, hotel rooms, the best table in the house, and.. ?"

"And you. Don't forget, I got you," he smiled. "Like the man said. I'm very lucky. Do you want some wine?"

"Some bottled water, S'il vous plair," looking for approval. "How's that?"

"You could fool me."

She smiled, "I already did," surveying the room.

"Bonjour. Monsueir, Mademoiselle." The waiter was elegant in his formal attire.

"Good evening." Darci chimed in. "Comment allez-vous?"

"Tres bien," he responded.

"You amaze me." Michael stated.

"Don't get to carried away with me, sir. That's all I know. Except for the all important, *Ou est le lavabo?*" she smiled.

"Don't talk anymore French to her," he told the waiter. "She'll get both of us in trouble. I'll have a glass of Chardonnay, and a bottle of water for my wife."

They ordered an aperitif. The waiter suggested their world famous lobster soufflé. They savored the specialty, and lost themselves in each other.

Back in the room she displayed a small container of honey she had taken from the restaurant. "Desert!" She exclaimed.

"Honey? Don't you have to have something to put that on?"

"You must promise to be perfectly still." She smiled.

* * * * * *

They saw most of Paris. Darci most particularly liked the Eiffel Tower, The Arc de Triomphe, and the Avenue des Champs-Elysees with its wonderful shops. Her favorite store was the Dalloyau where they pigged-out on outrageous chocolate.

They were disappointed when they could not find a floating Jazz restaurant they had seen, on the Seine, after dinner their second night. The following night they searched and searched the length of the Seine but, could not find the restaurant.

"We must come back and find that place." Michael announced.

* * * * * *

In the first days of autumn, just as Michael and Darci were running off, opposing factions were at work planning to take control of the resort. Pernicious Nugari, unhesitatingly put the wheels in motion. He sought out Norah Laude at her home in Pacific Grove on the pretense that he would be there on business. Nugari knew of her sister's relationship with Michael, and planned to use her to solidify a new deal at Sundance Lake.

"I'm going to be on the Peninsula for a couple of days. Would you join me for dinner at Pebble Beach?"

"I am going to meet my sister and her friend there for dinner tomorrow night," she suggested a safe encounter. "Would you like to join us? About eight?"

"Great! Can we meet for cocktails before dinner? Say, six-thirty or seven?

"Yes. Seven at Stillwater would be fine. Goodbye."

"Until then."

The sun was starting to set over the Pacific Ocean as Perni watched Norah make her entrance into the lounge. Her raven hair was combed back to a small, elegant ponytail adorned with a rust hued bow. Her tailored, two-piece cream-colored wool suit presented her long legs as an exquisite extension of her sleek form.

Heads turned to acknowledge her. He waited until she was directly in front of his table before rising.

"You are absolutely gorgeous."

"It's good to see you, Perni." She ignored his compliment.

They chatted about old times, their encounter in Barcelona, and what they had been doing for the last year. Perni used their past relationship as his reason for locating her. He nonchalantly, and without much detail, explained his part in a resort development. It wasn't any problem segueing into his relationship with a resort developer without tipping his hand. After all, he spent his entire professional life successfully deceiving the other side.

"How did you actually get together with this mysterious developer?"

He apologized for his obscurity, but disclosed how they met at El Toro without actually revealing Michael's name. She knew from his story that he just had to be in charge of the entire air show. Perni was pleased that they were able to reminisce, and that he could set the stage before the others arrived. The plan was working. Busy had taken the bait, and was ready to sell it to Bobbi.

Bobbi arrived ten minutes before her friend, and used the time to her best advantage. It took her only a few minutes to find out why Perni was in town. Busy, true to her nickname, filled Bobbi with all the unnecessary information.

The sisters ignored Perni while quietly scheming to connect him and Guy together on Michael's project. They quietly agreed to use *all their talents* to accomplish the task. Bobbi knew her part would be easy. After all, Guy came to her first and really wanted more than a business affiliation. Busy suspected that Perni wanted the same. The girls were determined to profit from their efforts.

Guy Nestor arrived irritated and exhausted. He plopped down hard on the couch next to Bobbi. "The damn chauffeur was screwing some bitch in the back seat of my limo, and I had to wait." He was percolating like an old fashioned coffee pot.

"Were you watching?" Bobbi teased.

Guy grumbled.

"Was she cute?" Perni chimed in.

"Who the hell are you?" he quizzed him. The anger subsided.

"Aren't you going to say hello?" Bobbi asked.

"Oh! Sorry. Hello my dear." He kissed her cheek, then whispered. "Who is this fellow?"

"Guy Nestor. May I present, Mr. Nugari. He's a very good friend of Biz, and a long time family friend." She added a little white lie.

They shook hands. "Not the hotel chain Nestor?"

Nestor replied with an affirmative nod.

"Guy's here to invest in a quality hotel development, and Bobbi's helping him. You two should get together." Busy suggested, then turned to Guy. "Perni is involved in a really great project in Nevada, but it's all hush-hush."

The two men did a great deal of talking about hypothetical projects, skirting around the facts to protect their specific interests. They gave each other just enough information to agree on a business meeting in a few weeks.

Nugari's sense of loss after Michael's exclamation to find another project, made him determined to balance the equation. He knew that Bobbi and Michael were lovers. Concerned about her relationship with Nestor, he decided to offer her anything she wanted in order to influence Michael, and he was sure Busy would help for her own selfish reasons. He reveled in his conjuring as he sipped his brandy.

"Perni!" Busy called abruptly. "Where did you go?"

From across the table he winked and confidently said. "You really don't want me to say in front of these people."

"Bobbi has a great idea." Busy said with excitement. "We're going to throw a party at the lodge and invite everybody. She has someone that both of you should meet."

"I'll make all the arrangements and let everyone know." Bobbi spoke with the confidence of an experienced social director. "It'll be the week before Thanksgiving, on Saturday evening."

They looked at each other, nodding positively.

"Then it's all settled." Busy chimed in. Then abruptly, noticed someone across the room. "Excuse me." She got up and walked to a table where two men were having dinner. She stopped and struck a pose from her favorite fashion magazine.

The men placed their utensils down and immediately arose, as if a real Princess had come to bestow an honor on them.

"Good evening Miss Laude." The short one said.

"Good evening." She responded with her eyes on his tall muscular companion.

"Have you met our new associate golf pro?"

She extended her hand only slightly towards him with a demure smile, and waited.

He had to move around the table to accept her invitation to shake hands. "Good evening *Miss* Laude? My name is Dave Roberts." He was a well-proportioned six feet-two with salt and pepper hair cut in a butch. His face was a golden tan from the sun showing perfect white pearls when he smiled.

"Norah! *Miss* Norah Laude. How wonderful to meet you. I was looking for an excuse to work on my game." She turned her coy approach into a transparent flirt.

"I have an opening in the morning. Can you come at ten?"

"I can come then." She became coy once again.

The short man asked. "Would you join us for a drink?"

"Thank you, but I have to get back to my friends." She brushed against Dave slightly as she moved past, continuing to the women's rest room.

Bobbi had watched the encounter, and went to meet her sister in the girl's room. "Who's he?" She was barely inside.

"It's Mr. Wonderful, and I've got to have him. Isn't he gorgeous? He's a golf pro, and he has two first names. Dave Roberts. I've always wanted a man with two first names. What do you think, Bobbi?"

"You've got to get him to take you out first."

"I'm seeing him tomorrow."

"That's fast."

"He's going to give me some golf lessons."

"You don't need lessons, Biz."

"He doesn't know that, my naive little sister."

They rejoined Guy and Perni.

* * * * * * *

Charlie was waiting for Mr. and Mrs. Orcini at the airport. He handed Darci a huge bouquet of fresh cut wild flowers. "Welcome M--Mrs. Orci--n--ni."

"Oh! Charlie!" she exclaimed, "They're beautiful." She thought for a moment. "But wild flowers aren't in season. Where did you *ever* get them?" She never bothered to ask about Puca T. She knew that Charlie had taken care of her special friend.

Charlie just smiled.

After they settled in at Darci's home, Michael checked his service for messages. They were numerous. Wu, upset. Contedetto, very upset. deVillefrance cordial, and let's get together and work it out. Nugari, upset, but he has an alternative plan. Keleigh wants to know where he is . . . must talk, J.T., Sumner, Rebecca, Hans, Hector, Guy, and Spike all need to talk. Ponci has some important information. Bobbi is giving a party, and he must be there. The Commander is ready to be picked up.

Michael rearranged the messages into his own priority list, and called J.T. at home.

"Popinski residence."

"Hello, Armella. This is Michael Orcini calling."

"Mr. Orcini! Hello. Jan has been trying to get through to you. Just a minute."

"Michael. How have you been? We've been.. "

Thinking he asked, "*where* have you been?" Michael responded. "It's a long story. I'll explain when I see you. Set a meeting for tomorrow afternoon, and be sure that Hector is there a half-hour before everyone else."

"Sure, Michael. Are you okay?"

"I'm fine. I'll be in about ten. Ask Keleigh to be there about ten thirty-eleven."

"She won't be in tomorrow. She's out of state 'til tomorrow night."

"You'll call everyone else?"

"Yes. Good to know you're back." Assuming he was gone.

"Thanks. See you in the morning."

The next call was to Henri. "Ciao." Came a feminine voice from the telephone.

"Hi, Cam. This is Michael Orcini."

"Where have you been? Henri has been worried sick. I told him not to worry, that you probably just ran off and got married." She said smartly. "Where are you?"

"I'm here, in Las Vegas, in my new wife's home." he replied just as briskly.

Henri had picked up the extension. "See, It's just like I said." Cam declared smugly.

"What?" A long silence before, "You're joking, Michael." It was Henri's voice this time. Tell me that you're kidding."

"You're going to love her."

"I knew it." Without hesitation. "*Your Princess*. Right Michael?"

"Right. Cam."

"Tell us all about her. I want to know everything." She demanded. "Wait!" She exclaimed. "We'll fly up and have dinner with you tonight. I've got to meet the woman that finally hooked you, Snickers." She paused and took a big breath. "You can pick us up at the airport. What do you think, Henri? She didn't wait for his answer. "Give me the phone number there." She demanded. "We'll call you when we leave."

He gave her the number, and hung up the phone.

"You look puzzled, darling." Darci said as she sat on his lap.

"Henri and Camuela are flying up to have dinner with us?" He frowned.

"That's okay? Isn't it?"

"Yes, but I wanted to spend our first night back with you."

"I'll be with you," she assured him, playfully.

"I meant, *alone*," he reassured her.

"You are uncommonly romantic. Michael Orcini, and I love it." She kissed him, and started to wiggle where she sat.

"Lap dancing will get you into trouble. I'm a married man, ya know."

"I know." She continued the playful excursion.

They made love.

"I'm glad we came here first, Michael."

"Me too."

It was love at first sight. Henri and Camuela immediately bonded to Darci.

"She is heavenly, Michael." Cam took his arm, and led him aside. "Where in the world did you find such an angel."

"That's exactly what I thought when I first saw her, but I couldn't put any words to what I was thinking." He looked at her then back to Camuela. "She *is* an angel."

They went to a quiet restaurant where the covenant was strengthened.

When the night was over, Michael asked. "How long are you staying?"

"We're flying back tonight. Will you take us to the airport?"

"Sure. What time is your flight ?"

"One-thirty-five."

They hung-out at a nearby casino before going to the airport. Camuela adopted Darci as her new best friend. In the months ahead their relationship would become openly more congruous than most blood kinships. They became like sisters.

Henri was concerned that Darci would be taking up too much of Michael's time. "Bring Camuela along, and they can do girl things while we build the resort," he said quietly.

"I heard that." Her voice seemed to come out of nowhere. "I want to know all about it." She was smiling when he turned to look. "But you might be able to buy me off from time to time."

Henri put his arm around Michael's shoulder. "They'll make real good friends." He said with a chuckle. "Let's go."

* * * * * *

Darci woke enraptured in his arms. "I wish we could just stay here all day, like this," she snuggled tight against him, "but, I'm going to have a busy day. I have a million phone messages to answer, and your stuff must really be piling up. Huh?" She rolled over on top of him. "Speaking of piling up." she wiggled a little, "I've got time for a quickie."

Their first breakfast at home as newlyweds was different from the past few weeks. It was time to get back to their normal ways. Darci went through her ritual lemon ablution followed by a whole grain toast and juice. She brewed Michael's favorite French roast, which she brought back from Paris, and prepared hotcakes with syrup. Puca T watched in wonderment, but accepted his new master as a friend.

* * * * * *

Darci's small office appeared cluttered, but had a unique sense of organization. It fit her perfectly. Maggie was there working at her computer when she bounced in through the stained glass door. "Missus Darci Orcini has arrived," she announced, holding her hat on her head with her hand while she twirled, stopping short of Maggie's desk.

"You look absolutely radiant," she remarked. "And, your hair, it's beautiful. I don't think that I've ever seen you wear it that way."

"Michael likes it down. Well--ll," she stretched it out, "he's never actually said so, but I'm sure he does."

"Tell me everything," Maggie instructed her.

"Later. Right now I've got to get things back on track." She recognized the pout on Maggie's face. "Okay! But only the highlights for now, then we go to work."

Maggie wanted to know all *about* Michael. Darci described the trip to the Caymans and how he proposed, leaving out the personal adventures. "We can talk about the rest when I get the pictures developed, but now I need you to do something confidential for me. I want you to call Pete at our title company and get as much information as you can on the property around Sundance Lake. Tell him it has to be hush-hush. I want to know who is buying and what offers have been made in the last twelve months." She handed her a package of coffee beans and a small electric grinder.

"What's this for?"

"I want to learn how to drink fresh ground coffee."

"He must like it. Huh?"

"Yeah. And I'm planning on becoming an expert."

* * * * * * *

He had just placed her picture on the credenza next to his telephone when Martha came in with his coffee. "My, my, Boss! She's beautiful!" Checking his reaction.

"Thanks."

Martha planted her feet firmly, and poised both fisted hands on her hips. "Well?"

He looked up. "Well. What?"

"I *am* your personal secretary, and I'm supposed to know."

"Know what?"

"Mr. Orcini!" She set her hands into her hips. "Who is *that* in the picture?"

"Oh," he said casually, "that's my wife, Darci."

"You don't have a wife. You're just teasing me. I heard how you tease."

"Yes I do."

"Harrumph."

"But you have to promise not to tell anybody. Okay?" He knew she didn't believe him. "Please ask J.T. to come in."

"Good morning, boss! I'm real glad to see you."

"Please don't call me that," he pleaded, "where you able to set the meetings?"

"Yes. I had a little trouble with Ruby, but I threatened him."

"Close the door before you sit, and let's move over there. It'll be more comfortable." He motioned to the seating arrangement opposite his desk.

J.T. sat on the small leather couch, placing his briefcase on the adjacent cushion. "I've been going over some of these.. "

"I must talk about something first." He turned on his most serious expression.

"Yes. Of course, boss." J.T. pushed back in the couch, and waited.

"I did something on the spur of the moment. It's why I was gone."

"I know."

"You know? How can you know? Only Charlie knows. Did he.. ?"

"No. We go to the same church. Pastor Jim has become a good friend."

"Have you told anyone else?"

"No. We thought, with the, well we thought that you should do the telling."

"Thanks."

"When will we get to meet her? Mr. Orcini," he said with a serious tone. "I hope you'll be able to concentrate on the resort. No disrespect, sir, but I know from experience when Armella and I first got married I wasn't much good around the office for quite some time.

"Would you let me know when I get off track?" he pleaded.

"I'll do my best, sir."

"Let's get down to business. What time is Hector due?"

"Two thirty. The rest will be here at three."

"Good. Thanks."

The two men settled into planning the entire business structure for the resort.. Michael immediately recognized the value of his CFO. The session lasted through the lunch hour, and they sent out for sandwiches. When Hector Ruby arrived they had the basic organizational charts outlined and ready to incorporate into the general plan.

"Discharging the Ceres proposal so abruptly could cause some tension for you, Michael," Ruby expressed his concern, while trying to be diplomatic.

"I haven't ruled them out, but they are becoming much too forceful for me."

They went over the key employee contracts. "Ruby, you'll have to rewrite these to include the five year incentive programs," Michael instructed.

"I don't think it's a good idea . . ."

"This is what I want." His voice became firm and precise. "Please put it in the proper legal jargon. Without an incentive we leave ourselves open for a revolving door syndrome. I want to keep my key people for the duration."

Reluctantly Hector Ruby agreed to rewrite the agreements. "I'll have these for you in a few days."

"You were pretty tough on him," J.T. said after Ruby left.

"I'm getting a strange feeling about him," Michael explained. "I can't put my finger on it, but he doesn't seem to have our best interest in mind."

"I'll review those agreements when he's through, if it'll help."

"Thanks J.T. It will." He talked to the intercom, "Martha, have the others assemble in the conference room. And I want you there, too. "

"Here's some fresh coffee for you boss," Martha sang as she directed the others to take specific seats. "Miss Cody-Ives won't be here sir," She whispered to him, making sure to leave the chair directly to Michael's left empty.

"Ladies and gentlemen! Before we start I have an announcement to make." He paused looking at Martha for some reaction. "You all realize by this time that I've been gone for a couple weeks." He studied their faces. "I got married, and was away on a honeymoon. It happened rather quickly, and I didn't have time to inform you." He sighed with relief. "I apologize if there has been any inconvenience."

There was a long awed silence broken by, "Congratulations, Boss." from J.T., followed by insincere scattered applause.

J.T. immediately took over the meeting focusing on the issues at hand. Michael sat back, and watched his CFO regain the staff's involvement. He was masterful at control and organization.

Michael wondered how he should tell Keleigh. He knew she would be hurt because he didn't involve her in the ceremony, not thinking that her hurt might be much deeper.

* * * * * * *

Their first conflict happened when Darci wanted to spend Thanksgiving with her parents at their farm in California. Going to meet her parents, and spend the holiday wasn't the problem. The idea of sleeping in separate beds was unacceptable to Michael. Stella Tashmit, an old fashioned mother, didn't recognize the marriage since they weren't wed in the Catholic Church. "You hardly know him," she said when Darci broke the news. "And you know what Father Martin will say."

"Momma. I don't go to that church, anymore. I have a different church."

"You must have Father Martin marry you. Some things *do not* change."

"Can I talk to Daddy? Is he there? Can you put him on the phone?"

"Here's your father." In the background, "Don't let her sweet talk you."

"Hi, baby."

"Hi, daddy."

Darci tried to convince him about Michael. "You're gonna love him, daddy."

"You know your mother when she gets something set in her mind. I'll talk to her," he assured her.

They decided that he would try to soften her up.

"Thanks Daddy."

"It would be difficult for me to be with you for the entire weekend and sleep in separate beds." He pouted a little. "Besides, I made a commitment to help the homeless at the mission. Why don't you go, and I'll go down to L.A."

"She'll love you. Just give her a chance." She pleaded, but agreed to the necessary separation during the Thanksgiving holiday.

Stella Tashmit finally succumbed to Darci's groveling about the marriage, but not without the constant phone calls from Michael. The turning point occurred when he flew, unannounced and alone, to the Tashmit farm. The small grass landing strip hadn't been mowed in a few weeks, which made the landing precarious. Michael was grateful that the Commander sat high above the ground.

Jason Tashmit ran out, with his nine gauge shotgun poised, to see who was landing on his property. He recognized Michael from the photographs that Darci left the week before, and welcomed him like a son.

Michael not only convinced them that the marriage was befitting, but also to join him and Darci at his parents home in Cape Cod for the holidays. They ate a large, country style lunch, and talked about Michaels plans for the future. A relationship was formed that day that would endure the events to come.

Michael put Nugari and company on hold while he waited for Nestor and Hans to complete their proposals. Meanwhile, J.T. took the helm of the resort, as if it were his own, and finalized the organization.

Bobbi and Norah were making plans for their party at Carmel, and the coup that they thought would bring many people together for Michael's resort.

* * * * * * *

The evening was changing, like a kaleidoscope turning from sun-soaked beaches to a rusty shimmering ocean with coral skies supporting a fireball preparing to drop into a sizzle, as Bobbi made the final preparations for her party. The peace and serenity of the natural and man-made wonders at Pebble Beach was a matchless backdrop for her *haute couture affaire*. A lone Bagpiper that strolled along the beach of The Inn at Spanish Bay, at sundown, was brought over to the magnificent eighteenth green just below the Lodge, to add a special touch to the party. Roberta Azure carefully chose this time and location because she knew that there was only a small window before the holidays when the resort was unusually slow. Her party would be the highlight of the season

The guest list included the mayor of Carmel, local dignitaries, and a varied selection of movie stars and other rich and famous people. To be sure she accomplished her primary goal, she carefully selected all of Michael's associates and personal friends. Bobbi systematically planned this affair, and was prepared to put an alternate into action if her initial scheme went awry. She scrupulously aligned the dinner seating arrangement to maximize her expectations. The celebrities were invited specifically to mask the intent of her endeavor. She had triumphantly manipulated people into business situations to suit her own needs many times previously, but to bring this many self centered entrepreneurs together for one project was a major coup. Bobbi Azure would soon find out that situations outside her control were taking place, and that soon she would be playing in a different league.

Guy Nestor's limousine was among the first to arrive promptly at seven thirty. He was joined by his son Ian, and Norah Laude. The celebrities were traditionally late in order to be seen. Michael's Las Vegas contingency arrived, as planned, at eight o'clock. He was astonished to see Nugari, Wu and deVillefrance there.

"Hello Michael," Busy said as she approached with Nugari at her side. "I'm so happy to see you again."

"Hello Biz." He turned and uttered a callous, "Nugari."

"You two know each other?" She was truly surprised. "I don't believe that I've had the pleasure." She put out her hand to Darci.

"I would like you to meet Darci," Michael announced. "Darci Orcini. My wife."

Busy stood in complete shock, not knowing what to say.

Nugari moved forward. "I'm Pernicious Nugari, Mrs. Orcini, and I'm pleased to meet you. I didn't know you were married." he said, turning to Michael.

"It was that or her father's shotgun," he joked.

Busy inspected Darci before commenting, "I must say we had no idea." She looked to Michael then to Darci. "Darci. That's an unusual name. Did I pronounce it right?"

"Yes, but you must be used to people . . ."

"Do you know where we are seated, Biz?" he interrupted their volley.

"I believe that you're sitting with Bobbi and Guy, and . . ." She studied his face for a moment. "I can't wait for Bobbi to.. " Her words faded until nothing could be heard.

As they walked to their table, "She doesn't like me," Darci held his arm tightly.

"Remember I told you that I was dating her sister Bobbi?"

"Yes. It's coming back."

Bobbi got up and rushed to embrace Michael. "Michael darling," she sang as she wrapped her arms around his shoulders pulling herself up and intimately close to him.

"This is his wife," Busy proclaimed just as Bobbi started to kiss him.

Bobbi slid down resting on her heels, but still holding on. "Whose wife?"

"My wife, Bobbi." He pulled back. "This is my wife, Darci." He shifted his weight, putting his arm around Darci.

Bobbi quickly composed herself. Choking a little, "Darci?" she managed.

"Yes." She put her hand out.

Bobbi looked at her hand, then to Michael in disbelief, then back to her hand, and reluctantly rendered a very light, unmistakably unwelcome hand shake.

"Excuse me! I must attend to my guests." Bobbi headed toward the Tap Room, and went directly to the ladies room with Busy close behind. "That son of a bitch! How can he do this to me?" she cried.

Busy comforted her. "There, there."

"I'll show him. That bastard. He can't do this to me."

"Pull yourself together. There's nothing you can do right now. Come on dry your eyes, and fix your face. We've got a party to give, and a lot of very important people who expect you to entertain them."

"Okay. Give me a minute." Her voice was toneless. "Damn, damn." Her eyes bore straight into Biz. "The wolf will be at his door."

In less than five minutes Bobbi emerged like a model strutting the runway of the most prestigious fashion house in the land. "I've said it before, Bobbi, you're amazing."

"Let's give the damnedest party ever. I'll show him." She looked at her sister.

"I don't like that look, Bobbi."

"We're going directly into plan 'B'." A conniving expression shown through her soft facade. I have work to do, and you, well, you'll have to sleep with Perni. Real soon!"

"What's going on inside your head?"

"We've got to get Guy and Perni to take over Michael's project."

"You've got a plan?"

"Just be sure to get him to do whatever you want."

The party was a huge success. Perni and Guy got the *pleasure* they believed they had to work for, and assured each other that they would do business in the near future. Wu and deVillefrance were in awe of the celebrities, and did not pursue any business contacts. Ian Nestor was disappointed that Keleigh did not attend. J.T. and the rest remarked that it was a party to remember.

Darci got an uneasy feeling about many of the people involved with the resort, and vowed to herself that she would check them out as soon as they returned to Las Vegas. "I don't like Nugari!" she scowled, as they drove to the airport.

"He's not my favorite person either, but it looks like I may be forced to do business with him and Wu."

"Now there is another piece of work. That guy is about as slimy as they come."

"Where did *you* come from? What happened to my sweet little princess? And.. that comment about Busy's name, where did that come from?"

"Some of these so-called business people get my dander up."

"So I've noticed."

"But, you still love me. Don't you?'

"Dander up or down."

* * * * * * *

The old Orcini Cape Cod home was the ideal setting for their first Christmas. Jason and Stella Tashmit arrived two days before Christmas, and settled in at the Orcini home by the ocean. Vittorio Orcini took Jason Tashmit around the Cape in his small sailboat while the women baked holiday cookies and candies. Michael and Darci trimmed the tree in a traditional old fashion way, with popcorn garland and handmade ornaments. The holidays were filled with a happiness that was long since forgotten.

* * * * * * *

"The ocean looks different than it does at your parents' place," Darci shouted over her shoulder. "Why do you think that is?" She walked to the kitchen where he was preparing sandwiches.

"Oh! I don't know. Maybe it's because the sun rises there and sets here." He tried to be analytical. "Or maybe it's because it's warmer here."

"How come you're so darned logical?"

"Which ocean do you like better?"

"They're so contrary." She eased on a stool wriggling her butt until she was comfortable, put her elbows on the snack bar, and propped her chin. "I think I like the sun rising on the ocean better." She sat straight, placing the palms of her hands on the counter, stiffened her arms as if she was at a podium, and pronounced, "Because it's the beginning of a new day, and we can do anything we want." Stopping to reflect for a brief moment, "The sun setting is just a memory of the day spent." She got off the stool and threw her arms around him. "I like Cape Cod better."

"I'm glad that I'm only logical, and not philosophical."

She punched his arm playfully. "When are we going to eat? I'm starved."

"Now. Get the lemonade and the napkins. I've got the sandwiches and chips."

"Michael?" She looked down at her half-eaten sandwich. "Can I work with you on the resort?" She kept her head down. "I want to help."

"What do you want to do?"

"I'm experienced in real estate. You know?"

"Okay. But, what do you want to do on the project?"

"I can help with the acquisition of the property and the parcel maps, and all sorts of that kind of stuff. It'll free you up to do other things, and, and."

"And what?"

"We.. ll." She drug it out impishly. "You won't have to pay me. Not in money anyway." She moved her foot up and down his leg. "You can take it out in trade."

"The price is right, but I've already got title to the property." He watched her face, "I've also quitclaimed the deeds to my parents. I'll fill you in on all that next week. We'll go to the bank and set up some trusts. Okay?"

"We.. ll." Surprised at his efficiency. "Okay, but what can I do to help?"

"There is a lot of work to do on the financing package. You know? Things like fees, investment returns for the financial partners, and cash flow projections."

"I thought that your CFO was doing that."

"He just set up the preliminary stuff. I still have to work on the final agreements, and then have Hector complete the legal documents."

"Your attorney?"

"Yeah."

"I don't like him. He's sleazy."

"He's an expert on Nevada's gaming law. So we have to put up with Mr. Sleazy Appearance," he assured her of his motives.

"It's more than just not liking his appearance. I don't trust him, Michael."

"So. Do you want to help out with the financial stuff?" He ignored her opinion.

"Sure. You didn't know that I'm pretty good with figures. Did you?"

"Sure do." He undressed her with his eyes.

"What are you going to do about it?"

"About what?"

"Undressing me. You can accomplish more with your hands than with your eyes."

Michael went around the table, took her face in his hands tilting her head back, and kissed her lips. His hands moved down her neck and across her waiting breasts. Finding the bottom of her tee shirt he gently lifted it up exposing her. Darci lifted her arms up around his neck, letting go when the shirt was to her face. She had set the stage, but now he had to orchestrate the play. He carried her to the living room where they made love in front of the fireplace.

"I'm a very good negotiator, Michael. I can meet with Nugari and Wu, and the rest of them. What do you think about that? Huh?" Her head was tight to his chest.

He stroked her hair. "They're ruthless. I told them to go find another project, but they still want to get a part of my project. I think that Nugari is up to something, and I can't put my finger on it." He rambled, "Wu and those Chinese delinquents of his are an ominous bunch, and Nestor is beating a path to my door. I think he wants more than he's willing to talk about. But, maybe you might have a good idea. You just might be able to use your charms to find out what these guys are up to."

Darci lifted her head tossing her hair back. "You really mean it?" Without waiting for his answer, "Oh Michael, I love you. I'll be great, you just wait and see."

"You are great."

"You've got a one track mind, Mr. Michael Orcini."

"It's a good thing that one of us does, Mrs. Darci Orcini."

She sat up, straddling him. "I am greater than you could ever imagine."

They spent the afternoon alternating between making plans for the resort, and making love.

Darci arose early and went upstairs to the kitchen where she prepared her first pot of coffee, Orcini style. She wanted to have it ready when he returned from his run on the beach. She was out on the balcony watching the waves crash on the rocks below when he approached. There was a sharp morning breeze blowing her damp hair across her face, and pushing her sweats tight against her body as she sipped the brew.

"Good morning, darling," he called as he ran up the wooden stairs toward her.

Darci stood motionless as if in a trance. Finally, as he entered the house, continuing out to the deck. "The ocean seems very angry today." She paused to determine why. "It seems to be coming right out of that black cloud way out there, and it doesn't stop until it crashes on the rocks with a vengeance. It doesn't even finish and another is right there pounding, pounding, pounding." Leaning back against him, "This El Nino is not through with us."

In the days that followed, Michael and Darci worked together at their Malibu home. She surprised him with her work efficiency, both mental and physical. She was as opinionated as anyone he had ever encountered. His beautiful new bride had a strong business sense coupled with a composed and unending source of energy.

One day they took a break from work and drove into L.A. There they met with Michael's banker who gave them the recorded land documents. They had lunch with Michael's personal attorney, Nathan Gregory, who had already created trusts in Darci's name, along with quitclaim deeds.

"What if I just married you for *your* money?" She joked.

"You probably have more than I." He enjoyed undressing her with his eyes, knowing every delicious spot along the way. "Besides, I plan on taking it out in trade," he retorted with complete confidence.

"Michael?" She was looking at Nate. "Do you think that I should do the same with my estate?" She turned to meet his surprised face.

"Do what?

"Put all my stuff in your name." Brushing a curl back from his brow.

He looked at Nate, his face questioned without words.

"We can set that up, Darci, if that's what you want. Okay, Michael?"

"It's okay with me, since I only married her for her stuff, anyway."

"You just like the sweet stuff," she exclaimed, kissing him with determination as she leaned forward and teased his thigh with her hand.

"Don't wear out the sweet stuff."

"Never happen."

"Ach hum," Nate sounded, "Darci?"

"I'm busy." She was seducing Michael with her eyes, while circling the small parting of her lips with her tongue.

"Darci!"

"I don't like you," she joked. "Yes I do. I'm just kidding, but sometimes I just can't help myself. You know what I mean?"

"Help me here, Michael."

"You're on your own, Nate. I'm still not used to her antics."

"When you think you are, I'll show you some more," she snickered.

The waitress broke up her playful salvo with a request for a desert order.

"Apple pie," Michael resounded without a moments thought, "with ice cream."

Nate and Darci declined, but she would have some of his.

"Have you met the vultures that Michael is talking to about the financing?" She quizzed Nathan as she returned to her silent, obstinate seduction of Michael.

Nathan Gregory did not know what to do with her pointed question, frosted with her obvious concern for Michael. He perused her face for any indication of a direction that she might be taking. Darci prolonged her silence. Finally, unable to decipher her meaning he spoke. "What makes you think that they're vultures?"

"Nugari wants the whole magilla for himself." Her face became flushed as she continued, "and, and, that, that slimy Wu creature." Her amorous subjugation turned to rage. Darci stiffened in her chair, and stared into Nate's eyes with the fire of her ancestors. "I wouldn't give the sweat off my ti. . . ." She looked apologetically at Michael, "Well, I wouldn't. They're crooks, Michael. They want your project, and I won't let them take it from you." Her heart in her throat, she slowly settled back with a sigh. What if Michael should hate her for being so outspoken?

He set the moment. "I love you sweet stuff." He slid his hand to hers, "These guys are in for a rough time. I'm glad that you're on my side." He changed the subject, and took control of the situation. "Nate, will you make arrangements to get together with my pugnacious partner, and set her estate in order?" He had a twinkle in his eye, "Don't forget your suit of armor."

"And, don't forget that Mafia grandmother. Now, there's real trouble."

"I'm amazed. What do you know about her?" Michael asked.

"See! Nate. Someone's got to take care of him. Don't you agree?" She didn't expect an answer. It was her turn to change the subject. She became seductive once more. "Don't worry, darling. Darci's here to watch over you. How's your pie?" She stuck her fork into the side with the ice cream, capturing their attention with her sensual savoring. "Yummy!" Her eyes closed. "Yum." An elusive glance, "Like you, Michael."

* * * * * * *

They reorganized the guest room at Darci's house into a home office for Michael. Darci made sure that it wasn't too comfortable. If he wanted to relax, he would have to go to another part of the house. Her need to maintain control of her own life spilled over into their relationship. Her charge was subtle and undetected by Michael. Without reservation she directed their personal and social activities with ease and little objection from him, except for the lovemaking. That was where she wanted Michael to dominate her, which he did with great pleasure. She had the guest room redecorated in a Southwestern motif with strong accents of rust, teal, and blue. Blue was his favorite color. The exquisite Indian maiden doll he had given her was placed in a corner across from his workspace, right next to an antique rack with the Jack Nicklaus golf clubs she gave him as a wedding present. A state of the art computer monitor took command of the workspace. With a view from the window to his side, she knew he would be contented enough to work, but sure that he would have to get up and move about from time to time. The workspace was large enough for the second chair upholstered in an obviously feminine color. She maintained her home office in the small alcove. She was comfortable there.

* * * * * *

It would be Spring in a few weeks, and the selection of funding partners had become more difficult. Nugari and Wu called Michael or J.T. every day with attempts to secure their own individual position. Guy Nestor was ready if Michael would concede to an unusual agreement that would give Nestor control until the initial investment was recaptured. Hans was still taking more time than Michael could handle. deVillefrance hated posturing between Ceres, Wu and Nugari, but worked as many angles as he could. He figured that the deal must go with Ceres, but was concerned now that Wu had introduced the Chinese Camorra. They were the most unusual combination of mercenaries that Claude had ever seen. He knew there was going to be a war, and quickly recognized that he was not a soldier. He saw the conflict between Ceres and Wu from the start, but always figured that they would balance the control issue to accomplish their own needs. It was time to use Nugari and his skills to negotiate the consortium.

In the populous anxiety of the days that followed, he never suspected that the others were planning to remove him from the financial equation. Even Bobbi suggested to Nugari that deVillefrance was unnecessary to the project, and that he would only get in the way. Claude deVillefrance blindly continued to ingratiate the cast of characters, attempting to bring them all together. He was not a patient man. His naiveté fueled the agony of his expectancy as he waited for these people to come together. Intuitively he knew that he must train himself as a sponge, to absorb the nuances of the others, and combine the patterns into a workable arrangement. Thoughts raced through his head adding to the apprehension. Must he bow to Nugari? Perhaps, but it had to look like Nugari needed him to make the deal. Only recognition now. He decided that there must be another way to accomplish his task without the pretense of friendship with Nugari. The humiliation of kowtowing to Nugari and Ceres had to change. His mind was on overload. It was as if a light came on. Of course,

Orcini's new wife. He would go to her, and stand before her as a man who could help her husband with his project. Claude praised himself for the brilliance of his idea.

* * * * * *

Darci was disturbed, but strangely excited when the image of a Greek sea captain showed up unannounced at her Las Vegas office. Maggie, the protector, made him sit and wait while she eased in behind the glass partition that separated the reception area from Darci's small office. Closing the door, "There's a Mr. deVillefrance here to see you. Says he met you at a party in Carmel, and wondered if you had a few minutes." He sure looks weird. D'ya want me to get rid of him? I can tell him you're very busy."

"He's someone that Michael might be working with on his project at the lake."

"Really?" she questioned, "what's he do?"

"He introduces people with money to people who need money."

"Oh!" still unsure, "What kind of money?"

"Lots of money. Gazillions."

"But he sort of looks like a bum. How?"

"I don't know, but I want to find out everything about this bum."

"You ready to see him now?"

"Yes, but first I would like a cup of your finest coffee." She smiled at Maggie. "If I'm going to look out for *my* Mr. Orcini, then I want to drink like *my* Mr. Orcini."

"I'll make a fresh pot, and *then* I'll send him in. Okay?"

"Yes. Thanks." deVillefrance carefully laid out how he became involved with Nugari and Wu, and how Ceres fit into the picture. The entire tale was tainted with lies that appeared so very plausible on the surface that he was sure she would not hesitate to fall into his web. He planned the deception to the smallest detail so she would intervene with Michael.

Darci watched his movements like a hawk watches her prey. She thought how every word he spoke must have been meant for someone else. It was like a foreigner who just gave his life history in a language she could not understand. She wanted to tell him how sleazy she thought he was, and that he should take his pack of lies somewhere else. She sat back in her chair looking incredulously at the time just spent. Then she knew why she had to be tolerant.

He watched her as she savored the last of her coffee. She dominated the moment. Slowly she swiveled her chair. First right, then left, pausing momentarily off center, just enough to look past him, then she continued to her extreme left side. She had taken him off guard without the least effort.

She had to be tolerant because she wanted to know everything about these people, and exactly what they wanted from Michael. "You were right to come here today, Mr. deVillefrance." She wanted him to think she believed his story. "I will be helping my husband with the contract negotiations," she looked over his shoulder, "with the successful financial partner candidates."

"Thank you, Missus Orcini. May I call you Darci?"

"No," she looked him straight in the eyes, "not until I'm in a comfortable business relationship with you."

"Well then," he rose to leave, "I'll not take any more of your time."

Darci looked up to see him struggle his large frame out of the chair.

"I trust that you'll tell Mr. Orcini that I'm here to help in any way that I can."

"I'll tell him that you were here. Goodbye."

Maggie watched him leave, and sat herself down in front of Darci.

Darci was starring towards the ceiling in the corner of the room. "There's a spider in the corner weaving his web."

"I don't see any.. " She glanced back to see Darci's devilish smile. "Oh! You mean the insect that just left. Huh?"

"It's time to get to work on all the rest of the spiders. I'm not going to let Michael get caught in any of their webs." She took a pad of paper and began to write the names of the people to be investigated.

"Darci?"

"Yes."

"Are you writing what I think you're writing?"

"What? she already knew."

"I have *all* the names of *all* those sleaze bags, and I've started checking them out."

"Let's see what you have."

Maggie went to her desk, and returned with an expandable folder with a mountain of papers and photographs.

"Where did you get all this?"

"I was talking to Charlie, and he said that his friend, the Police Commissioner, had a dossier on most of the guys. This one," she retrieved an official government document, "on Nugari, I got from Colonel Rojam's office."

"Michael's friend?"

"Well.. actually his girl friend, Traci."

Darci stared a blank stare.

"She's been a friend of mine for quite some time now." She became defensive. "Charlie introduced us."

"This is only military stuff," she grimaced. "*I-need-dirt,*" She emphasized, "civilian stuff, ex wives, business deals gone wrong. Ya know?"

Darci picked up another folder. "What's this?"

"That's on Jami Wu," she said proudly. "I got that from a friend of mine in the State Department." Maggie swung her shoulders back and forth in a little rooted dance.

"This is great stuff. Who or what are the Camorra?"

"They are like the Chinese Mafia."

"Bingo!"

"This one's on Donna Una Maria Antonia Ceres. She lives in a mansion they call Casa Trinacria. That's the ancient name for Sicily. They say she married this guy, Ceres, so she could come to America, and then had him killed so she could take over his fortune. Some say that she actually murdered him herself."

"Sounds like a real dreamboat. Do they think that she's Mafia?"

"Everybody thinks so, but nobody has any proof."

Let's see what we can dig up." She stood up thrusting her shoulders back and her breasts forward in a movement of authority. "We can do it!"

* * * * * *

On a starlit evening eight days after deVillefrance's visit, Darci sat across from Michael on the deck of their Malibu home. She was anxious to share the information she gathered on his potential business partners. She wore her most unattractive sweatshirt and baggy pants with paint from her last decorating venture. She knew how easy it was for her to distract Michael, but today she didn't want any diversions.

"Coffee?"

"Thanks. What in the.. ? What is *that* you're wearing?"

"Just an *old something* I found laying around. I thought I might seduce you. Pretty sexy, huh?"

"Uh.. right--tt." He drug it out in disbelief. "What are you up to?"

"What makes you say that? Just because I put on something pretty for you, you gotta think that I'm up to something?" she questioned playfully.

"That outfit is so terrible, you might just have to take it off." It was his turn to play with her. "The thought of that seems to make it very sexy. Turn around. I want to see if you have any paint on your rear."

"Michael," she sang sweetly, "I have something serious to talk to you about."

"I've got it. Those aren't really paint spots.. they're a great big.. "

"Damn it Michael Orcini!" she shouted, "get serious." The pout that he had come to know so well appeared on her pursed lips.

He put his cup on the small table beside him, and grabbed her hips pulling her down to sit on his lap. "Hi, Gorgeous."

"I dress frumpy so you'll listen to me seriously, and what do you do? You get amorous." The pout came back. "Maybe I shouldn't ever wear any clothes," she caught his smile. "Never mind."

"What's so important that you have to be serious? Are you pregnant?"

"Nope, not yet." She kissed his cheek. "Wanna practice.. later.. after my serious stuff is done?"

"What makes you think that practice isn't serious?"

"It is, and so it my stuff."

"I know. You've got some pretty serious stuff." He fondled her breast.

"Well, I guess we better just forget *any* of my serious stuff," she started to pull away, "until you can get serious."

"I'm sorry, but I just can't help myself."

"I know, and I love you too, but we got to talk sometimes."

"Okay. Let's see what you got. Oops, sorry. I mean.. "

"Never mind." She got up and retrieved her case from just inside the door, "I've been working for you.. like we talked.. okay.. so.. okay.. here's what I've been doing."

Michael had never seen her so nervous. He sat patiently while she rummaged through her case.

Darci glanced up and cautiously grimaced. "You're not going to be too happy with this stuff. First let me tell.. no.. I'd better wait.. I.. uh.. "

"Wait for what?"

"For you to see this stuff." She took the papers out, and neatly arranged them on the small table next to him, rearranging to fit some sort of an order of importance.

Michael watched her intently, but couldn't see past the seriousness of her face. "You're extremely beautiful when you work.

Did I ever tell you that?" He watched as her expression remained focused on her task. "I could sit here and watch you forever." Somehow he was sure she wouldn't answer, but asked, "Are you listening to me?

"No." She moved one last paper into place. "Are you ready?"

"Sure, let's see what you have been working on."

Darci took each group of documents and explained their meaning to Michael. She started with the people that she considered having the least impact on Michael's predisposition with getting the financial partner for the resort.

He listened as she went over each report page by page, describing the situation as she envisioned it. He was amazed at her painstaking attention to detail. When she was finished, she asked, "I'm not going to be killed if I know too much, am I?"

"It seems to me that you asked that very same question on our way to the Cayman Islands. Your wonderful imagination is only surpassed by the absolute wonder of you."

"Michael, I'm dead serious. This stuff is dynamite. These guys play rough, except for Guy Nestor and Hans, and the vote's not in on those two yet. Does this stuff really still happen?" She tried to catch her breath, but was too emotional to stop the questions. "Must you do business with these guys? Can't you just go to the bank and get a loan?" She looked pleadingly at him. "I don't want you to come home someday with your legs broken at the knees or maybe worse." Her face became drawn with despair.

"Deo juvante, my darling, we will see it through. Deo juvante."

"Save your Italian for the Mafioso." She set her brow and looked enraged.

"It's not Italian, my love. It's Latin."

"What's it mean?"

"With Gods help, my love." He smiled, "I added the last part."

"You mustn't do any business with those crooks. Promise me. You must promise. Tell me you won't."

He studied her for a long time before answering. She was shaking, and he wasn't sure if it was because of her obvious anger or some unknown fear. His voice was resonant, and almost in concert with her pulsing frame when he finally spoke. "I've come too far to turn back now. Don't worry, I'll be just fine." He had never lied to her before, but he saw her terror, and could not allow her to carry the pain. It was the same anguish that was in her face, that first night on the highway.

"I don't like any of them. Can't you at least wait for Hans? Promise me that you will have your detective friend look at this stuff and arrest them, or something," she pleaded.

"All right, I'll have him check. But if we don't move on this soon, well.. I don't think I have to tell you the consequences." He got up, and reached for her hand. "Let's go in, darling."

"I'll be there in a moment."

* * * * * * *

It was windy and cold, and it had been raining for more than a week the afternoon they returned to Las Vegas. A chill ran through her and deep into her bones as they drove up the winding road to their home. It was frightening.. frightening because she knew that it had nothing to do with the weather. She silently damned the entire resort project, and all those corrupt, power and money hungry bastards who wanted to take it from Michael. Suddenly, as if by a vision, she saw the resort in all its splendor with her name on the very top. Darci-O. She was terrified, and shivered like someone lost in a snowstorm. The chill permeated so deep into her that it seemed to freeze her very soul. What did this mean? She wondered why her name was on the resort building, and why did this picture seem so real. She decided not to tell Michael of this vision, or about the feelings of freezing. He would laugh at her imagination, and tell her that was what he liked about her. No, it was better left unspoken. She would only tell her journal.

She started to get out of the car when Michael said. "Let me put the car in the garage first, I don't want you to get wet and freeze."

She looked away and muttered a shaky, "Okay."

"You look tired, darling. Go on in. I'll get our things."

"Do you want some coffee?"

"Absolutely."

Michael checked in with the office. Martha said that Keleigh was very upset and wanted to see him as soon as he returned. "Tell her that I'll see her tomorrow at the office." He thought for a moment, "Set meetings with Nugari, Wu and Ceres at the office as soon as possible, but first I have to meet with J.T. and Hector. Oh.. get all the rest of the crew together for a staff meeting."

"What time do you.. ?"

"I'll be in all day, so use your discretion.. oh, and find out when Guy Nestor can be in Las Vegas. I want to see him. Tell him that I have some ideas, and want to go over his proposal. Tell him that.. ," he looked over at Darci to be sure that she could hear, "tell him that I want to explore some new possibilities, that I want to revisit his proposal, but don't make it sound like I'm too anxious.

"You've got it boss. Are you at home in Las Vegas?"

"Yes. You can reach me here. I don't want to talk to anyone, except you, today."

"I'll take care of everything here. You take care of the missus. What time can I expect you in the morning?"

"I'll be in at eight."

She was standing at his side when he finished the call. She snuggled her hip to his shoulder, and gently pulled his head to her breast. "I love you, Michael Orcini."

* * * * * * *

The next day, while Michael was at the office, Darci continued her investigation of Wu, and discovered his real relationship with Ceres. Her source came out of the blue with shocking information that set her on her heel. During a recent lunch with Father Martin, Pastor Jim learned that Donna Ceres was putting a lot of money into a project at Sundance Lake. Her Pastor was concerned that it might be with Michael's project, and wanted Darci to intercede. "She is a very questionable person," he tried to be diplomatic, "some say that she has ties to the Mafia. What do you know about her? You should tell Michael this news."

Darci decided to keep this critical information to herself until she had documented proof to show Michael. She made Pastor Jim promise to keep their secret until the right time. Faithful Maggie didn't have to be sworn to secrecy, but promised to nag her when the pressure got too be too much.

"There was a call from a Mr. Roberts. Says that he's a friend of Norah Laude, and wanted to see if you had time for lunch. He said that he was going to be in town for a couple of days this week."

"Norah Laude?" she pondered. "Oh yes, Busy."

"Busy?"

"That's her nickname. She's Michael's old girlfriend's sister. I met her at the party in Carmel. I wonder what they're up to?" She looked out the window. "Bobbi.. " she waived her arm as if to shoe a fly, and turned back to Maggie, "that's his old girlfriend.. " she gulped, "we--ll, she wasn't very happy to find out that Michael and I were married. I'll bet she has something to do with Roberts. Now come to think of it, she invited all the people that might be involved with the resort to her party. This is starting to make some sense. I think that she wants to horn in on the deal. Did he leave a number?"

"Yes, but you shouldn't.. "

"Let me have the number."

Maggie gave her the number in the midst of stern instructions not to call.

Darci met Dave Roberts for lunch at a small restaurant next to his hotel in downtown Las Vegas. It was off the beaten path, and seemed to be appropriate for the situation. She noticed how unsettled he was as he explained his relationship with 'Biz', and how he could be an asset to Michael in the development of his resort. Darci watched the unobtrusive way the self-proclaimed golf pro presented himself, and how she loathed his impertinence. Everything about him reminded her of the filthy insolence that she associated with Nugari. They were like two peas in a pod. They would sell their soul to the highest bidder, but right now he was trying to sell her. Why? She was curious, but not enough to bring herself down to his level. She would not ask what he wanted her to do. Her mouth no longer had the shape of tactfulness. Her lips set tight. He saw it.

She excused herself to go to the ladies room, but she just wanted to feel superior and confident . . . confident that he would not attempt to bribe her in any way. She purposefully lingered in the powder room while setting a plan into action. She would turn the tables on him. Yes that's it. She went back to the table.

He had almost seemed like a human being, and not the centaur she just had lunch with a few moments ago. She did not apologize, but instead responded to his interview as she remained standing. "I'm a very selfish woman, Mr. Roberts. I always expect to get paid for anything I do. Don't misunderstand, I mean anything and everything." She was proud of her pagan directive, and the power it seemed to have over him. "Call me at my office when you decide exactly what it is that you want from me. Goodbye." She left before he could respond.

* * * * * * *

After the next two exhausting months it was rewarding to see progress in the resort development. There was a renewed interest for Michael to work with the Chinese, especially with their acquiescence to make changes in the agreements. Everything changed but the players, giving Michael more options. Nugari and Wu were still trying to cut out Ceres. Ceres and deVillefrance had maneuvered the Chinese into a subordinate position with their latest proposal, and deVillefrance was still working every angle.

Bobbi was determined to get her retribution. She always held tight to things that *she knew* belonged to her. Michael was one of these hypothetical possessions. Roberta Azure, a disdained woman, was ready to take action. True to her tradition where she succeeded by creating an atmosphere of unseen competition among her adversaries, she had Biz introduce Dave Roberts to Nugari as a special emissary to the Donna and Wu. With a false dossier to give him credibility, he would keep his finger on the pulse of the resort development. His ostensibly pleasant and casual attitude towards both men and women of a higher stature than his own, gave him a decisive edge. After being seduced by Busy, Nugari agreed that Dave was a good complement to their combined cause.

Guy Nestor had reinforced his offer with a cash incentive for Michael if he could guarantee that Keleigh would be included as a part of the deal. Michael refused to make a commitment based on the Keleigh contingency. Keleigh had conceded to the sublime achievement as the casino operator under Guy, even though it did not include Michael as she thought it should. It was after her disastrous meeting with Michael when she found out about Darci, that she yielded to the job for what it was, and euphorically found a deep sense of belonging to these strangers. She was utterly shameless in her outrage, and castigated Michael, in front of the entire staff, for not telling her about the wedding. He found out what everyone else suspected about Keleigh, but he was too blind to see. Upset with Nestor's demands and the current turn of events, Michael continued to hold out.

Hans Gruber worked desperately, hoping to complete his gathering of funding commitments before Nugari put the ultimate pressure on Michael. At this point it looked like Nugari was holding all the aces.

* * * * * * *

Once again, El Nino had unmercifully discharged its fury along the entire west coast of the United States. It was only a matter of time before it would return and unleash its wrath on Malibu Beach. Michael kept in close communication with the Sheriff and his oceanfront neighbors. He prepared himself for an immediate trip, and had his bag ready at the front door. Most of his files for the resort were in his laptop computer or on disks.

Sheltered from the rain that had been falling all day, Darci stood on the deck listening to the wind, desperately trying to sort out the feelings that haunted her. She knew it was useless for her to argue with him about the hazards of driving to Malibu in the storm. If only there were a way to quiet her fears and not hurt him. If only the time didn't go by so slowly when he was gone. If only.. if only.. she started to miss him terribly, and he hadn't even left. What if.. what if.. what if she never saw him again? She must let him know just how much she needed and depended on him. But if he knew her weakness, he might never, never love her again. As she turned to go in she became aware of him watching her. Now, more than ever she was aware of her charm and the affect it had on him, she decided that the risk was worth taking. They did not speak. Darci took Michael's hand, much like the first time, and led him to *her* bed.

The rain was falling even harder than the night before when they awoke in each other's arms. "I love you, Michael Orcini," she kissed him softly, "and don't you ever forget it." She rolled over on top of him and loved him as passionately as any woman had ever done since the beginning of time. When they finished, she lay quietly by his side and told him of her fears.

"I love you, Darci-O. More than anything in the whole world."

"What did you say?" She sprang up, turned away from him, and started to cry.

"I said that I love you. What's wrong?"

He called her by the same name that she saw on the resort in her imagination. 'Darci-O'. She wondered how he could know a name out of her vision. This is one fear that she just couldn't share with him.

"Why did you call me Darci-O?"

"Did I say that? I don't have the slightest notion."

"But you never.. "

"I guess it's because you're Darci Orcini. Darci-O. Is that okay?"

"Sure, but.. "

"You're just stressed. I'll drive very carefully. It's open highway most of the way. Besides, you need some time away from me, so you'll appreciate me more."

"I don't like it when you're away. I want you here, so I can take care of you." She never *wanted* to take care of anyone before. For the first time in her life she was ready to commit to a desired responsibility to care for another human being. Not just doing things for family or friends, because they were family or friends, but actually caring for someone because she wanted to be a completion of his existence. Getting married was fun and exciting, but this, this was the reason she was born. He was her soul mate, and they were destined to be together forever. She was as sure as the sun came up every morning.

"I'll be right here with you, darling," he pressed his hand to her breast. "Take care of me, here, in your heart."

"Oh, Michael, don't you know by now that I always do?" It was time for her to get up. We'll have a big breakfast," glancing over her shoulder, "then we can make love before you leave me."

"I want to get to the bottom of this," he said, slapping her playfully on the butt.

"You will." She picked his shirt from the floor and put it on as she left.

The drive to Malibu was slow and arduous in the pouring rain. The freeway was jammed as he came to the San Fernando Valley. He deviated from his normal route, headed toward Topanga Canyon Boulevard, and down through the west end of the valley. The rain subsided, but now the wind howled between the red rocks, and ominous black clouds blanketed the sky as far as he could see. Shortly after he reached the canyon entrance the foreboding cloak released a downpour that made it impossible to proceed. He found a turnout and parked. Lightning was not a common site in these canyons, but today El Nino was breaking all the rules. Radio reception was virtually non-existent, so Michael attempted to use his cell phone to check on traffic. He couldn't make a connection. It looked like it was going to be awhile. He tilted the seat of the Explorer, and took a nap.

It was still raining when he woke, but not as hard as before. The clock on the dash told him that he had slept for more than an hour. He tried his cell phone again, but to no avail. Once he was back on the road it became apparent that the rain had brought about rock and mud slides. He readjusted his position leaning deliberately over the steering wheel, contemplating the possibilities at each turn. He smiled when he saw the small ceramic angel that Darci must have attached to the center console. It seemed odd that he hadn't noticed it before now. He dodged fallen rocks and some minor mud slides for the remainder of the distance to the coast. Now all he had to do was get to the house.

The damage to Casa Orcini by the Sea, as Darci called it, was limited to the stairs that led down to the beach. The entire lower half, from the sand to the intermediate landing, was gone. The rest of the stairway, above the landing, was hanging from the side of the house. It would go down to the sea with the next barrage, unless he set some supports. His neighbors had sand bagged the areas that traditionally were most susceptible to the waves and all along the entrance from the road.

He had been there only a few minutes when a couple of nearby residents appeared. One of them asked, "Need some help with those stairs, Michael? We should probably lash them back to the house. I'll get some rope." He left, but the other, a teenaged boy, remained.

"What can I do to help, Mr. Orcini?"

"There's a block and tackle in the garage. We'll need it to pull the stairs."

The three worked until it was dark, and the neighbors left as quickly as they came. There was no need to say more than *thanks guys*. There was an unwritten mandate in the colony that preceded any formality. They helped each other against the weather. It was expected.

The phone was ringing when he went in. "Hello," he said in a tired but clear voice.

"Michael, where have you been? I've been trying to get through to you for hours. Are you all right? Did you get there okay?" she said foolishly. "Of course you did. But where have you been? I've been worried about you. Tell me that you're Okay."

"I'm okay."

"Is that it?" She raised her voice.

"No, but I'm very tired. It was a long drive, and the stairs to the beach were damaged. Some neighbors came over, and we just finished securing them to the house."

"That sounds kinky." She laughed.

"What's kinky?"

"Tying the neighbors to the house, silly. What are you going to do with them?"

"You are doing it to me again."

"If I were doing *It* to you, you'd.. "

"Okay, my love. How are you?"

"Better now."

They talked for an hour or so. He dried himself as he told her about the storm coming, and how he had to stay and help everyone in the colony. Darci talked about all the things that they were going to do together when the resort was finished.

Suddenly she had an outright disregard for the present. The future was most important in her mind.

Generally, Darci would not have given it a second thought. Today, now, was always the most important time for her. But somehow she knew that there must be more than today. There must be a time when they would be together without the strain of business and relationships on their backs.

"There's someone at the door. Probably the neighbors. I'll call you tomorrow."

"Goodbye, Michael."

"Goodnight, Sweetheart, I'll talk to you in the morning."

Bobbi was standing at the door, exactly as she was a few weeks

ago, drenched and cold and crying. "My car stopped, and I didn't
know what to do."

"Bobbi! What are you doing here? Let's get you out of those
wet clothes."

"Well.. I.."

"Never mind. It can wait. Go into the bedroom and put on
something dry. You can tell me your story later," he ordered her, "I
can hardly wait to hear this one."

"Hear what?"

"Never mind, I'll get you some brandy."

After ten or fifteen minutes he became concerned. "Are you
alright?"

"Why don't you come here and find out for yourself."

"Your brandy is getting cold."

She sauntered out or the bedroom as she had done many times
before, a portrait of beauty and excitement. "How does brandy get
cold?" She struck one of her usual poses, exposing her thigh from
under one of his silk shirts, knowing precisely how to make it
drape in the most sensual way.

Roberta Azure was not the kind of person to drop in unannounced, but here she was again, in the middle of a storm. Cold
and wet, and beautiful.

"What brings you to Malibu, and where is your car? I looked
outside. It's not anywhere in sight. What are you up to?" He slid
behind the kitchen counter, "well--ll."

"I just wanted to see you," she said honestly, and climbed on
a barstool.

"But what are you doing here in Malibu?'

"I drove down to see you."

"From Big Sur?"

"Well, not *all* the way from Big Sur."

"Roberta?" He was getting irritated with her chicanery.

"I was staying with the Robinsons for a few days," she pointed
past her left ear, "up the road, you know."

"But you don't like them, Bobbi," he said quizzically.

"We became good friends."

"Him or her?"

"Both."

"Why are you staying with the Robinsons?"

"Why must you always be so precise?" she returned his interrogation.

"Roberta As--ure," he drug out a definite command, "why are you here?"

She bent over the counter exposing her breasts. "Becauz--zz--zz." she sang.

He frowned at her, trying to ignore her seduction.

"Well to tell the truth.. "

"That would be a novelty," he interrupted.

"I knew that you would be down here because of the storm and all--so--oo, I arranged to have car trouble right in front of their house, and they invited me to stay with them until my car is better." She wiggled a little on the stool. "Are you happy to see me?"

"There's nothing wrong with your car?"

"Of course not silly. I just switched a few spark plugs down the road, and *voila*. Pretty good idea, huh."

"You've gone to a lot of trouble to see me. What do you want?"

"I told you, Michael darling. I just wanted to see you. It's been a long time. Can't I see an old friend if want to, without having to have a reason?"

"You've never done anything without a reason," he gazed at her half exposed breasts, "not as long as I've known you." His eyes moved to hers, "Cover yourself. We're not boyfriend-girlfriend anymore. I'm a married man now."

"Tsk.. tsk. Do my bare tits bother you?"

"You know they do, so please cover up."

"We can still play, even though you went off and did something dumb."

"It wasn't dumb."

"You hardly know her, and we're good together."

"You're right, Bobbi, we *were* good together, but that's changed now."

"How is it changed? Because of a little piece of paper? No! You're still the same, and so am I. We both want the same thing. Money, power, and sex. And I know that you still want me. I can see it in your eyes." She slid off the stool, undoing the one button that held the shirt in place. "See. This is what you need."

Michael fixed his eyes on her hardened nipples, and began to move restlessly behind the counter. "You're a beautiful and desirable woman, Miss Azure."

"Desirable woman.. humm? So, d'ya want those desires fulfilled?" She still hadn't moved toward him. She wanted him to make the all-important gesture.

He moved from behind the counter, and took her chin in his hand. She lifted her eyes to meet his. He kissed her lightly on the lips, and moved his hand to her waiting breast, tenderly massaging her nipple. Softly. "You'll always be sexy to me." His voice became stern, " Now get dressed and go back to the Robinsons." He walked away.

Stunned. Bobbi shouted, "You son of a bitch," Tears streamed down her cheeks, "You'll pay for this, you bastard. You can't just throw me away." She stormed into the bedroom. "I'll get even, just you wait and see. I'll get even."

In a few minutes she came out still wearing his shirt, but now it was tucked into a pair of dungarees. Her hair was set in a small ponytail, and she was wearing a golf cap she bought for him at Pebble Beach. The calm facade was covering her internal rage. Her voice was sweet, "I'm going now, Ciao." With a small sweet smile, matching her voice, she walked to him, and kissed the air next to his cheek. "I always get what I want." Her eyes penetrated his, and he knew she was going to be a problem. "I'll be seeing you."

Michael was relieved that she was gone, but the look in her eyes stayed with him.

* * * * * * *

During the weeks that followed her party in Carmel, Roberta Azure became obsessed with her plot to sabotage Michael's resort development. At first she only wanted to profit by her involvement with Guy Nestor. But since she lost Michael to Darci, she put her new plan into high gear. Her scheme involved Nugari and Wu, but she had no concept of their connection with Ceres.

She hated them, these crooked smiling wheeler-dealers, who wanted to control all the arrangements. Especially Guy Nestor, whom she must sleep with to get what she wanted. Oh, how she hated sleeping with him. Not because he was undesirable, but because he was a means to an end. Why did Michael go off and marry someone he hardly knew? She had a revelation. She would invite his bride to lunch, and pretend to be her friend. All her life she had to fight for what she wanted, and she still wanted Michael. She was sure that Darci was only a whim, and that he would tire of her when he found out that she was just after his money. Positive that Michael was naive, Bobbi resolved that there must be an alternate plan. Somewhere, from the back of her mind came a notion. She pondered it.. she would succeed. She was determined to be by his side when it was over. She vowed that they would be together.

Busy went on ahead to Las Vegas and rented a furnished condominium. She asked Perni to make arrangements for a tour of the Sundance Lake property. She knew that he was still trying to impress her, in spite of the fact that they had become intimate on several occasions. He scheduled the use of a yacht for an entire day, and found it an exceedingly easy task by using Guy Nestor's company name. So easy that he arranged for a limousine, and a catered lunch on the yacht.

Guy Nestor flew into Carmel where Bobbi joined him. They had lunch at a small café nearby, and then flew to Las Vegas. He was disappointed that she was sharing a condo with Busy, but graciously dropped her off on the way to his hotel. He was convinced that she was genuinely interested in him as a lover and friend. But she concealed her true feelings, like an actor playing the part of her life.

Bobbi rushed into the condo almost knocking Busy down. "I must make some phone calls before we go out to the Lake."

"Well, don't say hello," Busy planted her feet firm with her fists on her hips, "I'm only your sister."

"Sorry." They exchanged their ritual of kissing the air next to each other's cheeks.

"Who do you have to call in such a hurry?"

"Darci."

"Darci?" she questioned, "Michael's Darci?"

"Yes, I want to take her out to lunch," she said as a matter of fact. "We must become friends, or this whole thing won't work."

"I don't like the look in your eyes."

She fumbled with the phone book. "What's her last name anyway?"

"Orcini." Busy rendered a snide, lip-curling smile.

"Right."

Darci picked up after the first ring, hoping it was Michael. "Hello," came a soft sexy vociferation.

"Oh, boy," was the return. "Uh, hello. Darci?"

"Yes."

"This is Roberta Azure, Michael's friend from Big Sur. We met at my party. "

Darci didn't know how to respond.

"At Pebble Beach. A few weeks ago."

"Yes, I remember. I'm just surprised to hear from you."

"I'm surprised too. Believe me. But I'm in town and I thought it would be a good thing if we had lunch or something."

Perplexed she answered. "Well, I guess, sure why not."

"It's settled then. Tomorrow. At one. I'll pick you up at your office."

"I'll be working at home, tomorrow."

"That's fine. Give me the directions."

Darci gave her the address and her usual directions.

"I'm looking forward to.. I'll see you tomorrow. Goodbye."

"Goodbye." came a bewildered response.

Norah Laude sat mesmerized. She didn't seem to understand what possessed her sister, what drove her to this sweet revenge, this passion to punish Michael for being human. Why couldn't she just confine her actions to the business at hand? It all seemed so unnecessary, a lot of effort to get even. She had to ask, "Why, Bobbi?"

"Someone has to teach him."

"Teach him what?"

"You know . . . what it's all about."

"And, just what is it all about, dear sister?"

"I have to get ready to go to the lake."

"You don't have to get ready right now, and you know it."

"Michael and I, well.. you know.. we.. we were.. " She couldn't finish.

"You and Michael were screw buddies, and that's all."

"We were more than that, you just don't understand. I loved him." She became enraged, "We were going to.. that son of a bitch." Trembling, she walked to the window and pulled back the curtain, "He was going to take me to the Cayman Islands before she showed up. I was supposed to be involved with him on the resort. That.. that.. that rapscallion isn't going to get away with it."

"Rapscallion? Now you're sounding like gramps, and you remember the kind of trouble he used to get into."

"Rapscallion, smapscallion! I'm going to get even with that.. o--hhh. Damn him."

"Don't do anything that you'll regret, Bobbi."

"Sure."

"Promise?"

The chauffeur arrived promptly on time. "Miss Laude?"

"No, I'm her sister," Bobbi flirted," Who are you?"

"I'm your driver. I'm here to take you to meet Mr. Nugari."

"Biz. Are you expecting a driver?"

"What?" She shouted from the bedroom.

"Did what's his name say that he was sending a car?"

Busy came into the living room. "No. He just said that he'd pick us up."

Bobbi whispered to Busy, "He's cute, what do you think?"

"Not a good idea," she whispered back, looking around Bobbi. "He does have a cute butt. We'd better go" She walked toward him. "Where are you supposed to take us?"

"We will meet Mr. Nugari and Mr. Nestor at their hotel." He executed a slight bow with a courteous gesture, suggesting that they follow him. "Ladies, if you please."

"I please." Bobbi winked at him, and brushed his hand with her derrière as she turned and paused, "Coming Biz?" She looked back at him, and winked again. He did not move his hand. "Let's go." She exited with Busy close behind.

* * * * * *

The yacht was positioned at the dock ready for their excursion. A ruddy sailor appeared on deck, walked to the guardrail, and looked out over the lake. He seemed more like a Greek sea captain than a sophisticated yacht captain.

Nugari rushed ahead of the others. "What are you doing here?" he demanded of the unkempt boatman.

"The captain is an old friend from Southern California. I figured that it was only a matter of time before you made your move. You're very predictable. You know?"

"Commodore deVillefrance. It's *so good* to see you again," Bobbi articulated in her best yacht club, nasal, vernacular.

"Miss Azure. It is *indeed* a pleasure." He bowed slightly, since she had not extended her hand. He knew, all too well, the drill and its opportunity for rejection.

Guy and Busy were right behind Bobbi, commenting on the natural beauty of the setting for the resort in the middle of the desert. "But it's so far away from everything. Why, it's out here in the middle of the desert," Busy observed.

"Everything's out here in the middle of the desert," Guy Nestor explained. *"Las Vegas* is out here in the middle of the desert," he emphasized.

The captain maneuvered the boat out onto the lake. They sailed around the entire perimeter, stopping for a late afternoon snack in a small cove. Pernicious Nugari pointed out the entire plan for development of all the lake property. The others were certainly impressed by his knowledge of the master plan.

It was time for Bobbi to take over the reins. She laid out her plan to get Guy and Perni involved without Wu and Ceres. She included deVillefrance, but only because he was there. Her plan did not include him. She didn't know, even though the highest bidder could buy him, that his strongest allegiance was with Ceres. The plan was complicated and required some up front capital to grease the right palms. Guy liked her ideas and assured her that he would transfer two hundred thousand dollars to her account within the next few days. She had control, now she must eliminate Michael from the equation. Bobbi was cautious not to tell Guy that she wanted to eliminate Michael. She would delineate a plan to him that was irresistible, and take his share without his slightest inkling as to what happened.

They said goodbye to the Commodore, and returned to the lights and excitement of Las Vegas. They gambled, dined, and drank a lot of champagne, finally ending up in separate hotel suites. Both Nugari and Nestor believed that they had made the conquest, but the girls knew better. They continued their conniving long into the night. They were experts at getting most men to do their dirty work. Before the sun rose they would have these two men eating from the palm of their hands, and the entire resort would be theirs for the asking. deVillefrance paid an unexpected visit to Ceres. He told her of the plot by the conspirators to take over the resort. She assured him that he had done the right thing in telling her of this conspiracy. She was curious as to what he knew about Orcini's new wife, and why she was digging into her affairs. He said that he knew nothing, but would check her out.

* * * * * *

Bobbi was deliberately late for her lunch appointment. But much to her dismay, Darci was so wrapped up in her work, she didn't even notice.

Darci gave her a short tour, which excluded her bedroom.

"This looks like it should be Michael's office," Bobbi invoked as a matter of fact.

"There's a little café just a short distance down the road. They have nice salads and fresh breads. We can go there." Darci offered as she ignored her comment.

"Sounds perfect. You better take your umbrella. It's raining again."

"Still."

"What?"

"It's still raining. It has been for weeks."

"There has been a terrible storm all along the California coast. I was in Malibu the other day, and you couldn't see to drive. I had to stop and stay with a friend." She didn't bother to look for Darci's reaction, she intuitively knew. "Can we take your car? I hate rentals."

"Sure," she said, still unsure of what was going on in this woman's mind, "let's go. I just realized that I'm very hungry."

They started down the rain soaked road to a confrontation that Darci was sure should not be happening.

"This is a nice car. Its a Shelby Mustang, isn't it."

"Yes, a special edition. It's a Cobra GT 500 KR"

"I didn't know they made a Shelby convertible in this year. 68?"

"Yes. You know about cars?"

"I married a Frenchman who loved racing hot Mustangs."

"What happened?"

"He loved his cars more than he loved me," she lied, "but he gave me Alexandra, my most prized possession."

"A car?"

"Alexandra, my daughter."

Darci wanted to change the subject. She was sure that Bobbi would start telling her about her other possessions, and was afraid that one of them might be Michael.

"I have a classic Jaguar at my place in Big Sur, and.. "

"This road is really slippery during the rains. They've never put guardrails or anything along the sides. You can see almost straight down along here. Why do you want to see me? I'm sure it isn't just to talk about your possessions and our cars."

"I just want to get to know you. After all, we *do* have something in common."

Darci reached the bottom of the hill and turned into a small parking lot in front of a turn of the century heritage style house that had been converted into a quaint café.

They ordered salads and herbal tea. Dreading the answer, Darci asked the question. "Just exactly what do you think that we have in common?" She cringed within waiting for Bobbi's response.

"We're both in real estate." She took her lunch partner off guard.

"Real estate?" Darci began laughing uncontrollably.

"What's so funny?"

"Oh, it's not funny that we're both in real estate, it's.. well it's.. "

"You thought that I was going to say Michael, didn't you?"

"As a matter.. yes I did."

"That's over for me," she lied once again. "I have someone new, and I think that we should be friends. After all, we might be able to help each other in our line of work."

They talked about the real estate market, classic cars and the resort. Darci was careful not to disclose anything of real importance, but she did say that she didn't like Ceres and her henchmen. Bobbi agreed, and mentioned Nugari, just to get a reaction.

"I think they're all slime bags, if you know what I mean."

On the short trip back, Bobbi decided that they should do this again, and Darci reluctantly agreed.

"I'll call you the next time I'm in town." She put her hand out, "I'm glad that we had a chance to get to know each other."

It was Darci's time to lie. "Me too. Drive safely." Half hoping that she would crash.

* * * * * *

Perni and Guy met the girls at the casino in their hotel. They gambled a while and had dinner in a quiet corner of an elegant restaurant on the strip. They talked about their common interest, the Resort at Sundance Lake. Guy convinced Bobbi to go with him to his room for some relaxation. She silently winced as they had sex. When they were through she showered and invited him to go casino hopping with her, hoping that he would make an excuse to stay. She wasn't disappointed. He said that he was too tired, but might join her later. He was asleep when she returned in the early hours of the morning. Still a little wet from the night rain, she undressed quietly, took a quick shower, and slid under the covers next to him.

* * * * * *

Darci worked at home as it rained the entire day, and now the black night sky was shattered with God's electrical display, and a thunderous orchestra played somewhere in the background. Darci hated the lightning. Her father told her stories of warriors coming down on each bolt to find a soul to take back to the heavens, but only if their work on this plane was finished. Her Indian grandmother left the Earth plane on a night like this, and it was well known that she returned time and again to finish her work here. She had not meditated all day, and now seemed to be an appropriate time. She fixed some herbal tea, lit the candles, as she always did, and started to disconnect the phone bell when it rang. The answer machine began recording. "Mrs. Orcini, this is the Memorial Hospital Emergency. It's Mr. Orcini." She jumped at the sound, and without thinking said, "Hello."

A woman's voice came intermittently over the crackling line. "Mrs. Orcini?"

She could barely make it out. "Hello." The static was crackling unbearably loud.

"Mrs. Orcini," it was difficult to hear over the static, "can you hear me?"

"Yes, This is Darci Orcini. Can you speak a little louder? I can hardly hear you."

"How's this?"

"It's a little better," she shouted.

"Mrs. Orcini, this is Nurse Johnson at the Emergency Department at Memorial Hospital. There's been a serious accident. It's Mr. Michael Orcini. Can you come right away?"

She dropped the phone and screamed so loud that you could hear her over all the thunder. "MI.. CHAEL!.. MI.. CHAEL !" Her screams became even louder turning into ear shattering outbursts as she fell to her knees crying his name over and over until nothing would come out.

She knew that she must go to him, she must garner the strength to get up off the floor and.. my God.. how long had she been there on the floor? She got up, eyes filled with tears, she struggled with her coat, and started for the door. What was she forgetting? Pukie. Where was he? She called to him but no words came out. There he was, on the love seat in the alcove. She put him under her arm and rushed out the door.

The wiper couldn't go fast enough to clear the windshield. The road became nothing more than a momentary flash of a picture between the swish of the wiper blades and Darci's sobbing. Suddenly the sky lit up like the fourth of July, and she saw where the road curved sharply. With quick reflexes she jerked the wheel. SNAP came the awful sound, and the wheel turned freely on its hub as the car continued straight. There was no barrier to stop her. The Mustang sailed for an eternity before it hit a rock, and tumbled over and over, crashing, slamming, again and again until it came to rest, upside down. Lightning struck the ground, seven times, all around her, and the thunder shattered the night sky.

* * * * * *

The flashing red lights in the rear view mirror, and the intermittent siren of the Highway Patrol Cruiser were the only lights and sounds along this lonely stretch of highway between Stateline and the Blue Diamond Turnoff. The rest stop a few hundred feet ahead was the logical place to pull over.

As his car came to rest, Michael Orcini saw two familiar faces coming toward him. Michael's best friend, Charlie Swift, and two other men who looked very official flanked Dominic Poncerelli.

"What did I do now?" He said as he lifted the gull wing door.

They stopped short, except Charlie who continued, "There's been an accident." He took his best friend's hand, "It's Darci.. Michael.. Darci is dead."

Stunned, he fell back against the SL. Ponci was quick to his side. They helped him to one of the concrete picnic tables where they sat and waited until he spoke.

Charlie thought in advance and brought a small bottle of brandy and a plastic cup.

"What happened?" he asked, half crying.

"Her car went off the road in the middle of a blinding rainstorm," Ponci said.

"Where?" He drank some of the brandy.

"She was coming down the road from her house." Ponci continued, "There aren't any guard rails along that stretch of road. She went over the side and down into the canyon. She never had a chance. I'm sorry Michael."

"Why was she going out in the storm? She hated driving in the rain, and especially on that road when it was wet." He was in

shock, and babbled on, "Did you know that she was on a committee to get barricades installed up there. She said they wouldn't do
it until somebody got killed. He looked at Charlie, and questioned,
"She's gone, Charlie?"

"Yes Mikey, she's gone." He said gravely and without a stammer.

"Why is the sheriff here?" He recognized the Deputy from his
first date with Darci.

"They want to know why she was out in the storm, and where
she was going. They thought that you might have some ideas."

"Why do they want to know that?"

"Her phone was off the hook, and it looked like she left in a
hurry. The front door was wide open."

"Puca?"

"He was with her. He's gone too."

Ponci moved next to Michael, and quietly said, "The steering
mechanism was tampered with, and we think it was deliberate."

Michael's eyes glazed over and he became enraged. He slammed
his fist down so hard on the concrete table that he cried out in
pain.

"Michael, I think that you should stay at my place tonight,"
Charlie pleaded

"Okay. But right now I need to be alone."

The deputy put his hand out to Michael. "I'm sorry sir, she
was a fine lady. I'll be in touch with you in a day or two. If you
think of anything that might be important, please tell Commissioner Poncerelli, and he'll know where to get in touch with me."

"The cruiser will stay with you to see that you are alright,
Michael," Ponci said in a truly concerned tone.

"Thanks."

"Where are you going, Mikey?"

"I'm going to drive out to the lake. I need to be alone."

They hugged for a long time.

Michael got in the SL, and took the back roads where he raced
at top speed. The Highway Patrol could only watch his taillights.

They finally caught up with him when he stopped on a ridge overlooking Sundance Lake. They waited a distance away, and allowed him the privacy he needed.

Michael put Darci's favorite CD in the player, and began to cry. He remembered how she loved the two singers' love song that sounded like an opera.

The rain had stopped, and the cumulonimbus clouds moved out over the lake. Suddenly, like a pyrotechnic show, lightning came out of the awesome cloud formation, and struck the lake. Not once, but seven long, everlasting times. Michael waited for the thunder, but there was none.

He got out of the car looked up to the heavens, and finally cried out. "Oh God, why have you taken her from me? She was everything that I ever wanted. It's not fair.. it's not fair.. it's not fair.. " He fell to his knees sobbing, "Why?.. Why?.. Answer me.. answer me.. there must be some reason.. I loved her so much.. "

The latent thunder clapped with its echoes resounding across the desert floor, and then it was silent.

Michael sat exhausted, and meditated until the sun rose. When he was at peace with his Maker and himself he stood up and vowed, "I will find your murderer, Darci my love, even if it takes the rest of my life. This I promise you." He stopped by the cruiser on his way. "Hey, guys. Thanks for the vigil. You can go home now," he said in a somber tone.

He drove directly to Charlie's place, and slept for two days.

Charlie called Keleigh, and together they went about the unpleasant, but necessary process of contacting family and friends.

THE GHOST

Chapter Three

Darci felt herself float up and away from the wreckage at the bottom of the canyon with Puca snuggled tight under her arm. A silver thread trailed her, somehow keeping her connected to something on Earth. In an instant she was transported from the canyon to the middle of a large room with a high, open pyramidal ceiling made completely of lavender colored glass. The space seems to be part of a larger structure floating in the middle of a lake. Darci was drawn to a figure seated at a desk at the far end of the space. As Darci reached the desk, the figure, a tall, slender, and extremely beautiful woman rose from her chair.

"Welcome, Darci. I am Aditi."

She didn't speak a word, but Darci heard every word in her mind.

"Don't be frightened. We do not have any need for a voice as you did in your physical life on Earth." Her face shown with a radiance that was indescribable. Darci only knew that she wasn't afraid. "Come here, I want to show you something." She moved without taking any steps.

"Why am I here? What is this place?"

"This," she pointed to the water outside the space, "is Sundance Lake."

'But, I don't understand. Am I dead? The car. I remember that awful sound. The steering wheel snapped, and I drove over the edge."

"Yes, you have passed over to this side."

"The lightning. Seven. My soul left on the seventh.. Sundance Lake? But why am I here?"

"This is the next plane for you."

"I can look out. Can people look in?"

"No one on Earth can see the inside of this place," Aditi transferred her thoughts. "It will only be here for a while, and will be moved somewhere else when it has served its purpose."

"What's its purpose?"

"You will learn that soon enough. But first you must learn why you are here, and what is expected of you before you can move on."

"Why? What do you mean? Where am I?"

"This is the first level of advancement before you can join the Ultimate Power."

"How many levels are there?"

"Do not be concerned. You just have to complete the requirements of this level. We are not in any hurry here."

Darci moved over to a painting supported on an easel. "This is very beautiful, but I can't tell if it's a painting or a photograph."

"It is neither."

Darci studied the neither painting nor photograph. She instinctively knew without counting that there were forty-nine white roses in a crystal vase with one silver rose set directly in the middle. "What is the significance of this.. ?" she coated a sort of gesture at the neither-nor item.

"You will learn the meaning as a part of your spiritual training."

She felt a movement under her arm, and realized that Puca was still with her.

"He is here to help with your task." Aditi knew her thoughts.

"My task?"

"Yes, you must help Michael find the one who murdered you."

"Murdered? Michael's all right? But I was told that he was hurt."

"It was a stratagem to upset you and get you driving fast down the hill."

"But something happened to my car."

"Yes. A linkage on the steering device was sabotaged."

"Who did this thing to me, and why?"

"You will learn why when you find out who was responsible, and tell Michael."

"How do I tell him? What means do I have to communicate? Can I talk to him?"

"I will help you with the spiritual tools for you to accomplish the task."

"How much time do I have to do this task before I have to move on?"

Aditi laughed. "You are not of the Earth any more." She moved back to her desk. "Here we do not measure anything in terms of time. But you must finish your obligation before you can move to the next level."

"Where do all these levels lead?"

"To the Highest place. You must advance spiritually before you can join the Ultimate Power."

"The Ultimate Power?"

"Yes, Darci. Come with me, it is time to start your spiritual training"

They instantly moved to a place high above the Earth where Darci could see forever. The images of her grandmother and grandfather were as clear as if they were alive and right there with her.

"How can.. ?"

"You will learn all there is to know in a little while," Aditi promised.

* * * * * *

Rays of sunshine streamed colorfully through the stained glass windows of the small Presbyterian Church as friends and family gather for the memorial service. There never was a morning as long as this that Michael could remember. For a moment he could not recollect where he was or what he was doing here.

A hush came over the gathering as the main doors opened to expose the casket bearing Darci's remains. Darci's father and Michael agreed that Darci's remains along with her beloved Puca would be cremated and cast over three places where she felt the most love and belonging. The first was the fields of the family farm, the second was over the ocean near their home at Malibu, and finally across Sundance Lake, a place she desperately wanted to share with Michael.

The choir loft was filled to capacity with musicians dressed in formal wear, instead of the usual choir in their robes. Spike Hawley arranged for two celebrated entertainers to perform A Time To Say Goodbye, Darci's favorite. The orchestra began to play as the casket was brought forward, attended by Michael, Charlie, Darci's father and brother, Maggie, and Michael's father.

Everyone who knew Darci and Michael were in attendance. Old friends and new alike were there. Hans Gruber left an important negotiation in Aruba to be with Michael, Guy Nestor and his son Ian flew in from London where they cut short a meeting with members of two major world banks. Guy diverted his private jet to Paris where Alexandra Azure joined them. He would do most anything for Bobbi. Roberta Azure connected with them at his hotel in Las Vegas. Norah Laude was accompanied by her most recent conquest, Dave Roberts, while Pernicious Nugari came alone.

Dominic Poncerelli stationed a large number of undercover detectives among the other guests. Ponci figured that the murderer would be there, and wanted to be available if any attempt was made against Michael.

Jami Wu accompanied Claude deVillefrance, who was dressed in a dark blue double-breasted blazer and gray slacks, and almost unrecognizable without his trademark Greek captain's outfit.

Michael's entire office staff, except Keleigh, arrived early. Keleigh didn't want to be there at all, but finally, accompanied by Charlie's girl friend, quietly made her entrance through the side door, and joined the others just as the orchestra began.

"The Lord has.. " Pastor Jim stopped, and stared down the aisle to the rear of the sanctuary.

The double doors open, and Donna Una Maria Antonia Ceres, flanked by Connie and Mario, entered. A mournful, "O--hh," was heard from many as they turned to watch. Pastor Jim waited until they were seated, and continued with the funeral service.

Charlie eulogized Darci without a stammer. He told of the way she changed his best friend's life. "If there are any angels on this Earth," he said with tears in his eyes, "Darci was.. " he choked, and stopped to wipe his eyes, "Darci was an angel." He looked up from the pulpit toward the heavens. "I don't know if she is with God yet, but I can feel her right here with us." He looked down, first at her parents, and then at his friend. "She will always be with us."

Pastor Jim signaled for the orchestra to begin. They played A Time to Say Goodbye again, and the ushers accompanied the casket to the waiting hearse.

"That was the song that Michael played for me the first night we made love," she looked at Aditi, "isn't it beautiful?" Darci moved to Michael's side, "Can I.. " she asked Aditi, "can I kiss him?"

Aditi nodded.

Darci kissed him on the cheek. "I love you Michael Orcini."

Michael touched his cheek as a tear fell.

Many of the heavyhearted gathered in the adjoining multipurpose building to share in food and drink, and extend their condolences to her parents and Michael.

"Waat will you do now, mon?"

"I don't really know, my friend. Thanks for coming on such a short notice. I know that you were in the middle of some very important business."

"Dis is waat friends har for." His blue eyes were sorrowful. "I feel your pain."

Charlie left his girl friend, and joined them. "Hans, this is my best friend, Charlie Swift. Charlie, this is Hans Gruber, a very special friend."

The men nodded, and shook hands.

"I think thot you should cahm to de islands for a while. Sort out your life."

"That's a good idea, Mikey."

"Only if you come with me."

"You got it." Charlie hadn't stuttered all day.

"We can take the Commander."

Guy Nestor approached them in time to hear their plan. "My pilot is at your dispose," he put out his hand, "and my jet will get you there a lot faster."

He introduced Guy to the other men. "That's a very generous offer, Guy."

"Taahk it mon."

"He's your competition," Michael said to Hans.

"No mahter." Hans looked serious, "Eht ehs for you."

"You are a gentleman and a friend."

"I like the idea Mikey."

"No strings attached," Guy reinforced his proposition.

"Thanks, Guy. In that case, I'll take you up on the offer."

"I'm taking Bobbi and her daughter to Carmel, you can have the jet by day after tomorrow. Just let me know when you want to return, and I'll make the necessary arrangements."

Michael started toward Darci's folks when Alexandra intercepted him. "Michael, I'm so sorry for you." They hugged for a long time.

"Charlie," he tugged at his arm, "come with me, I want you to meet Donna Ceres.

"She has a lot of muscle around her." Still not a stutter, "You met any of them?"

"The bull is Mario, and the one on her right arm is Connie. I've seen the other one somewhere, but I can't remember where."

"Wasn't he at Bobbi's party?"

"Could be, I'm not sure."

Una Ceres stepped forward to meet them. "Mr. Orcini. I am grieved to hear of your loss. If there is anything that I can do for you, please do not hesitate to let me know."

He wanted to stop her in the middle of her dissertation, but ardently listened while she said the same unfeeling sentence that a dozen or more had already said.

Connie Contedetto extended his hand and looked to see who might be watching. "Mr. Orcini, we are sad that you should have to lose Missus Orcini to such a terrible accident. We have ordered many candles to be lit in our church, and the Monsignor will perform a special Mass in her honor next week."

Mario simply bowed his head.

The other man stepped forward, also extending his hand. "Dave Roberts, Michael. I don't know if you remember me, I'm a friend of Roberta Azure and her sister Norah.

"Yes, of course." Michael wasn't sure.

"I also would like to extend my condolences."

Michael went to Charlie's home in the desert and slept until the next morning.

* * * * * * *

It would have been her thirty-third birthday in a few weeks, Michael thought as he walked along *their* beach. He stopped and sat in the place where they made love. His eyes looked to the heavens for a glimpse of an answer, but all he could see were seagulls sailing the jet streams until they were out of sight. The islands were calm between storms, and the entire population was getting ready for the next one that was sitting out over the Atlantic Ocean.

Michael sat for hours, listening to the waves crash against the shore, meditating, searching for the truth of his lost love. In the waves he heard her voice crying out, "I'm here Michael. I'm here with you. Be strong, be strong." He wondered if he had actually heard her or if it was a dream. She often told him her theory of the dream state, and how what we thought were dreams was actually reality, and that what we thought was reality was just a dream.

Felicia was running, calling him, "Senor Orcini.. Senor Orcini." He was jarred back to his conscious state. "What's wrong?"

"No som ting wrong Senor," she caught her breath, "de Patron, he wo-rees bout jew." Her accent was more Spanish than Jamaican. She fussed with her blouse, and ordered him. "Jew cum to eat now." Felicia turned in her bare feet, and ran back, disappearing into the lush vegetation between the beach and the house.

The men retreated to the study to enjoy brandy and cigars. Michael was surprised to see Dominic Poncerelli and another man sitting by the fireplace. He looked at Charlie. "Do you have something to do with this?"

Charlie nodded.

"Hello Michael," Ponci uttered softly and apologetically, "I hope this isn't going to be inconvenient for you."

"I must say, I'm overwhelmed." He looked quizzically at the other man.

"This is agent Arden of the FBI."

"FBI?" a puzzled retort. "What's the FBI doing here."

"It's very complicated Mr. Orcini," the agent said. "Let's sit down and I'll try to explain what we think is going on here."

He didn't think that they had any intention of leaving, so he sat, drank brandy, and smoked a cigar while Arden and Ponci laid out the situation as they saw it. They told him how the agency had been watching Ceres for a long time. She never broke the law, but always seemed to be right on the edge. Her financial holdings were suspect, but under the law, the State of Nevada never shared income information with the IRS, and everything was in order with the SEC. But still they cautioned Michael not to do business with her.

"You didn't come all this way to tell me how to run my business." He went to the bar, filled his glass, and continued, "Did you?"

"Mr. Poncerelli thinks she might have something to do with your wife's death."

Michael trembled as he heard the words. "You think she had Darci killed? Why?"

"Your wife was digging in to her past," Poncerelli got up and put his hand on the mantel, "and investigated everybody who worked for her. She was even checking on some people in my department." He sipped his brandy, and waited for a response.

Michael started to rise and then sank back down as agent Arden spoke. Could she have found out something that was so horrible that Ceres would have her killed? He thought that she shared everything when she showed him those files back in Malibu. There must have been something.. something he didn't think was important. He felt a knot forming deep inside his stomach, tightening, twisting, and burning his entire insides. There was a brief interval of relief, then the sensation returned as if a mule had kicked him. He doubled over in agony, and only the tears released the pressure.

"Mr. Orcini.. I."

Michael raised his hand to let him know that he as okay. After a moment he looked at Ponci and Arden and asked, "What proof of this do you have?"

Agent Arden moved away from the fireplace, and relit his cigar. "We were hoping that you might help. We know that your wife had extensive dossiers on Ceres and her Chinese partners, but they weren't to be found in your home in Las Vegas."

"You searched my home?"

"There was a crime, and, well.. "

He looked at his friend. "Ponci. Did they have a search warrant?"

"I, uh.. "

"Is that a no?" Michael's eyes blazed with anger at the FBI agent. "What right do you have to.. " He stopped as the anger turned within. He shouldn't have let her go so far. She tried to warn him about these people. Why didn't he listen? Her voice echoed from the depths of his soul. "I'm not going to be killed if I know too much, am I?" With pain in his voice he apologized, "I'm sorry. I'll look for the papers."

Hans ordered some dessert brought in, and the men discussed the many possibilities well into the morning hours.

Charlie caught up with Michael during his early morning jog on the beach. "Hey, Mikey," he shouted over the sound of the waves, "wait up."

They walked the entire length of the white sandy beach, and talked about Michael's involvement in the investigation. Charlie was emphatic that the police work should be left to those who were trained to find clues and motives and so forth. Exhausted from the conversation, Michael agreed to let Ponci, and the Sheriff, and the FBI, and everybody else handle the investigation while he concentrated on the resort. He figured it would be difficult dealing with any of these people until the case was solved. His promise to Charlie was lacking depth since he never would stop until her killers were brought to justice.

The seagulls were sailing high this afternoon, and Michael wondered if they ever slept. He remembered one of his favorite books about a seagull and his spiritual growth, and wondered if a distant shore held the soul of his love, or if she could watch him.

One of the gulls, a brilliant white creature, dove down.. right at him.. then swooped up and away to circle around, and did it again.. and again.. and again. Michael swirled around and around with every gull skirmish, and began to laugh. He plopped himself on the sand, and watched the gull as he came in for a perfect two point landing.

"I suppose you know where she is," he told the gull, half questioning.

Darci sat next to him as he tried to communicate with the gull wishing that he could hear her. She wanted him to know that she was in a new place, but that she was not without concern for his anguish. She kissed his cheek as she had at the memorial service, and once again his hand touched the curious sensation on his face.

* * * * * *

He stood in the center of his Malibu living room looking around at every wall, in every corner. The two story gray walls with their blue accents, paintings by Dali and black and white masterful Ansel Adams photographs he acquired just last year, somehow seemed bare and lifeless. He remembered how they made love on the off-white leather sectional in front of the massive flagstone fireplace. The thick, white bear skin throw rug had stains where she spilled wine the first night after they returned from Paris. There was a small picture of Darci on the black lacquered baby grand piano. Her arms were stretched out, and draped in a shawl he had just bought her in a little shop along the avenue des Champs-Elysees. He recalled that they just finished lunch at Lucas-Carton and were going to walk along the Seine. She acted out the child in her by dancing in circles around him.

He guided his hand over the black granite kitchen counter where she rolled lemons, each morning, before squeezing for the juice. He took her special rainbow coffee mug down from behind the beveled glass cupboard door, and embraced the memory of her attempt to like French Roast coffee as he did. He moved his finger lovingly over the rainbow image, stopped at the top, and whispered, "Somewhere, my love."

The warm earth tones, with their brilliant blue and coral accents, could not mask the empty, passionless ambience of the master bedroom. He threw himself across the king sized bed, hugged her pillow, sobbed, and slept until late the next morning.

Rain soaked from his trek along the beach, Michael took time to prepare his coffee before taking a shower. He stood in the sunken black granite stall, with the pulsating, hot water beating on his weary body. He rubbed his chin as he wiped the steam from the mirror, and decided not to shave. He searched for her face, but the image did not come.

He drank his coffee from her cup, and reviewed the barrage of telephone messages from the last week. The calls from J.T. and Keleigh were his priority.

"Sundance Resort, how may I direct your call?"

"This is Michael Orcini, may I speak with Keleigh, please?"

"Oh! Mr. Orcini. Am I ever glad to hear from you. Everybody has been calling. I'm sorry to hear of your loss, and.. "

"Candace."

"Yes, sir."

"Let me talk to Keleigh."

"She's not in right now, sir."

"Tell her to call me at the beach. Let me talk to Mr. Popinski."

"Yes, sir."

"Michael. How are you doing?"

"I'm fine. Ask Martha to talk to Candace about the way she answers the phone."

"Sure. Any suggestions?"

"No. But Martha and Keleigh can come up with something." He continued. "Where's Keleigh?"

"She's been meeting with her staff away from the office. They're getting their marketing plan put together. You've got quite a girl there, Michael. I couldn't have picked a better person to run the casino operation. I'll ask Martha to find her and give you a call. Are you here or at the beach?"

"I asked Candace to do that. I'm at the beach"

"I'll ask Martha. She'll get it done."

"Can we get a teleconferencing system set up in the conference room?"

"We're working on that, it should be in place by the end of the week. Keleigh wants to set it up on each of the executive PC's. I think that it's a good idea."

"Sounds like Keleigh has taken the helm. If you talk to her before I do, would you ask her to arrange a setup here too?"

"You've got it boss. I've got a million things to discuss with you."

They talked about the potential financial partners, and their ability to fund. It was their consensus of opinion that Nestor had four hundred million dollars ready to commit, but it would take a little while longer to bring in the rest. Michael still didn't like his overall proposal. He wanted the verbiage changed. Michael thought that as far as Wu and Ceres were concerned, the money was in the bank and ready to put into escrow. J.T. said that he got a call from the bank, and Nugari had authorized the transfer of fifty million to their checking account. Michael reiterated his earlier instructions for Nate Gregory to review all transactions before any action was taken. But J.T. already instructed the bank to fax the documents to Nate for analysis.

It was obvious that Nugari was trying to position himself for a takeover. Neither of the men was ready to jump into bed with Nugari.

Hans Gruber was probably the best deal in town, but he wasn't moving at the same pace as the others. Michael decided not to tell J.T. about Poncerelli and the FBI agent's visit to the islands.

"Sumner had an interview with Seth Hobson, and put him to work."

"Hobson?"

"He's the fellow you wanted to use in the catering department."

"Oh, yes. Does he think that Hobson will work out?"

"I don't know. You'll have to talk to Sumner."

* * * * * * *

Ethereal sounds became louder until they filled the entire pyramid. The serene music cast a magical spell of calm and contentment through Darci's soul. Birds were singing in tune with a cello, to a song that had to be composed by angels. Aditi was seated on a white wicker chair, with an enormously high rounded back, rising more than ten feet above her head. Like a throne, with an intricate collection of geometric designs surrounded by a wreath of lavender flowers, the chair dominated the grand space. Aditi's long dark hair was the only contrast to the otherwise pastel palette of the room. She called to Darci in a voice that complemented the melody. "It is time to start your journey."

In an instant they were standing in a field of flowers. There were millions of white roses everywhere she looked. "What do you see here?" Aditi asked.

"A gazillion beautiful white roses." Darci danced like a child.

"What else?"

She stopped her choreography, and looked around. "Just the clear blue sky.. and you." She began to swirl with her arms stretched out.

"Concentrate.. there is more."

Darci pouted like a small child. "I don't see anything else. Just you, and me, and the flowers, and the sky.. and.. that's all."

"Take a rose in your hand, child."

Darci inspected the flower. "There aren't any thorns." She looked at Aditi in amazement, "These roses don't have any thorns."

"Why should that be so special?"

"Because we're in Heaven?"

Aditi smiled.

"If we're not in Heaven, then where are we, and who are you?"

"I am your guide, and I will be your mentor on this level. I have told you that you have a task to accomplish, and I am here to teach you how to do what is necessary." She waited for Darci's answer to her question.

"The rose has no thorns.. because.. because.. " she became somber, "because roses don't *have* thorns." Delighted with her answer, she began to dance once more.

Her mentor waited patiently. "Oh?" She seemed to stare right through Darci.

"Roses don't have thorns, because.. because it's the bushes.. they grow on thorn bushes." She got serious.

"What does that mean to you?"

Darci thought for a while before she answered. "That.. maybe.. there is beauty to be found in a thorny bush?" She wasn't sure.

The slightest acknowledgement shown through Aditi, but she did not answer.

"What about the one silver rose?" Darci was ready to move on. "You were going to tell me about the one different color rose in the picture. In the non-picture."

The messenger examined her from her head to her feet.

Wonder came over her as she looked down to see that she was adorned in the most beautiful sterling silver gown she had ever seen. It appeared to be made completely of rose pedals. "Am *I* the rose in the non-picture?" she questioned as she turned, and slowly gazed out over the field of flowers. "One silver rose in this garden of a gazillion white roses?" she still questioned. "Michael said that I was one in a million."

"You are ready Darci. Come."

Once again they were transported to another place. This time it was familiar to Darci. "It's Michael!" she shouted with joy.

Michael was alone on a beach with a gull swooping down at him.

"What is that bird doing to Michael?"

"Do not worry, he's a friend. Watch."

The bird landed in front of Michael as if to tell him something.

"Can I.. ?"

Aditi acknowledged without words.

Darci sat next to her lover, and listened to his request. She kissed his cheek.

"Aditi," she exclaimed, "he felt my kiss."

"We must go."

Darci was standing in her own bedroom, at the foot of the bed, her eyes transfixed on the picture of an Indian Princess above her bed. "It's you," she said without moving, "I've always loved this painting."

"I have been watching over you for a long time."

"Why did you bring me here?"

"This," she said seriously, "is where you must wait for Michael."

"What am I supposed to do when he gets here? I can't talk to him. He doesn't even know that I'm around." She turned and looked in wonderment at Aditi. "Does he? I mean.. when I kissed him.. uhm, why must I be here? Is this some kind of punishment?"

"This is not any kind of admonition. Remember what I told you about helping Michael?" She looked at Darci's puzzled face, and continued with yet another astounding revelation. "He'll be able to see and hear you." She waited for her declaration to register, "But not until he is *ready* to come here.. to this place where you first gave yourselves to each other. Only then will the time be right."

Aditi went on to explain the limitations of Darci's presence on Earth. "No one else will be able to see or hear you, except Puca. Michael will not be able to see you when other people are with him. Do you understand?" She didn't wait for an answer. "Sometimes you will be able to observe, but you are not permitted to invade on anything mortal. Puca will help you. He can see things that you are not allowed to see, so you must pay close attention to your little friend." She picked up a cameo broach that Michael had given Darci for Christmas, and turned her head to show off her profile. "Good likeness. Don't you agree?" She handed the cameo to Darci, and disappeared.

* * * * * *

It was seven in the morning when Michael returned from his jog on the beach. It was a cold and damp April morning, and the aroma of a fresh brew coming from his kitchen stimulated his thoughts of a hot cup of coffee.

"Hi darling," came an exuberant welcome as Bobbi appeared from behind the counter and handed him a cup.

"How did you.. ?"

"I still have a key." She was wearing an elegant, pale rose, tight fitting jump suit with the front zipper lowered to her mid-section. "Would you like some breakfast? I was going to fix myself a waffle."

She brushed his hair back, "I can have something ready by the time you're done with your shower."

Flabbergasted, he said, "A waffle would be fine," he frowned. "There's syrup in the pantry. I like it hot."

"I know how you like *it*," she smiled and turned to the kitchen. "*I know*."

"I had forgotten what a good cook you are, Bobbi," he said as he finished off his second waffle. "But.. ?"

"What?"

"I don't remember having any bacon around here. I, uh.. "

He was about to continue when she got up and began massaging his shoulders. "I brought it with me. And.. d.. I've got some steaks, and fresh veggies, and a wonderful desert for later. And, oh, don't get the wrong idea." She stopped and kissed the top of his head, "But I just knew that you probably haven't had a proper meal in a while." She continued with the massage.

He pressed his cheek to her hand, and said. "Thanks."

"There," giving him a slight shove, "that's all for now. You go and do your work, and I'll clean up."

Bobbi interrupted his phone conversation. "I'm going down the coast. Got things to do, you know. But I'll be back to cook your dinner." She pulled his face gently towards her, and kissed him lightly on the lips. "Ciao."

"What's going on?" Came the voice on the phone, "Who was that?"

"That," he paused, "was Bobbi."

"Bobbi!" Keleigh's enraged voice blurted out, "She sure didn't wait very long."

"It's not like that, Keleigh. She just wants to help."

"You never asked me to help," she said soulfully.

"You're doing a lot. You've single-handedly organized the entire company, and now you are taking care of the marketing with a vengeance."

Her heart pounded as if she had just run a hundred yard dash.

After a long period and a deep sigh, she said. "You're right. Let's get on with it."

Michael detected her indignation, but wasn't ready to get into a confrontation over Bobbi. "How's the teleconferencing stuff coming?" He changed the subject.

"Didn't I tell you? Everything is in place here, and they'll be coming by your place later today to install your equipment. They're 'sposed to call first."

They talked about how she was coming with the rest of her department, and what she knew about how everybody else was doing. When they were finished, Michael sat back in his chair , and relaxed. "You.. are.. great.. , sweet cheeks."

"You don't know how great," she whispered.

"What?"

"Nothing."

"See yah soon."

"See yah bye."

The expected dial tone sounded.

Michael returned all the calls he wanted to answer, leaving the ones to Nugari, Wu, and deVillefrance for another day. The call from Ceres had him perplexed. She always had Contedetto call and make arrangements. She asked for him to come to lunch. There was someone she wanted him to meet. He decided to wait until he talked with J.T., Keleigh and Sumner. He called Martha and asked her to set up a conference call with them, and to be sure to include Nate Gregory. The teleconferencing technicians arrived a little after noon and had the system operational in a couple of hours.

Bobbi returned a little after five, and immediately went to the kitchen where she began preparing dinner. She neatly organized charcoal and oakwood chips in the massive built-in charbroiler on the opposite end of the kitchen. The steaks she marinated earlier were ready to cook, and she started to combine the ingredients for her special creamed pearl onions and an outrageous Enoki mushroom soup. The potatoes au-gratin were prepared in small individual crocks and placed in the oven.

She was as quiet as possible, but he was totally aware of her presence and the aroma that came across to his work place.

After a while she quietly placed a small tray with warm sake' next to his computer keyboard, and quietly left the room.

Michael sat back and poured the rice wine into the small cup, savoring the warm elixir as it made its way passed his lips. "Are we having Japanese?"

"No. But the sake' is a nice way for you to unwind," she called out from the kitchen. "Dinner will be ready in about twenty minutes."

"This is absolutely fantastic," he smothered his words with the food still in his cheek. "Where," he shamelessly swallowed, "where did you learn how to cook this stuff?"

"What stuff?" She pursed her lips, and acted hurt.

"The steak.. and.. and.. these little onions.. I mean.. well.. and ohhh," he sighed with pleasure, "that mushroom soup was out of this world." He pierced the steak and cut off another piece, and without missing a beat, replaced the one he had just swallowed.

"Michael, Michael."

"What?"

"Sometimes I just don't know what I'm going to do with you." She stretched her arms backward with a little squirm, and pushed her breasts forward knowing he would stare approvingly. "You should save your animal ways for a later time." She brought her arms forward sliding them down over her breasts and pushing them together to form a more pronounced cleavage. "Want some desert?" She asked playfully.

Michael gulped the last mouthful.

Before he could answer, she got up and started clearing the table. "I made a special treat for you. Your favorite."

"You did? What?"

"Lemon meringue pie. Want some?"

"I always have room for lemon meringue pie."

"Go sit by the fire, take off your shoes, and make yourself comfortable."

Bobbi snuggled her derrière tightly against his thigh as she placed the tray on the coffee table. She turned and leaned against him. "You can pour the coffee, darling." She smiled a sweet smile and moved a few inches away.

They ate their desert quietly, glancing at each other when they thought the other wasn't looking. When they finished Bobbi asked, "D'you want s'more?"

"No thanks. I'm full."

She purposefully maneuvered her posterior for him to enjoy as she picked the tray from the table. "I'll be right back."

Michael propped his feet on the table and pushed back into the couch, and began to daydream about Darci.

"A penny for your thoughts?" came a soft whisper in his ear.

"Wha--what?"

"You had such a big smile, I just know that.. Is anything else getting big?" She stroked his crotch. "Ouuu.. uh. I like that." She moved, pressing herself against him, kissing his ear and neck while her hand continued the stimulation. Bobbi knew just how vulnerable he was, and intended to take full advantage of him.

Michael moved his hand under her blouse, and enjoyed touching her soft, excited breast. Soon they exchanged passionate kisses and feverishly worked the pleasant chore of removing each other's clothes.

"Let's go to the bedroom," she instructed him. "Come on, we'll finish undressing on the way." She tugged at his belt buckle. "Come on." She took off her blouse, thrusting her breasts towards his face, and jumping up to tease him. "Come on." She danced to the bedroom door where she stopped and slowly caressed her body with her hands, following each curve with the explicitness of an experienced seductress.

Michael rose with her blouse in his hand, and walked slowly to the doorway where she waited. He inspected her sexy stance, starting at her breasts, then down to her peach colored panties, and back up, stopping momentarily at her breasts before looking into her eyes. He sweetly kissed her pursed lips. "You forgot something," he said as he handed her the blouse.

"I won't be needing it for a while. Come." She took his hand.

"I can't. Not now.. it's too.."

"It's still her. Isn't it?" She set her chin and glared angrily at him. "You know that we're right for each other. We always have, and always will." She moved against him, and grabbed his buttocks, pulling herself tight against him.

"It's too soon," he said softly. "It's just too soon. I'm sorry."

"I can wait." She pouted. "Poor Mikey."

He pushed her away. "Enough."

Bobbi dropped her head with the move of an actor, "I'm sorry. Please forgive me." He put his arms around her, as she knew he would. She burrowed her entire body against his as tightly as she could, and once again felt his arousal. Satisfied that she had won the moment, she whispered. "Let's go to bed," with a coy smile, "I'll take the guest room."

"Thanks."

Michael fell into his bed with a desire to have sex with Bobbi, but a longing for Darci that precluded his craving. He tossed and turned with the anxiety, then fell into a deep sleep. His reverie felt as real as if he were awake. Suddenly he realized that someone was right there, with him, in his bed. He jumped, only to be smothered with kisses. Fear and delight came over him simultaneously. Then reality kicked in. It was Bobbi. She had slid under the sheets while he slept. They argued fiercely until he could stand it no more.

"I'm leaving," he said.

Bobbi sat up and stared. "This isn't over. you can't run away from me."

He dressed and departed.

She looked at the clock by his bed. It was only two a.m. She pulled the covers over herself, and went to sleep.

* * * * * *

Restless and anxious for Michael to return, Darci decided to leave for a while, and discovered that she can move to almost anywhere she wanted in the flash of a thought. First she walked down the 'Strip' and experienced her first encounter with people who can't see her. A very large man with a beard and long hair, wearing blue jeans and a tank top walked right up to, and through her. More people came along, and she experienced the same thing. Having had enough of these inconsiderate beings, she stepped away and onto the street, where a long black limousine, moving slowly, stopped, then moved again. It took forever to drive through her. "I don't know if I like this being dead stuff, Pukie" she said to her little dog. "A girl could get hurt, if she doesn't watch out."

She conjured herself into a casino, and moved quickly into the pit area where everybody wasn't walking through her. She intuitively knew what cards were coming up next, and how the dice would land. She even knew what some of the people were thinking. What to play, how much to bet, sexual desires and fantasies. It was too much for her first time out. At a blackjack table she saw Nugari and Wu. She wondered how it was that they were at this casino, or if she had actually directed herself to where they happened to be. She stood behind the dealer and listened to what they were saying.

"We must move faster," Nugari said, "Ceres wants Orcini to accept the fifty million that we have put in the bank." He motioned for the dealer to 'hit' him, once more. "Damn." He threw his cards down.

"He is being very cautious. We shouldn't push him so hard. He might panic and go somewhere else."

"Nestor and the German don't have enough funds together yet. Nestor could be close, but the German has a way to go," Nugari affirmed. "I'm concerned that Nestor might convince Orcini to get started with him now, with a promise to bring in the rest of the money later."

"But *we* have all the money now," Wu whimpered. "What is he waiting for?"

"I think deVillefrance has gotten to him with another deal." He watched for Wu's reaction, "I thing that he is trying to take control and cut us out."

"How can he do that? I brought the money in from China."

"I'm not sure, but he's been spending a lot of time at the Ceres mansion."

Jami knew of deVillefrance's other proposal, but it only cut out Nugari, and gave a little more control to Ceres. He also knew that she wanted to take the entire resort from Orcini. He wondered if they would try a double cross on him. It was time to reinforce the Camorra, and to show force, if necessary. As he looked up from his cards, he saw the same woman he had seen at Casa Trinacria. She was standing at the end of a Black Jack table just across the pit. If he could make friends with her, maybe he could find out what the Donna was planning. Just as he got up to go over to her, a tall, athletic looking man, whom she kissed as if he were an old friend, joined her. It was Dave Roberts. He saw Roberts with Ceres before, and wondered about their connection. He settled back on his chair, but continued to watch her.

Darci's mind was no longer free of thought, and her interest grew as she heard their conversation and read their thoughts. They were truly planning to take Michael's resort away from him, both of them, separately and maliciously with this Ceres person. She went over to Roberts and the Asian girl to see what they would be talking about. Embarrassed by their conversation, she turned away and heard, "You were to stay at your home on the mountain, Darci," Aditi chided her.

They were standing in the middle of her living room once again. "You are not permitted to plan any revenge to those responsible for your untimely passing over." She turned with a sweep of her gown, "You may only show the evidence to Michael. He will pass it on to the authorities."

"But.. "

She was stopped by a thought wave, as Aditi departed without a word.

* * * * * *

It was the end of the workday, and Michael was totally exhausted. He had been at the office since he drove up from Malibu in the middle of the morning. The sun had gone down, and he still procrastinated about going home to their place in the hills. The memory of Darci would be too overwhelming, and he wasn't ready to undertake the emotion that was sure to erupt from the sojourn.

Keleigh offered the guest room at her condo with dinner thrown in. Michael was so numb from the events of the past few weeks, that any kindness, however motivated, was a welcome intrusion into the hubbub of his life. He accepted, and she went on ahead.

It had been such a long time since they were together, in someplace other than a restaurant or work place, that he had dismissed her as a real close friend, replacing her as a good buddy, a pal, and business confidant. He drank his favorite brandy that she so thoughtfully poured in the proper snifter, and remembered the time they got stinking drunk together. "Hey Kel. Do you remember the time we got drunk, and I got.. uhm.. "

"Yeah. I should've let you," she said with a quick look from the kitchen, "only I was too bombed to know what you were up to." She thought a moment and then turned quickly toward him, striking a pose with a large wooden spoon in one hand, and her other hand in a fist on her hip. "It probably wouldn't have been any good anyway." She nodded her head in affirmation, and maintained her pose.

"Yeah," he forced a tired smirk.

She swirled the spoon with a nonchalant, whoop-de-do, who cares gesture, and spun around with a little wiggle.

"Pretty good, *sweet cheeks*," he emphasized

She intently wiggled her *sweet cheeks* and withdrew from the room.

They ate most of the simple meal in silence. Keleigh was aware that Michael was emotionally and physically exhausted, so she didn't initiate any meaningful conversation. He was talked-out and couldn't even muster up any nonsense to lighten up the evening.

When dinner was done they sat on pillows by the fireplace, drank wine, and talked about their times in college.

Suddenly he remembered that he was to meet Henri early in the morning. "I'd better call him."

"Stay there," she said, "I'll get the portable phone."

He lay on his back and watched her leave the room.

She handed him the phone. "Here, he's on the line."

"Henri," he looked up the length of her legs before she continued to the kitchen, "uhh.. hum." he sat up, "oh, nothing. What time are you coming in tomorrow?" He listened, then hollered to Keleigh. "Kel. Can we pick him up at McCarran about nine and go out to the lake?" He talked back to the phone, "Just a minute Henri."

"Sure." She peeked out from the kitchen. "How much time are you planning to spend out there?"

"Couple hours."

"As long as I'm back by noon for my lunch appointment."

"We'll pick you up at nine. See yah then. What?" He listened, "Oh, good. Bye."

"What's, *oh good*?"

"He's bringing Cam."

"We should get to bed," she looked away from him, "I fixed the guest room for you. What time do you want to get up?"

"Six-thirty."

"I'll wake you," she turned to leave, "night Michael."

"Night.. Kel."

She turned back, gave him a sweet smile, then slowly sauntered off to her bedroom, and closed the door behind her.

He started to the guest room, pausing momentarily at her door, "Nah." He uttered softly to himself, shaking his head.

Keleigh took a long hot shower. She pondered on how easy it would be to take advantage of his vulnerability and just join him under the sheets. But the opportunity of his rejection was more overwhelming than she was willing to risk. She lay on top of her bed, stroking her loins, and decided to use her seductive charm on him in subtle but constant ways. She would tease him when they were alone or at work, but he would have to want her, and make the first move. Satisfied with her plan she slid under the sheets and went to sleep.

* * * * * * *

There was a light rain falling as they stopped at their temporary office trailer on the shore of Sundance Lake. J.T and Sumner had been there for more than an hour, and had the place warmed, coffee made and fresh Danish rolls spread out on the work counter. The trailer was totally equipped for Henri and two technicians. Drafting tables, computers with telecommunication set-ups, and a large spread table for plans and a model of the project. In the corner were a fax machine, printers and plotters, and flat files for the drawings.

"Save one without any nuts for Michael," Keleigh cautioned the others, "He's the boss, and.. "

"I was just getting that one for him," Cam chimed in.

Henri looked at Michael and shrugged.

Spike Hawley and Rebecca Greydove arrived an hour later with their departmental requirements and wish lists. The entire team worked relentlessly for the whole day. Their mid-day was broken up by a surprise from Sumner. He arranged for their lunch to be brought in by their new Catering Director. Keleigh called and canceled her lunch appointment.

Seth Hobson arrived, wearing coveralls, and a blue and green plaid shirt. His curly brown hair hung carelessly down to his shoulders. He was clean-shaven, but had a ruddy, down-home look about him. His two helpers, a man and woman, carried insulated containers that looked like they came from a space ship.

Sumner T. Williams, III said, "We can clean the work table." He motioned to the others, "Bring the food here." He pointed to a spot at the end of the table.

They ate in wonderment. "You make all this?" Keleigh said with a full mouth.

"Yes ma'am, Miss Keleigh," he beamed and rocked from foot to foot, "I sure did, with the help of Jack and Jill."

"Jack and Jill?" Came two or three voices at the same time.

"That's what I call them. 'Cause first time I saw them, they were carrying a pail of water.. "

Everyone laughed.

"Seth," Michael said, "I would like you to create a special menu. Get Spike and Sumner to go over it, and show me what you would do for our grand opening. It'll have to encompass foods from all around the world. Can you do that?"

"Yes sir, boss."

Michael leaned over to J.T. "Would you please ask Martha to send out a memo asking everybody not to call me boss"

"Yes. But I don't think it'll work."

"Thanks."

When they finished their workshop, Michael asked. "Henri, are you staying over?"

"I would like to stay for a few days. Can you put us up?"

"You can stay with us," J.T. said, "we'd like to get to know you better."

Michael and Henri shook their heads in agreement. "Their bags are in my car." He threw the keys to J.T.

"Where do you plan to stay tonight, Michael?" Keleigh asked as they headed back toward Las Vegas.

"I think that I better stay at the house," he pondered. "Got to sooner or later."

"If you're not ready, you can always stay with me."

"Thanks." He looked at her. "But, I would like to use your shower. I have a dinner appointment with Poncerelli and Charlie."

"Sure. I have to finish up some stuff at the office, but you can just go on over. Do you remember where I hide the extra key?"

"Do you still keep it under the clay pot by the front door?"

"Sure do."

He dropped her at the office, and went to her place to change.

* * * * * * *

Dominic Poncerelli was waiting at the bar, in a small Italian Restaurant out on Charleston Boulevard. At forty-five, wearing an oversized sweater and designer blue jeans, his black hair parted neatly and slicked back, he didn't look like a cop or a politician. He could easily be taken for an insurance salesman, but never a cop. He looked over the top of his oval shaped glasses, and said, "Hello, Michael."

He walked right pass him. "Oh, there you are. How are you?"

"I'm fine, Michael. The question is, how are you doing?" He took off the glasses and slid a bow under his sweater allowing them to hang down his chest.

"I'm doing okay. Not one hundred percent, but," he hesitated, "but, I'm okay."

They shook hands.

"Let's eat. Charlie is going to be late, but will join us for a drink later." Ponci said with assurance, and motioned for the hostess. "We'd like a table now."

After they ate, Dominic Poncerelli opened a small note pad, turned the page, and said. "I have made a list of suspects." He studied Michael's reaction. "Keep an open mind as you read these. You'll be offended, but I must include everybody, and every possible motive, before we can start weeding them out." He handed him the tablet, "There's no particular order. I jotted them down as I got them."

"Wow! I guess you've got almost everybody here."

"Almost? Who'd I forget?"

"Well for one, the Governor." He was being facetious. "You've got Keleigh, and Bobbi, and Norah. I've known them for a long time. None of them would do such a thing." He looked at him in surprise. "Will you investigate me too?"

"Yeah." He looked serious. "It's what I do."

Charlie joined them.

"We're going over a list of suspects. You and the governor are the only ones who didn't make the list."

"Who's at the t--top of your li--list, P--Ponci?"

"The most obvious. Ceres. I'm sure if she were involved, you'd find one of her henchmen, like Contedetto or the big one, Mario, the prime suspect. But outside the obvious, I've got my bets on Nugari."

"Nugari, huh?" Michael thought a moment, "Why him?"

"He's been working every angle, and then when Darci found out about his abused daughter and threatened to exposed him.. "

"Wait a minute.. hold on.. " he took a breath, "What abused daughter? Who? And just when did she find this out.. and.. and.. how do you know what she found out?"

"Slow down, Michael," Ponci cautioned him, "I'm just look-ing for motives."

"Don't you think it has to do with the resort and what she found out about the Mafia type guys or the Chinese guys?"

"Well it certainly is the direction that I'll probably take first, unless you two can shed some light in another direction."

"I made a copy of all her notes and the stuff she gave me in Malibu," he handed the copies to Ponci. "There isn't anything in there about Nugari's daughter. Where.. ?"

"I got that from her assistant, Maggie." He shuffled through the papers, "Who is this Dave Roberts?"

"I think he's a golf pro that Busy was having an affair with."

"Busy?"

"Norah Laude, Bobbi's sister."

Ponci looked at Charlie. "Do you have any ideas?"

"Yeah, b--but I'll wait 't--til Mikey's not around."

"Why?"

"C--cause you'll get m--mad at m--me."

"Why would I get mad at you? Come on, tell us who you think it is."

"N--no, M--Mik--key." He was getting very nervous, "B--be--s--sides, you should l--let t--the pol--l--lice handle it."

"Charlie's right. Let us do our job, and you build your resort."

"Where are y--you st--staying tonight, Mikey?" He was a little less anxious.

"I'm going home."

"To Malibu?"

"No. Here." he paused. "At our place." He paused once a gain, and looked sadly at his friend, "I'm going to stay at Darci's place."

* * * * * *

He sat in the driveway for a long time before going into the house, but thoughts eluded him. His mind was as empty as he knew the house was without her. He was afraid to go in, his stomach tightened with panic, so uncontrollable that he doubled up over the steering wheel. Then he heard it. That song. The one she loved so much. It sounded like was coming from inside.. waiting for him. The terror subsided as he slid out of the seat and dropped his feet to the ground.

The front door was closed, but unlocked. The timers for the lights had turned on some of the interior, and all of the exterior lights. He stood in the entry waiting for her to come and throw her arms around him. He shut the door and leaned against the jamb while he set the alarm. He moved slowly to the kitchen and ground the last of the coffee beans she had brought from Paris. This emptiness felt like he had reached the end of the world. He looked for her favorite vase, the one that he loved to have her reach up to get, but it was not there. He pretended that she was reaching, and his hands slid under her breasts.. and.. and he began to weep.

He wandered about the living room and the alcove.. touching.. feeling everything, chairs, couch, pillows, and her cherished books. He took one from the shelf. It was about astral travel. The whole idea of out of body experiences seemed to take on a new meaning. He contemplated whether or not he could communicate with his beloved if he learned to travel outside of his body He thumbed through the pages, but shook off the thought, and replaced the book. When the coffee was done, he poured a cup, and started for the bedroom. But he could not bring himself to go into that room just now, instead he went to his office, and worked. He woke, slumped over his computer keyboard. Stretching his stiffened neck, he decided it was time to go to bed.

He walked around the room aimlessly, looking here, looking there.. when suddenly it struck his eye. Her favorite vase, it was there, there on the nightstand with a fresh sterling silver rose, and a few twigs of baby's breath. A chill came over him, and he drew a long, deep breath letting it out slowly. He called out her name. "Darci," quietly at first, "Darci," it became louder, until finally he was shouting, "DAR.. CI!" It dragged out.

"I'm over here, Michael."

He froze at the vision. But his eyes shown with an effervescence created by pure ecstasy. He tried to speak but no words came from his lips. He thought how beautiful and radiant she was standing there in her silver gown.

"Thank you," she said, 'I'm glad you still think that I'm beautiful."

Not knowing what to do, he said, "You know what I was thinking?"

She smiled and nodded.

"This is crazy. You're.. you're.. "

"Yes, darling. Isn't it terrible? I mean, that I had to die like that, and without getting the chance to say goodbye."

"You know what happened.. that someone killed you."

"Yes. But enough for now. How are you doing?"

"I don't know. I thought I knew, but now I'm not sure."

"All of this is very confusing."

"If you think that you're confused, try getting in my skin for a while."

"I don't know if Aditi will let me do that."

"Aditi?"

"Yes. Come sit by me Michael." She sat on the bed, and motioned for him to join her. "Aditi. She's my mentor and spiritual guide." She pointed to the picture over her bed, "That's her there."

"I want to touch you, but I know that I can't."

"I know. But you *did feel* when I kissed you on the cheek."

"That *was* you." He fidgeted where he sat.

"Do you remember when?"

"Of course. At the memorial service, and then in the islands, when I was on our beach." He touched his cheek.

"That's all that I'm allowed to do, and there are limitations to that."

"Like what?"

"Well, nobody else can see me, and I can't be seen by you if someone else is around. As a matter of fact, I can't see you or talk to you when somebody is around."

"What about the memorial service?"

"I got special permission for that."

"So.. I can see you, and talk to you. But why? Does everybody get to do this?"

"I don't think so. The way Aditi explained it was.. well.. It's because of how much we love each other, and how I was killed and taken away from you by someone evil."

"So.. how long can this go on?"

"She says until we find the murderer."

"We?"

"Yes, you and me," she paused, "and someone else."

He looked even more puzzled. "Who?"

"Puca," she waved her hand toward the corner, "my little dog."

"But how can he help?"

"Do you remember what his name means."

"You mean.. "

"You guessed it."

"I don't have to sleep, and you do." She got up and walked across the room, and looked out the window.

"You don't sleep? Can you look through walls, and stuff?"

"I don't know yet. I haven't tried any of that, But I can be somewhere just by thinking about it."

"Like the beach?"

"Like the beach."

"I want to hug you and hold you just like before."

"Me too, Michael. Maybe we can come near and just close our eyes and wish it."

He closed his eyes, and Darci put her arms around his neck and kissed him.

"I could feel you." He trembled, "Tell me I was just imagining it."

"This isn't supposed to happen."

"You felt it, too?"

"Yes, but.. but.. I'm scared Michael. I'm scared." She got excited and disturbed. "I don't know what this means."

"This must be a dream. I'll wake up and.. and.. it's just a dream. Isn't it?"

"We both can't be having the same dream. Besides, I don't dream if I don't sleep."

"So.. what do we do?"

"I don't like this being dead stuff, Michael."

"We gotta go slow," he shivered, "can you ask your Indian guide?"

"I'll go to find her." She kissed him. "Go to sleep my love, I'll be back soon."

Michael believed that this must be a dream. He hugged her pillow and slept.

THE PROJECT

Chapter Four

Henri Piaget looked out on Sundance Lake from the window of the temporary office he had been working from the last three intense and exhausting months. The conceptual design was complete. The hotel and casino had taken shape, and the other uses were assigned spaces that were characteristic to their specific function. Although Henri embraced the design philosophy of the late Le Corbusier, he substantiated his planning arrangements utilizing the systematic views set down by the great Chicago architect, Louis Sullivan. He designated most of the forms to follow their individual functions, thus complementing each contiguous space.

He walked about the room, stopped at each of the large renderings of the various aspects of the project, and studied the completed delineations. He was pleased with his accomplishment, and was ready to prepare the construction documents as soon as the approvals were obtained from the planning commission. Today, as he studied the final designs, he jotted notes for his presentation to the commission. Both he and Michael spent a lot of time with the city and county planners, and they didn't expect any resistance from the commission or any of the local politicians. They were prepared to accept the normal condition that required the specific approval of the State Gaming Commission. Over the last two and a half months Keleigh worked interminably with the people at the Gaming Control Board, and completed everything, with the exception of documenting the financial partner aspects of the project.

Henri stopped and sat on a draftsman's stool in the middle of the room. Since his intention was not for just the visual presence of the structures, but a consciousness of all the spaces melded together to form one homogeneous environment, he searched and studied every facet to verify that the completed design was obedient to his philosophy. He added a separate page to his notes, entitled *special considerations*. He noted; the balustrade along the water's edge must not look quite so nautical.. more sophisticated.. the cupola was too ornate.. the stairs from the main garden must be formal.. formal, not as ostensive as his delineator had shown. He spent the rest of the day preparing his critique for the final design development before they started the working drawings.

Michael called and asked for a dozen copies of eight by ten glossies of all the design drawings for final meetings with his potential investors. Henri promised to have them delivered to his office before noon the next day.

The next afternoon, four people stayed at the office for what had to be the most important meeting of the resort project's development. Michael Orcini, J.T. Popinski, Sumner T.Williams III, and Keleigh Cody-Ives sat around the huge conference table after everyone else had gone for the day. Nathan Gregory flew up from Southern California, and joined them for this all-important meeting.

The largest hurdle was still the selection of their financial partner. Hans Gruber had the cleanest proposal with the most favorable conditions, but his group had not completed their compilation of the funds. As much as they liked Hans' proposal, his documentation was not adequate to make the deal happen. Guy Nestor had half the capital in the bank with a commitment from his bank to fund the remainder in nine months. J.T., Sumner, Keleigh, and Michael were equally concerned about the availability of the final capital contribution. Nestor assured them that he had friends with the cash if the bank could not meet its commitment.

In the meantime, Nugari had beseeched Wu to sweeten the pot. He ultimately persuaded the Wu-Ceres group to increase their ante by another fifty million, which they deposited in Michael's bank with a letter of credit from a major U.S. bank for the balance of funds. Una Ceres personally called Michael with an unusual offer to meet at his home to complete the deal. Michael said that he would meet with his board of directors to make a decision, and get back to her as soon as they agreed on their choice for the financial partner.

Michael shuffled the packets containing the proposals and the eight by tens, and slid them to the middle of the table for the others to take. Keleigh glanced at him across the table and saw his tortured face calling out for help. She resented the presence of the others in the room, because she alone had put most of the project together, and wanted to be the only one whom he would turn to for help. Keleigh wanted to take his face and bury it between her breasts, and.. suddenly his eyes met hers, and he smiled a painful smile. She did not understand the full meaning in his eyes, but for that brief moment, she almost hated his impertinence. Then as she watched him, she thought that he wanted her.

"Keleigh, I want you.. Keleigh." Michael saw a distant smile on her face.

"Yes, Michael." Her lazy reply seemed to brighten the smile into a glow.

Sumner snickered. "Are you with us, Kel?"

She stiffened. "I'm sorry. I must have drifted for a moment."

"He must be something." Sumner joked.

"He is." She gave in to the reality of the moment. "What is it Michael?"

"I want you to give your assessment on the financial candidates first."

"Me?"

"Sure. You've done more than anybody here to bring us to where we are today, so I thought that it would be appropriate for your opinion to be heard first." His face became sincere.. as genuine as the day he first told her about the project. "How about it?"

She was confused. Was this a sublime triumph for her, or merely a passing of responsibility? Keleigh thumbed through the papers and photos searching for her notes. "I need a moment."

He respected her wish, "While Keleigh's getting ready, we can look at the drawings that our architect has prepared." He demonstrated by picking up and pointing out the eight by tens in his packet. "These are copies of our presentation to the planning commission. I think you'll agree that he has done a terrific job."

They spent a short time inspecting the photos.

"How're you doing Kel?"

She found her notes, "I'm ready Michael."

"Then the floor is yours."

Keleigh remained seated, but adjusted her position and sat straight. She began with an official voice, "I've labored over the proposals from all the major candidates, and have a recommendation that is apart from their individual offers." She distributed a short scenario, and gave them time to read her single page abstraction. "As you can see, I would embrace the combining of the Hans Gruber Group and Nestor Enterprises. Gruber is my first choice, but he is slow to bring the funds to the table. Nestor, on the other hand, has half the funds ready now, but his take-out financing package is shaky." She took a sip from her glass, "Then there is.. "

"What if.. ?" Sumner started to speak, but stopped when Michael gestured that Keleigh had the floor.

"Then there is the WU-Ceres Group." Her inflection followed by a pause that denoted her disdain for the motley coterie. "They are too pushy, and I think that Nugari wants to force a hostile take over before the project is completed." She looked up, and surveyed each face with determination. They knew she had something else to say, something that wasn't written in the scenario. "If we combine the two, perhaps we could start with Nestor, then use Gruber as a back-up for the take-out." She didn't wait for their reactions. Keleigh's face was exceptionally beautiful when she set her mind to express a logical statement. Her emerald eyes sparkled with the excitement of a child on Christmas morning. "The Nestor-Gruber combination is a perfectly wonderful solution to our circumstances." She looked away as she rose, and walked around the table, touching each man's shoulder as she passed. "Nestor can put up the money to begin, and Hans' people can bring in the balance later. We'll have to work out the timing, but I think it's a good plan if we can get them together." She was careful not to have eye contact with anyone during her monologue, except Michael.

Keleigh went on to lay out her plan in detail, finishing with a predetermined look that would end all questions. She deliberately looked at each one as she panned their faces, finally stopping where she burned her gaze deep into their unsuspecting attorney, "No intelligent human being would turn down such an offer." Keleigh turned away from the table, and without looking back she said, "Please excuse me. I'll be right back."

The men sat quietly until J.T. spoke. "She's got it in for somebody. But I think she just might be on to something. It could work, if Guy and Hans would come together."

"Why did she pick on me?" Nate Gregory asked.

"She wasn't picking on you Nate. You just happened to be at the end of the line." Sumner intoned.

"Guy is a control freak. I don't think that he would go for the idea." Michael chimed in, "But I would like to give Keleigh's idea a concerted effort. What do you think?" He waited for an answer.

It was J.T.'s turn. "I feel the same as you boss. Let's map out a plan of how we're going to present this to those guys."

"If I know Keleigh, she's already got one." Michael reported.

"Yeah. You're probably right."

"Yes sir. I'll bet she does." Sumner added.

"I wouldn't run this by Ruby if I were you." Nate instructed.

"Why not, Nate?" Sumner asked."

"Let's just say.. wel--ll, I think we should keep it in this room for now." His quick response seemed determined.

Keleigh returned with a fresh, almost spiritual, glow on her face, and went directly to her place at the table. She knew that all eyes were on her, and played all her feminine cards with the right amount of sophistication. "Wel--ll?" She sat down slowly, easing herself all the way back in the chair. She swiveled to face Michael.

The men looked at each other. Michael nodded to J.T.

"We'd like to see your plan, Keleigh." J.T. requested.

"Don't you mean that you'd like to hear my plan?"

"No. I think that you've got one for us to read."

"Think so, huh?"

He remained silent as she looked first to Sumner, then to Michael for assistance.

"You guys think you know me, don't you?"

"You amaze me," Michael said in a less than business voice, "You came up with such a brilliant idea, that we're sure there must be more. You obviously gave this a lot of thought." He looked thankfully at her, more like a friend than a boss.

Keleigh looked around the table soaking in the distinct respect of these experienced executives and glowed with pride. "I did prepare a little something," she reached into her briefcase, "this is how I'd structure the proposal." She passed the papers around.

"A little something?" Nate quizzed her after scanning the half-dozen pages. "If this job doesn't work out for you, come and see me. I could use you in my office. He felt Michael's stare. "Sorry Michael, but she's good."

"That's what I've been trying to tell him all along."

"Kel. Will you set up a meeting with Guy and Hans?"

"Sure boss."

"I don't think that they should know what the plan is.. I mean.."

Keleigh interrupted J.T. "I know exactly what you mean."

"Michael turned to Nate. "Do you want to add or modify any legal terminology?"

"Like I said before, she's good." He smiled at her. "Not a word, Michael, not a word."

"God help me." She fidgeted in her chair, "I think I'm starting to like a lawyer."

They all laughed, especially Nate Gregory.

* * * * * * *

She sat on the couch near the fireplace. The reflection from the soft glow of the flames seemed to dance in her smooth, black, silky hair. Her silver, rose pedal, gown appeared strangely transparent exposing her creamy skin. Darci Tashmit was beautiful. She was the epitome of everything Michael wanted, except.. except she wasn't alive.

"Hi!"

"What are you doing here?"

"What do you mean?

"It's a perfectly valid question. Besides you're not supposed to answer my question with a question."

"This is my home. Remember?"

"Sure, but.. you know what I mean. don't you?" He put his briefcase on the side chair near the couch. "I'm very confused by all this."

"I know, darling, and I have a lot of answers for you. But first you must sit and relax. I'll pour you a glass of brandy. Take your shoes off, and I'll be right there."

He knew that none of this should be happening, it couldn't be happening, but he wasn't in any mood to try to figure it out tonight. "How long have you been here?"

"We don't have any time where I'm at, so I really can't answer you."

"Did you have a talk with your Indian friend?"

"You mean Aditi. She's my guide and mentor. Yes, I had a long talk with her." She brought the brandy, and sat at his feet. "Here, darling."

He felt the touch of her finger as she placed the stem in his hand.

He trembled, "How can you hold a glass? I mean how can.. how do.. how is it that I can feel you.. ? I just felt your touch. Am I imagining it or.. ?"

"Patience darling. Just rest now."

Michael sipped his brandy, and gazed down at the beautiful image before him.

"Tell me about your day," she said, "What did you do?" She rose up on her knees, propped her arms on his lap, and looked up into his eyes. She sensed that he was uncomfortable, and slid back slowly resting on her feet.

He told her of the meetings and their decision to go with the latest idea and try to get Guy and Hans together.

"That's a great idea. I've always liked Hans. D'ya think it'll work out? Whose idea was it anyway?"

"You haven't changed.. still are full of," he paused, "questions."

"Wel--ll?"

"Well, naturally I hope it'll work out. Time will tell."

"Wel--ll?"

"Well, what?"

"Well, whose idea? I'll bet it was yours, and you don't want.. "

"It was Keleigh. She not only thought up the idea, but had a complete scenario laid out for us. Nate didn't want to change a word in her proposal."

"Keleigh?" She got up and walked to the kitchen.

"What?" He got up and followed her, "What's wrong that Kel dreamed up the plan? She's got a good business sense." He sat on a barstool. "But I gotta tell you, we were all flabbergasted when she presented the idea." He watched her pout, but continued. "I asked her to be the first to present some comments on our situation. And.. ya know.. no one else did after she was done."

"Did what?"

"Comment on the candidates."

"Candidates?"

"Yes. The financial partners."

"Oh, them."

"Okay. What's going on in that pretty head."

"I've been gone just a little while, and now.. *another* one is making her move."

"You think that Keleigh is hitting on me?" He watched her lip purse a little more, "Can you tell that sort of thing from where you are?"

"Well, no." She sashayed a little. "But I can tell.. as a woman. That's what."

"Look darling, Kel and I have been like buddies for a long time. She's just trying to do a good job. She knows that she doesn't have to impress me."

"Okay, Mister Can't See Past His Nose." She fussed with the rose pedal gown.

"Did you know that I can see right through your dress?"

"Do you like what you see?"

"Of course I do. Why shouldn't I?"

"Is it the same as before? She lowered her head and swung her shoulders like a shy schoolgirl. "I mean, do I look the same as when, when.. when I was.. you know.. ?"

"When you were alive?"

"You don't have to be so.. so.. darned blunt."

"Yes, except for the fact that I *know* you're different. You look fan--tas--tic." He stretched the affirmation, and examined her from her head to her toes. "It's much easier to undress you with my eyes than it was before." He smiled, a satisfied grin. "But, I must say that imagination certainly has its place in a relationship."

"I always liked it when you did that."

"That?" He examined her again. "Undressed you?"

"Like that with your eyes." She moved toward him. "It turned me on."

"Does it still?"

"Still what?"

"Turn you on. I mean, do you still have those sort of feelings?"

"Yes, it's strange. My feelings for you are a lot stronger now.. now that.. " She edged a little closer, "I want to.. " She looked at him dolefully, and turned away.

"You said that you had a long talk with Adehty," he mispronounced.

"Ah--dee--ti." She was very phonetic.

"Yes, Aditi. What did she tell you about the touching stuff?" He got up and went over to the fireplace. Resting his arm on the lintel he continued, "Did she explain why, or how we're able to feel the touch. What I mean is, well, how can I feel you when you're not really here?"

"It has something to do with how much I loved you when I was alive."

"Don't you love me anymore?"

"Of course I do, silly." She sat across the couch, like it was a lounge. "I love you more than before. It's like everything is magnified hundreds of times."

"But, lots of people love a great deal. Do they get to do this?"

"I don't know, I just know about us."

"How much *so much* did.. I mean.. do you love me?"

"Oh, Michael. I never did tell you how much." Darci raised herself up on her elbow, and readjusted her position, "I promise that before this is over, you will never wonder about that again. Ever."

"I wish.. I wish.. "

"Don't be wishing for that, my darling. We're not ready for that, yet."

"You mean.. can we.. no.. no that would be too much. I mean I don't.. " He began to stammer, "It was just a thought. We could never, could we?"

"I think we can, but neither of us is ready."

Michael sat down on the edge of the couch next to her, and looked longingly.

"If I get scared, I'll go somewhere else."

He shifted away a little. "What else did she tell you?"

"Like I told you before, I'm supposed to be here to help you find my murderer. I can go places just by thinking about where I want to be."

"Anywhere?"

"So far. Once I went to a casino to check things out, but Aditi zapped me back."

"She did what?"

"She brought me back here. She wanted me to stay here and wait for you. I guess I wasn't ready for a bunch of people walking through me."

"Walking through?"

"Yeah. They can't see me, and as far as they are concerned, I'm not here. I'm a ghost for everybody except you."

"You're a ghost! You're a ghost!" His face got red with anger. "It's not fair."

Darci sat up and opened her arms for him to come to her.

"You're not going to disappear, are you?"

"I don't think so."

They hugged for what seemed like an eternity to Michael.

"I can feel your heart," she said as she broke the spell. "I feel very close to you."

He felt a mysterious magnetism and trembled with excitement. "It would be so bizarre if we could have.. "

"I told you that we can't go there yet."

"But.. " he leaned forward only to find that she was gone.

"Michael." She was standing by the fireplace, "lets just talk for now. Okay?"

"Okay. How about if you talk for awhile, and I just listen." He condescended.

"Aditi said because of how we were together when I was alive, that we can be that way now.. well.. almost the same way.. for a while anyway." She went on to explain in detail that they could have a relationship together, but only when they were alone. She wasn't able to be with him at any other time. If he was with anybody, anybody at all, she couldn't intrude. "As a matter of fact,

Aditi says that I can't even wish myself to see you when somebody else is in the same space with you." She waved her hand at the diminished fire, and the flames responded with a remarkable new brilliance. "I didn't know I could do that." Her face was puzzled.

"I'm going to have to keep you around."

"I wish you could, but I don't think that you have anything to do with me being here. What I mean is.. oh!.. I don't know what I mean." The pout returned.

He sensed her exasperation. "We can talk about this some other time."

"No. I want to tell you everything I know about this ghost stuff."

"What else is there?"

"I'm learning a little every time I see Aditi." She became serious, "I can stop time.. well sort of.. it's like.. like people and things don't talk or move or.. anything when I want to move around them. It's hard to explain." Darci looked at his bewildered face. "Then there's Puca. His powers are not clear to me yet."

"What does he do?"

"Aditi says that she'll tell me soon. Michael, I've got to go to work on this mystery, and I'm not sure how to start."

"How can I help?"

"You just have to wait until I can get some more experience at this ghost stuff."

"So, where do we go from here?"

"I must go to Aditi for my next spiritual workshop."

"Spiritual workshop?"

"It's where she teaches me what to do." She moved toward him, "I must go now. I'll see you soon, my darling." Darci bent over and kissed him on the lips, and disappeared.

* * * * * *

The city was still enveloped in a sea of light as J.T. Popinski maneuvered his new Cadillac Sports Utility Vehicle down the freeway and towards Sundance Lake. He mused at how all the towers looked strangely alike even in their attempt to be different. The sun rose over the hills and cast a mysterious hue across the lake as he pulled up to the temporary construction office.

"Good morning, Jan," Henri came out to greet him, "It's good to see you on this beautiful day." He stopped at the edge of the entrance platform, and spread his arms out and up, as to welcome a Spiritual Presence.

"Are you welcoming the Gods?"

"I need all the help I can get. Come over here." He stepped down, and beckoned him to follow. "Look at how the sun reflects on the lake." He waved his hand to illustrate.

"Okay. It's very nice. Am I supposed to be looking for something special?"

"Look how it stops right there in the middle, and continues on a little further over there," he pointed across the lake, "it's like something's in the way." He studied J.T.'s doubtful face. "The same thing happens at sunset."

"Must be some sort of phenomenon. There's a lot of strange things out here in the middle of the desert, you know, like mirages and other things like that." He squirmed a little, and changed his demeanor. "Do you think it's a sign?" He was flippant.

"It wasn't there.. like that.. when we first started here." He motioned toward his car. "Come, let me show you something.

They drove a short distance, to a place where a condominium development was under way. "Let's walk over there." Henri instructed.

The men stopped on a small knoll and gazed out across the lake. "Look!" Henri pointed, "the sun shines clear across the lake when you look from here. Nothing gets in the way from this side." Henri stood motionless for a moment, "It's almost like there's something in the middle of the lake, but it's only there when you look from our site."

J.T. became uneasy. "You don't suppose that it has anything to do with.. ?" He was afraid to continue.

"Don't know. But it only seems to happen when you're at our project." He repeated himself. "Don't know."

"Let's go back to the trailer."

They drove the short distance without saying a word. When they arrived, the men walked over to the same place, still not talking, and stared at the sun's interrupted reflection on the lake. They looked at each other in disbelief.

"How long has this been going on?"

"Camuela noticed it the day after Darci's memorial service."

"Is it like this every day?"

"Yeah." Henri started toward the trailer, stopping he turned back to J.T., "It's really weird at sunset, when the sun shines back this way." He needed to ascertain J.T.'s reaction, and carefully chose his next words. "It almost as if you know there's something out there in the lake. Something big, but invisible, and.. and the only way you know it's there is when the sun shines on the lake." He saw the bewildered expression. "You think I'm crazy, don't you?"

"Does it happen at night.. with the moonlight?"

"Don't know. I haven't been out here at night since it started happening."

They agreed to return at night, and see if the phenomenon occurred.

"By the way Jan, what brings you out here anyway?"

"I wanted to get your opinion on the construction timeline for the project. I was wondering if we could phase the project, from a design standpoint." He walked over to the table where the plans were spread out. "Can we do any of the construction now, and phase some things for a later time?"

"Are you worried that someone might hold out on funding the remainder of the money after the construction has begun?"

"No. Actually I'm trying to anticipate.. it's ah.. " He slammed his fist on the table, "We need to get started, and I'm afraid that Michael will jump at the wrong offer.. "

"You want me to say that we could hold off on some of the facilities, and still have our resort? You want a start-up resort with phase two ready to go at some later time, and you want me to validate your plan. Right?"

"Well, I wouldn't put it exactly that way."

"How *exactly* would you put it?" Henri was very short with him.

"Don't get me wrong, Henri. I just want to do what's right for Michael."

"What's right?"

"We're trying to put Hans and Nestor together on the deal. Guy has half the money now, and I think Hans can put together the rest but, he needs a little more time."

"You'll never get those two to go in together. Hans might, but Nestor wants his own deal. He wants control. No, I can't see them as partners."

"Michael and the others want to give it a try. You know that the alternate is Ceres and the Chinese. I have to meet with them and the attorneys to establish the basic agreements. Wu has put a lot on money into an escrow account to entice Michael to move forward in a hurry. Keleigh thinks that Nugari has plans to cut Michael out of the deal."

"How can he do that? After all *this is* Michael's resort."

"I don't know, but I trust her intuition, and so do Sumner and Charlie."

"I see what you mean. Let's consider what options can be incorporated."

Two hours later, J.T. headed back to the office impassioned with the knowledge that there was a light at the end of the tunnel. He only hoped that Hans Gruber and Guy Nestor could understand, and come together as their financial partners.

He was strangely excited about coming back to see the sunset over the lake. The sunrise phenomenon had his interest aroused, even though he wouldn't let Henri know.

The mid-day sun had completely gone behind the dark gray clouds when he reached the city limits. The absence of the sun left the skyline over Mount Charleston with an eerie profile that seemed to blend reluctantly with the storm hovering above.

The cold, moist wind blew as he ran from his car to the office building. The light rain had turned to hail, and the walk alongside the structure was covered with ice pebbles the size of grains of rice. Intoxicated with the excitement of his earlier accomplishments, but aware of the hazard, he carefully restrained his gait and slowed to a snail's pace. Once inside he rushed to the elevator, and made his way to resort offices.

"Candace, come to my office, and bring your pad." He fired his command.

"Yes, sir."

His eyes danced with excitement as he dictated a memo of his tour de force. He paced back and forth with anticipation as Candace wrote awkwardly in her own style of shorthand. She did not understand the melodrama, and constantly interrupted with an abundance of misinterpretations. Finally after his message was done, he said. "Ask Martha to help you with this. I want a rough draft back ASAP."

"Yes, sir. Excuse me for asking, but is something wrong?"

"Everything's fine, just get that memo done for me. And, uhm . . . oh yes, please ask Keleigh to come in. I want to see her. Another thing, ask Martha to call and confirm my three o'clock with Nugari, Wu and Mr. Ruby."

"Yes, sir. Where's the meeting?"

"It's here," he cleared his throat, "when's Mr. Orcini due?"

"He just called. He's on his way."

"Let me know when he gets here."

"Yes, sir. Is there anything.. can I get you some coffee?"

"Thanks, coffee sounds good. Thanks."

"You wanted to see me?" Keleigh peered around the door jamb.

J.T. glanced up, "Come in Keleigh.," he continued working the keyboard of his desktop computer, "I'll be right with you." He gestured for her to sit across from him.

"Save as," he said to the computer, and turned to her. "We have a meeting with Nugari and Wu and Ruby and, and.. " he smiled, "They are going to try to force the issue of an agreement. I don't want to close the door on any opportunities while we try to put your plan into action, so we must play the game."

"My plan?"

"Yes. Your plan for Guy and Hans."

"Do you like my plan?"

"Yes, as a matter of fact, I met with Henri this morning. We have some ideas to help your plan. You'll get a memo from Candace in a little while. Together, I think we can make this work. It'll take some time, and we must convince Michael that it's worth the effort."

"They have time on their side, and they know that Michael wants to get going. How are we going to stall them, and at the same time convince Michael to wait?"

"Stalling them will be relatively easy, but Michael.. yes, Michael.. wel--ll, that's a horse of a different story."

"Color."

"What?"

"It's color. A horse of a different color." She smiled a devilish smile, "Or do you say it different where you come from, Mister Popinski?"

"You're cute, Miss Ives-ski." He retaliated.

"Touché."

"Thanks."

"For what?"

"For lightening things up."

"You *do* get too serious sometimes."

"I know. I'm sorry.

"How do you plan to stall them?"

"That's easy. We'll put enough stumbling blocks in the contracts to keep the attorneys busy with changes. Those guys will love us, 'cause they get paid by the hour."

"Yes, but Michael is no dummy. He'll see right through our scheme, and want to get right to the core of it."

"That's where you come in."

"Where I come in?"

"Michael listens to you. He listens to you more than anybody, even his attorney."

"You really think so?"

"Sure."

"What should I do?"

"Be positive in the meeting this afternoon, but when you can, get Michael alone. Maybe you can take him out to dinner, and convince him to be a little patient and wait for your plan to kick in."

"Excuse me sir," Candace came in with a rough draft of the memo. "Will there be anything else?"

"Just a minute while I read this," he handed it to Keleigh, "it looks fine for now." He looked at the secretary. "You did a good job. We'll make some notes, and have you finish it in a little while."

"Thanks." She smiled proudly, and left.

"I like your ideas Jan," Keleigh said in her most serious voice, "the phasing plan could just make the whole thing work. You're a genius."

"Henri is the genius. I admit that the phasing idea was mine, but he made it work."

"Can I write on this?" she referred to the memo.

"Of course. I want whatever ideas you have."

She finished writing. "Here. What do you think of your idea now?"

He smiled. "Perfect." He punched the control on the intercom, "Candace. We're ready for the final draft."

The meeting with the vultures, as Keleigh called them, was long and meticulously boring. Michael winced a few times when J.T. interjected his arguments that set the attorneys off into their legal embattlements. After two grueling hours, the only thing they agreed to, was to return in a few days, and continue negotiations.

"I think it went well." Hector Ruby said as he prepared to leave.

The others echoed his remark as they left.

"What's going on with you two?" Michael snapped.

"What?" They intoned in concert.

"You know exactly what I'm talking about. Why the stall?"

They looked at each other with Keleigh shrugging her shoulders.

"And?" Michael insisted. "The stall. Why the stall?"

"No stall, Michael. We just want to be sure that all the pegs are in the right holes. Don't want to have any loose ends, especially with these guys."

"That's right," Keleigh mimicked. "Michael. How about having dinner with me tonight? My treat. I have a lot of things to talk to you about, and that's the only way I seem to be able to get to talk to you alone, anymore."

"Seven-thirty?"

His quick response was unexpected. "Uh.. sure.. seven-thirty." She stammered.

"I'll pick you up at your place."

J.T. gave her a thumbs up when Michael turned away, but was unaware that he saw the signal in the mirror across the room.

"Oh!" Michael remembered and turned to J.T., "please get with Sumner and Henri, and interview the general contractors on our list. I'd like a short list by this time next week. Henri needs to get his interior decorators lined up too."

"Okay boss."

"Anything on the Guy and Hans team yet?"

"I'm working on it." Keleigh said.

"Kel. Would you stop at Sumner's office, and tell him that I'd like to see him before he goes home?"

"Absolutely." She smiled and turned away. "Don't forget, seven-thirty." She called over her shoulder without looking back.

"Seven-thirty."

* * * * * * *

The city's pulse throbbed from the street and highway battlefields as commuters made their way in every direction. Cars and trucks and busses and an assortment of minivans and sport utility vehicles roared towards their own special destinations. The fires of excitement would soon glow from the neon that was attached to the casinos and hotels. Las Vegas was more than a city of gambling, it was a constant traffic jam, and J.T. Popinski couldn't wait to get out to the lake.

Henri and Cam waited in their car while he walked to meet them.

Camuela opened her window and pointed. "Moon's going to be full tonight."

J.T. looked up to see it peering from behind the black clouds. "I'm not exactly sure what we're doing here." He looked toward Sundance Lake. "Do you really think that Darci's ghost is out there?"

"Let's take a look," Henri interrupted as he got out of the car, "can't see anything from here." He opened Cam's door, and pleaded with her. "Coming?"

She stepped out slowly and intently. "I'm not even breathing hard, darlin.. "

"We'll see about that." He slid his arm around her waist and pulled her tight against his groin while he kissed her passionately."

"You can do that later. I came here to see if anything's really happening out there on the lake." He started away, glancing back, "Coming?" he mocked.

Camuela straightened her blouse, and took Henri's hand. "Later," she whispered.

The moon had positioned itself with a soft glowing ring directly between the storm clouds. It's *interrupted* beam danced on the water as if to encourage them to look beyond the ordinary and find an uncommon meaning.

"It looks the same as it does during the day." Cam's voice shivered.

"Except," J.T. said with definite trepidation, "there seems to be a shape to whatever is *interrupting* the ray of moonlight. Look," he directed. "look, over there."

They stood in silence as the *interruption* seemed to take shape.

"Let's go around and get a better look." Cam tugged at Henri and simultaneously burrowed tight against the safety of his large frame.

They drove silently to a vantage point on the opposite side of the lake. The *interruption* became more apparent as they stopped on a small hill where another hotel would be built. A translucent pyramidal shape seemed to define the anomalous phenomenon. They sat transfixed at the sight, as the moon moved through the clouds casting distorted rays, and creating more wonder in their minds.

Finally Camuela spoke. "Do you think it has anything to do with Darci?"

The men were quiet.

"I mean, the way she died and all. Maybe she's a ghost or something, and is trying to tell us something. Something about the resort and the lake or.. something." She punched Henri. "Say something."

"It's weird," Henri retorted, "and it started right after she died. I suppose that maybe it could be some sort of harbinger. Maybe she's trying to tell us something. Maybe she's trying to warn us about Ceres and Wu and those guys." Perplexed, he sighed, "I don't have the slightest clue."

"In the islands there were always signs that we watched for when somebody died in an unusual and sudden or mysterious way. They always told us a story about the ghost and how it's soul couldn't rest until we knew what really happened." She looked woefully first at Henri and then J.T. "There's a Ghost at Sundance Lake." She said with certainty.

* * * * * *

"Come in Sumner," Michael motioned for him to sit on the couch across the room from his desk, "over there, I'll be through with this call in a moment." His face drew tight as he listened to the voice on the phone. He squirmed in his chair and finally blurt out, "I don't like where this is going." He listened. "Yes, I understand, but I must know," he said softly, "I really need to find out . . ." He listened again. "Thanks. Keep in touch."

"Is something wrong, boss?"

"That was the police. They still don't have any new information about Darci's.. uhm.. accident."

"What about that fellow, Poncerelli? Has he been any help?"

"No, but he seems to be more in touch with the situation than the other cops."

"You must be patient." Sumner got up, and gestured for Michael to join him. "We have work to do." He invoked. "Why'd you want to see me?"

"Yes, you're right. He regained his composure. "I want you to get together with Henri and work out the interior designs of the common areas and hotel suites. We'll have to start buying fixtures and furnishings soon if we want to get good deals."

"I've had an interior designer call me several times, says she knows you."

"Really? What's her name?"

"I have it here in my notes . . . let me see," he shuffled through his files, "oh yes here's her card. Gina Santiago."

Michael looked doubtful.

He read the quote on the card. "Rules and models destroy genius and art," a slight pause, "unusual." He searched Michael's face. "Do you know her."

"We met briefly at the airport, before I met Darci, and.. well.. I um.. sort of promised that I'd look her up."

"Do you want me to call her?"

"I guess it wouldn't hurt to talk to her and see what she's got to offer."

"Sounds like you've already done that."

"It was an innocent meeting. We just passed the time. Okay?"

"I'll give her a call. Anything else?"

"Would you meet with Keleigh and Henri with regard to the promenade that connects the hotel and the casino?" He looked smug. "I noticed something which looks like an interference of flow near the area where the concierge is supposed to be available to both functions." The boss pushed back into the couch. "I want you to be sure that the hotel doesn't look as though it's dependent on the casino. It must appear to stand alone, and the casino must also have it's own distinctive quality." He studied his hotel chief. "I'm fearful that Keleigh may have exerted her enthusiasm for the casino beyond the total concept. I trusted that Henri would keep her in check, but as you probably noticed, she does have a way in getting what she wants."

The phone rang. It was Martha. "Una Ceres is on the phone and wants to come over here to meet with you."

"When? Why?"

"She didn't say. Do you want to talk to her?"

"Tell her that I'm in a meeting, and I'll call her back."

"I've already told her that, but she insisted."

"Then, I guess that you'll just have to tell her again. Please?"

"Yes, sir."

He barely put the phone down and it rang again. It was Martha. "She said that she was on her way over and would be here in fifteen minutes, and hung up."

"Harrumph," he uttered, "I guess we're all in for a showdown. Get Wyatt Earp and Doc Holiday and meet me at the OK Corral." He said imitating John Wayne.

"What?"

"Oh, never mind. Let me know who she brings with her."

"What are you going to do about her?"

"Play along." He got up, crossed over to his desk, picked up a picture of Darci, and said, "Until I know for sure."

Know what?" Sumner intoned.

Michael moved back toward Sumner. "Until I know if she had anything to do with Darci's death." He put her picture on the coffee table.

"What will you do if she did? I mean, she's still the prime candidate as your financial partner." He rose to meet Michael's eyes. "You may not know for a long time if she was involved. If she was, then what?"

"Don't know, I don't know."

"Do you want me in this meeting?"

He thought for a moment. "Yes."

"I'll drop in after you start. Okay?"

Donna Ceres arrived with Connie and Dave Roberts, and was ushered into the conference room where she waited impatiently.

The door opened and Martha entered. "Can I get something for you?"

"Tell Mister Orcini that I am waiting."

"He is aware that you are here. He is on an important call, and will be wth you in a moment. Anything?"

Donna Ceres removed a handkerchief from her sleeve, and waved her off, dismissing her like a servant.

"She acts like I work for her," Martha said with a whine, "I'm not one of her henchman." She looked soulfully at her boss. "You're not going to let her have anything to say about how things run around here, are you? I mean if she puts up the money."

"What did she do to you?"

"She waved her handkerchief at me. Like I was a minion, or something."

"Minion? He repeated.

Martha nervously straightened an imaginary wrinkle in her collar, and waited for his response.

"Minion." He repeated. "Well. Minion. I think that you'll have to rub her out."

"Rub her out? You mean like the Mafia does?" She frowned. "You must be joking, Mister Orcini."

"Yes, of course I am."

"I told her that you were finishing a call."

"Thanks." He smiled. "Ask Mister Williams and Mister Popinski to join us."

"Anyone else?"

"No, thanks."

Ermano Contedetto and Dave Roberts rose when Michael entered. Connie began to walk to meet Michael, but was stopped by a motion from Ceres.

"My senior officers will be joining this meeting."

"But, I only wish to speak with you, Mister Orcini."

"It doesn't look like you wanted to be alone."

"They are here to protect my, how should I put it? My interests."

"Then you, of all people, must understand my position."

Sumner and J.T. entered and quickly sat on each side of Michael without speaking.

"Shall we begin?" Michael looked up as Martha rushed in with steno pad in one hand, and a tissue in the other.

"I'm ready when you are sir." She waved the tissue in the direction of Ceres, and sat directly across from her.

"Tell us why you are here."

Donna Ceres looked at Michael, and ignored the others. "I must know why it is taking so long for you to complete our arrangement? Attorneys meeting and meeting. Papers here, papers there, everywhere more papers. We have an agreement, no?"

"These things take time." Sumner invoked.

"Mister Orcini?"

"Everything must be in order first." Followed J.T.

"Mister Orcini?" Donna Ceres raised her voice. "I came here to discuss our arrangement, and you are being very rude."

"Rude?" Michael knew that she must stay on the defensive or he would have to succumb to the agenda of her forced meeting. "How am I being rude? Why did you come here? What is this meeting about?" He bombarded her with questions.

"I want to talk to you about our arrangement, and you bring in these other people." She gesticulated an all-encompassing wave.

"We don't have an arrangement, and these other people are necessary to my operation. You just drop in without any prior notice. We are very busy. Please state your purpose or be kind enough to leave."

Donna Ceres didn't like being put on the defensive. She stared at Michael, and then motioned to Dave Roberts. He took some documents from a large case on the floor, and handed them to Michael.

Michael glanced at them, and passed them to J.T.

After a while J.T. said "Your position hasn't changed, except to give you more control. I don't think there is anything to discuss, unless of course , you have something to add." He looked at Michael. "They are taking a stronger position of control with nothing for us on the down side. Granted, their group would be taking most of the financial risk, but they could also walk with the entire project if you defaulted in the slightest way, from operation right down to an ambiguous statement about design." He slid the papers to Sumner.

Sumner quickly went to the section about the corporate control. "I agree. We would have to give up something that has not been discussed to this point." He handed the papers to Michael.

"I am not willing to start from the beginning with you or anyone." He said in a masterful tone. He waited for a moment, and rose. "If you want to deal with me you will have to agree to my terms. Put all of your investment in escrow, agree to the terms originally set forth, and notify my attorney when the documents are ready to execute." He slid the documents half way across the table toward the Donna.

Sumner and J.T. pushed their chairs back and stood.

Martha closed her steno pad, but remained seated.

"You are a difficult man, Mister Orcini." Donna Ceres remained seated in an attempt to regain control of the meeting.

The three men stood motionless.

"I like you Mister Orcini. You will have what you want. No more delays." She motioned for Connie to help her up. "Have Mister Ruby come to my home for the final paperwork. He can complete them with my people."

Her attempt to control was met with Michael's response. "Mister Ruby will not prepare the final review. Send the papers to me." He looked at Dave Roberts. "What is your position in this project?"

"I am an advisor to Donna Ceres."

After they left J.T. looked at Michael. "Looks like we have a project."

"I'm concerned," Sumner interjected, "first Nugari and Wu with their back stabbing, and now Ceres wanting more, but conceding without a fight. Something's not right here, Michael. Something is terribly wrong. And, and . . . who is this guy Roberts?"

"Let's wait and see." Michael turned to leave, and stopped. "Martha get Nathan Gregory on the phone, and tell Charlie that I want to meet with him and Commissioner Poncerelli."

"Michael." Pleaded J.T.

"Let's wait and see."

* * * * * * *

Charlie's home, like that of many small independent contractors, was in a state of constant reconstruction. The main entry floor, which leads to the Great Room, was covered with hardboard to protect the new granite tiles, while the walls were waiting for the finish plaster coat. The entire rear wall of the great room was gone, replaced by a temporary sheet of transparent plastic that separated it from the patio. Dominic Poncerelli was sitting on the patio gazing out over the valley when Michael arrived.

"Out there somewhere," he said without acknowledging Michael's presence, "is the one person that can tell us what we want to know. It is pure torture to know who that person is, but not be able to . . ." he paused, stood straight filling his lungs until they were ready to burst, and let out the air of disappointment, "because she's covered her ass."

He became silent as the muffled sounds of the city came to this remote sanctuary on a soft, cool wind from the west, as if he was waiting for an answer. He turned to Michael and blurted out, "You know that Charlie's grandfather got it through a tribal dispute with a Southern Paiute. The Paiutes didn't have any claim to this place . . ." he paused.

"Who?"

"The Paiute? Oh I don't remember his name. Some old Indian."

"No. Who covered her ass?"

"Who covered.. ? Oh yes, yes. Ceres. She's got it all covered. We haven't been able to find out anything. Each of them uses the other for an alibi. None of them were anywhere near Darci's house, or office."

Charlie joined them carrying a tray of sandwiches and drinks. He placed the tray in the glass top table, and sat across from Ponci. "Have something."

"There are other suspects."

The commissioner told the two men about the investigations that Darci had been into as well as her meetings with deVillefrance and Roberts.

"She had meetings with them?" Michael asked.

"Yes. One of my men found out from her secretary."

"Maggie knew about these meetings? He looked at Charlie for an answer. "Why was she meeting with them?"

"Sh--she d--didn't trust any of th--them. She was afraid that the--the--they were t--t--trying to st--steal your pr--pr--project. Sh--she wanted t--to p--p--prote--te--tect you."

"Who else did she meet with?"

"You name them, and she probably met with them. She even had lunch with your old girl friend, Roberta Azure."

"Bobbi? Why would she investigate Bobbi?"

"The way I get it is that Miss Azure invited her out to lunch. Maggie said that she tried to dissuade her, but Darci was curious, and wanted to see what she was up to."

"Commissioner. What would you say if I were to hire a private eye?"

"He might get in the way."

"No disrespect, but I need to see some results."

"We are getting results. We're eliminating the suspects one at a time."

Suddenly he despised Poncerelli because he was indifferent and unemotional towards the whole case. He abhorred the matter-of-fact attitude this policeman used. He wanted him to be passionate in this task. He wanted it to be his only concern, instead Poncerelli was confined to the protocol of his department.

"Can you put more men on the case?"

"More is not always better. Detective work is not a menial task, but a tedious one. Time is on our side. Be patient, my friend. The guilty one always makes a mistake."

* * * * * *

The sky was gray and forbidding as Pernicius Nugari turned his BMW into the long drive leading to Casa Trinacria. An appropriate ambiance for the colorless and sinister task at hand. He must convince Donna Ceres to eliminate deVillefrance from the equation. He knew what was facing him if he failed. He must be forceful, but ready to sacrifice a portion of his own stake in the project. He knew that his entire share could be snatched away if he made the smallest mistake. The Donna was not a person to cross, but her need to be in control made her the obvious factor to his plan. She must be persuaded to direct her greed against this unnecessary sycophant who will only get in the way. He must succeed in convincing Contedetto first before taking the scheme to The Donna.

The Asian girl who met him at the front door distracted Nugari. Her diminutive tennis attire revealed more than would be acceptable on any upscale court. She led him to the library while she teased his senses with her provocative moves, and ended her sally at the granite top bar.

"May I offer you something?"

"Depends on what you're offering." He moved next to her, put his hand on her back, and slid it down to her derriere.

"The last man who tried that.. " She looked over her shoulder.

"What?"

Mario stood in the doorway.

"Mister Contedetto will be in a moment. Please sit down, sir."

Nugari whispered to her, "Another time, another place."

"A rum and coke, sir?"

"Yes." He glanced back, wondering how she knew.

Connie Contedetto entered with his usual semi-important demeanor.

"Mister Nugari, it is of wonderment that I am to see you." His hand extended.

"Hello Connie." Not even Connie could mistake his disdainful tone.

He remained seated.

Connie sat across the coffee table from him and listened while Nugari mapped out his plot to force deVillefrance out of the entire project, suggesting a small finders fee, and a job well done as the only consideration.

When Connie was sure that he was done, he threw a curve that not only stunned Nugari, but also shook him to his core. Ceres had already planned to remove deVillefrance, but she also wanted to exclude Orcini and his entire group. The fact that Ceres was neither kind nor magnanimous was a foregone conclusion, but the total apathy for the man who started the project was frightening. Still another curve ball. She had manipulated Wu's funds electronically, and transferred it to her account in the Cayman Islands. If she could eliminate Orcini and all the competition, why would she need him? Would he be the third strike? Would he be out?

Connie finished with still another surprise. "The Donna wants for you to make for other specific arrangements with Mister Orcini's attorney, Mister Hector Ruby. You are to make a switch in the contracturals at the last time of appropriateness."

Nugari squirmed in his chair.

"Do not to be concerned, for Mister Hector Ruby is in the employ of the Donna."

* * * * * * *

In the center of the highly polished Philippine mahogany conference table at Orcini Properties, Inc stood an unassuming crystal
vase containing a sterling silver rose surrounded by eleven white
roses, and a modest selection of baby's breath.

Another outsider called a surprise meeting. Dave Roberts admired the floral selection as he waited for Michael. He was there to
gain Michael's confidence, and attempt to be rewarded for information he would share about the Ceres takeover. His status as
consultant to Ceres left a lot to be desired. She had promised him
a position in Michael's project, but he saw the preverbal hand-
writing on the wall. He was to be just another henchman. He
knew if he gained Michael's trust, he would be able to move into a
position of stature.

He stood erect with his hands on the back of a chair. He looked
like a model out of the latest fashion magazine, painstakingly
groomed, wearing a finely tailored pinstripe, with a pastel colored
shirt, power tie, and matching pocket square. His tanned face was
clean-shaven, and he smelled of aftershave lotion and the outdoors.

Michael entered. "I believe that we can dispense with the normal overtures and get down to business." He signaled for him to
sit. "Martha tells me that you have important information regard-
ing our project." He reached for the phone. "Excuse me. Martha,
where did these flowers come from?" He listened. "Here in the
conference room." He replaced the receiver.

Martha entered and looked . "I don't know, Mister Orcini.
Shall I remove them?

"No."

"I'll check if anyone knows." She said as she left.

He knew.

"Sorry for the interruption."

Then Roberts spoke. He spoke at great length, first nervously
from his chair, then rising and pacing. He put his hands on the
back of his chair to make a point. Sometimes he would emphasize

a point by pounding the chair. He had practiced his speech over and over, like an actor getting ready to go on stage. Michael raised his eyebrows when he talked about deVillefrance being removed, not knowing if it was a Mafia removal or just being cut out of the deal.

It was when Roberts delineated their plan to cut him out, completely, using Ruby and Nugari to switch the documents, that he became inwardly enraged.

Roberts finished, and sat down relieved that he had done well.

"I think that you're smart and ambitious, and that you have another agenda." Michael turned in his chair. He believed the repertoire, but wanted to know why Roberts risked his position, or maybe even his life to present this scenario.

Roberts sat forward and began to speak, but Michael raised his hand with the palm forward to signal restraint. He slumped back.

"You came here to tell me about Ceres, and Nugari, and my attorney, and their plot to take my project. Do you expect me to believe that you came here without regard for your own future? What is the real reason for your being here? What do you want?"

"I have seen the way this project has turned from a developer's dream into a Mafia nightmare. You can still save your project, if you let me help. All I want is a position in the casino. And, and a small share of the take."

"But, you have already told me everything that I need to know. Why should I negotiate a position with you if you haven't anything else to offer?"

"I have heard that you are a man of honor, and a man of honor will do what is right."

"How do I know that you're telling the truth?"

"What I have told you can be corroborated."

"I'll have to get back to you."

Dave Roberts rose like a whipped puppy, and started for the door, "Don't take too long. You don't have much time left."

* * * * * * *

Michael Orcini had conceived The Resort at Sundance Lake, lived with the planning, agonized over the selection of his key staff, labored with the financial aspects, and took her to bed with him every night, afraid of what might cause him to lose her.

At first his experienced competitors laughed at him, laughed because his dream was unfounded, and unlikely to succeed. Now they aren't laughing. Most of them, the big ones, are desperately trying to capture their portion of the niche market that lay dormant. Michael took their remarks with quiet presence, commanding respect while he set the wheels in motion. Some of the very same Presidents and C.E.O.'s applied for senior positions, articulating the merits of this gaming maverick's concept. The very thought of resurrecting the Societe des Bains de Mar style of gaming in a resort by a desert lake in the United States has brought out the latent desires of many gaming executives throughout the state. Michael was confident of his success.

Now there is the dread of losing everthing to greedy and unscrupulous people who will stop at nothing to steal the Resort, even before the first shovel hits the ground.

Michael wondered if he played their game, if he beat them to the punch, if, if, if. "Damn, damn," he thought, "if only, if only?" Once again the voice of his mother came through to settle his mind. He remembered how, when he was a small boy, his mother would tell him, "If's are just irrelevant fantasies." He never knew what she meant, never before, until now.

He decided to call her, and tell her that he finally understood, but the idea triggered a thought of Darci's mother. He should call her, too.

* * * * * * *

A Greek Captain's hat lay crumpled on the circular drive at Casa Trinacria as the wind swirled leaves past it. Soon it was caught up in the ritual, and tumbled to a far end of the drive where it rested in the limbs of a dead bush.

Commodore Claude deVillefrance came to Casa Trinacria to complete his negotiations with Donna Ceres, and then return to the Yacht Club in Southern California with the future of his world secure. He was escorted to the bungalow near the pool where the sexy Asian woman would entertain him until the Donna was free. She handed him his favorite elixir, a Manhattan straight up, and watched while he savored his last drink.

* * * * * *

His car was in the shop, the Donna's limousine was late, and the sun had settled over Mount Charleston as Pernicious Nugari waited under the Porte-cochere of his hotel. A well dressed, but extremely intoxicated young man was dispensing his anger at the undeserving valet because he would not retrieve his car. The fragrance of a nearby woman distracted him with thoughts of Biz. He wasn't fond of her nickname and chose to call her Baby when they were alone. His thoughts turned into fantasy as the limousine arrived.

"Mister Nugari." Snapped Mario as he opened the curbside door.

Mario's silence during the drive to the Casa was welcomed, and Nugari returned to his fantasy. He imagined himself as an important executive at the Resort Casino, and Baby as his arm ornament and plaything. He would not marry her, but would keep her hostage as long as she pleased him, then he would release her. He silently chuckled, more sure of himself as he had never been before.

The air was still as he stepped from the car. An uneasiness came over him as he walked the few short steps to the main doorway. Mario had signaled from the main gate and the Asian woman opened the door just as he reached the top step. She wore a flowered silk, Chinese style dress with a high collar, tight around her tush with a slit from the floor to somewhere near her hip. The kind he had seen in WWII movies.

"Shalimar." he whispered while he passed as close as he dared with Mario watching. He went directly into the study, continuing to a spot behind the bar. "Let me guess." he said with a smirk, "poison on the rocks." He took a tall glass from the display behind the bar, and turned to see her smiling. He raised the glass, "What's your poison?"

"I disperse the poison here," She winked as she squeezed by him, "but you must make room for me."

He did not budge. She took the glass from him, and mixed a rum and coke.

"How do you.. ?" He stopped, "of course you'd know. What about you?"

"Another place," she smiled, "another time." She mimicked his comment from their last encounter.

"Come to my hotel tonight." He put his electronic key card on the counter. "If I'm not there, wait for me."

To his delight, she took the card and slid it inside the mid section of her dress, just below the bodice. She whispered, "I'll be there."

His excitement was squelched as quickly as it appeared when Jamie Wu announced his presence.

"Perni, my dear friend," He looked at the woman, "did I interrupt?" He answered his own question, "Of course I did." He made sure that Mario heard his declaration.

"Would you like something?"

"I'll have the same as Nugari."

"Rum and coke?"

"Never mind. Wine, perhaps. Yes, I'll have a glass of white wine."

"What are you doing here?" Nugari asked.

"Contedetto called and said that we were meeting with the Donna. I thought you knew." He looked puzzled, "Why are you here?"

"Same reason."

"Donna Una Maria Antonia Ceres!" Exclaimed Mario as the matriarch entered the room.

The two looked at each other, then to the Asian woman. She merely shrugged.

Donna Ceres went quietly to a small mahogany table that served as her desk, and shuffled some papers. She took the ruffled kerchief from her sleeve, and signaled as she prepared to sit. Connie motioned for the men to take their places across from her. They knew not to sit until she was seated, and Connie gave them permission.

Donna Ceres raised her eyes with a look of determination. "Sit." she commanded.

"Ermano, come here by me," She said softly, "here by my side."

Connie responded without a word, taking his place as second in command.

"We will have an agreement with Mister Orcini in a few days. I have personally met with him, and concluded the arrangements," she lied. "The attorneys are drafting the final papers for my approval. Mister Wu. The money that your group has deposited in escrow has been transferred to my off-shore account."

Enraged, Wu jumped up shouting and waving his fist, "What? You cannot do this. That money belongs to my family. I.. "

Wu was grabbed from behind by Mario, and forcefully seated.

"I have control. It is my money now, Mister Wu. If you wish to remain involved in The Resort at Sundance Lake, you will do as I say, and you will join me. Otherwise I will be forced to administer an alternative." Her voice was soft and determined. She was not inclined to enter into the International legal arena, but neither was she ready to concede to Wu that her disposition was tenuous, and that she would eventually have to return the money. She played her cards close to the vest when she offered him a surrogate place in her scheme of the project. A test to see if greed would take its place above family ties. She was certain that she held the trump card, and that Jamie Wu would agree to her proposal. She intuitively knew that he feared the Camorra's wrath more than saving face. Her proposal would accomplish both, and make him an ally. "Will you join me, and become a part of my organization?"

Jami T'ing-fang Wu knew that he could not struggle any more. That his desires had to be set aside, and he would have to accept the pain of defeat. Somehow, though, he felt an unusual complacency in the pain. The pain of acceptance seemed better than the pain of defeat. This was to be his choice, not hers.

"What do you want from me?" He was composed.

She studied his face, and looked for any sign dictated by the language of his body. "Jami, you are a wonderful business partner," She spoke softly at first, more like a lover that an adversary, ending with a tone of undeniable excitement, "you and I are going to get along just fine, you'll see. Now let's move on with the project."

Pernicious Nugari wasn't certain about what just happened, but he was sure of one thing. He was sure that it wasn't going to be easy dealing with Ceres. He decided that he would have to outwit this Sicilian at her own game. He would turn the tables on the old woman.

"Where do I fit into your new plans?" He asked abruptly.

"I don't see any change in your future, Mister Nugari." She lied again. "You will exchange the documents as we discussed." She was careful not to disclose any more for Wu to hear.

"Then why was I asked to this meeting?"

"I wanted you to have first hand information about Mr. Wu and his group."

"But, Donna Ceres, I am not sure about his group. Exactly what part do they play now that you have control of their funds?"

"They have paid for the privilege to learn how to run a casino. That is why they came to me in the first place. No?"

* * * * * * *

Connie quietly followed Donna Ceres down a long hall to an elevator that took them up to the Master Quarters. She went directly to her boudoir where she painstakingly removed her makeup and her padded outer garments. She removed the netting from her head, unfastened the matronly bun, and let her silky black hair fall to a point midway between her shoulders and her waist as she stood and turned to him.

"You are as beautiful as ever, Maria," He said without the usual forced vernacular, "how much longer must we carry on this charade?"

At forty-three Maria Ceres had the physical appearance of a well-proportioned lingerie model. Her skin was endowed with an olive tone that exaggerated the curve of her breasts, and accentuated her nipples as she exposed them to her lover.

"Soon, my darling, it will be over soon. But, now I must have you."

Maria and Ermano planned to retreat to their villa in Sicily after the project gave her the appropriate presence in the United States. She would instruct her servants to start a rumor that she was at an exclusive spa undergoing a complete change. There would be reports that he died in an accident. Minor plastic surgery, change his hair color back to its normal color, and a new identity. After a much-publicized whirlwind romance, they would emerge as the talk of Europe.

"Did you lock the door?"

He picked her up, and carried her to a turn of the century four-poster with fringed canopy. He pushed a concealed switch that exposed a full mirror under the canopy.

"Hurry."

* * * * * *

"Could we meet for a drink when you finish work?"

Pernicious Nugari was vague, but dangled enough carrot to whet Michael's appetite. He wanted to see what anvil would be dropped on him this time. Nugari wouldn't disappoint him.

"Charlie, can you meet me at the Nugget? I am meeting with

that vulture, Nugari, and I could use your support." He listened for a moment. "Sure, same as always. What?" He listened again. "I've got it covered. He's gonna have me paged. See you at seven. Thanks, Charlie."

"Mister Michael Orcini to the white courtesy phone, Mister Orcini to the white courtesy phone." The voice over the loud speakers was almost intelligible over the sound of the Friday night gamblers.

Michael led Nugari to the table where Charlie sat. "You remember my friend, Charlie." He said as a definitive.

"Charlie Swift. Good to see you again," he lied, "you didn't tell me that you were bringing reinforcements."

"Charlie and I were planning to have dinner after our meeting. I was sure that you wouldn't mind. Now, what is this astonishing change of events that you couldn't discuss over the phone?"

"But, I.. "

"Charlie is my best friend and confidant. You can say anything in front of him, and be assured . . ." he noticed Nugari's nervous hands, "What's on your mind?"

Pernicious Nugari set out the course of events that had taken place over the last few days. It was almost like he had memorized Dave Roberts' script without the dramatics. Michael was surprised when he added the Chinese synopsis as the frosting on the cake. Michael and Charlie listened without comment until he was done.

Charlie decided to bait him. "What do you think we should do?" He said without a stammer. "We are ready to choose a contractor."

Michael said a silent prayer of thanks for his most trusted friend.

Nugari stared at Charlie, and then turned to Michael with a questioned silence.

He remained as quiet as a poker player with a straight flush.

The expert military negotiator was about to lose the sinking ship for the sake of saving the cargo, which had overburdened the ship in the first place. Much worse, he was afraid of going down

with the ship. Pernicious Nugari attempted to regain his importance to the project with a new offer.

"Michael," he hesitated until he was sure his concern did not
show through, "I have another money source for the Resort. I have
given them all the information, and they are ready to move. They
knew about the Resort, but needed an inside contact that could
make it happen. They heard that we were affiliated and contacted
me."

"Where did this source come from? Michael has been working
on this for a long time. What makes you think that an equitable
agreement can be made to coincide with our timeline?" Once again.
Not a hint of a stammer.

Nugari questioned Michael again with his eyes.

Michael was not ready to turn over his cards. Not just yet.
But, he was ready to 'up the ante'.

"I need nine hundred fifty million."

"Then you'll meet with them?"

"I assume that they are foreign investors."

"I can have them here next week. Just say the word."

"They have to be approved by the State Gaming Commission,
you know? That takes time."

"They have Gaming interests in Nevada. I don't see any problems."

"Would you give us a moment?" Charlie asked.

Nugari went to the bar where he could watch the men, and
wait for their signal to continue.

After a short discussion they decided that they needed more
time, and didn't want to be pressured as Nugari waited. Charlie
waved for Nugari to join them.

Before he could sit, Charlie announced, "Will you call tomorrow afternoon? We will let you know then."

"I'll call right after lunch."

* * * * * *

The scent of Shalimar filled the room. A small light shown from the half open bathroom door. He made his way toward the light when he noticed her laying on his bed in a semi fetal position. Her hands were together under her cheek as if she had been praying. He gently touched her arm with one hand, balanced himself with the other on her tush, bent, and kissed her lightly on the cheek.

She smiled a soft sweet smile, as if she were awakened by an angel, turned on her back, and put her arms out to receive him. He tried to kiss her lips, but she lowered her chin allowing his lips to meet her forehead.

"I must get to know you first. Before we kiss on the lips. It's customary."

"Okay. My Name is Pernicious Nugari. What's your name?"

"Dominique."

"Dominique? Is that all?"

"Yes. Just Dominique." She forced a frown. "No more for now."

"How can we make love, if we don't kiss? You did come here to make love?"

"That's different. Kissing on the lips becomes involved. The rest is just physical."

"Just physical?"

"You want what you see?" She swung her long legs over the side of the bed, and stood in one quick movement. She wore a pair of baggy pants, and a loose fitting, semi-transparent silk blouse that clung to her nipples. "You must feed me first, then we make love."

* * * * * *

The single Sterling Silver rose, with drops of water clinging to its pedals, seemed to fill the crystal vase by his bed. Her fragrance was everywhere. An ethereal scent combined with Tiffany Perfume

He knew she was there, but decided to wait until she was ready to show herself.

"Don't play that waiting game with me, Michael Orcini. You only get to control me when we . . ." She stopped. "I love you, Michael, and . . ."

"Where are you?"

"I'm right here. Beside you."

He turned left then right. "Where? I can't see you. Are you playing a game?"

"No, I'm right here. Close your eyes." She kissed his lips.

He opened his eyes, and there she was. Right there, no more than a heartbeat away. She looked as alive as she ever did before.

"That was no ghost kiss." He put his arms around her, and realized that he could feel her. Frightened he loosened his embrace.

"Move your hands down, big guy, that's where you always loved to put them." She took his hands and guided them down her back, along her full hips, and finally to her tush. "Wha-d-ya think?" She smiled, "How about this," She pushed her thighs against him, "don't you just love it?"

He couldn't help but respond to her actions, and pulled her tight so that she could feel his excitement.

"What's happening? How can this be? Did you come back to life?"

"Remember what I told you about our love being so strong?"

He shook his head, but wasn't sure.

"Not sure, huh?" Aditi says that we can have it all back while I'm here helping you." She tightened her hold around his neck. "We can have it all, Michael. Do you have any idea what that means?" She kissed him long and hard.

"I've got to think."

"Don't hurt yourself." She giggled.

"I'm going to take a shower."

"I'll help."

"No, just me. Okay?"

"Okay."

When he finished, he looked for her, but couldn't see her anywhere. "It must have been a dream," He thought, "thank God, it was just a dream."

"Not."

She was in bed, and holding the sheet up inviting him to join her. The moment he did, he knew that this was like nothing he could have ever dreamed. They made love more passionately than ever before. Michael fell asleep full of love for this angel. She was an angel. There could be no other explanation. When he woke there was only her fragrance to remind him of the ecstasy of the night. He called for her, but to no avail. He could never share this with anyone, because they surely would think he was crazy.

He decided to work at home, and called the office to let them know.

"Oh, Mister Orcini. You must come right away." Candace was sobbing.

"Get a hold on yourself. What's happened?"

"Here's Martha."

"Mister Orcini. You'd better get here as soon as you can. It's Mister Williams. He was working late, and they came and wrecked the place, and they, they beat him. They beat Mister Williams."

"Martha. Martha, get a grip and tell me is he going to be okay? Where is he?"

"I found him this morning when I got here. The paramedics took him to Memorial Hospital. They said that he would be okay. Mister Orcini?"

"Yes Martha?"

"I'm scared. Please come soon."

"I'll be right there."

* * * * * *

Puca sat on the couch barking at him as Michael came in. It was the first time since the accident that he heard any sound from the little dog. He dismissed it as being just another phenomenon that came with his new relationship with Darci.

"Where is she?" He asked the ghost of a dog, "What is she up to now?"

"Arf. Arf." Came his response. Followed by a series of dog grumbles that somehow made sense. Michael intuitively knew that he was warning him of an eminent danger, but what?

"Darci. Are you here? Darci." He went into the bedroom, the bath, everywhere. She wasn't there, or at least, she wasn't making herself visible to him. "Darci. I need to talk to you. Darci."

He went to the kitchen, and ground some coffee beans. Puca jumped up on the counter. "Pukie. You know that you're not allowed." He went to pick him up, but his hands passed right through the little dog. Surprised he jumped back. Puca grumbled again. This time his little noises became intense, but now they sounded like muffled words. He sat up as if he was begging, moved his paws like he was scratching some invisible object, and looked at Michael with soulful puppy eyes.

"Sorry I wasn't here when you came home," Darci appeared next to him, "But, Aditi kept me after school." She kissed his cheek. "Has Pukie been bothering you? She picked him up from the counter, "You know you don't belong there. Just because.. "

"I think that he's been trying to tell me something." He finished his ritual. "It feels like there is some danger that.. " he noticed Puca squirming in her arms. "See how nervous he is?"

"What is it Pukie? What's wrong?"

The seer licked her face, and uttered strange sounds from some long forgotten language. He looked at Michael, and back to her.

She walked out of the kitchen looking up, and down, waving her arm. Wandering aimlessly about the room, she silently, desperately summoned her mentor. Aditi appeared, and told her that she must tell Michael of the danger that Puca senses.

"Can't you do something about it?" She cried real tears for the first time in her new life. She continued her telepathic plea. "Why can't I help?"

"You can. You must tell him to leave this place until it is safe to return. You must tell him to go with his friend, Charlie."

"Can't I go with him? I can take care of him, love him, and be with . . ."

"No you must not break the rules. You must always remember why you are allowed to be with him. Tell him that he must hurry, but tell him that he must not be alone. Tell him." Aditi delivered her first command to her.

"You were talking to her, weren't you? Something's wrong."

"Yes, my love. Yes." She was crying again.

Without a second thought, he wiped the tears from her face. "You're actually crying. I didn't know that you could do that."

"Neither did I."

"What's wrong? He took her hand and led her to the couch. "Tell me."

"Pukie says that they want to kill you, and take the Resort for themselves."

"Who?"

"I don't know. He isn't clear on that."

"I'll call Dominic Poncerelli. He'll know what to do."

"How can he know what to do when we don't even know who it is. Besides, how are you going to explain that you got your information from a ghost and her dog?"

"I guess you're right." He walked to the window, and looked out over the city. "This is a precarious time. I'm at a point where decisions must to be made about the financing and start of construction. How can I leave now.?"

She moved to his side. "Aditi said that you must not go alone. You should call Charlie. As much as I hate the thought, maybe you guys can go airport hopping or something"

"How about this? Why don't you and I hide out at the beach house?"

"That's probably the first place they'd look if you weren't here, and . . ."

"And, what?"

"I can't go with you. It's not allowed."

"You can't go?" He opened the door and went out on the deck. "Not allowed?"

The alyssum and gardenias sent their sweet bouquet across soft breeze. He had transplanted some of them from the clay pots on her bedroom deck. He searched the skies, and the tall pines for some sign, some kind of omen. A blackbird hovered over its nest in the pine adjacent to the bedroom deck. He looked inside. She was there, watching him with an ethereal beauty that saddened him. He could hear her voice in his mind, telling him that he must hurry. Michael cried.

* * * * * * *

Charlie always turned off his cell phone and pager when he was working in the field. The answering machine wasn't the way to get through to him in a hurry. He called his subcontractors, suppliers, architects, and finally the civil engineer who designed the site work for a project in Mesquite. The engineer's secretary said that they had a meeting at the job site that afternoon. He'd have to hurry to get across town in time to catch them.

He wheeled the Explorer through the opening in the chain link fence, across the open dirt field, and skidded to a stop next to Charlie's car, leaving a small dust storm in his wake.

"Wha--what's up?" Charlie hollered from the steps of the construction trailer.

"I've got to talk to you."

"W--we'll be fi--fi--nished so--soon. C--come on in, I just p--put some c--coffee on." They hugged like good friends.

Michael had never shared his relationship with Darci's ghost. Not with Charlie, or with anyone for that matter. How could he convince him without looking like an idiot? It hit him like a ton of bricks. "I'll tell him the truth," he decided, "I'll tell him everything. Just the way it happened. He'll understand." He smiled. "He won't believe the part about the sex." He figured it would be wiser to leave that out.

They drank coffee as Michael mapped out his dilemma. When he was through, Charlie looked puzzled, and did not speak for what seemed an eternity.

"None of this makes any sense, Mikey." He poured out the remainder of his cup, "I hate to disappoint you, but my plate is full. I have meetings from now to the end of the month." He said without a stutter. "C--can't g--go alone?" He saw his friend's nod. "Take Keleigh. S--she's t--the only one wh--who w--will unders--st--stand."

Michael agreed that he would. They should take the Commander and fly to some remote place, but not so remote that he couldn't communicate with his office. They decided that he shouldn't file a flight plan. That would be an obvious way to find him. Charlie agreed to follow up on Nugari's new financing plan, but not to share it with anyone until he returned. He would tell Nugari that Michael would call him in a few days.

Keleigh had to restrain herself. Go away with Michael, and not let anyone know. It sounded dangerously romantic. She tried to make it sound as if she had things to do that couldn't wait. She deliberately chose business excuses that she knew he would say could be handled by J.T. or Sumner, and graciously gave in to his plea. She was grateful that his request was by phone, and not in person. She could never have masked her excitement.

They met at the airport, and parked their cars in the Commander's private hanger so they would not be detected. Michael prepared the Commander, and they took off for parts unknown.

THE ESTRANGEMENT

Chapter Five

Michael Orcini guided the Commander out of Henderson Executive Airport, away from McCarran's Class B airspace, and set a course toward Sacramento. They would fly southwest along the Silver Peak Range, and then he would alter their course for Tahoe. He didn't tell Keleigh why they were going away or where they were going. "Just pack your tooth brush, flannel jammies, warm clothes, and a smile." Was all he told her. He wasn't surprised that she never questioned him.

"How does Tahoe sound to you, cute buns?" he asked his side-kick.

"Tahoe? Isn't Tahoe the other way? She pointed to her right, "Or is this going to be one of those, I ran out of gas dates?" She tried to look serious. "I've heard stories about you pilots. Take a girl up, and if she doesn't go down, join the mile high club, or whatever, you take her to some remote landing strip until she does." She pretended to inspect the map he gave her. "And, mister smooth talk, when did I graduated from sweet cheeks to cute buns? "

"We're going to head in this direction first, and then swing around and go up this way to the big blue spot." He pointed to the map.

"That takes us over this military practice range. We can't get shot down, can we?

"Not at this time of the year."

"All of a sudden this is starting to look more official than just a fun trip." She realized that he didn't answer all her questions, and she wasn't about to let him off the hook. "When?"

"When, what?"

"Don't be so coy with me. You know exactly what I mean?"

"Since you took my advice and threw away those baggy pants."

"What makes you so sure that I threw them away." She leaned over and kissed his cheek. "Thanks for noticing. By the way. Why are we going to Tahoe?" She decided to put it all out for his reaction. "You didn't ask me to bring any files or reports or notes or anything."

"I asked you to bring your tooth brush."

"Does this have anything to do with my recent graduation?"

He didn't want to give her the wrong impression. He skirted the issue, and decided to tell the truth. "I didn't want to frighten you, but someone is out to kill me."

"Yeah, me. If you don't answer my question." She used a terrible James Cagney impression. She realized that he might be serious when he didn't laugh. "Don't kid me, Michael. That isn't funny."

He told her that he had just found out himself. He left out the part about Darci and Puca. His story was an expansion of the office robbery and Sumner beating.

"But, I thought that Sumner was hurt because he just happened to be there. Are you telling me that he was beaten on purpose, and that the break-in was a cover up?"

"Yeah. I think they were really after me, and got pissed off when they found out that I wasn't there. Sumner was in the wrong place at the wrong time."

"Shit."

"Keleigh?"

"I'm sorry, but that really makes me mad. D'you have enough gas in this puppy?"

"Yes. You want to change the subject?"

"No, I don't want to change the subject. But, why is that fuel gauge jumping around like that?"

"She was full when we took off." He tapped the instrument panel, "these other gauges are acting funny too."

"Just exactly what does funny mean?"

"Don't know yet," he checked some more, "the instrument panel lights aren't on either. Looks like we are experiencing some electrical problems."

"We're not going to crash, or anything, are we?"

"No. Probably just a loose wire. I'll just check a few things."

Sput-sput-sput! The engine sounded. The engine sputtered a final time, and stopped.

He checked the magneto switches. First the Right then the Left, and returned to the 'Both' position. He switched the fuel selector to the other tank, switched the fuel pump off and then back on. The engine gauges were of no assistance.

"What's going on? Michael, I'm scared."

"We have to find a place to put her down." He dialed the transponder to 7700, and the radio to 121.5, the emergency frequency, clicked on the microphone, and said, "Mayday-mayday-mayday." After one minute he turned the transponder off, looked at Keleigh, and said calmly, "Turn the transponder back on in five minutes."

"This one?"

"Yes."

"What happens in five minutes?" Tears appeared in her eyes. "The engine stopped. Can we keep flying for five minutes?"

"This is what needs to be done. Please do what I ask. I'll fly the plane."

He grabbed the emergency checklist from behind his seat, and followed the procedure; Airspeed-Glide, Fuel selector-Fullest tank, Fuel pump-on, Mixture-Rich, Carb heat-on, Magneto switch-Both, Flaps-up, Gear-up, and finally, Seat belts fastened.

"Now help me find a place to land her."

"Okay, boss." Five minutes passed, and she clicked the transponder on, and looked out the window. "What am I looking for?"

He set the flaps to ten degrees.

"Any place that is a lighter green or brown color."

"Light green?"

"Dark green, or black is the big pine trees, light green or brown will indicate grassy or clear areas."

After what seemed an eternity to her, she shouted, "There, there," she pointed, "over there, Michael, look."

He saw a light green patch at two o'clock about two miles ahead.

"Keleigh?"

"Yes."

"From now on I don't want you to ask any questions. Understand?" He didn't wait for an answer, but saw a frightened nod from her. "Pull your seat belt as tight as you can. This might get a little bumpy."

He had set the flaps to ten degrees earlier to slow their descent, but now he set them to the full position, and 'crabbed' the plane. He wouldn't have time for any other procedures to slow her down.

"Were going sideways," she shouted, and grabbed the controls instinctively, "We're going . . ."

"Take your hands off the controls." He shouted back.

He saw the panic on her face, and said quietly. "I'm just slowing her down, It's okay, Keleigh, it's okay."

He maneuvered her like he was putting a thread into a needle's eye. Without thinking, he reached behind his seat for his oversized WWII leather flight jacket, and pushed it into her lap.

"Here. Wad it up, and hold it in front of your face and chest."

"But.. "

"Do it, damn it. Just do it!" He exclaimed.

The ground rose quickly, and the green area became a lot smaller than it appeared from above. It turned into a field of tall curled grass and wildflowers that wanted to reach out and grab the landing gear. He pulled hard on the controls, manually retracted the landing gear, yanked the handle to return the flaps to a clean position, and set the tail down first.

The Commander responded as if it were made for a tail first landing. Her nose came down with a thundering splash as the propeller engaged the grass. She bounced. First forward, then back, continuing the cadence until she skidded sideways in an abrupt stop against a juniper outcropping.

Michael wiped the small amount of blood that trickled down his face, and looked over at Keleigh. She sat motionless.

"Kel. Kel." He shook her gently.

She was hunched forward, crying into the lining of his jacket. She pulled back, and inspected the WWII pin-up sewn into the lining. "I've got Betty Grable's butt all full of my snot." Her tears turned into laughter. "Are we dead?"

"I don't think so. Are you all right?"

"Michael, you're hurt." She touched his forehead.

"It's nothing." He took her hand, placed it on his cheek, then to his lips, and kissed it. "Let's see what damage we've done."

"We?"

"My door's jammed."

He reached across her, and released the safety catch. "Try it now."

She turned the handle, and the door popped open. "Yeah." She said relieved.

"Wait 'til I get out before you jump down on the wing."

"Isn't the captain supposed to be the last to abandon the ship?" She snickered, "This thing isn't going to blow up like they do in the movies, is it?"

He pushed his door open, looked down at the wing. "She looks okay, here goes nothing."

He eased his leg out, and stepped down in the wing. His ankle gave way, he let out a yelp, and fell bouncing off the wing onto the ground.

Keleigh jumped out, and ran around the plane to find him holding his ankle. "Here let me take a look at that." Gently, like a mother lifting her baby out of a crib, she took his foot and eased it to the ground. She slipped off his shoe, and kneaded the ankle, looking for any sign of a break. "Nothing broke," she chuckled, "take two aspirins, put some ice on it, and call me in the morning."

"What?"

"Looks like you dislocated your ankle. I'm gonna have to pop it back into place." She gazed mischievously into his eyes, "Wanna bite the bullet, or do I have to get the whisky from my saddle bags, pardner?"

He watched as she took charge without waiting for his answer. She talked quietly telling him what she was going to do, and did it before he could prepare himself. He screamed as she twisted the ankle back in place.

"There!" she exclaimed, "That wasn't so bad, now was it?"

* * * * * * *

Just before he left, Michael called and asked Charlie to phone his office, and tell them that he and Keleigh would be out of town for a few days with regard to a recent development. He promised to let Charlie know when they got to their destination.

"Where will you be going?" Charlie had asked.

"Under the present circumstances, it's best that you don't know." Was his answer.

It was three days since they left, and Charlie was worried. It wasn't like Michael to forget to call. "Unless," he rationalized, "Keleigh succeeded in seducing him." The thought was overshadowed by another, "He would make time to call. After all, I am his best friend."

He called John Rojam at his quarters off base. "Is Colonel Rojam there?" He asked the feminine voice that answered.

"Who's calling, please?"

"Tell him its Charlie Swift, Michael Orcini's friend."

Charlie told him of the situation at the office, with Sumner, and how Michael and Keleigh flew off to a safe place. John responded by telling Charlie he was premature in his concern, and that Michael and Keleigh had just taken advantage of the opportunity. Finally, after a lengthy conversation, he convinced the colonel that if Michael would call him from his honeymoon, he would have called now. John said that he would use his influence with the police and sheriff to get a search going. Both men knew it would be difficult to convince the authorities to look in an unknown direction.

There weren't any records that his plane left the Henderson Executive Airport. The only evidence was the two cars parked in the hanger instead of the Commander. There wasn't anything reported for an aircraft matching the Commander's description in the last three days. Charlie convinced Dominic Poncerelli to help find out if there were any small plane crashes. John Rojam contacted the FAA. They had an unidentified Mayday somewhere over the Silver Peak Range, but were unable to pinpoint its location. He called the local search and rescue team who set a rescue operation in motion. They coordinated with the authorities, and a full-blown air search was underway in a couple of hours. Helicopters and private pilots in their small planes joined in the search.

"Yes General, I know that we don't look for private aircraft, but he flew my wing for a long time, and we have," he paused and listened, "yes, General. A training mission over the practice area. I was going to suggest a similar plan." He listened to his superior. "I understand. We would have to initiate operation 'Watchdog'. Choppers, T-3's, satellite surveillance, and ground troops."

The General refused the use of ground troops, but allowed the Colonel to utilize the aircraft in a mock training mission. Charlie worked with the search and rescue team, and helped coordinate their efforts with the military operation.

"We've been looking for two days now, and have little to go on." Reported an Air Force Captain, "Without a transponder signal, or some coordinates, we are searching in the blind. A needle in the haystack, sir. If a small plane went down in those mountains, well sir, a dark colored plane among all those trees, I . . ."

"Give it one more day, Captain." Came the Colonel's order.

* * * * * * *

The newspaper laying on his desk declared real estate developer Michael Orcini and his casino operator, Miss Keleigh Cody-Ives missing and presumed dead.

Pernicious Nugari paced the floor of his condominium slapping his thigh with a swagger stick. He unconsciously performed the ritual as he planned an unscrupulous undertaking. It was time to make his move. He had his new investors in place to present to Orcini, but now he would take over.

He stopped, and stood rapping the palm of his hand with the swagger, like a teacher uses a ruler to emphasize authority to unruly students. Blandly, but determined he said out loud. "I am going to own your resort, Mister Orcini. No more Chinks or Dego's. No more toad eating, bootlicking submissive shit any more. They'll be coming to me. He still needed Ceres and her expertise, but no switching contracts. No more, no more."

He went to the desk, picked up the phone, but didn't dial. Instead he took a short memo pad and scribbled a note to himself, 'Call Norah'. His investors would be here tomorrow, and she would be his diversion. He sat down at the desk, crumpled the memo, and threw it aside. Definitive lines formed on his brow as he rested his chin on his fist. An emphasis as portentous as his plan, a peculiarity that consumed his features while the rest of his body became quiet in a noxious satisfaction. His stomach tightened as he realized that he still needed Ceres and her expertise.

* * * * * *

Michael and Keleigh worked feverishly to get the transponder to work, while the search to find them began. They continued to send out their distress signal, but he knew there was only a slim chance that the signal would transmit out of the mountain range. They removed the seats, and prepared the fuselage for the cold night ahead. Michael's survival kit had provisions for a week, and there was a multitude of elderberry, currant, and sweet pinion pine nuts to supplement their diet.

Michael's ankle had swollen, and it was unlikely that he would walk for at least a week. Keleigh's injuries were limited to minor cuts and bruises. Later that day, after the initial shock had worn off, she walked around the plane, and noticed that the windshield where she sat was penetrated by a tree limb. Michael was sitting under the right wing working his palm pilot in a futile attempt to communicate with the outside world.

"Oh, Michael," she said, "Look at that." She threw her arms around him, knocking him down, and fell on him. She kissed him with a passion he had never associated with her. She lifted slightly, pressing her loins against him, and saw the surprised look on his face. She got up, reached inside the cockpit, and got his jacket, "It's ruined. If you hadn't made me.. Oh, Michael." She fell to her knees, and began to cry.

He held her for a long time. This girl, this pal and sidekick just kissed him sending erotic waves through his body making him weak and defeated in one simple act. "It's going to be freezing out here tonight," Keleigh exclaimed, "we're going have to sleep together," she glanced at him with a twinkle in her eye, "to keep warm."

* * * * * *

She exchanged his hotel key card for a key to his condominium. The sweet smell of her perfume was as plain as day when he came into the entry hall. It was almost as if she had sprayed the air to welcome him. He remembered their time of passion, and followed her scent to the bedroom. He turned on the light, and saw her lying naked on his bed. Her face was buried in the pillow. Her silky hair was orchestrated evenly across her back, leaving her exposed butt and slender legs as an invitation for his pleasure. She looked peacefully seductive as he moved to the side of the bed. He picked up a bath towel from the floor, and placed it on her backside. "Don't you like?" She turned over. "I thought that my ass got you excited."

"It does, but I've got to talk to you first."

"What's so important that it can't wait until after we have sex? She moved her hands from her breasts slowly down to a point just below her abdomen. "I might not be ready for you later." She kissed the air.

He knew that she would leave, and he needed her for his new plan with the Donna. He removed his clothes as she turned over to her original position. When they were through, he took her to dinner, and laid out his plan. She was to get a percentage if she could use her influence with the Donna.

Dominique's surprise at his offer triggered a gift of her own. She shared the secret of the Donna and Contedetto. He was flabbergasted. "This is great." He kissed her hand as if they were more that just casual lovers. "And, we are going to be great, together. You and I, my dear Dominique, are going to be a great team."

"It will not be easy to convince her."

"I'm going to have to change directions a little. She can't afford to be exposed."

"You must be careful. She is ruthless. Besides, what about Wu and his people?"

"She has their money, and just wants them as a front. She doesn't have a choice. My new investors are waiting in the wings, and ready to go." He looked down from her eyes to her half exposed breasts, "I'm holding all the aces" His eyes returned to her eyes.

* * * * * *

They laid in the cold darkness of the fuselage with her arm across his chest, as her leg moved restlessly across his thighs. "Warm enough?" She snuggled, sliding her hand down to his hip allowing her arm to rest on his obvious excitement. "Humm." She said no more, but gently kissed his cheek and went to sleep.

Michael felt a new hunger in his midsection.

Michael slept as Keleigh slipped out of the plane. She jotted a quick note, stuck it by the door where he would see it, took the compass and map, and went off into the chaparral. He had marked their position on the aeronautical chart, and explained how to interpret the various lines and symbols. She found the indication for a stream, and with containers for water and anything else she might find to bring back, went to investigate.

He was sitting under the wing and was working some wood with a hatchet and large knife when she returned.

"Hey, Sleepyhead," She shouted, "it's about time you got up." Look what I found. She was carrying a container of mountain stream water, and a myriad of fruits and nuts. "What'cha makin'?"

"You shouldn't go off by yourself.. "

"You wanna go off with me?"

He ignored the innuendo. "You can get lost very easily out here."

Not so. "See." She pulled out the chart and compass. "You marked where we are. All I had to do was drop the bread crumbs, and here I am." She looked down at his work. "You didn't answer. What is that thing?"

"I'm making a brace for my ankle so we can get out of here. That long tee shaped stick ," he pointed, "is my cane."

"I saw a small cabin over there," She aimed her finger like a pistol, "further down the stream." She spread the chart on the wing. "Right about here," she showed him, "right here by this symbol. Well as near as I can figure, anyway."

"That's a bridge. Makes sense. Could be an old way station or prospector's cabin. They used to look for silver in these mountains."

"Are you up to traveling?"

"Sure. How long do you think it'll take to get there?"

"It shouldn't take too long. Three, maybe four hours." She inspected the support. "How much longer on the brace?"

"Another hour or so."

"That'll give us time to settle in before dark."

Keleigh fixed food for them, while he worked on the brace. When they finished eating she filled their knapsacks, bundled the woolen ponchos, and made a sign to indicate where they went.

"What's that for?" He asked.

"It's in case someone finds the plane. They'll know which direction we went. I'll make another when we move on from the cabin. Can you mark the cabin's bearings? You know. Exact location and all." She handed him the pencil.

"I'm sure glad it's you that I'm stuck with."

"You haven't seen stuck yet."

"What?"

"Never mind."

He wrote the coordinates on the chart, gave her the pencil, and secured the brace to his ankle and leg with the seat belts. "I'm ready when ever you are."

The narrow trail was almost a constant and parallel dozen feet from the stream, until the current was diverted by a large stone wall. The man made deflector widened the waterway and sent it rushing away.

Keleigh stopped to see where the water was heading.

"Let's keep going. As long as we can hear the water, we should be okay." She hollered back to him.

"Keleigh. Wait."

"Are you getting tired?"

"I'm okay, but look," he pointed, "it's heading way over there. I think that we should cross, and stay with the stream. Didn't you say that the cabin was next to her?"

"Okay, Michael, but it's too wide to cross here. There was a narrower spot back down the trail." She gestured, and immediately started back.

The stream was just wide enough, and fast enough, to make the crossing questionable. They threw their provisions to the opposite bank. Michael tied a rope around her waist, looped it around a tree, and said, "You first. When you get to the other side, tie the rope around a tree, and I'll follow." Once safe on the other bank, the two continued their journey.

The sun moved slowly behind the mountain, and the temperature started to fall. "It's gonna be dark soon. Let's pick up the pace." He commanded. He looked to the sky. "We have about an hour of light left."

"We should have been there by now. Shouldn't we?" Her voice showed signs of fear. "Michael," she stopped and turned, "are there any wild animals around here?"

"Just me."

"You're all talk." She kissed him for a second longer than normal, and continued her trek.

The log cabin was smaller than it looked from her vantage point earlier that day. Keleigh ran to the door, stopped abruptly, turned and exclaimed, "I'm home. I'll never be homeless again." She ran back to him. "You'll never regret this."

He laughed, louder and louder until it became a roar. "You're crazy."

The stone fireplace with its massive hearth took up most of the twelve by twelve room. Firewood was neatly stacked in the corner, and there were large pots hanging from the railroad tie mantel. A carved pine table was off to the side with two small bench like chairs. A porcelain bowl and pitcher were on a block table, next to a rectangular metal tub, which served as a sink. Keleigh inspected the feather mattress that took up the remainder of the room. "We'll have to be careful on this." She said. "Never saw a mattress on a dirt floor before. Have you?"

"No. I'll get a fire started."

Keleigh lit the candle over the mantel, and unpacked the knapsacks.

"I want to look at your ankle where you're done there."

* * * * * * *

Somewhat indebted to Dominique who paved the way, Pernicious Nugari took his new proposal to Donna Ceres.

"Are you sleeping with my associate?"

"Is that a problem?"

Dominique entered the room, and Ceres summoned the Asian girl to her side with a simple royal like gesture. Dominique glanced obliquely at Nugari, giving him a small smile topped off with an assuring wink, which denoted that her initial suggestion was well received.

"Dominique has been with me a long time. Her allegiance will be with me, even if you did offer her a stake in your share. She can get sex anywhere. So don't think that you have an advantage over me. Is that understood?"

Dominique shifted her weight to her leg that was closest to the Donna's chair, pressing lightly against her shoulder while partially exposing her other leg to Nugari. He read it as a signal that she was playing Ceres, but was on his side.

"Maria, Maria.," Nugari said smugly, "but I do," he paused, "I have a definite advantage over you."

Contedetto moved toward Nugari.

He turned to meet him. "What will you do? Kill me? I think not." Ignoring him, he turned back to Ceres. "I did not come without protecting my position. The information that I have about you has been left in a sealed envelope with instructions to be sent to the police if anything happens to me."

Ermano Contedetto spoke without his usual forced dialect. "What do you want from us? Do you have any idea . . ." he was enraged, "You'll never get away with this."

"I already have, partner. Now sit down, and listen."

Mario entered the room just as Contedetto and Nugari began their volley, took an obvious deep breath, and moved toward Nugari as he finished his command.

Pernicious Nugari calmly opened his jacket revealing a handgun. He reached across his midsection and placed his hand on the weapon.

Mario stopped in his stride, and looked to Ceres.

"Come over here by me." She said to the bull of a man.

His eyes shot right through Nugari with a look of death.

"Mario." She commanded.

Nugari's thumbs released the leather strap that held the gun in its holster. His military training, once again, clicked in, and he stood ready for any confrontation.

Mario looked at his employer as color rushed into his face. She was making her usual matriarchal gesture for him to come to her side. He reluctantly moved to her while watching Nugari every step of the way.

Donna Ceres took his hand, as a mother would to a child who wanted to play with a precarious dog that might hurt him. She pulled him close, and quietly spoke in a tone that Nugari could not hear, "You'll have your time with him, I promise." She looked at Nugari with contempt. "We will accept your proposal with some minor adjustments."

"Minor adjustments?"

"You are willing to come to an agreement?" She smiled a wry smirk. "You are an experienced negotiator, are you not?"

Pernicious Nugari instinctively knew that his position was tenuous, and decided that the negotiation should not include his own life. "I believe that we can come to a resolve that will be acceptable to both of us, Donna Ceres." He ended with a sarcastic tenor. "I would be more comfortable if everyone left us to talk alone."

"Alone?"

"Do you have a problem with that?"

"Well I . . ."

"They leave or I will take my deal somewhere else." He closed his jacket leaving it unbuttoned. "You *do realize* that I have control of Orcini's property." He lied.

"Ermano must stay."

He figured that his bluff had to be played out completely if he was to win. "Alone."

She tugged Mario's hand, pulling him to her once again, and whispered, "Stay just outside the door." She looked at Ermano, "Go. I'll be fine, go." She motioned with her hand, as if she was shooing a fly away. "Go."

When they were gone, Donna Ceres got up and walked directly to Nugari stopping only an inch from him. "You've got some big cuchonies, but remember that I too, hold a winning hand." She stepped back a foot or so and looked up and down stopping to stare into his eyes. "I am not afraid to have you eliminated from the equation, no matter what you might know about me. I've survived many who were much more determined than you." She repeated her inspection, "But there's something about you that I like. You're a formidable opponent." She put her hand on his lapel and stroked it as if she was checking the quality of the fabric, "Partners don't have to agree, just work together. Besides you could get to like me when you know me better."

He grabbed her hand firmly, leaving it as it was. "I would like to see what is under all that makeup. I'm sure that," he paused. It was his turn to inspect. "Aren't you uncomfortable wearing all that, that stuff?" He slapped the padding on her hip with his other hand.

"You do have . . ." She stepped back, "let's get back to business.

* * * * * *

J.T. Popinski's usual bright color was sapped away as he addressed the employees. The gray-white face seemed almost sinister as he began to speak. "The facts, as we know them, seem to indicate that Mr. Orcini and Miss Cody-Ives are lost and presumed to be dead." Martha's sobs interrupt him. After a moment he continued. "We plan to continue with Mr. Orcini's dream. Mr. Orcini's parents have title to the property, and want us to continue with the project. Mr. Williams and I have been in daily contact with the Orcini family and have continued negotiations with the financial partners on their behalf." The color began to return as he exhaled a sigh of relief, and continued. "Mr. Orcini's long time friend, Charlie Swift, will be joining our team. He will be taking over the position of C.E.O."

Candace stood and tearfully blurted out. "Will there be a memorial service?"

"Yes. Mr. Swift will be making the arrangements."

* * * * * * *

A shower, a bath anything to bring her back to civilization. But, all there was in this small cabin was a porcelain bowl and a metal sink. "I'm gonna heat some water in the fireplace. D'you wanna take a bath? We both won't fit in the tub, so you'll have to bathe alone today." She laughed at the mental picture of her and Michael in a small metal tub with suds flowing over the sides.

He looked at Keleigh, he was amazed at what he felt. She was no longer just his pal, and his buddy, she was an incredibly delightful and sexy woman who was alone with him, and passing out sexual innuendoes like a doctor hands out lollipops to little kids for being good. He couldn't make up his mind whether he was just missing Darci, or whether he was becoming attracted to Keleigh. What he did know was that he was aroused by her slightest touch, and the sound of her voice. He remembered how she would linger against his touch when he patted her butt. Now they were alone, stranded, in this small space, and it would soon be time to sleep. He looked at the feather mattress, and knew they would sleep there. Another part of his mind told him that he must remain true to Darci, especially now since she had returned in such a special way. But, she was dead, and Keleigh is alive. He watched her hang the huge pot of water over the fire, and realized that she was wearing form-fitting slacks because he had made an issue of her baggy pants. He enjoyed the view, but decided that if there was to be sex, that she would have to be the aggressor.

"It's gonna take a while for the water to heat. Let me look at that ankle," She knelt in front of him, and began removing the bandage. "It needs to breathe." She attended to him with a gentle caring that stirred her own sexual emotions as she stroked his ankle. "The swelling has gone down a little. I think that we should leave the bandage off for a while. But, you must promise not to get crazy on me, and. . . ." She looked up into his eyes, wishing that he would. "uhmm, we-l-l, go slow, I mean, oh you know what I mean." She sat back on her legs, and decided to change the subject. "What's going to happen to the project now that you're gone? Will J.T. and Sumner be able to hold things together?"

"It looks like we are going to be out of touch for a while, and with no sign of the plane well, they've got to think that we're dead. The vultures are going to try to take over. Nugari is ruthless, and Ceres," he straightened his leg pressing it to her thigh while extending his foot with a soft touch on her crotch, "Ceres has wanted my project from the beginning." Michael was aware of the warmth of her crotch on his bare foot, and the sweet smile on her face. "Then there's Hector Ruby. Did you know that he works for Ceres?"

"I never liked him. It doesn't surprise me." She adjusted the way she sat, moving forward a little, pressing against his foot. "What about Guy and Ian, and Bobbi. I'm beginning to distrust everybody. deVillefrance. Now there's a real piece of work. He'd sell his mother for a song. Where is he anyway? I haven't heard you talk about him in a long time." Keleigh closed her eyes. "I hate them all. I hate them. Damn, damn. Everything's changed but the game is the same. The players move here and there according to the rules. Oh yes the rules, their forms change but they are masked by new forms, new rules that are changed again and again every time some player decides that he in now in charge. New investors, old investors, and we must go on. Michael can we. . . ?" She got up. "I've got to check the water."

"Can we what?"

"Nothing. What happened to the Frenchman?"

"He seems to have fallen of the face of the Earth. You'd better use a towel or something."

She looked puzzled.

"The pot. Its handle is going to be very hot. Find a towel."

She obediently did as he said, and took the pot from the fireplace, and placed it on the block table next to the metal sink. She tested the water with her hand. "It's warm not hot but it'll do just fine." With her back to him she took off her blouse and bra, and began splashing the warm water on her face, neck, and breasts. Keleigh hummed a soft melody as she enjoyed this simple down-to earth luxury.

"Need some help?"

Surprised, she turned around dropping her hands to reveal herself. Excitement rushed through her making her shiver. Her breasts swelled and the nipples hardened as she responded. "Yes." She slowly unbuttoned her slacks, and let them fall to the floor. "Yes." She said quietly. He would have to come to her. He would have to struggle with his sprained ankle if he wanted her. Keleigh decided that now was the time to be the player in charge. The new unspoken rules would be hers. Aware that her damp skin glistened in the amber light of the fire she adjusted her position making her form even more desirable as she moved her hands to a point just inside her peach colored thongs.

"Want me to wash your back?"

Keleigh pouted, and turned back to the table exposing her butt. "Sure."

Michael pulled himself up and started toward her, taking off his shirt as he moved. As he reached her, she handed him a wet cloth over her shoulder. He took it and started to wash her butt. "I've always liked your tush." He patted it lovingly with the cloth while his other hand moved around her waist to stimulate her excited breast. He kissed her shoulder and neck as he pressed his excited body to her.

"Let's go to bed." She whispered.

* * * * * * *

The fast moving clouds that were driven by the same winds that rattled the windows of Michael's Malibu home hid the moon sporadically. The semi-dark night was an advantage for the two men sent by Pernicious Nugari. They moved around the house to the stairs that lead to the beach. At the top landing they unlocked the door with a key that Nugari got from Hector Ruby. After they entered, one of them punched-in the security code at the alarm panel just inside the door. The men searched until they were convinced that the quitclaim papers to the Sundance Lake property were not there. The shadow of one of them stood on the balcony talking on his cellular phone. "It's not here Mr. Nugari. We've looked everywhere. He must have the papers at his office. What do you want us to do?"

"Did you find a safe?"

"No. If there's one here, it's well hidden."

"Try his office in Vegas. But, this time be sure that there's no one there. Use the key that I gave you. Be sure to reset the alarm, and lock the door when you leave."

The two men drove to Las Vegas the next day, staking-out the office until they were certain that everyone had gone home. Again they were unsuccessful.

Desperate, Pernicious Nugari went to a disreputable Real Estate Agent who was known to forge documents. A man wearing granny glasses greeted him and ushered him to a room in the back. The back room looked like a scene from an old 'B' rated movie, complete with the single warehouse type hanging incandescent light.

The man sat down in a wood swivel chair at an old roll top desk. "You said that Claude deVillefrance sent you. How is the old salt?"

"He's taken a trip."

"A trip? Where?"

"Don't know exactly. He was vague."

"What exactly do you want?"

"I need a quit claim for some property." He handed the man a large brown envelope. "This is all the necessary information."

The man took the papers out and read them. "Sundance Lake. Yes, of course. This property belonged to that guy whose plane was lost somewhere in the Silver Peak Range." He put on a green visor. "This will be complicated. A hundred thousand. Cash. Fifty to start. The rest when you pick up the papers."

"One hundred thousand? That's pretty steep."

"Any more discussion and the price goes up."

"What? This is highway robbery."

"Like what you're doing isn't? A hundred-fifty."

"A hundred-fif . . ."

The man handed him the envelope. "Come back when you're ready to pay."

"Okay. One hundred thousand. I'll be back with the cash in a couple hours."

"One-fifty or nothing. Remember what I said about more talk?"

"I'll be back."

"Bring seventy-five. Cash"

"How long will it take?"

"A week, or so."

* * * * * *

The front door slammed behind her and she was alone in the house. It was Norah Laude's first time in Darci's house. She still wasn't sure what led her to be an uninvited guest in a dead woman's house. She found herself saying a silent prayer for her own safety in this house when the realization hit her that it was Michael's house too, and he was also dead. She believed in the afterlife and was afraid that a ghost might have summoned her. Her fear of an imminent peril was so overwhelming that she brought a small handgun with her. Her heart was pounding so hard that it seemed to explode through her skin. Deep breathing eased the pulsation. Once the gun was firmly in her hand, the feeling began to leave. "What in God's name am I doing here?" She asked the empty room.

Darci answered, "To help me find my murderer." But she knew that Norah couldn't hear. She had to direct her to the clues she left for Michael, using telepathy to plant ideas that would seem to be her own.

Norah became her busy self, looking here and there not really sure what to look for or if she would recognize something important. Busy floundered from one room to another and finally back in the living room as the phone rang. She jumped at the sound and was tempted to answer when the machine clicked-in. It was a sales pitch for a life insurance policy. She stared at the machine. "Life insurance. Hmm, I wonder." She said aloud. When the machine stopped, she pushed the rewind button. The second message toned back. "Mrs. Orcini, this is the Memorial Hospital Emergency. It's Mr. Orcini." A click, then, "Hello." Followed by a crackling sound. "Mrs. Orcini?" Busy listened to the entire message. She heard a thump as the phone fell to the floor, and Darci's screams that followed. "Oh my god. She was set up. Oh my god, oh my god." She said it over and over and over until she began to cry. Still sobbing she rewound the machine and removed the tape. Then she talked to the room again. "Why didn't the police find this?" She instinctively knew. The phone was off the hook, and they must have assumed that she was talking, so there wasn't any reason to check the machine. "But why didn't Michael find it?" She knew this too. It was too soon to hear her voice. She rationalized. She also knew that this must be why she was drawn to this place.

Darci liked Busy's rationalization but was disturbed by the thoughts that she was reading. Busy received a package in the mail from Claude deVillefrance that was to be opened in the event of his death. She thought it was just one of his weird come-ons. It was tossed in a corner of her home office in California. She must get the next plane out. Guy was in town. She would ask him to fly her home. "On no," she thought, "what if he's involved in this? What if he had her killed?" Busy decided to keep this information to herself until she could piece things together.

With her discovery secure in her handbag, and her self-justification raising her spirits, she looked around the empty room once more. "No ghosts, no more signs, just furniture and stuff." She inwardly assured herself. She turned off the lights and left.

Anxious to get home, she quickly drove out the driveway not noticing the two men in a car parked just across the road.

* * * * * * *

Keleigh, sitting in a Buddha-like position, was picking feathers from an opening in the mattress when she decided to wake up Michael. She took one of the feathers and waved it slowly under his nose. She giggled each time that he would rub his nose from the tickle. Remembering the ecstasy of the night, she closed her eyes and unconsciously began stroking her nipples with the feather.

"They're beautiful."

"Not just my tush anymore. Huh?"

"Nope."

"Want s'mores?"

He put his hand on her breast. "Are these s'mores?"

"They're boobies. S'mores are everything."

"Like last night?"

"Last night was just a sample. You've only opened the package. There's more to come. Want the whole package?"

"Come here."

They made love and went back to sleep in each other's arms.

Michael woke first. "Listen," he said gently moving her from atop him, "listen."

Still half-asleep she mumbled an unintelligible sound.

"Sounds like a helicopter. Come on." He rolled over her, stopping for a brief moment to feel the softness of her butt against his genitals.

"Be careful of your ankle," she said, "I don't want you to keep me here on some dumb pretense."

He grabbed the makeshift cane and went to the door. The helicopter circled and continued over the ridge. "They're gone."

"Did they see you?" She asked as she slid her arms around his waist.

"I don't think so."

"Good. I want you all to myself," She slid her hands slowly down to his thighs and inward until she found the beginning of his excitement. "all---" she hesitated, "ways." Abruptly she moved away leaving him standing in the doorway. "Want something to eat?"

"What do you have to offer?"

"What you see is what you get."

"I thought that you were talking about . . ."

"I was but." She looked soulfully.

"But what?"

"Michael? She tied a towel around her waist. "Are we doing this just because we're here alone together, or, or---we-l-l, I mean?"

"You're irresistible and, and it feels good. It feels right."

"You better get out of the doorway before somebody sees you."

"Keleigh? Can't we just enjoy what's happening and see where it goes?"

"We were shot down over a mountain range, trudge through the black forest, brave the elements, fight off bears and Indians, I nurse you back to health, and you say let's see where it goes."

"The cold breeze on you is very sexy."

"Get used to it."

"I'll try."

Keleigh turned to the table and began preparing something to eat. "Michael?"

"Hmm?"

"We should try to find a way out of here, shouldn't we?"
"Yes. As soon as I'm able to travel."

* * * * * * *

Norah Laude, geared up by the glasses of brandy, called Dave Roberts to tell him of her discovery. Instead she invited him to have dinner with her at a popular place in Cannery Row. She had almost four hours to re-read, to study the contents of Claude deVillefrance's envelope. She wasn't sure what it all meant, but decided that she would take one document with her to convince him that she had evidence about Darci's murder. She had to tell somebody, and she was sure that Dave was the only one who wasn't involved with Darci. She couldn't even tell Bobbi for fear that Guy would find out. Satisfied that she had enough information committed to memory, she wrapped the remaining documents and the message tape in aluminum foil and placed them in the crisper drawer of her refrigerator.

The night came as Busy closed the shower door and adjusted the showerhead to a soft pulsating stream. She lavished in the warmth as she acted out her presentation to Dave in her mind. It was one of the few times that Busy slowed down her normally self induced hectic pace. Fifteen minutes was a short shower for her.

Two men quietly entered Busy's home and made their way to the sounds coming from the bathroom. They waited in the dark hallway and watched as Busy finished, patted herself dry, and applied lotion to her body. With her hair still wet, and totally unaware of their presence, she moved to the bedroom and dressed. Suddenly she sensed their presence and turned to see them standing at the door. The warmth of the shower drained from her body leaving her cold and afraid. She knew why they had come. Her attempt to scream was met by a soft moist cloth over her mouth and nose. One of the men grabbed her as she slumped to the floor. He lifted her and carried her out while the other looked around, turned off the lights, and closed the front door behind them. They put her in their car and drove off.

Dave Roberts waited for twenty minutes before he called her number. He shrugged it off and dialed another number. "Hey baby. It's Dave. How'yah doing?" He listened for a moment. "Do you want to party?" He listened again. "Great. I'll be there in about twenty minutes or so. See yah."

He called her at least a dozen times in the three days that passed since he went to meet her for dinner. Dave Roberts drove to Busy's home and rang the bell. When she didn't answer, he tried the door. It was unlocked. He went in and looked around. Her coat was lying on the bed next to a towel, and a pair of high heel shoes was on the floor. In the bathroom her make-up and hair-brush were positioned on the counter like she was going to use them. He deliberated and logically knew that something had to be wrong. Norah Laude was a tidy person and would be late before she would leave things lying around.

Back in his car he searched his daytimer phone list, and dialed his cellular phone. "Mr. Nugari please, Dave Roberts calling."

* * * * * * *

Pernicious Nugari stood on his hotel room balcony overlooking the Las Vegas Strip. He could smell the money coming from the casinos below. The streets orchestrated the sound of cars moving in both directions with people who wanted to win the big jackpots, and some who just wanted to party. He was ready to get his share. The time was drawing near when he would look from his own suite at his own hotel at Sundance Lake.

Unaware that Michael Orcini had placed the property title with his parents, Nugari filed the forged quitclaim deed for the title transfer in the County Recorder's office. He convinced Bobbi and Guy with the bogus documents, but Donna Ceres vowed that she would not to be cheated out of her share. A wicked smile crossed his face as he thought of the coup d'état he had just pulled off. Orcini's property was his, and there was nothing that anybody could do about it. He pondered on the other players. He would handle Ceres. She would not risk exposure and possible deportation. Donna Una Maria Antonia Ceres was a phony and he could prove it. But he might still need her if his new partners don't follow through with the money. He decided to continue the deception as long as it was of a benefit to him. Jami Wu had been defeated long ago, and Claude deVillefrance was nowhere to be found. Nugari figured that the Donna had him eliminated. Permanently. The German had no investment in the project, except for his time. His face grew taught as he thought of Bobbi and Norah. He knew that he had to be cautious with them. Especially Bobbi. She expected her share and would probably kill for it, even before Ceres. He decided to call her.

"Bobbi, this is Perni. How are you?"

The voice on the phone said, "Busy is missing."

"She probable went off with someone" he lied, "Dave Roberts called me the other day and asked if she was with me. I guess he thought that we were seeing each other."

"This isn't like her. She'd tell me."

"Is she dating anyone? I mean regular. Is she seeing any. . . ?"

"Listen to me. Something's happened to her. She went snooping around Michael's house in Vegas. She flew back to the peninsula with Guy, and she hasn't been seen since."

"Snooping around? For what?"

"I don't know. Can you help?"

"Sure. I'll see what I can find out. Does Guy know what she was looking for?"

"I don't know. I was so worried about her that I didn't ask. Would you call him?"

"Sure. I'll talk to you later."

"Perni? Why'd you call?"

"It can wait. Bye."

"Bye."

* * * * * *

A dark green limousine with a crest on the door and Dave Roberts in the back seat arrived at the Ceres mansion just as the sun sank behind the mountain to the west. Mario went around and opened the door. Roberts was surprised to see the Donna standing in the doorway without the usual bodyguards flanking her.

"Welcome to my home Mr. Roberts. Please come in."

"Good evening." He wasn't sure if he should call her Donna or kiss her ring, or if he should just go in. She made it easy by extending her hand as a businesswoman.

"Come into the library," she took his arm and walked beside him. "This way." Connie Contedetto rose from his chair as they entered. "Mr. Roberts." He extended his hand, and they shook as businessmen.

"What's this all about? Why all the red carpet treatment?"

"We have a business arrangement to offer you." Ceres motioned for him to sit in the chair directly across from her desk. "You are aware of our involvement in Michael Orcini's project at Sundance Lake." She sipped from and elegant teacup. "How rude of me. Would you like something to drink?" She didn't wait for his response. "Mario, please get Mr. Roberts whatever he wants."

Mario came to his side. "Sir?"

"A beer. No, better make it something stronger. Brandy. I have a feeling that I'm going to need it."

"Yes sir." He went to the bar.

"You were talking about the Orcini project. But, didn't he die when his plane crashed in the mountains?"

"Yes, that is what the report says, and we have no reason to believe otherwise."

Mario came with his drink.

"Thanks." He sniffed and then sipped. "Very nice."

"My group is the major financial partner in the development. We have controlling interest in the project, and intend to move forward. There is another group, Chinese, represented by Mr. Jami Wu. But they only have a passive interest."

"What does this have to do with me?"

"I'll be blunt, Mr. Roberts. Dave. You are in a relationship with Norah Laude. We know that her sister, Roberta, and Michael Orcini used to be close. We also know that she may have information about the project that would be useful to us." She raised her hand when she saw that he was going to interrupt. "The information that Miss Laude has could be detrimental to our position. We must have her on our side, and we thought that you would want her to be," she looked at Connie, "safe."

"Safe. You had something to do with," he looked at Connie, then Mario who stood motionless, "you kidnapped her. Didn't you?"

"Kidnap? No. It's like having an insurance policy to have her with us."

"She's here?"

"Miss Laude is our guest."

"Here? In Vegas? When I can see her?"

"Later. But, first we must complete our business arrangement."

He drank down the brandy, and lifted his glass to Mario indicating that he wanted more. "Business arrangement?"

"You'll find my offer quite generous." She had dropped the 'papal we' to indicate that she was in charge. "How does David Roberts, Chief Executive Officer sound to you?"

He gulped the fresh brandy and coughed. "Chief Executive Officer of what?"

"The Hotel and Casino at Sundance Lake."

"Whoa." He got up and walked around his chair, put his hands firmly on the back and stared down at her. "Hotel and casino? The whole magilla? The entire.. ?"

Dave Roberts paced the room as Ceres and the others smiled at each other. They had their figurehead, their puppet.

Donna Ceres opened a manila folder, took out a business card, got up and walked over to Roberts. "Here Mr. Chairman. How does that look?" She handed him the card.

He read the card and asked, "Who do I have to kill?" He looked at Connie. "There must be a catch. You aren't just giving me this position for nothing."

Connie Contedetto looked at the Donna who gave him a small nod of approval. "It is a truth that you have spoken. The Donna Ceres wishes for you to be of her opinions to run the hotel and casino. You should be to the Board of Directors as she wishes that you should be. It is for your job to be the voice of the Donna. People have respect to you because of how you were a professional athlete. For this the Donna will show to you that she is gratitudinal to you in a most generous form." He took a document and a check from Ceres, and handed it to Roberts commenting. "The Donna also wishes for you to be knowledgeable of the fact that we do not kill people."

"Two-hundred thousand." He sat down and read the two-page document. "I just have to pretend to be the C.E.O. and you give me a bonus to sign with a contract for five years. That's it?"

Ceres smiled.

"What about Busy?"

She looked at Connie.

"Miss Laude." Connie invoked.

"She'll join you as soon as you agree to our business arrangement. Just sign below my name and give it back to Ermano." She handed him a pen.

Dave Roberts signed the agreement and gave it to Connie. "There, it's done. When do I start?"

"We have an executive apartment for you. Mario will take you there and help you get settled in. Tomorrow you will go to California and get your personal things."

The door opened and Norah Laude came in. Dave got up and turned to greet her.

"Dave?"

"I have come here to take you home."

She rushed to his arms.

"Can we go now?"

"Mario." She commanded, and made her unassailable gesture.

* * * * * *

The sun was setting over Pacific Beach when Dave and Norah got to her front door. She suspiciously inspected the front yard as she went to unlock the door. "It's unlocked," she exclaimed, "the damn door is unlocked."

"Let me go in first. Stay here." He said as he pushed past her.

"I'm coming with you." She whispered, and followed close.

They inspected the entire house, and were relieved when they found it empty. Nervously, Busy went to the refrigerator, opened the crisper drawer, and exclaimed. "It's still here."

"What's still here?"

She showed him the foil package. "This. This why they kidnapped me." She took his hand. "Come with me."

Norah carefully opened the foil wrapping and handed the papers to him.

"Where did you get these?"

"Claude deVillefrance sent them to me."

"What's that?"

She told him of her visit to Darci's home, and how she discovered the tape. Together they listened to the tape. She cried and got up, and Dave played it over and over trying to discern the message and the voice.

"I have a friend who works for the studios. He might be able to filter out the static and background noises. Maybe we can hear the voice better."

"What good will that do? We probably won't be able to recognize it anyway."

"I have to try."

"She was set-up, wasn't she?"

"It sure looks like it."

"Why would anyone want to kill her?"

* * * * * *

In those days at the cabin, Keleigh learned more than she wanted to admit about her friend and new lover. She instinctively knew, and painstakingly understood that he was still in love with the memory of Darci. As good as they were together, she knew that he was not devoting all his energy to their newly found relationship. Nonetheless, she was determined to do everything possible to make him want her more than the nostalgia. She would be his pal, his buddy, his partner in business, and his lover. She would not try to make him forget his past relationship with Darci, or anyone else for that matter but, she would make him aware of her total presence and devotion on a regular basis. She would not suffocate him with her love. She would be there for him, but she would tempt him, yes she would tempt him to want to be with her.

But this would not be enough. Michael was committed to building and operating the Hotel and Casino at Sundance Lake. It scared her when Rebecca told her about the mysterious pyramidal shape and shadows at the lake, and the reports of Darci's ghost at the project site.

A ghost in their relationship was one thing. On the other hand, Darci's ghost at Sundance Lake would be problematical not only for her but, for Michael and all the others. She wondered just how long Darci's ghost would stay between them.

The sun was in the western sky, and their first week on the mountain would soon come to an end. Michael had the fire roaring, and Keleigh was near the stream picking flowers when she heard the sound of a plane. She ran back to the cabin dropping her makeshift basket with her simple treasures, and shouted. "The plane, the plane."

Michael appeared at the doorway, and looked up. "That's a Comanche," he hollered at the sound, "it's Charlie, it's Charlie." His voice sounded louder than the engine. He limped back into the cabin and threw the moist wood chips he prepared for a smoke signal on the fire. Soon heavy white smoke billowed out of the chimney top.

"Looks like we just elected a Pope." She laughed.

"What?"

"He's coming back," Keleigh shouted to the sky, "on, no."

"What?"

"It looks like he's in trouble."

"He's tipping his wings," Michael explained, "He's signaling that he sees us."

Keleigh threw her arms around him. They stared at the sky as Charlie's plane flew out of site.

"Michael. Let's fool around as much as we can before they come to save us."

It was mid morning on the next day when they heard a helicopter circling. She ran naked out the door and began waving.

"Keleigh. Put some clothes on."

"Oh my God. I'm just so excited. Are you excited to leave our little paradise?"

"Let's get dressed cute buns," he patted her butt. "They'll be here soon."

The chopper set down in a clearing about a quarter of a mile down stream. The pilot and three enlisted men followed the stream to the cabin.

"Mr. Orcini. Are you okay?" The officer asked.

"Lieutenant Norris. It sure is good to see you."

"You sure know how to get stranded, sir," said one of the other men as he set his eyes on Keleigh.

"Where is your plane?" The lieutenant asked.

"We have it marked on this map." Keleigh sang out.

"We'll give this to the NTSB. Can you walk out of here?"

"I can, but he has a badly sprained ankle."

"We have a stretcher." Lt. Norris motioned to his men who unrolled the canvas from its supports. They made it down the trail, and onto the waiting chopper, which flew them to the bottom of the mountain where Charlie and Dominic Poncerelli waited with an ambulance and a Highway Patrol cruiser. Charlie cried as he hugged his friends.

Michael and Keleigh were taken to a remote hospital for a check-up. Charlie brought Michael up-to-speed on the Ceres-Nugari take-over. Michael asked the police not to let it be known that they were found alive. They made arrangements to send Keleigh to Michael's Malibu home with two around-the-clock policewomen. Michael went with Charlie to his home.

* * * * * *

"Orcini and that girl are alive," came the voice on the phone, "they were rescued about an hour ago."

Donna Ceres slammed the receiver. "Damn. He's alive, she told Connie, "Orcini. Orcini and the girl. They're alive"

"This changes things."

"Things will get a little hectic for a while but, Nugari has title to the property, and we have the money and control."

"He'll be pissed."

"Let him. It's time for us to use Roberts. We'll have to get in touch with Pauli at the Police Department, and find out where they took Orcini."

"I'll call him at home tonight and let Roberts know." Connie sounded confident.

Dave Roberts had just returned from his friends recording studio where they isolated the voice on the tape when Connie called. The Donna wanted him to make an appointment with Orcini as soon as possible. He was to offer him a seat on the Board of Directors with a generous compensation package.

"He's not going to go for that."

Connie reminded him that he was only the messenger but, he had to make it sound like he was on Orcini's side.

Michael and Charlie sat in the unfinished living room of Charlie's home discussing the unexpected electrical failure in the Commander, when the phone rang.

"You say that you want to speak with Michael Orcini." He said purposefully without a stutter as he looked toward Michael. "Haven't you heard than his plane crashed over a week ago?"

Michael jumped up and ran to the kitchen phone. Quietly he lifted the receiver.

"Yes," said the voice on the phone, "and I also know that he and Miss Ives were rescued yesterday. Tell him it's Dave Roberts, and I must talk to him. Tell him that I have important information about, well, tell him it's very important."

Michael shook his head with a no response.

"If he's alive, I'd sure like to know. Roberts you say. Give me your number."

"Okay. I know that he's there but, you talk it over and have him call me. Got a pencil? Remember to tell him, it's important."

Charlie wrote down the phone number. "I'll get back to you. Goodbye."

"How'd he know that I was here? There must be a leak in the Police Department."

"Or the Highway Patrol or the Paramedics, or the people at the hospital, or the Air Force." Still no stutter.

"Next, it'll be on the 11 o'clock news. So much for secrecy. I'm glad that Keleigh's in Malibu."

"So, tell me Mikey. How was a week alone in a twelve by twelve cabin with a gorgeous girl that's crazy about you? Did you fight her off?"

"Things happen."

"Keleigh had a sparkle in her that I've never seen before."

"This could get complicated."

"Keleigh and.. "

"No. I'm talking about Dave Roberts. Let's talk about Roberts. Do you think that I should meet with him?"

"Yes, but I should go with you. It could be a set up."

"No. If you're there he be intimidated. I've met with him before. He's a wus. He gets uncomfortable real easy. I'll go it alone."

"Okay. But only if Ponci knows that you're going."

"Poncerelli? Okay. Maybe it would be better if *you* call him back and set it up."

"He has a c--condo just of th--the st--strip. Here's the d--dir--rect--s---shuns."

Michael knew that Charlie was nervous when he started to stutter. "I'll be okay." Will you call Poncerelli and let him know where I am?"

Charlie nodded.

THE OFFERS

Chapter Six

It was almost nine o'clock when he pulled up in front of the condo. There was someone in a black sedan parked across the street. Michael figured that Poncerelli had some of his men posted as a precaution.

Dave Roberts greeted him as if they were old friends. "Come in Michael. Can I get you a drink? Brandy? I have Hennessy."

"Yes, thanks."

"It was good to hear that you and Miss Ives survived the crash."

"Let's get down to business. Shall we?"

"Yes. Of course."

Dave Roberts outlined how Nugari got control of Michael's property with the deed that Michael had given him, and wasn't about to return title without a legal battle. He let him know that the Donna and Nugari had formed a partnership, and that they appointed him as her CEO.

He looked pompous when he made his offer. "I have been empowered to offer you a very lucrative position within our hotel-casino project. You will be a paid member of the Board of Directors of the Hotel and Casino at Sundance Lake with full voting rights."

"You arrogant son of a bitch. How dare you offer me a position on the board of my own company?"

Michael stood up and turned away. He stopped and turned back to face Roberts, when he became enraged. With both hands, he slammed into Roberts' chest. "You no account back-stabbing bastard." His fist struck Roberts' mid-section with a crushing blow that broke at least one rib.

Roberts retaliated with a swing that missed Michael. A right cross from Michael sent him across the table smashing the light. The room fell into semi-darkness. A figure appeared from the bedroom door and threw a gun to Dave Roberts. He got up and pointed it at Michael. Instinctively, Michael rushed on his opponent. They struggled and the gun fired. Roberts slumped and fell to his knees. He clutched his abdomen, and stared at Michael.

"Help me," he whispered. "Your wife, ach, ach.. "

"What about my wife?"

"Killed, ach, ach, murdered."

"What do you know? Michael shook him.

"Bob.. bah.. ahh.. bi..ahh." He fell unconscious.

Michael found the phone and dialed 911. The figure from the bedroom had fled through the bedroom window. He looked for the sedan across the street. It was gone. The paramedics arrived in a few minutes, and rushed Roberts to the hospital. Poncerelli and some detectives questioned Michael. He left out the part about Bobbi. Bobbi. At least he thought that was what he said. Dominic Poncerelli vouched for Michael, and the senior detective told him that he was free to go but, not to leave town. He was glad that Poncerelli and Charlie were such good friends.

"It was a set-up," he told Charlie, "Someone was in the bedroom with a gun. He threw it to Roberts. They probably wanted him to kill me and take the rap."

"They?"

"There were two in a sedan across the street when I got there. I thought it was Ponci's guys." He took a deep breath. "Before Roberts passed out, he whispered something to me. He said that Darci was murdered"

"We know that."

"Yes. But, it's what he said next that floored me. He said Bobbi."

"He said that Darci was murdered, and that Bobbi did it."

"Well, not exactly. He said that something like wife, killed, murdered. Then I shook him, and he said Bobbi ahh."

"Was it Bobbi or was there more?"

"Now I'm not sure. But if it was Bobbi?" he sighed. "Why would she, and if it's true, how would he know?"

* * * * * * *

"It's all over the morning papers." Charlie said as he came into the kitchen. He tossed the paper on the counter. The headlines read, "CASINO DEVELOPER FOUND ALIVE".

Michael was pouring his coffee. "Want a cup?"

"Thanks." Charlie took the cup.

"I've been watching it on TV. They've got me and Keleigh cast in a sex hideaway for executives."

"It'll make good copy for the supermarket tabloids."

"Thanks, pal."

"I need to get my car from the airport and get to the office. It looks like I've got a lot of damage control ahead of me. Want some eggs and toast?"

Charlie nodded yes. "I've got some calls to make. Call me when it's ready."

Michael drove directly to his office where he was met by a raft of newspaper and television reporters. Still limping a little, he pushed his way through the entourage stopping short of the main entry. He raised his hand to stop their indecipherable questions. They became quiet. "We had an electrical problem with my plane, and had to make a forced landing in a grassy field. The transpon-

der failed and we were unable to get a message out. Miss Ives and
I were only shaken a little, and were finally found by my friend
Charlie Swift. My office will prepare a formal statement later to-
day. Thank you."

The questions began again. "Did you and miss Ives.. ?'" What
about the take-over?" "Who.. ?"

As the door shut behind him he was welcomed by big round
of applause. The entire staff was waiting in the reception area.

Martha was first to come forward with a cup of coffee in her
hand. "Welcome back boss." She walked at his side. "Mr. Swift
called and said that you were on your way."

Michael shook hands as he passed each of them. He stopped
to wipe the tears from Candace's cheeks. He turned back as he got
to his office door. "Thanks. Thanks. I know that you're wondering
about Miss Ives. She's just fine, but is taking a few days off to rest
from our ordeal." He looked at Martha. "Come in please." Duti-
fully she followed closing the door behind her. "I need to be brought
up to speed on what's been happening while I've been gone."

"Mr. Swift had the key personnel prepare reports. They're on
your desk."

"Charlie did?"

"Mr. Swift took over when they thought that you and Miss
Ives were.. "

"He never said a word."

"Mr. Nestor has called twice this morning and three times
yesterday. He's flying in today and wants to see you."

"Set it up for tonight, at eight, at my home. I want to see him
too."

Michael settled in at his desk. After he read the reports, he
dialed his parents. "Hi Mom. How're you and Dad doing?"

His mother cried as she tried to respond, but all she could say
was, "Here's your father."

The men talked for almost a half an hour. Vittorio Orcini told
his son that they had asked Charlie to take over. He confessed that
he knew nothing about real estate development, and that they

trusted Michael's best friend. He confirmed that he had the deed to the property in a safety deposit at their bank, and that he notified Nathan Gregory when they heard about the accident.

Michael summoned Martha on the intercom.

"Yes, boss." she said with a happy tone.

"I need to see Nathan Gregory. I'd like you to arrange a meeting at my home in Malibu for the day after tomorrow. Call Maggie and tell her that I need to see her at her office today, and ask J.T., Sumner and Rebecca to come in."

"Maggie, Sir?"

He recognized her confusion. "Maggie. Darci's Assistant, at our real estate office."

"Yes, sir. Maggie. Right. Yes sir."

After the expected salutations from his top executives, Michael expressed the need to get back on track. There would be meetings with Ceres and Nugari. He told them that he was meeting with Guy Nestor later, and would share the results with them tomorrow. They had been working together for more than two hours when Martha interrupted. She whispered that his appointment with Maggie was in thirty minutes.

Maggie Cunningham became Michael and Keleigh's partner when she took over Darci's Real Estate Company and Cody Travel. She was more that just a partner, she was Darci's best friend, and now Michael's trusted friend. She combined the companies and their names into Cody-T Enterprises, and expanded it to include foreign real estate opportunities for her travel clients. She was a young woman of twenty-eight with exceptional fortitude, who knew more about the real estate business than most seasoned agents. Darci used to tease her about her plump figure, and since the accident she trimmed down to a size eight, changed her hair style, and worked-out every day.

"Michael." She hugged him long and hard. "It's good to have you home safe. I was sure that we lost you and Keleigh. I could never make it without you guys."

He stepped back and looked at her. "Maggie? What have you done with yourself?"

"D'you like?" she moved back and twirled. "It's the new me."

"Wow."

"Don't say any more or you'll embarrass me."

"I need your help, Maggie."

"I've made some coffee."

"No thanks."

"Darci taught me how."

"In that case.. "

"What can I help you with?" she asked, as she filled two cups. "I still use cream. Can't get used to it black." She indicated that they should sit at the two overstuffed, love-seat-size, chairs in the corner, and placed the cups on the small coffee table that completed the ensemble. "Sit, please."

"I need you to check on a quit claim deed that was filed against my property at Sundance Lake. It was probably filed under a Corporation. Check under Nugari or Ceres. This has to be in the strictest confidence. Do you know somebody at the recorder's office that you can trust?"

"Yes. I can get Kasha to do it." She noted his uncertain look. "She's Pastor Jim's wife. You should remember her from.. " She became uneasy, and reached for her cup.

"It was pretty hectic that day." He was a master at changing the demeanor of an uncomfortable situation. "I trust your judgment."

He laid out all the facts about the deed, but he deliberately left out the detail that his parents held the deed in a secure place.

"I'll have the information by tomorrow."

* * * * * * *

A flagman stopped him half way up the road, and walked to the car. "It'll be just a moment sir."

"What's going on?"

"We're building a guardrail along the side of the road. A girl was killed not so long ago when her car went over the side."

Michael remembered Darci's words from their first date as if it were yesterday. " . . . I'm heading up a committee to get some barricades installed along the edge. They probably won't do anything about it until someone gets killed." The flagman waved him on. There was a small marker with some wild flowers at the point where her car left the road. Michael stopped and approached the workmen. "I would like to put a permanent marker here. Whom should I talk to?"

"Was she.. ?" One of them started to ask.

"My wife."

"I'll take care of it sir, just tell me what you want."

"Tomorrow?"

"Yes sir."

Michael thought it was odd that the front door was unlocked, and cautiously entered. He checked every room. Confident that everything was intact, he methodically went to the kitchen and made some coffee. He took a quick shower, poured the coffee into Darci's favorite cup, and sat down at his desk.

"What are you doing?"

He answered without thinking. "I'm designing a roadside marker for you."

She took his hand, and he followed her to the bedroom.

* * * * * * *

Guy Nestor arrived promptly at eight with Roberta Azure at his side.

Bobbi rushed in and threw her arms around Michael's neck. After a short moment, she pushed her shoulders back forcing her thighs and groin against him. "I'm so-oo happy to see you. We thought that . . . Are you surprised to see me? I was on my way to Big Sur when Guy told me that he was meeting with you, so-oo," she pushed her groin tighter against him, "I canceled my plans, and we-ll, here I am."

He put his hands on her hips and gently pushed her away. "When did Guy tell you that we were meeting?"

"Yesterday," she glanced at Guy, "yesterday afternoon."

"Hello Michael," he said slightly embarrassed, "she has a way of insisting."

"Hello, Guy. Come in."

They sat by the fireplace and spent about fifteen or twenty minutes having a drink and exchanging insignificant social repartee.

"I think it's about time to get down to business." Guy said. "You've had a lot of problems with the Italians and the Chinese, and, well we all know that they want your project. Then there's Nugari. He's claiming that he has the title to your property. I have a proposal for you. If it's true about Nugari," he hesitated, "I have."

Bobbi chimed in. "Guy has an option on the property just across the lake from your property."

"Bobbi. Let me." He got up and put his elbow on the mantel. "It's like Bobbi says, I did take an option on that piece of land but, you need to know, I want to finance your project, whether it's on your property or across the lake." He looked intently at Bobbi to be sure that she didn't interrupt. "Here's the deal in a nutshell. If we go across the lake, we can still use the plans that you have with only minor adjustments because of the topography. The plans still belong to you. If we stay on your property, well I think that's obvious. It'll be fifty-fifty split right down the middle, and you keep all your people just as they are, except for Keleigh. She'll have to go." He smiled at Bobbi.

"One thing right off the top. Keleigh stays or this conversation is over."

"You're sleeping with her. I knew it." Bobbi's face reddened.

"There's no discussion on this point. It's not a negotiable item."

"You'd throw the deal away for one insignificant person?"

"Not negotiable."

Guy Nestor looked down at Bobbi, and shrugged his shoulders. "What other issues do you have?"

"Keleigh?"

"Okay. She stays in. What else?"

"I have controlling stock with ten percent off the top going to my non-profit foundation, same as before. I have complete control of employee and management."

"Do we have a deal?"

"Not until I see it in writing, and my attorney approves every paragraph."

"I'll be in touch with you. Come along Bobbi."

"One more thing. I have control of the name of the project."

"I thought that it was called the Hotel at Sundance Lake." Bobbi said.

"I'm thinking about changing the name."

"To what? Keleigh's Place?"

"Send me your contract and be sure to send a duplicate to Nathan Gregory."

The men shook hands, and Bobbi left without a word.

He went back to work on the marker but, was constantly interrupted with a blurred vision of a figure tampering with Darci's Mustang. When the vision went away his mind raced with a myriad of questions. How did Guy know that he was back yesterday? Why was Bobbi hitting on him with Guy standing next to her? How did Guy know about Nugari and the deed? Why did Bobbi want Keleigh out of the project? Was it jealousy, or was there another reason? Did Guy think that the Italians and the Chinese were just going to roll over and play dead? What about Hans Gruber? Did he really have the money now?

"You have a lot going on in that brain of yours." She appeared with a distant guise about her. Her ethereal beauty was somehow transformed into an earthly concern, which mystified him. "Don't concern yourself with the vision, remember to accentuate only the positive, and eliminate the negative."

"I know. But, I have to find out who killed you."

"You need to talk to Norah. She found out something that will lead you to the person that you are looking for."

"Norah? Biz? What does she know?

"I'm not sure. I only know that she has an important clue. How's the marker coming? Any ideas?"

"I'm confused. I don't know what to write."

"A heart with an arrow through it, and the words 'Darci loves Michael'."

"For an angel you should come up with a better idea."

"It's not my job, and I'm not an angel. Not yet. You'd better get some rest."

"Will you stay with me?"

"Now *that's* my job."

* * * * * *

Henri Piaget was surprised when Pernicious Nugari showed up at his door. They hadn't spoken more than a few words in passing, and now he came unannounced.

"May I come in?"

"What do you want?"

"It's complicated, May I?" He gestured as he took a step forward.

Piaget blocked Nugari's advance. "We have dinner guests. We're entertaining some clients at the moment. It would be awkward."

"This will only take a moment."

"I'm sorry. Not now. Please leave." He stepped back and shut the door.

* * * * * *

Michael pushed the hands free answer button on the dashboard. "Hello. Orcini."

"Hello Michael," came the response, "I have some very interesting news for you."

"Good morning, Henri," he recognized his architect's voice, "what's up?"

"Nugari came by last night."

"That son-of-a-bitch. What did he want?"

"I don't know. I didn't let him in. We had dinner guests."

"Interesting. Say, while I've got you on the phone, what do you think about adapting your design to another site across the lake?"

"Move across the lake?"

"I'm not sure. If we had to, could it be done?"

"We'd have to get a topo and a soils report, and make a new study."

"What if I had the topo and report? How long would it take?"

"I could make a quick study in a week, but we'd have to have the full blown grading plans, and the foundation designs might change."

"How much longer to get our permits, if we stay where we are?"

"I should have a grading permit next week."

"Okay. Stay on track. I'll call you if there are any changes."

* * * * * * *

Keleigh sat on the fog-covered beach wearing a double layer of her heaviest hooded sweats when Michael got to his Malibu home. When he couldn't find her in the house, he went out on the deck and saw her hunched figure on the sand. He knew that she wouldn't hear him call, so he rang the brass ship's bell on the wall. He kept striking it until she turned around and waved. She got up almost instantly, and ran in the soft sand tripping a few times along the way. Her hiking boots sounded like thunder on the wood steps, and she tripped again as she got to the top.

The door slammed back against the wall as she burst into the house. "Where are you?" She hollered.

"In the kitchen."

She slowed down her anxious pace and pouted as she got to the kitchen. "I thought that you'd meet me at the door."

"You looked cold, so I decided to make you some hot chocolate."

She went around the counter and they embraced.

"It's really damp out there. You're clothes are all wet."

"Help me take them off?"

"Go take a hot shower while I finish your drink."

"Okay." She dashed off submissively.

He put her drink on the bathroom counter and paused to watch her through the clear glass shower enclosure that was beginning to steam up. She turned to face him, and pressed her breasts against the glass, then she turned around and did the same with her butt, leaving their impressions as she went back to her shower. She was not the same Keleigh that he had known for all those years. She was totally uninhibited with him. He wanted to join her but, the image of Darci's ghost flashed in his mind. He went to the kitchen and poured himself some coffee.

"What's wrong, Michael?" She snuggled to his back.

"It's uh . . ."

"It's a long drive from Las Vegas. You must be tired. I'm sorry, I wasn't thinking, I was just being selfish."

"Thanks. Let's sit down."

It wasn't the trip. It was Darci. Michael wasn't sure what to do. He knew that he had to tell her about Darci's ghost. She would surely think that he was crazy. He wanted to be with her but, he was still in love with Darci. How could he have an intimate relationship with Keleigh as long as Darci was there, ghost or not. How could he continue this ghostly relationship with Darci? He must see Biz, get the information, and find out who killed Darci. Then she be would free to leave this world, and he could get on with his life. His voice rang out in his mind asking if he really wanted her to go.

They sat on the couch by the fireplace.

"I want you to go abroad and get things started with your list of high-rollers."

"When do you want me to go?"

"Next week. But first, I have to go to the Cayman Islands to see Hans, and I want you to go with me."

"Why me? Don't get me wrong, I'd love to go with you but, wouldn't it be more productive if you took J.T.?

"I have my reasons."

"And you're not going to share them with me." She put her cup down and turned to him. "I thought that you had a deal with Guy Nestor. Wait. That's not it. You're not just covering your bets, there's more. I know." She pursed her lips for a serious proclamation. "I've got it. You plan to run out of gas, or get shot down for a second time, and feign a sprained ankle so you can seduce me again."

He took her face in his hands and kissed her tenderly.

* * * * * *

The BMW convertible fit in but, as soon as he got out, the worsted suit complete with dark shirt and silk tie, and his over-sized briefcase characterized Nathan Gregory as an outsider to the colony at Malibu.

"You're early. I didn't expect you for another hour."

Nate looked at Keleigh wrapped in Michael's robe. "Sorry. My deposition in the Palisades ended sooner that I expected. Am I interrupting something?"

"No. We're finished. I'll go and put some clothes on."

"Come in and make yourself comfortable. And take off that coat and tie."

"I didn't know," he glanced toward the bedroom, "that you and Keleigh . . ."

"She just got out of the shower. That's all."

"Right. She's a pretty girl, Michael, and she's had a crush on you for a long time. I can't blame you, I mean. . . ."

"You're my legal counsel, not my counselor."

"Touché."

The two men spent the next couple hours going over Nestor's extensive proposal. When they were through they asked Keleigh to join them. She was given a quick overview, and asked her opinion.

"First, I'd want him to put all of the money in an interest bearing escrow account. Personally, I don't think that he has enough to complete the project, much less the operating capital for the first year. Second, I'd want to see the active gaming licenses of all the investors, and finally I want to know what Bobbi and Busy get out of this. Other than that, it sounds like you guys have a good handle on it. Oh, by the way, what about Hans? How does he fit into this?"

"Hans is.. " Nate began.

"We'll talk about that later, Keleigh." Michael cut in.

"Yes boss." She got up and headed for the kitchen, "Are you staying for dinner?"

"I can't. But thanks, Keleigh."

* * * * * *

Except for the usual pseudo religious vagabonds, Bradley Terminal at the Los Angeles International Airport was relatively quiet when they checked in.

"Is this all the luggage that you're bringing?"

"The last time you told me to bring my flannel jammies and a warm smile. This time all I brought was the warm smile."

Hans Gruber had his driver meet them at the airport. Marianna welcomed them at the door just as she did when he brought Darci there.

Felicia and Simone giggled as before, and waited for the ritual, "Allez mes paresseuses! Vite! Vite!" Followed by the handclap from Marianna. They responded, and carried the bags up the stairs. "Please follow me Senor, Senorita. Dinner will be in one hour."

They were the same connecting rooms that he remembered.

After the servants left, Keleigh went through the connecting door to Michael's room. "I could live here. Couldn't you?" She looked back to her room, and then to him. Intuitively she knew. "You've been here before. With her." She sensed that this was more than just a business trip for Michael. "This is why you wouldn't tell me about the trip." She felt a mysteriously warm and gratifying sensation fill her entire body. In another time she would have been furious about the situation she found herself in today. But, now she felt his pain of letting go. He had to let go before he could commit to her. She would see it through. She kicked off her shoes as she walked to him. "It's okay, Michael." She put her arms around him and they embraced.

Keleigh was standing at the arched dining room windows overlooking the garden when Hans entered.

"Cahmm sit here, by me, Miss Kahl-lee."

They dined in the same elegance as was the custom of the house. Hans did not want to talk about politics or social events. He wanted to know all about Keleigh. He looked at Michael to fill in the missing parts that she wouldn't reveal. It seemed as if Michael remembered everything about Keleigh since the time they first met. He found himself offering recollections of events that even she had forgotten.

Abruptly Hans changed the subject. "You shuud not do bezhnahs wid dat mon Nugari or dat Mafiah wooh-mon. Nestoohr duz not haav ehn-huf mohn-ee." He wiggled his palm down hand indicating a tenuous amount. Hey haas four huhn-drahd mill-yoohn. I haav de rest of dah mohn-ee dat you need. I wehl trahns-fohr et to yohr ah-count en dah mahrn-nahn eff you wish."

"Five hundred million?" Keleigh questioned.

"Yes."

"What do you want for your investment?" She asked.

Hans looked at Michael. "I luvh your new wooh-mon." He set his eyes on her, "twahntay pahrsahnt fohr Nestoohr, twahntay-fahv pahrsahnt fohr meh, ahnd fefthtay-fahv pahrsahnt fohr you, ahnd," he looked at Michael, "heyhm."

"Michael's foundation gets ten percent off the top, and our people manage the hotel, the casino, and all the retail stores."

"Ohf coohrss."

Without taking her eyes off him she said, "We wish."

Hans smiled.

"I don't know why I came."

"So you could thank me later."

Keleigh went for a walk in the garden while Hans and Michael had the traditional brandy and cigar, and completed the negotiation. Hans disclosed that Nestor had already come to him for the money. The finances would soon be in place without conflict.

Keleigh had taken off her summer dress and was lying across his bed, asleep, wearing only her peach thongs. He sat next to her and gently stroked her shoulders.

She woke and turned over to greet him. "You smell like a stale cigar."

"Then I'll only kiss you where you can't smell . . ." He kissed her breasts, and started to move his mouth down her abdomen when she pulled his hair. "Ouch."

"Which room did you sleep in before? This one or that one?"

"This one."

"Then we sleep in the other one." She got up and headed to the other room.

"We do?"

"If you want to sleep with me we do."

His eyes followed the purposeful sway of her derrière, and he went to her room.

After breakfast they took Hans' yacht and sailed to a remote cove where Michael told her about Darci's ghost and about finding the killer. He left out the fact that they could touch and feel each other, and of course, the sex.

"Whew. That's a lot to swallow." She wanted to run. Get away from this fantasy. "But she'll be gone when the killer is found. Right?"

"That's what she told me."

"What about the information that Busy has? How do we get that stuff? So what do we have to do to find him? The killer."

"Not we, cute buns. Me."

"I want to help."

"No. It could be dangerous. I'm just helping the police when I can, besides you've got work to do."

"Can you touch her?"

"She's a ghost. What do you think?"

* * * * * * *

It was mid morning when he dropped Keleigh off at her house. "I'll see you at the office this afternoon." The light morning rain left the road up the hill slippery. He slowed down as he approached the monument. The work crew chief recognized his car and motioned for him to stop.

"It's in place, Mr. Orcini. Just park over here." He pointed. They walked, and Michael fell to one knee in front of the marker. "Is it what you want?"

Michael studied the granite marker. A half-open single rose with it's stem piercing the simple inscription; 'Darci my Love' was chiseled into the face. He looked intently at the monument, said a silent prayer, and got up. "It's perfect. Thank you." He stayed for a few moments, and continued home.

He stopped for a brief moment as he stepped into the cold, damp house. Michael looked around to see if *she* was there, and set the thermostat to heat. He kept his leather flight jacket on, went directly to his office, and dialed the phone.

"Biz. It's Michael. How are you?"

The voice on the phone said. "Michael. I'm so glad you called. I wanted to call but, I was afraid that you didn't want to talk to me."

"Why would you think such a thing?"

"It's because of Dave, and . . ."

"Forget about that. I need to talk to you about what you found out about Darci's Murderer. Killer. What do you know?"

"Please don't be mad at me but.. "

"I'm not mad. I just want to know what you found out."

"I went to your house. Darci's house, and.. "

"I know that you were there. Please go on."

"Well, I don't know why I went there or what I was looking for but, after I searched and searched, the phone rang and the machine answered." She told him, in detail, about the message on the tape, and how Dave and his friend removed the background sounds to make it audible.

"Have you got the tape?"

"No. Dave has it."

"Did he play it for you after they cleaned it up?"

"No."

"Have you told anyone else about the tape?"

"No."

"Thanks Biz."

After he hung up she remembered about Claude's papers. "Enough for one day," she told the receiver, "enough."

Michael arrived early for his lunch appointment with Guy Nestor at the New York Deli, and chose a table along the rail in time to be seen by his twice cancelled dinner appointment.

"Mr. Orcini. I'm still anticipating our dinner engagement." The hotel executive said with a tempered sarcasm.

"I'm sorry. There doesn't seem to be enough time in each day. Tomorrow?"

"Eight o'clock. I'll have my secretary call your office with the details."

They shook hands over the rail, and he left just as Guy Nestor got there.

"You making a deal with him?"

"No. Just comparing notes. One has to be friendly with his competitors."

* * * * * * *

London, Paris, Madrid, Monaco, and many points in between were exciting and rewarding for Keleigh. Almost grateful for the three months abroad, she rationalized that her time away would give Michael time to sort out his feelings. She had more than half of the known high rollers committed to the grand opening. Many royal figures from smaller monarchies, and principalities expressed their commitment if she would promise that they would be seated with movie stars at the grand-opening extravaganza. With the success of her European adventure she almost detoured to Las Vegas while on her way to South America but, at the last moment determined that a romantic interlude wasn't appropriate. Instead, she called and they talked for almost half an hour.

Michael was pleased with her accomplishments, and agreed that she should continue while she was on a roll. "Aruba is beautiful this time of the year but, stay away from the beaches."

"I'll show off my buns if I want. You're not the only one that looks. You know? Besides it'll only be a few more weeks. See ya, bye."

The old familiar ending. She hadn't done that to him in a long time.

THE RETRIBUTION

Chapter Seven

Orcini Enterprises received their final approvals and building permits, and began construction on Michael Orcini's property. Nathan Gregory brought in a new local law firm, and filed a lawsuit against Nugari and Ceres. Nugari countered with an attempt to restrain Orcini from building on the land until the suit was settled. The presiding judge, an old friend of Charlie's father, ruled that the building permits were in order, and the risk would by borne by Orcini Enterprises if it proceeded before the a final decision was rendered.

Not to be outdone, Ceres, Wu and Nugari optioned another property across the lake, hired a large Newport Beach architectural firm, which was experienced in hotel and casino design, and began work on their own project. The architects had plans for a project that was approved but never built. After some adjustments to fit the new location, they submitted their project for approval, greased a few palms, and started a few months later.

Pernicious Nugari covered the agony of his defeat with a gregarious pursuit of the new project. His act convinced most of those who watched the competition unfold. He had fooled Jami Wu, and was out to get Wu's share back from Ceres. He approached Wu with a plan to not only get his share back, but also cut Ceres out. They would threaten to expose the details of the partnership to the Gaming Commission. This, he figured, would get her to release Wu's money back to the Chinese. He would take control. Wu liked the idea, and said that he would bring in the Chinese Camorra to strengthen their position. Nugari figured a war between Ceres and the Chinese would cancel each other out.

Donna Una Maria Antonia Ceres had other plans. She planned to frame Nugari for Darci's murder and get all the attention shifted to him, leaving her free to double cross both him and Wu. Nugari beat her at her own game. He brought in a phony witness who claimed to have seen Mario tinker with Darci's car the day of the accident. Mario was arrested and formally charged with the Murder of Darci Tashmit.

Confused by the allegations, Michael finally disclosed Dave Roberts' confession with Dominic Poncerelli. Ponci wasn't surprised with Roberts' accusation, considering his arrangement with Ceres.

"Did you know that Norah Laude tried to get him an executive position with Guy Nestor's group?"

"No. But, it doesn't surprise me."

"Roberts had a sweet deal all set up when her sister squelched the deal. He was out before he could catch his breath."

"I've known Bobbi for a long time, and she always wants it her way. She tried to get Keleigh out by using her influence with Nestor. But murder?"

"So, Roberts tried to get back at her."

"Even when he thought he might be dying?"

"But, he's not. He's out of the critical stage, and we've got a man parked outside his hospital room. He's not going anywhere for a while. We'll check out his story later."

* * * * * *

From her boudoir she called to him. "Call Pauli and find out what's happening with Mario." Maria Ceres told her lover.

Connie Contedetto resented being ordered around when they were out of character. "Call him yourself," he shouted back, "I'm not your slave."

She slinked back to the bedroom. "Ah but, you are." She dropped her negligee to the floor revealing herself. She walked to him, pushed him back on the bed, and solicited, "Would you rather that I was your slave?"

When they were finished, *he* sat on the edge of the bed, called Pauli, and found out that Mario was ready to tell all for immunity and the safety of a witness protection program.

"Pauli says that they're transporting him up into the mountains in two days. To a trailer park in Pahrump. First Binion hid his money there, and now the cops want to hide Mario there. They could have been more creative."

"Mario has to be eliminated. We can't afford to be put at risk." She reached up and ran her hand through his hair. Suddenly she took hold and pulled his head to her breasts. "Here, here." She pushed his face down toward her abdomen until he became her slave once more.

* * * * * *

She stood by the edge of her bed as the bright sunlight streamed through the Paisley curtains. For a brief moment she felt alive and human again. She inspected the painting of Aditi, and swung around, expecting her to be watching over her. "Where are you?" She was surprised to hear her own voice. "What's happening?"

Puca appeared from under the bed with an, "Arf, arf," that surprised her, "arf, arf," came the diminutive sound, again and again.

She knew that she was supposed to hear him in her mind only. Once more she looked around for her mentor, but she wasn't there. She called out in her human voice but Aditi did not appear. She sat on the bed, and immediately Puca jumped on her lap.

"What is it, Pukie?"

The little soothsayer spoke to her in the ancient language that she was starting to understand. He was telling her about the sabotage of the steering column on her car. She wished that she understood everything that he said. He wanted her to warn Michael about somebody. Somebody that set the steering wheel to snap when she tried to turn.

"Rober, Robber, Robert. Is that what you're trying to say, Robert?"

"Arf," came the sounds, but sounding more like words. "Arf."

It all came back to her. The horrible cracking sound just before the Mustang went over the side of the road. She recalled with a quiver, how many times she gone down the road cursing it. With a whisper, she cursed again. "Damn him, damn him." She realized that she was cursing *him* and not the road. But, why wound he do that to her? She hardly knew him. Why didn't she have the answers for Michael? She should know these things she rationalized. She stroked her little companion thinking what a heartbreak that he had to die with her but, then again, she was grateful for his presence. She wished that Michael would hurry home so she could tell him the news.

The sun sank behind Mt. Charleston as he pulled into the driveway. He was glad that the workday was over. Warmed by the thought of a quiet evening he approached the front door, and started to put the key in the lock when it opened. Puca was sitting in the entry with his tail wagging and a look like he had just helped himself to the dinner steak.

"Hello my little friend. Where's Darci?"

"Arf, arf." He ran to the bedroom, stopping to make sure that Michael was following, "Arf, arf," then off again.

She looked like an angel standing there in an almost transparent silver gown. There was an unmistakable lavender colored aura that encircled her. Michael stopped and savored the manifestation. She looked the same but, out-of this world different. He feared that this angel-like appearance meant that she was leaving him.

"Don't be afraid. I'm not leaving you, Michael," she read his mind, "but, I do have important information to share with you. Come here by me."

Once again, he was taken aback by her telepathic ability. "You look different today, and Puca looks like the cat that just ate the canary. What's up?"

"Come here, and sit by me." Darci told him of the visualization that Puca had about Roberts and her car. She had a sadness about her as she told the story.

"Why are you so sad? Is it because you know who killed you, or because the knowledge of it will take you away from here?"

"It's not time for me to go yet. I'm sad because," she laid her head on his shoulder, "because he was a total stranger, and had no reason to do what he did. I have to stay and find the raison d'être for this dastardly act." She kissed his cheek. "I remembered that from our time in Paris."

"Poncerelli needs to know this."

"What will you tell him? That a ghost and her dog told you?"

"None of this makes any sense. Why would Roberts have the answer machine tape cleaned if it would incriminate him?" Are you sure that it's Roberts?"

"Well, Puckie said his name to me in his ancient language."

"Are you sure that you understood him?"

"Well—ll, I sort of had to drag it out of him. Kind of like charades."

"It was Roberts. Not Roberta?"

She repeated what her little friend had told her again, and again.

"Roberts. I'll go to the hospital and beat it out of him."

* * * * * *

Several Police cars, Sheriff and Highway Patrol cruisers, and a Federal Marshal's Sport Utility Vehicles drove in a caravan south along I-15 to the Blue Diamond turnoff, and headed up the mountain road to Pahrump. Mario Tasso was on his way to a new life and identity.

As the caravan neared the top of the first grade, a fully equipped attack helicopter rose from the depths of the valley and singled out the third SUV sending a rocket directly into it's hood. The SUV was instantaneously demolished. The chopper banked-off behind the side of the mountain, and disappeared. The surprise attack left Mario Tasso and three Federal Marshals dead. Attempts to track the chopper were futile. It was below radar detection, and seemed to vanish into thin air.

"They knew exactly what vehicle he was in." Reported one of the Marshals at the debriefing. "It was a hit and run. They never even came back for a second pass."

Dominic Poncerelli, along with a contingent of high-ranking police officers and detectives listened as the senior Marshal ranted on that there was a mole in their department, and he had to be flushed out. "We lost three good men in this operation. I want the records of everyone in this department." The debriefing went on for another two hours. Poncerelli and the Chief left the Feds to their task.

"We need to do some house cleaning. Have someone check all the outgoing and incoming phone calls from here and every cell phone in the department for the last three days. No make it a week"

"Who do you suggest, Chief? Who can we trust?"

"Pauli. He's been here the longest. Yes, have Pauli do it."

* * * * * *

"No, Poncerelli, this is serious. Mario didn't kill Darci. It was Dave Roberts. The same guy that tried to kill me. That whole thing with the chopper was a cover. Roberts works for Ceres, and Mario, well, he was expendable. You were getting too close to her operation, and she took him out so he wouldn't testify against her." Michael said with certainty. "Both of them were expendable. She'll have Roberts eliminated before you can lock him up." He pounded on the commissioner's desk.

The worn leather chair that Dominic Poncerelli sat in, as his friend made demands, was out of character with his tastefully decorated Art Deco style office. He grabbed the antique ceramic statue before it fell. "Please control yourself. I don't want you killing off *my* favorite lady. She holds the stars of my future."

"Sorry, but I don't think that she'll stop at anything to get my project." He quieted down. "First, deVillefrance disappears, then Darci was murdered when she got too close, now it's Mario. She's going to get Roberts. You'll see."

"We don't have any reason to suspect Roberts." He gestures for Michael not to interrupt. "Listen to me before you say anything more. We can't go around arresting people just because you think that they did something. You got to have proof. Do you have any proof about Roberts?"

He wanted to tell him, Oh God, how he wanted to tell him. "Nothing that you can put your finger on."

Come back when you do," he stood up, "and I'll arrest him." He put his hand out. "Goodbye Michael. Call me, and we'll have a drink. My treat."

"Thanks. . . ." He wanted to complete with, "for nothing." But, graciously left.

* * * * * *

She had been sitting in the private room for more than half an hour when the nurse came in. She looked at his chart. "It'll be awhile before the sedative wears off." The nurse informed Norah Laude. "Why don't you go to the cafeteria and get some coffee or a sandwich. I'll have someone get you when he wakes up."

"Where?"

"Come, I'll show you."

Moments after they left, a figure in a hospital gown crept quietly into Dave Roberts' room. Rubber-gloved hands prepared a hypodermic needle, and injected the intravenous apparatus with a deadly potion. The intruder searched the closet and found a brown envelope with a cassette tape.

"I forgot my cell phone," Norah said to the nurse, "wait here, I'll be right back."

Quickly and quietly the killer left, brushed by Norah, covering her face from view with the plastic wrapper from the syringe, and went into the adjacent linen supply room and removed the gown and gloves.

Norah Laude paused and noticed that the person who bumped into her was wearing spike-high heel shoes instead of the traditional hospital sneakers. She shook it off, retrieved her cell phone and continued to the cafeteria.

"Hi."

"Bobbi?" Norah was surprised to see her sister. "What are you doing here?"

They hugged and kissed the air by each other's cheeks.

"I'm in town with Guy. He said that he dropped you off here, and was going to come back and pick you up. I told him," they sat down, "well, here I am. I'll drive you back to your hotel. How's Dave?"

"He was still sedated when I got here. The nurse was going to call me." She looked at her watch. "It's been a while, let's go up."

There were nurses and doctors hovering over his bed as the two women got to the room. "You can't come in here." A hospital orderly said, and ushered them out.

"What's happening?" Bobbi asked.

"He's had a relapse. You'll have to wait and check at the Nurses' Station."

They watched the door as the doctors and nurses left his room. Norah jumped up and grabbed a doctor's arm. "How is he?"

"I'm sorry," she said, "we did everything we could. I'm sorry."

Dominic Poncerelli was first on the scene with two detectives and two uniform officers. Poncerelli made a phone call, while the detectives questioned the staff and visitors.

"Hello."

"Mr. Orcini. Dominic Poncerelli here."

"Why so formal?"

"You were right. They got to Roberts. He's dead." He told him how it happened. "We found a surgeon's smock and some rubber gloves, and a hypodermic needle in a nearby supply room." He cleared his throat. "Something else that I think you should know. Your friends, Norah and Bobbi were there."

"At the hospital?"

"Norah claims that she was visiting him, and Bobbi came by to pick her up."

"Are you holding them?"

"No. We'll question them later."

Michael wondered who would be next on Ceres' hit list.

* * * * * *

The argument between Pernicious Nugari and Jami Wu was as intense as it could be without being physical. Jami threatened to bring in the Chinese Camorra if his family's money wasn't returned to him by the end of the week. Nugari countered with his own threat. He would have Wu cut out of the deal completely.

Nugari decided not to take any chances, and pretended to rescind his threat. "I'll see what I can do."

"Nugari is on his way here," Ceres warned Connie, "he's going to be trouble. I think that we should cool him off for now."

"How cool?"

"I'll make myself unavailable. Let's play the game."

"He's not going to buy it anymore."

"Tell him that I'm out of town, and find out what he wants."

The road to Casa Trinacria had a sense of the unknown pressing in on him as he came around the last turn. Nugari slammed his brakes as a coyote darted across the road and disappeared into the brush. He sat back and sighed a sigh of relief but, the weight of the mysterious phenomenon became heavier. His military training kicked in once more. He knew that action would suppress the fear, and jammed the accelerator to the floor spinning the wheels on the decomposed granite drive. The car sped to the front door where he slammed on the brakes and skidded to a stop. Two men in black came out to the car, and escorted him to the mansion. Dominique waited in the open doorway.

"Come in Mr. Nugari." She articulated in a manner that excluded their personal relationship. "Follow me." She led him to the library. "You'd better leave." She said as she closed the large doors behind her. "Tell them that you changed your mind, and go." Her voice trembled as she spoke.

"I'll be okay. Its just business."

The door library doors opened, and Ermano Contedetto entered the room flanked by two massive men in black. "Leave us." He instructed Dominique. When she was gone he asked. "What do you want?"

"I've come to talk to you and," he eyed the henchmen, "Donna Ceres."

"She is not here. Tell me what you want."

"It's the Chinese. They want their money back, they," he paused, "I must see her. I know that she's here"

"The Donna is not here."

"She'll see me or . . ."

Connie nodded to the two men beside him.

They moved quickly toward Nugari. He reached inside his jacket, and drew his gun. One of them hit him square in the stomach, and grabbed the gun as he doubled over. The second man came around his backside and struck several blows to his kidneys. They beat him until he could not move.

"Get him out of here, and finish him off."

* * * * * * *

"He's not worth it. I mean, getting all upset over Dave is, well, it's just not worth it." Roberta Azure tried to console her sister. "He tried to screw everybody out of their fair share of the project, and well, he got what he deserved."

"He didn't have to be murdered."

"What makes you think that he was murdered? The doctor at the hospital said that he had a relapse."

"But the police were questioning everybody, and.. "

"The police always question everybody."

"Bobbi?"

"What?"

"I never told anyone, but.. "

"But, what?"

"I saw someone come out of Dave's hospital room. She was wearing one of these green hospital gowns. Like the ones that doctor's wear."

"She? Doctor? What are you trying to say?"

"She actually bumped into me. I think that she killed Dave."

"You're imagining this."

"No I'm not." She was wearing high heels and perfume. I specifically remember the perfume; because it was the same perfume that you always wear. That's how I remember."

"Let's talk about something else."

"No, no. You were wearing that perfume when I saw you that day at the hospital. The shoes. You have the same.. " She got up and began to pace. "It was your voice on the tape. It was your perfume, your shoes, and your voice on the tape. You didn't come to the hospital to give me a ride back to the condo. Did you? You were there to, to do what?" She looked long and disgustingly at Roberta. "You went to shut him up, and to get the tape from him. It was you. You killed Michael's Darci, and now you've done the same to Dave Roberts. Roberta. You did it. You killed them. Why."

"That bastard dumped me for her. Now he will have to come back to me." With a smile of satisfaction she stroked Norah's cheek and continued. "You can't tell this to anyone. Remember, I'm your sister."

* * * * * * *

Jami Wu had waited almost a week for Nugari to return his calls. Finally he placed a call to his family in China. Jami T'ing-fang Wu had lost face, and was to be replaced. A large contingent of the Camorra was dispatched within a few days. By the end of the first week, Wu's replacement confronted the Donna with a proposal to reestablish the business relationship. She refused, and had him beaten and forcibly removed from Casa Trinacria. Two of his fingers were cut off, and he was dumped in an alley.

Outraged, the Camorra retaliated in a true old-fashioned Mafia format. They launched their response with an attack directly on Casa Trinacria. Maria Ceres and Ermano Contedetto had just left for Italy when the unexpected rocket launcher and mortar shell volley began. They stopped their car and looked back in horror as the beloved Casa went up in smoke. The attack was quick and decisive. The Casa Trinacria was destroyed.

THE GHOST STAYS ON

Chapter Eight

The Darci-O Hotel and Casino Resort at Sundance Lake was completed on schedule, and the patrons were getting ready for the gala party that would begin when the sun set on Sundance Lake. The kitchens buzzed with activity as the chefs prepared the pre-selected multi-national orders for the entire house. Breads and pastries that would rival anything in the world were prepared in the Resort Bakery. Wines, liqueurs, and international drinks from all over the planet were ready to be dispersed at a moments notice. Nothing was left undone.

Keleigh Cody-Ives had spent most of the last fifteen months traveling around the world. She invited all the rich and famous, and some of the rich but not so famous to the grand opening of the Darci-O Hotel and Casino Resort.

Michael Orcini, on the other hand, spent all of his waking hours administering the construction and decoration of the resort. He worked relentlessly with his key staff to bring every facet of the resort in concert with all the other aspects of this mega-resort.

World famous entertainers rehearsed their acts. Spike Hawley had engaged the largest ensemble of the most popular stars ever amassed in one place. Celebrities that were not a part of the show were given complementary rooms at the hotel. Many extended their stay as paying customers.

Michael stood at the top of the Grand Staircase, which led down to the main casino. Thirty minutes earlier, Keleigh threw the dice that started the gaming. The casino was reminiscent of Monte Carlo, filled with men in formal attire, and women wearing one-of-a-kind gowns. Darci appeared at his side wearing a silver and white gown that had to be designed by the angels. It was simply adorned by the antique cameo brooch that he gave her for Christmas. Her hair was parted slightly off center, and fell softly across the side of her face down past her breast to her bodice. He wondered why she reappeared after all these months.

"It's your vision, darling," she read his mind, "I'm here with you to fulfill your dream. Come on. They're waiting." She took his arm, and they started down.

Soon the entire room became silent as they descended. Some whispered that they saw the ghost of Darci on his arm. "I hope they don't fall out." Darci whispered. "It's part of your reverie."

He remembered, looking down at her cleavage, and smiled.

They stopped as they neared the bottom of the staircase. Almost instantaneously, the rich and famous clientele rendered a standing ovation. All those in his fantasy, and a few more greeted him. They worked the room, and moved to the veranda.

"I was wondering . . ." he started.

"Special permission because it was a part of your dream, and besides, I wasn't really intruding. I'm so happy that I could be here to share your dream." They stopped walking. "Goodbye, darling." She kissed him sweetly and disappeared.

Michael walked across the veranda, stopping at the classic Mediterranean style stone railing, and looked out over the moonlit lake. The image of the pyramid was still visible. "Goodbye, my love."

He turned and watched the people dancing to the music from inside.

Keleigh came across the veranda. "Hi." She gave him a social hug. "She was here, wasn't she?" She looked around, and then continued quietly. "I could swear that she came down the staircase with you." She froze at the sound of her own words. "I'm sorry. I shouldn't have . . ."

"She was here." He took her hand. "Let's dance. He twirled her around and brought her full turn to face him. With her tight in his arms he whispered in her ear. "She had to complete the dream of the grand opening. She said goodbye a little while ago." Their interlude from the reality of the day was interrupted by a pit boss that needed an approval from Keleigh. "Will I see you later?"

"I'm going to turn in early. I'll see you tomorrow."

"See ya, bye."

He smiled.

Michael worked the casino again, moving to the smaller private gaming rooms. The ones that were by invitation only. He saw a Prince and his entourage creating a commotion over a famous movie star couple. Diplomats with colored bands of silk across their royal attire, and politicians with consorts that were obviously not their wives or husbands acknowledged him as they partied.

J.T. Popinski, his wife Armella, and Sumner T. Williams were in the hotel lobby with the Governor and his wife when Armella spotted Michael. She excused herself, and rushed across the length of the lobby to greet him.

"Hello, Mr. Orcini." She took his arm, and they walked slowly to meet the others. "It's a great success. Everything is so beautiful. The hotel, the casino, its all just so magnificent." She stopped him. "Tell me. Was she here?"

"Was who here?"

"Darci. Was Darci here?"

He resumed their walk. "Of course she was. Good evening Governor. Ma'am."

Michael complemented his executives on the success of their hard work, and excused himself. He retired to his suite. On the table next to the living room sofa was a large crystal vase with forty-nine white roses and one sterling silver rose in the center, which he ordered as a tribute to Darci. After a quick shower, he returned to the living room, took the silver rose, and went into his bedroom where he continued the tribute. A tall crystal vase that contained a few sprigs of baby's breath sat on the table by the side of his bed. Michael placed the symbolic rose into the vase.

Darci appeared between the satin sheets, and turned back the cover to invite him in. "Our work is not done, darling."